THE WIDOWS' CLUB

Amanda Brooke is a single mum who lives in Liverpool with her daughter, Jessica, a cat called Spider, a dog called Mouse, and a laptop within easy reach. Her debut novel, *Yesterday's Sun*, was a Richard and Judy Book Club pick. *The Widows' Club* is her tenth novel.

www.amanda-brooke.com
@AmandaBrookeAB
@AmandaBrookeAuthor
www.facebook.com/AmandaBrookeAuthor

Also by Amanda Brooke

Yesterday's Sun
Another Way To Fall
Where I Found You
The Missing Husband
The Child's Secret
The Goodbye Gift
The Affair
The Bad Mother
Don't Turn Around
The Widows' Club

Ebook-only short story
The Keeper of Secrets
If I Should Go

THE WIDOWS' CLUB

AMANDA BROOKE

HarperCollins*Publishers*

HarperCollins*Publishers* Ltd
1 London Bridge Street
London SE1 9FG

www.harpercollins.co.uk

A Paperback Original 2019
1

A catalogue record for this book
is available from the British Library

ISBN: 978-0-00-821921-5

Set in Sabon LT Std by Palimpsest Book Production Ltd, Falkirk, Stirlingshire

Printed and bound in Great Britain by CPI Group (UK) Ltd, Croydon CR0 4YY

MIX
Paper from
responsible sources

FSC
www.fsc.org
FSC™ C007454

For my daughter and my best friend, Jess

Hope is the thing with feathers
That perches in the soul
And sings the tune without the words
And never stops at all.

Emily Dickinson

STATEMENT

The Widows' Club @thewidowsclub
In response to unprecedented media interest, we confirm that the deceased was a member of the group but are unable to comment further. We kindly request that the privacy of the group and its members is respected at this difficult time.

1

As April Thorpe stood outside Hale Village Hall on a damp September evening, she didn't know if she was ready to join the group she spied through the windows. A dozen or so chairs had been arranged in a circle, but so far no one had taken their seats in the glass-fronted room on the lower floor. They had gathered in the foyer, sipping tea and chatting, and when someone tipped their head back and laughed, it felt wrong. How could they look so relaxed and happy? Who in their right mind would want to be a member of this exclusive club? April certainly didn't.

She was tempted to scurry away home and scream into her pillow, but she knew from experience that wouldn't lessen the pain. It was time for a new approach, but April's feet refused to move. She was scared, and her fear was echoed high above her head in the low rumble of a plane making an approach to land. Hale was directly beneath the flight path for John Lennon Airport and in the darkened sky, the noise carried a sense of foreboding.

'I don't belong here,' she mumbled to herself. 'I'm too young to be a widow.'

A passer-by might say the same. Widows weren't thirty years old with bright auburn hair and a feathering of wrinkles around sharp, green eyes. They were older, with laughter lines and watery eyes that captured decades of memories. Such women might point out that a lifetime wasn't nearly long enough, but it was longer than the five years she and Jason had been married.

Widowhood had been thrust upon April seven months and twelve days ago on a cold, February morning, and whether she liked it or not, she had earned her place here. She imagined Jason prodding her shoulder to get her moving, and her body swayed ever so slightly.

'Are you coming in?' someone behind her asked.

April turned to find a smartly dressed woman offering her a smile. She looked like someone April might bump into at the office, someone normal, but her tote bag gave her away. It had the phrase, 'Hope is the thing with wings' emblazoned across it.

'Erm. Sure,' she replied.

Swept along by embarrassment rather than purpose, April stepped into the foyer to be greeted by the one person who wasn't a stranger. Tara was in her mid-thirties and reminded April of a tall Audrey Hepburn with her dark hair pulled back into a chignon. The look was completed with a black-and-white striped top and a pair of pedal pushers. She didn't look like a widow either.

Tara had stumbled into April's life by chance a couple of weeks earlier when delivering boxes of exquisite cupcakes to the office where April worked as an internal auditor. The cakes were the finishing touch to a lunch-time baby shower the team had organised for one of their colleagues. Sara had

had a difficult pregnancy, not least because her boyfriend had dumped her soon after she discovered she was expecting, but on her last day at work, her belly had been taut, her smile broad, and her happiness suffocating. April had no right to spoil her friend's moment and in her haste to escape, she had almost knocked the cake boxes out of Tara's arms.

'Bad day at the office?' Tara had asked later when she found April shivering outside the building.

April pulled out her earphones. She had been listening to one of Jason's playlists on Spotify, feeling safe with songs her husband had chosen rather than risk new releases he would never get to hear. 'I'm sorry about before.'

'I don't suppose I can expect everyone to fight over my cakes. I'm Tara, by the way.'

'April,' she replied as she took a closer look at her new companion. That day, Tara was wearing a vintage print tea dress with a pale yellow, round-necked cardigan. Her dark eyeliner flicks accentuated eyes that scrutinised April's features.

'I don't normally do the deliveries,' Tara said, 'but I had to be on this side of the water anyway. I'm on my way to Clatterbridge Hospital next. I go back every year.' She left a pause before adding, 'My husband died there eight years ago today.'

'That's lovely,' April said. She blinked. 'Sorry, I mean, that's awful, but it's nice that you go back.' Her cheeks flushed. She was usually on the receiving end of such a clumsy response and it felt odd to have the situation reversed. She hadn't been prepared to meet another widow so much like herself. 'You must have been quite young when you lost him.'

'Twenty-eight.'

5

'I was twenty-nine,' replied April.

'I know,' Tara said. 'I spoke to your friend Sara and she mentioned why you might be upset.'

'Then maybe you could explain it to me,' April said, and for the first time she felt like she was talking to someone who might actually know why she felt the way she did. 'I'm happy for Sara, and it's not like Jason and I ever lost a child or suffered a miscarriage. We weren't even trying for a baby.'

'And now you'll never get the chance,' Tara replied. 'While everyone else is working out their future paths, the ground in front of you has fallen away and you're balancing on the edge of a precipice.'

'I am,' April said with a nod that threatened to spill the tears welling in her eyes. 'I woke up one morning and everything I thought I had was gone. Jason died in his sleep. A subarachnoid haemorrhage. There was no warning. Nothing.'

April could remember how she had stretched out her arms when she awoke that morning. Her hand had touched something cold and even the memory made her recoil. She had no idea how long she had been lying next to Jason like that, but it would have been hours and there was no doubting he was dead. Her first reaction had been to scramble backwards off the bed, and she had landed hard on the floor. Unable, or unwilling to process what was happening, she had started to scream. Luckily they lived in a flat, and one of her neighbours had heard her.

Staring into the distance, April was back on her bedroom floor. A part of her had never left.

'It will get easier,' Tara assured her. 'The grief might stay with you for ever but the shock each time you remember your loss will become less intense, or else you'll simply get used to that stabbing pain in the centre of your heart.'

'It really is a physical pain, isn't it?'

'Oh, yes.'

'How did you get through it?'

'With a lot of help from a close network of family and friends. My daughter Molly was only two at the time, and Mike and I ran a business together, so there was no choice but to keep going.'

'Gosh, that must have been hard. I don't know how I'd cope if I had a baby to look after as well,' April admitted, which only confused her emotions about the dreaded baby shower.

'You seem to have a good group of friends around you too,' Tara told her.

'They must be sick and tired of walking around on eggshells. I don't know how I feel from one minute to the next, and if I can't predict how I'll react, how can they? I know I'm being irrational half the time.'

'Talking helps.'

April shook her head. 'I don't have any siblings, and I can't offload on my parents, or worse still, Jason's. I keep telling myself I should open up to friends, but Jason and I had known each other since school and we worked for the same council. His mates were mine, and vice versa. I can't talk to them. It's too painful. It's too complicated.'

'If you're interested, I run a support group called the Widows' Club. We were a bit short-sighted when we came up with the name because quite a few of our members these days are men, but we were all widowed under the age of fifty. We meet once a month to share things that would probably sound crazy to anyone else. We cry, we vent, and occasionally we have a laugh too.'

April bit her lip. 'I don't know,' she said, edging away. 'I should be getting back to work.'

Tara chuckled to herself. 'I know how this must look, but I promise, I'm not some recruiter for a weird cult. Here,' she said, pulling a business card from her pocket. 'My mobile number's on the back, or you can look up the group online. Have a think about it and if you're interested, come over to my shop and we'll have a proper chat.'

The embossed card with cursive script was for Tee's Cakes and above Tara's phone number was her address. 'You're in Hale Village? I live in Eastham.'

'Then we're practically neighbours,' Tara said, dismissing the fact that the Mersey flowed between the two villages. 'If you can get there, you'd be very welcome.'

Meeting another young widow had felt fated and, despite April's reservations, she had visited Tara's shop the following week where she found herself being inducted into the group. Tara's offer of friendship had proven difficult to resist and she didn't look in the least bit surprised when her newest recruit arrived at the village hall for her first meeting.

'I knew you'd come,' she said, giving April's arm a squeeze.

'I didn't,' April replied, stunned that she had made it this far.

There followed a blur of introductions that left April dizzy. After months of isolation, she was now one of many. Someone made her a coffee and another offered her a carefully crafted cupcake, presumably from Tee's Cakes, but a combination of nerves and dread churned April's insides. She was lucky to make it past the pleasantries without throwing up.

8

When it was time and they all took their seats in the circle, April didn't know if she would talk, or what she might say if she did find her voice. With dark, unspeakable thoughts swirling inside her head, she stared into the depths of her half-empty mug until she became aware of the room falling silent. She looked up, and it was Tara's face she saw first. She was sitting opposite to keep April in her line of sight, while the group's other administrator, Justine, sat on April's right. She was the one who had greeted April outside the hall.

Justine was around the same age as Tara, although her style was far more conservative. She wore a tailored dress and her sleek blonde ponytail swished as she bent down to take a clipboard from her tote bag. Tara had described her as the organised half of their partnership, and April was beginning to see why.

'Shall we get started?' Justine asked.

'Sure,' Tara replied. 'Welcome back everyone. I'd like to start by introducing not one but two new members to the Widows' Club. For those who haven't had a chance to say hello yet, we have April sitting on Justine's right, and on her left is Nick.'

There was a ripple of greetings and nods directed at the newbies, but April latched on to Nick's smile. Wearing a suit and clean-shaven, he was in his late thirties and had spoken with a soft Liverpool accent when they had been introduced earlier. She had been too dazed at the time to pick up that she wasn't the only curiosity in the room, but now that she knew, she felt drawn to him. They all had stories, and like the rest of the group, she wanted to hear his.

'On behalf of all of us,' Tara said, 'I'm so sorry that you find yourself needing this group, but we're in this together.

9

Please contribute as much or as little as makes you comfortable. No one is here to judge.'

'No Faith tonight?' asked one of the men.

'She's passed on her apologies, but I'm sure our new members will have the pleasure of her company at the next meeting,' explained Tara. 'Right then, who wants to contribute first?'

As the conversation began to flow, April took time to familiarise herself with the faces that turned occasionally in her direction. The women outnumbered the men, but their ages were more evenly spread. There was at least one woman who looked younger than April, and a couple of members in their late forties, giving the group an age range that spanned more than a quarter of a century.

April tried her best to memorise names and keep a mental note of their individual circumstances, but it was difficult to keep track when her thoughts kept tugging her back to why she was there and how much she should share. What she did manage to glean was that some members had endured watching their loved ones' health decline whilst others had suffered the shock of losing their partners in the blink of an eye. Some had children, others did not. They were all different, and yet whenever someone raised a gripe about a world that didn't understand them, there were nods of agreement around the room.

'I told myself I should get out more,' a woman was saying. She glanced over at April and Nick to catch their eye. 'I'm Jodie, by the way. My husband went out to play five-a-side one night and never came home. Heart attack. He died right there on the pitch two and a half years ago. He was twenty-seven.' Jodie pursed her lips and there was a spark of anger, or was it disbelief behind her eyes? April had felt both.

'I'm sorry,' April replied, her first contribution to the group beyond a couple of indecipherable mumbles. Nick had been quiet too, listening intently as he pulled at the starched cuffs of his pristine white shirt.

'So, where was I?' Jodie asked with forced cheeriness, only to find she couldn't continue. She tipped back her head and blinked hard for a second or two before straightening up. 'You'd think I'd be able to control these flipping tears by now. Can you believe I went a whole week without crying last month? Honestly, I'm so sorry.'

'You don't have to apologise, not here,' Tara reminded her.

'I know, but sometimes it would be nice to say what I want to say without breaking down. It's not like it was something sad, not really. All I wanted to share was that I bit the bullet and went out clubbing with my mates the other week,' she said. 'I wasn't looking to meet anyone, but all my friends are in couples and they're desperate to hook me up with someone new. They spent the entire night striking meerkat poses to check out potential candidates.'

'Did you mind?' asked Justine.

'Not really, or not at first. I know they just want to see me happy again.'

'Only you can know when the time's right,' Steve said. He had introduced himself earlier, explaining how he'd nursed his wife through treatment for ovarian cancer. It hadn't worked, the disease had been detected too late because a thirty-four-year-old mother of two presenting with symptoms couldn't possibly have cancer. 'You shouldn't feel pressurised, Jode. It could be they're only interested in pairing you up because they're worried you'll sink your claws into one of their husbands. The last time I went to what had been one

11

of our regular couples' nights, the men were ridiculously possessive of their wives. Probably explains why I wasn't invited back.'

Blood rushed to April's cheeks as she thought about her inner circle of friends. They had all rallied around her after Jason died, but April had slowly distanced herself. It was too painful to go out without Jason and, like Steve, she had detected a growing awkwardness too. She didn't think her friends saw her as any sort of competition, but it did happen, didn't it? People formed inappropriate attachments to their friends' partners all the time, and you didn't have to be widowed for it to happen.

Jodie rolled her eyes. 'Seriously, Steve, I'm not a threat, and my mates know it. The idea of being with anyone else still feels like cheating on Ryan, and I couldn't do that to him – especially with one of our friends.'

April took a breath. This was it. This was why she was here. She needed to delve deeper into Jodie's theory about what friends would and wouldn't do – what Jason would or wouldn't do. Finally, she could tell a group of strangers what she couldn't share with anyone else; that when she grieved for her husband, she felt a burning anger and a growing fear. Was it normal to suspect your dead husband of cheating on you? She needed to know.

2

April was about to share her darkest fears with the group, but before she could muster the courage, Nick cleared his throat to speak. The breath April had been holding escaped with a soft gasp, and she was left feeling crushed but temporarily relieved. What if she were wrong to suspect Jason? Worse still, what if she were right?

'I've no idea how I'd fare in a new relationship,' Nick began. 'How could anyone compare to Erin when I choose to remember only the best parts of our relationship? I'll never love anyone like I loved her. She was perfect.'

Nick turned to meet April's gaze. He was seeking reassurance, but April lowered her head and closed her eyes as a rush of sacred memories assaulted her. She had once thought Jason was perfect too.

'Would you like to tell us about Erin?' asked Justine.

'Sure,' Nick said. He pulled at his cuff, unable to continue until it was straight. 'Erin found a lump in her breast and pretty soon after we were told it was cancer. She was only thirty-two and it didn't seem real.' He paused a moment before adding, 'I should explain that Erin and I weren't married, but I asked Justine and she said it would be OK with you guys.'

Justine nodded. 'I told Nick we recognise the love between two people and not what's written on a certificate. Our differences bring us together, they don't set us apart,' she said. 'Lisa and I had a civil partnership, but I've never been treated any differently in this group.'

'Not marrying Erin is one of my deepest regrets,' Nick admitted. 'I was stupid. I didn't appreciate what I had until it was too late. She had treatment, but there were secondaries and she never did get the all-clear we were praying for. The last thing Erin said to me was not to waste my life thinking about what might have been. I couldn't believe how brave and noble she was, right up to the end.'

'I'm sure you were brave too,' said a woman sitting next to Steve. Nadiya was another thirty-something with three children to bring up after her husband had drowned on an ill-fated boat trip.

'If you'd seen me, you wouldn't have thought so. I was useless to her.'

'My husband had cancer too,' Tara explained. 'And I remember feeling that sense of impotence. It was their fight, their suffering, and we were the bystanders.'

'How did you cope?' Nick asked.

'I have no idea,' Tara said, but she glanced at Justine and added, 'Actually I do. I had family and friends like Justine who looked after me and my baby so I could look after Mike in his last months. I'm sure I appeared brave, but I was a mess inside.'

'Two years on and I'm still a mess,' Nick said, head down as he tugged at his shirt sleeve. He sniffed back tears before adding, 'Sorry.'

There was a pause that no one tried to fill until it became clear that Nick had said as much as he could for his first meeting. One or two people glanced at April. It was her turn, but after listening to Nick, her emotions were pinballing between the pain of her loss and her anger.

Steve was close enough to hear her gulp as she struggled to swallow a mouthful of cold coffee and he offered her a reprieve. 'It's not all gloom and doom,' he said. 'There are some of us who make new relationships work, aren't there Tara? Where's Iain tonight?'

If April wasn't mistaken, there was a blush rising in Tara's cheeks. 'At home looking after the girls.'

'Your place or his?' asked Nadiya, quick to join in the teasing that brought light back to a room crowded with ghosts.

'My flat, although I won't be living above the shop for much longer. Iain and I have put an offer in for a house around the corner on Pebble Street,' Tara replied. She bit her lip as she waited for the group's reaction. It was Nick and April's frowns she noticed first. 'Sorry, I should explain. Iain's another member of the group and this lot have had to listen to us debating whether or not to move in together for a while now. We each have a daughter and we didn't want to rush things.'

'And how are the girls taking the news?' Nadiya asked.

'We haven't told them yet, but I know Molly's going to be thrilled. She'll be glad not to have to share her poky little bedroom with Lily whenever she stays over.'

'And what about Lily?' Justine prompted.

Tara shifted in her seat. 'That's going to be more of a challenge. She'll have to move schools, and, whereas I can keep the flat so we can rent it out, Iain's putting their house

15

in Widnes on the market. It's not going to be easy for Lily to leave the place where she lived with her mum, but I hope there are enough positives to outweigh the negatives.'

'We had to move house because we couldn't afford to stay where we were,' said Nadiya. 'The older two were sobbing their hearts out on the day we left, but they settled eventually.'

'It's a new start for all of us.'

'Do you think Iain will keep coming to the group?' asked Justine. 'He's missed a few now.'

'You'd have to ask him that, but maybe he has got as much out of the group as he needs,' Tara replied. Smiling, she added, 'Possibly more than he was expecting, but that's the thing, we have each other now and a future to look forward to.'

Justine played with the corner of her clipboard. 'You make it sound like you're considering leaving too.'

April tightened her grip on her mug. The others were lovely, but Tara was the one who had persuaded April to join the group and she didn't want to lose her so soon.

'No, I have no plans to escape just yet,' Tara said, falling short of giving them an absolute assurance. She gave a chuckle, but her smile was tight when she added, 'And who knows? Blending two families could go horribly wrong and we might need you all more than ever.'

After another pause, Justine sat up a little straighter. 'Are we about done for tonight?'

The thought of leaving without making any contribution was enough for April to regain the courage that had failed her earlier. 'Can I say something?' she asked.

'Don't feel you have to talk about Jason until you're ready,' said Tara.

The sound of Jason's name falling from the lips of someone

16

who had never known him, in a place he had never been, evoked such bittersweet emotion. April was angry, confused, and possibly paranoid, but she had never lost sight of how much she missed her husband, or how much she had loved him. No one in this room was ever going to meet Jason, but he was the reason she was there. He was what connected her to each and every one of them. She inhaled slowly and her breath vibrated over the thump of her heart.

'I'll admit my feelings are confused,' she began, 'so I apologise if what I'm about to say doesn't make sense.'

'Why don't you start at the beginning?' suggested Tara. 'There's no rush.'

April nodded. It was as safe a place as any. 'Jason and I were childhood sweethearts and we managed the whole long-distance relationship while I went off to do my accountancy degree and he took an apprenticeship as a surveyor. When I came back, we ended up working in different departments for the same council. We moved in together and eventually got married just over five years ago. Our lives were perfectly synchronised until the night Jason died in his sleep,' she said, surprised her voice held despite the crushing pain that made it difficult to breathe. 'He was gone, just like that.'

'It happens,' said Jodie. Nadiya was also nodding.

'I was told the bleed on his brain had been sudden and catastrophic,' she said. 'No one could have known there was a time bomb ticking inside his head, but I do wonder if there were signs. Jason changed in those last few months. I couldn't do right for doing wrong but we got through last Christmas, and by February, he seemed like his old self. The night before was just an average Tuesday evening at home watching TV, eating pizza and going to bed.'

17

April didn't mention the sex, but it had been intense, followed by leftover pizza and slower, more languorous sex until they had fallen asleep utterly and completely sated.

'I'm pretty sure I woke up with a smile on my face,' she continued as she closed her eyes and recalled how she had felt that morning. There had been a sense of relief that they were back on track. Whatever had been wrong between them had been fixed.

As the scene played out in her mind, her blood ran cold.

Justine leant in. 'You don't have to do this,' she whispered.

A sob escaped, but April swallowed the next one back. 'I keep going back over our life together and challenging *everything*. All the things I should have said, or should have asked but didn't. I want to know what Jason was thinking. I *need* to know. There are so many questions. I want . . . I want . . .'

Justine patted April's back as she gasped for air. 'Maybe that's enough for one night.'

Through vision blurred with tears, April looked to Tara, who asked, 'Is that OK with you, April? Do you want to stop there?'

No, thought April. I want to tell you how I spend most nights going through pages and pages of phone bills, emails, and bank account statements as if I'm reading a book that's been carefully edited so as not to reveal the final twist. If an undetected bleed on the brain hadn't caused Jason's change in behaviour, April wanted to know what – or who, had? She didn't think the group could give her an answer, but she might feel better for asking it. Unfortunately, the only sound she could utter was another sob as someone passed her a tissue.

'In that case,' Tara continued, 'thank you all for coming,

18

and if there are any cupcakes left in the foyer, please take them home.'

'And before you leave,' Justine said, raising her voice above the scrape of chair legs, 'if there's anyone who hasn't paid the deposit for the Christmas do, can I have it as soon as?'

Everyone was up on their feet, but rather than heading for the exit, they gravitated towards April and Nick.

'If you're in need of a stiff drink,' Steve said to April, 'a few of us are going over to The Childe of Hale for a quick one.'

'I'd better not, I'm driving,' she replied as Jodie approached and wrapped her in a bear hug.

'It will get better, although I can't promise the tears will dry up anytime soon,' she said.

'I can vouch for that on Jodie's behalf,' added Steve.

Jodie poked him in the ribs. 'For that you can buy the first round.'

As the group thinned out, Nick approached April and he too gave her a hug. 'We can do this,' he whispered.

Nick was slow to pull away and for a split second April had an irrational fear that he was going to cup her cheek in one of his broad hands as Jason had once done. She turned her head quickly.

'You both did really well and I hope you'll be back next month,' said Justine, laying a hand on each of their arms to give a gentle squeeze. 'And it would be lovely to see you at the Christmas party too. I know it's only September, but it's a dinner-dance and these things need to be booked early.'

'Sure, how much is it?' asked Nick, slipping a hand into his jacket pocket.

'We're asking for a £40 contribution and the rest will be

made up from our end-of-year surplus,' Justine said. Glancing at April, she added, 'We're very careful about how we manage member subscriptions and we don't like to build up too much in reserves. Can we tempt you too?'

'I'm not sure. I haven't been planning that far ahead,' April stuttered. She had so far declined any and all plans for Christmas and New Year. Knowing how she might feel three months from now was an impossible task.

'There's no rush,' Tara said, coming to her rescue. 'If you want to decide nearer the time, I'm sure we can sneak you in.'

Justine's mouth twitched, but she didn't overrule Tara. She took the money Nick handed over and said, 'Come with me and I'll sort out a receipt.'

'No, it's fine. I trust you.'

'Honestly, I insist,' Justine replied, taking his arm and pulling him away.

Nick looked back over his shoulder at April. 'See you next time.'

Tara waited until the smile April had returned to Nick began to fade. 'You don't have to wait until next month if you need to talk sooner. Ring me anytime. That's an order.'

The invitation was almost too much, and April came close to blurting out all those thoughts and feelings she hadn't managed to share with the group. She needed someone like Tara in her life.

'Thank you,' she said, 'but you might regret the offer. In case you hadn't noticed, I'm pretty messed up.'

Tara smiled. 'I'll let you into a secret,' she said in a hushed voice, 'we all are.'

3

Once the last of the lunchtime customers had been served, Tara shut up the shop. She closed early on Wednesday afternoons and would normally use the time to make up cake orders, but she had other plans today and had already sent her deputy manager, Michelle, home early. Molly, Tara's ten-year-old daughter, was still in school, and Iain was home in Widnes, decluttering the house while eight-year-old Lily was out of the way. Tara would need to have a pre-move clear-out too, but with the limited space available in the flat upstairs, she had learnt a long time ago to be ruthless with keepsakes. Even so, it would be a wrench for both families to step away from the past, and as Tara enjoyed a rare moment of calm, she stopped to appreciate where she was and how far she had come.

Tee's Cakes had the feel of a Parisian patisserie, with a high counter running along one side of the shop to display intricately crafted cakes and tarts, and a line of padded booths on the opposite side for customers to sip their coffee and whisper secrets. Additional seating could be set up outside, weather-permitting, and the kitchen in the back was state-of-

21

the-art to meet the demands of daily visitors and a thriving online business. Mike wouldn't recognise the place.

He had originally opened the shop as a traditional café serving English breakfasts and sandwiches to both the locals and returning visitors who had stumbled upon the village and discovered its secrets. Hale was an often overlooked settlement on the edges of the Mersey, and boasted two pubs, a church, and a post office. It had a rich history that stretched back to Roman times, with several points of interest including a nature reserve at Pickering's Pasture and a lighthouse at Hale Head, and no visit was complete without a trip to St Mary's church and the grave of John Middleton, better known as the Childe of Hale. The history of the village's four-hundred-year-old resident, who had reportedly measured nine feet four inches tall, was well known. Sadly, few would stop to remember Michael Thomas Price, who had been dead just eight years.

Tara had known Mike as a friend, a boss, and briefly as a flatmate before they realised there was a spark between them that couldn't be contained. Tara had grown up in Hale and, after coming top of her class at catering college, she had turned up at Mike's café one day looking for a job. Her plan was to save enough money to move to Paris where she intended to perfect her craft, but it wasn't long before Tara had created a successful sideline for Mike by selling her cakes. They worked side by side and with the days so long, it made sense for her to crash out in his spare bedroom above the café. She never did make it to Paris.

Looking around at the transformation, she hoped Mike would approve of how she had used the money he had left her. Of one thing she was certain, he would approve of Iain. In those last days before cancer stole her husband from her,

Mike had made it very clear that he wanted Tara to find someone else. If anything, he would ask why it had taken her so long.

Drawn to the window, Tara looked out across the small car park that served Ivy Farm Court; a parade of shops of which Tee's Cakes was one of eight units. She could see the entrance to Hale Primary School on the opposite side of the road where Lily would join Molly once the house move was complete. The main road continued up towards the park and the Childe of Hale pub where it hit a sharp bend at the war memorial, which formed its own little island between the lanes.

In the aftermath of Mike's death, Tara had often pictured the regiments of war widows standing before the sandstone cross to remember the husbands who hadn't made it home. She had imagined them drawing comfort from each other and, longing for something similar, she had created the Widows' Club with Justine's help. It was her way to reach out to others, and she had taken far more from it than she could ever hope to give. She was yet to decide if she had given enough.

As Tara stared off into space, her mind unable to form a clear vision of the future, she didn't register the flash of Faith's white Range Rover until her friend pulled up directly in front of the shop. Tara unlocked the door and beckoned her inside.

Faith had dropped into Tara's life three years earlier when she had visited the shop to pick up a large order of French pastries. This was in the days before Iain had used his Internet wizardry to establish Tara's online business, and when Faith had explained that the cakes were a thank-you gesture to colleagues who had supported her after the loss of her husband the year before, Tara had hooked Faith in. She was good at that.

23

'You look nice,' Faith said with more generosity than was entirely deserving of Tara's current ensemble.

Having a job that required crawling out of bed at an ungodly hour, Tara had grabbed random items of clothing from her wardrobe in near darkness and only as the sun rose did she notice that the mustard yellow swing skirt clashed brazenly with the pink checks of her vintage blouse. Her customers were used to her eccentricities, but she wished she had tried harder today as Faith slipped off her bright yellow rain jacket.

'And you look stunning,' she said as she admired Faith's dove grey cashmere jumper paired with black cigarette pants. At forty-six, Faith maintained a seemingly effortless beauty. With penetrating grey eyes and a flawless complexion, her make-up was understated and she had caught up her tousled blonde hair into a messy ponytail that left stray curls to frame her face perfectly. This was Faith's idea of casual. 'Make yourself comfortable and I'll sort the coffee. Do you fancy a slice of cake?'

'Why else would I be here?'

Five minutes later, Tara set down two cups of coffee, one opera cake, and three plates and forks.

'Please don't say Justine's joining us!'

'I wouldn't do that to you,' Tara said, only to feel a pang of guilt. Justine had been there for Tara long before Faith dazzled her way into her life. 'I wouldn't do it to Justine either.'

Faith pulled a face: the clash of personalities was felt on both sides. 'So how was the meeting the other week? Did I miss anything? Was there lots of blubbing?'

'It was a good session and I think our new members are

24

going to fit in well. You should have been there,' Tara said pointedly as she served up a slice of cake for each of them.

'It was probably safer that I wasn't. We'll be running out of space if you recruit any more.'

'The numbers are fine.' Tara played with the cake on her plate, carefully separating the intricate layers of coffee-soaked almond sponge, ganache and buttercream. She didn't look up when she added, 'Iain wasn't there either.'

Faith cocked her head. 'And was that a problem?'

'It did raise a question in the group about whether he was thinking of leaving. We have talked about it, and, while Iain's not going to make a firm decision just yet, he's doesn't need the group like he did before. He wants to focus fully on the future.'

'Easier said than done.'

'I'm not suggesting we airbrush out the past,' Tara said, suddenly aware of the strong aroma of coffee that was a stark contrast to the smell of sizzling bacon she associated with Mike's café. She had held on to the life insurance money for almost three years before plucking up the courage to have the place remodelled. The café's reincarnation had a distinct French vibe, but Tara had ensured there was a place for treasured mementoes too, including Mike's chef's cap pressed flat inside a frame on the wall behind the counter. 'But Iain and I have each other now, and if there are any issues to face, we should deal with them as a couple.'

Faith's cup was halfway to her lips. 'You make it sound like you want to leave too.'

Tara didn't answer immediately. 'Funnily enough, that was something else the group picked up on.'

'Anyone in particular?' Faith asked with a raised eyebrow.

25

'I bet Justine would love it if you left. I keep telling you, she doesn't like being overshadowed. She must be champing at the bit to run the group on her own.'

Tara refused to entertain the idea that there were cracks developing in her friendship with Justine. It was true that, occasionally, it felt like there was an element of competition when it came to opening and closing the meetings, but Justine admitted herself that Tara was more natural when it came to leading the discussion. 'She was as concerned as the rest of the group that I might consider leaving,' Tara insisted. 'And if I did go, I'd make sure there was someone else to pick up the slack.'

Faith had managed to take a sip of her coffee this time, and she spluttered. 'I hope you're not suggesting me?'

Tara laughed. As good as Faith would be at controlling the group, they could all agree that she and Justine would not make the ideal partnership. 'It doesn't have to be you. Steve or Nadiya might be willing.'

'Justine wouldn't work with any of us. She might say the right things, but she'd push us out eventually.' Faith leant forward when she added, 'It's what she's doing now with you. You just don't see it.'

'I'm not leaving ye—'

'Good,' Faith said before Tara could add the caveat. 'You keep chairing the meetings and Justine can carry on as the bean counter. Speaking of which . . .' She took an envelope from her handbag and slid it across the table. 'Here's my balance for the Christmas party.'

Tara wrinkled her nose. 'I'll take it on the condition you tell Justine I've given you a receipt. She's become obsessed with keeping the accounts squeaky clean since finding out one of our new members is an auditor. Like April could care less.'

'I like the sound of April already.'

'That's good because she's on her way over. The extra plate is for her,' Tara said, watching for Faith's expression. She didn't disappoint.

'And you call yourself a friend? Why are you doing this to me, Tara? She's going to cry, isn't she?'

'Quite possibly,' Tara said and went on to explain April's nightmarish discovery of her husband's body. 'She needs us, Faith, and I think she'll talk more if it's just me and you. A large group can be overwhelming and in hindsight it was a mistake to have two new members starting at the same time. You sidestepped the last meeting, but you're not getting out of this.'

It was no coincidence that Faith had made her excuses. Introductions were often cathartic for new members, but their raw grief could be harrowing for those who were further along their journey.

'I was busy with work,' Faith insisted.

'If you say so.'

Tara didn't push further. Faith put on a convincing act, but she continued to feel her husband Derek's loss keenly. Unlike April and Nick, it had taken several sessions before she had been able to share her story with the group, but she too had cried.

Faith was unlike anyone Tara had ever met. She could be as charming as she could be blunt. She had no time for fools, but for the lucky few she let into her heart, she was fiercely protective, hence her animosity towards Justine for her perceived attempts to undermine Tara.

'You're going to like April. I promise.'

Faith scowled. 'And what about the other newbie? Is he invited too?'

'No,' Tara replied. 'He'll manage just fine with the group.'

'What's he like?'

'His name's Nick Malford, he's thirty-eight, and he lost his partner two years ago. It was Justine who enrolled him so I don't know all the details. What I can say is that he's genuinely heartbroken, and he's not afraid to shed a tear,' she teased Faith. 'But he has a certain confidence about him, so I expect he'll integrate with the others quite quickly.'

'So we're left with the problem child.'

'We're left with someone who needs some extra attention.'

'You're lucky this cake is so good,' mumbled Faith as she stabbed it with her fork. 'And while I gorge myself, tell me where you're up to with the house move. You look stressed. Are you stressed?'

'You said I looked nice before,' Tara reminded her, but she was smiling. Most people assumed she could cope with whatever life threw at her and it was a rare thing for someone to stop and ask if she was OK. Tara should have known that person would be Faith. 'But you're right, things are getting very real. There's a bit of wrangling over the house on Pepper Street after the survey picked up a couple of issues, but that's nothing compared to the stumbling block we've hit with Iain's house. He thought he had a buyer, but apparently they haven't secured a mortgage yet.'

'It'll happen.'

Tara felt her stomach clench. 'Maybe that's the issue.'

It had felt like fate was giving them a nudge when Iain had been made redundant over the summer, and they had planned

28

their future while sitting on a bench in Pickering's Pasture. Everything had seemed to click into place as they gazed out across the mirrored surface of the Mersey with the girls close by taking turns birdspotting with a pair of binoculars. With the online business taking off, Tara's fortunes had taken a turn for the better. She needed more help with the admin, plus a part-time delivery driver, which conveniently added up to a full-time job. To the background noise of their daughters' giggles, they had struck upon the perfect solution. She and Iain would join forces and become partners in every sense of the word, but as the summer faded and the days shortened, the imperfections in their plan had become difficult to ignore.

'Don't tell me, the pieces don't fit into place as neatly as you imagined,' Faith said.

'Barring a few adjustments, the house move and the business set-up will work out fine,' Tara replied. 'If there are delays, we'll manage.'

'Then what's the problem? Are you having second thoughts about Iain?'

'Absolutely not,' Tara said quickly, her heart clenching. 'I know we've only been together for a year, but I couldn't love him more. It feels right, and I know he'd say the same. Our families might be two broken pieces from different puzzles, but we can fit together, given the chance.'

'Ah, so the girls are the problem.'

'Iain and I took them for a walk to the lighthouse at the weekend and explained we could be in our new house by the end of the year. Molly was over the moon, but Lily was worryingly quiet,' Tara said as she pictured them walking back to the village.

Molly had raced ahead, but Lily had slipped her hand into

her dad's. When Tara had offered to take her other hand, Lily had refused. 'My mummy's holding this one,' she had said.

'It's natural that they'd react differently,' Tara told Faith. 'Molly was practically a baby when Mike died and she's never known any different. It might take her some time to adjust to having a father figure, but she can't wait to move out of the flat. Lily on the other hand was five when she lost her mum. She has memories and emotional ties that are intrinsically linked to the home Iain's trying to sell from under her.'

'Is it a deal breaker?'

'No,' Tara said, pulling back her shoulders to shift the weight pressing down against her chest. 'But it's going to make the next few months far more interesting than I would like. Now enough about me, tell me your news. How come you've taken the day off work?'

Tara had been pleasantly surprised when Faith suggested calling into the shop. They tried to meet up at least once a month between group meetings, but Tara had all but given up hope of finding time between one crisis and another.

'I had a date with a man,' Faith said, raising an eyebrow.

'What for? A manicure? Pedicure? Indian head massage?' Tara asked with a smile.

'A quotation, actually,' Faith said, pushing away her empty plate. Her smile disappeared. 'Lily's not the only one with emotional ties that are about to be cut. I told myself I had to do something about the house this year, and I've finally made a start.'

'Are you selling up?' Tara asked, unable to hide her shock. Faith talked about her house as if it were a shrine to her husband, and Tara couldn't imagine her letting it go any more than she could imagine Faith letting go of the place Derek occupied in her heart.

'Looking at things rationally, the house is too big for one person, and you never know, it might be fun living in some stylish city apartment with beautiful views.' She took a moment to consider the possibility, then shook her head. 'But no, Woolton is my home. I can't leave.'

'So explain. What was the quotation for?'

'There are rooms full of furniture that have been left to gather dust,' she said. 'Assuming the antique dealer I met can improve his offer, and I'll make sure he does, I can at least empty the rooms I don't use. That way, if and when I do pluck up the courage to move, it should be less traumatic.'

'One step at a time,' agreed Tara.

'And if Ella happens to notice, I might tell her I've donated all her family heirlooms to charity,' Faith said, referring to her grown-up stepdaughter. 'I doubt she'd care, but her mother would be apoplectic.'

Tara couldn't believe some of the stories Faith had told her about Derek's embittered first wife, Rosemary. Their daughter had grown up believing all the tales her mother had spun about her father, and sadly Ella and Derek had been estranged at the time of his death. Tara felt sorry for her, but as for Rosemary, any woman who continued to use her daughter to eke out revenge on a man long since dead deserved Faith's spite. 'You are wicked.'

'I know,' Faith said with a glint in her eye that faded as she looked over Tara's shoulder. 'Your stray lamb has arrived.'

After greeting April with a hug, Tara guided her towards the booth where Faith had remained seated. There was an

31

awkward moment where April dithered, seemingly unable to decide if she should offer Faith a handshake or a hug, but, to Tara's relief, Faith stood to embrace the new arrival.

'Faith isn't one of life's huggers, but after three years of group therapy, we're getting there,' Tara quipped.

The two friends scowled at each other before Tara retreated to the counter to make April's coffee. From the corner of her eye, she watched April take her seat opposite Faith.

'I hear you're an auditor,' Faith said, raising her voice above the gurgle of the coffee machine. 'We were hoping you'd cast an eye over the support group accounts to see if Justine's been skimming something off the top.'

'Actually, I'm an internal auditor so I deal more with governance issues, but I could take a look.' April's eyes were wide when she turned to Tara as she approached. 'Is there a problem?'

Tara placed a steaming cup of coffee in front of April and took the seat next to her. 'No, there isn't. Justine's far more likely to add money to our fund than take from it. Faith's teasing and she really shouldn't.'

Faith took the reprimand with a polite nod. 'Sorry, that was mean of me, but I don't like the way she's been trying to overthrow Tara. Justine hates that Tara's looked upon as the group leader while she's left to do the admin.'

'Which she does really well,' Tara added in Justine's defence.

Tara and Justine had been friends since school and had been there for each other during the most difficult times of their lives. Justine had been a source of great strength at Mike's funeral, never guessing that she would be the next to wear the widow's mantle three short months later when her wife died from sepsis.

Together, they had sought out an existing widows' group,

but they had stood out from the start. Tara was in her late twenties, Justine only thirty, and as much as the older women had welcomed them, their experiences of widowhood had been markedly different. There had been no talk of childcare, careers, or the pressure society placed on them to reinvent themselves. If anything, the others envied Tara and Justine's youth and their potential to start anew.

'And Justine doesn't only manage the budget,' continued Tara. 'She takes care of all the social media, and puts a lot of time and effort into organising us all. I couldn't do what she does, but someone could easily replace me.'

'That's not going to happen,' said Faith.

Turning to April, Tara said, 'I don't want you to get the wrong impression. The group is a family of sorts and Justine is like a sister to me. There really isn't a problem between us and if ever there was, I would deal with it.' Tara knew Faith had good intentions, but she didn't want anyone taking sides. There were no lines to be drawn, not on her behalf. To Faith she added, 'So can we please leave her alone?'

'Noted,' Faith said as she and Tara locked eyes. The moment passed and they both relaxed as they turned their attention to April.

'Can I tempt you with some cake?' Tara asked.

'I haven't had much of an appetite lately,' April replied, 'but it looks beautiful.'

Ignoring the refusal, Tara cut a slice and left the plate within reach. 'You can take some home for your mum and dad, if you like.'

'You're living with your parents?' Faith asked. 'Oh, sorry. I heard what happened to your husband. No wonder you moved out.'

'I'm not sure I could have slept there again even if I'd tried,' April agreed with a shudder. 'And being looked after is probably what I need right now, but to be honest, I didn't have a choice. Jason and I had been renting our flat, and I couldn't afford it on my own. I had to rely on family to cover the cost of the funeral, and my first priority is to pay them back before looking for a place of my own. Jason didn't have life insurance or a pension.'

'It happens more often than you'd think,' Faith said. 'My Derek died in a car crash just over four years ago. He was twelve years older, so you'd think he'd be better prepared, but he'd cashed in his pension as part of the divorce settlement with his first wife. He left me his business, but I don't know the first thing about imports and exports and most of his contracts were verbal. I was lucky to keep the house when the company folded and its assets were stripped. My parents died when I was a teenager, so there was no one to bail me out.'

Tara looked over the rim of her coffee cup. 'Enough of the sob story. Tell her about the compensation.'

Faith's expression was sheepish. 'OK, so maybe my financial circumstances weren't as dire as I'm making out. Derek's accident was caused by a mechanical failure that was supposed to have been fixed. He'd taken his car back to the dealership several times, but my guess is they simply reset the warning light and charged us a small fortune for the privilege. I agreed an out-of-court settlement, but I'm starting to regret it. I could have taken them to the cleaners if I'd been in a better frame of mind, but I'd just lost my husband. Derek's death was needless, that's what hurts me most.'

'That's awful,' said April. 'And what a thing to go through while you were in mourning, although I can understand why

34

you settled. It feels wrong moaning about the money side of things. It shouldn't be important, should it?'

'But it's a reality we can't ignore,' Tara replied. 'Life would be so much simpler if we could deal with the emotional and practical elements of grief separately, but when the worst happens, everything hits you at once. So yes, April, you are allowed to complain about the financial mess you've been landed with, to us and the group. And don't feel guilty about being angry with Jason once in a while.'

April's laugh was hollow as she pulled the slice of opera cake towards her. She teased a corner of the cake onto her fork and didn't look up when she said, 'I've been angry with him so much lately.'

Tara's eyes narrowed. Her instinct had been right – there was more to her story than April had been able to share so far. 'Do you want to talk about it? Was there something you needed to say at the group meeting but couldn't?'

Above their heads, there was the roar of an aeroplane climbing to the skies and April finally lifted her gaze.

'In the months before Jason died . . . he'd changed. He had been a constant in my life, and suddenly he wasn't – it was like he was somewhere else, or maybe he just wanted to be. There were times when he wouldn't look at me and other times when he couldn't do enough.'

'But you said at the meeting you thought his change in behaviour could have been linked to his brain haemorrhage,' Tara said.

April shook her head. 'It's what I've tried to tell myself, but according to the doctors it would be unlikely. I think Jason was up to something.'

Faith was blunter, as always. 'Was he having an affair?'

'It crossed my mind at the time, but not enough for me to accuse him. There was nothing specific, and then shortly before he died everything seemed to right itself. Stupidly, I thought I'd got my old Jason back,' April said, blinking away tears. 'And I'm glad I didn't say anything. He would have died believing I didn't trust him.'

'And if he was having an affair, chances are he would have denied it anyway,' Faith replied.

'Exactly, but now that he's not around to challenge, my nagging doubt has become a full-blown obsession. Am I being paranoid? Is this some cruel side effect of grief?' April asked. She continued to look at Faith: she would pull no punches.

'We're blessed with natural instincts for a reason,' Faith said. 'Only people with something to hide, or something to hide from, dismiss it as paranoia. Have you checked his messages? His emails?'

'Yes, and I hated doing it, but I hated myself more when I couldn't find anything more incriminating than Snapchat on his phone.'

'Sorry for being a techno-phobe, but why would that mean anything?' asked Tara.

'Messages are time-limited. You don't have to go to the trouble of deleting them and you don't run the risk of leaving an audit trail behind if something unexpected happens to you,' April said, mashing her cake with the fork. 'As far as I was aware, Jason never used it, so why was it on his phone?'

'And that's one of the questions you've been left with that Jason can't answer,' Tara said, recalling April's lament to the group.

'It hasn't stopped me looking,' April said. 'I was finally given online access to his bank accounts last month and

I've been going through his statements line by line. I'm not sure, but I might have found what I was looking for. There were some biggish cash withdrawals before and after Christmas, and I know for a fact Jason hated using cash. I can only presume it was to avoid any record of his purchases.'

Faith leant over the table and took the fork and plate from April before she pebble-dashed them with ganache. 'Was it enough to buy a hotel room?'

April shrugged, misery etched on her face.

'I'm sure there are lots of other explanations,' Tara suggested. She wondered if Jason might have been into drugs, although this theory was only marginally better than the possibility of an affair.

'Do you have any idea who he might have been seeing?' asked Faith, having already reached a judgement.

April didn't answer immediately. 'Not really, but what Steve said in the group about friends getting involved with other friends' partners struck a chord. I look at my girlfriends and wonder if one of them is grieving more for Jason than she should. I'm tempted to come right out and ask each and every one of them, but I'm not sure that's a particular rabbit hole I want to go down.'

'I'd say that's a good call,' Tara said, taking April's hand and giving it a squeeze. 'You don't need to come up with all the answers straight away. Take it one day at a time.'

April glanced down at Tara's fingers. 'Is that your wedding ring?'

'Yes,' she replied, lifting her right hand to examine the gold band. 'I swapped it over when I was ready to accept that my future was no longer as Mike's wife.'

'Same here,' Faith said, wriggling the third finger of her right hand.

'Did you find someone else too?' April asked.

'No chance. Don't get me wrong, I like the idea of love, and I'm over the moon for Tara and Iain, but it's not for me, not any more. I prefer being in control of my own fate.'

'I wish I could say the same.'

'Oh, April,' said Tara gently. 'It's early days and you have a lot to process.'

'I know, and I can't tell you how good it feels to talk about this at last.' April paused and chewed her lip. 'Will the rest of the group understand? Has anyone else gone through something similar?'

'None of us had perfect marriages,' Tara replied. 'As much as I loved Mike, I spent a lot of time resenting him for stealing my dreams. I had every intention of moving to Paris until I found out I was pregnant. I'm not saying I didn't love the life we made together, but there's a reason I've created a little corner of Paris in Hale Village.'

Tara wasn't sure if April noticed she had evaded the question, but Faith did.

'And you don't have to raise this in the group if you don't want to. It's none of their business, and besides . . .' Faith reached over to squeeze April's hand as Tara had done. 'You have us.'

Tara couldn't hold back her smile. She knew Faith would like April. 'And it's not as if the main group are ever short of things to talk about, so you'll still have lots in common with them. You're not alone, April. Not any more.'

RESPONSES

Petersj @Petersjhome
Replying to @thewidowsclub
I hope the police are investigating this so-called support group of yours. These were vulnerable people you were dealing with. The situation should never have been allowed to get out of hand.

Jodie @iamJPriestly
Replying to @Petersjhome @thewidowsclub
You're out of order blaming the group. It's been my lifeline and no one could have predicted what happened.

Leanne Thompson @LTReports
Replying to @iamJPriestly
Hi Jodie, I'm a freelance reporter and would love to hear your story. Can we meet?

Jodie @iamJPriestly
Replying to @LTReports
Fuck off Leanne

4

The tap of stiletto heels ricocheted off the walls as Faith Cavendish surveyed the empty room. Behind her, she heard the soft wisp of socked feet and the scratch of pencil on paper.

'Is that everything we agreed?' she asked.

'Looks like it,' the man said, stuffing a tattered sheet of paper into his pocket. He was middle-aged, but his voice sounded older, with the telltale rasp of a smoker. 'For a small fee, the lads could take those bags of rubbish too.'

Faith followed his gaze. 'Those bags of *rubbish* are my husband's clothes,' she said, 'and I'll decide what to do with them in my own good time. We agreed a fee and I expect payment in full, no deductions.'

The man gave her a broad grin, revealing tobacco-stained teeth. It was a shame because he might be attractive if he were to take better care of himself, not that Faith was interested. The antique dealer's only appeal was that he had offered the best price for furniture that had been in the house longer than she had.

'I authorised the payment not ten minutes ago, Mrs Cavendish. It should be in your account if you'd like to check.'

Faith let him wait as she used her phone to access her account. Her balance looked satisfyingly healthy. 'Fine, we're done,' she said.

As she led the way back out onto the landing, there was an echo to the house that hadn't been there before. Three of the five bedrooms had been emptied during the course of the day, leaving only her bedroom and the home office untouched. She had convinced herself that she wouldn't notice the difference, but she did. The house had been plundered.

Faith strummed her fingers on her crossed arms as she waited for the dealer to lace up his battered brogues at the front door. She regretted insisting that he and his workforce remove their shoes before entering the house. She wanted them gone, but this remaining invader showed no sign of leaving when he straightened up.

'If you change your mind about the other pieces we talked about, let me know. I have a buyer who would snap up that dining table.'

'I'll bear it in mind.'

'Or if there's anything else I can do,' he said. His grin suggested there was more than a business deal on offer. 'I'm sure it's a difficult time for you, but once you find a new place, give me a call.'

He raised his eyebrows expectantly. Faith had given him a sob story about losing her husband and needing to move out to clear his debts and the fool had swallowed it, hence the generous quote. He thought he'd sized her up; a lonely widow in need of a man to save her. How wrong he was on all counts.

She could tell him that she was more than capable of taking care of herself, that she had spent most of her life being happily independent before Derek swept her off her feet, but Faith didn't explain herself to anyone. 'As a matter of fact, I've already found a place,' she said. 'I'm moving to Marbella.'

His grin disappeared. Outmanoeuvred, the would-be Romeo stepped outside, but as he crossed the drive, he took one last cheeky look over his shoulder. 'I don't suppose you'd like to send me an invite when you're settled in Spain?'

Refusing to dignify the comment with a response, Faith was about to shut the door when a woman stepped through the gates the dealer had been closing behind him. Faith's stepdaughter, Ella, was in her late twenties but had none of the nonchalance of youth. Her back remained stiff as a board as she gave the antique dealer, the van, and then Faith a curious look.

'You're moving to Spain?' she asked.

Reluctantly, Faith opened the door wider and invited Ella inside before the neighbours could hear any more of their conversation. Despite the tall shrubbery and expansive gardens, someone had been snooping: Ella's arrival on the day a removals van was parked out front was no coincidence.

Derek had warned Faith that his divorce had been acrimonious but his ex-wife's bitterness was something to behold. Rosemary had been particularly aggrieved that her ex-husband had kept the family home despite her agreeing to a generous divorce settlement and plundering funds that would one day cost Faith her widow's pension. One or two neighbours had remained loyal to the first Mrs Cavendish, and Faith guessed she had Mr Newton next door to thank for Ella's arrival. A wronged wife of twenty-odd years was always going to out-trump the usurper widowed after only six.

Faith placed her hands on Ella's shoulders and air-kissed

her on both cheeks. With a reassuring smile, she said, 'I told him I was leaving the country just to get rid of him.'

Ella's shoulders remained tense. 'And who was he?'

'An antique dealer. I thought it was time to declutter.'

'You've been getting rid of stuff?'

'I've emptied some of the bedrooms, that's all.'

Ella's eyes grew wide as her gaze travelled up the sweeping staircase. One of the emptied rooms had been Ella's bedroom although she hadn't stayed a single night in the house since the divorce. Derek had let her take everything that was hers and it had remained a rarely used guest room ever since.

'Sorry, should I have warned you?'

'I know it's your furniture and you have a right to do what you want with it,' Ella replied, 'but . . .'

'You don't have to tell your mum,' Faith replied, feeling a swell of sympathy for her stepdaughter, caught in the middle of a battle that was already won as far as Faith was concerned.

'Can I take a look?' Ella asked, hanging her coat on the polished oak newel post.

She took the stairs without waiting for a reply and disappeared into the largest of the three emptied rooms. Her old bedroom was bare apart from the bin bags the antique dealer had offered to take away.

'I can't decide what to do with those,' Faith explained when she caught up with Ella. 'If there's anything you want, please take it.'

Unable to watch Ella tear open the bags, Faith pulled back a curtain and looked out across the gardens. The detached house was in a prime location in Woolton Village and although it was only six miles from Liverpool city centre, she could see more treetops than rooftops. Glimpsing the dense woodland that marked the boundary of Woolton Golf Course, she felt a pang of sadness as she recalled the raucous dinner parties she had hosted for Derek and his golfing buddies. Her heart suffered another blow when she turned to find Ella scavenging through the remnants of the life that had been wrenched from her.

'It's all his rubbish,' Ella said, straightening up. 'I don't want any of it.'

'Don't be like that,' Faith replied, clenching her jaw. 'He cared a lot about you.'

'Dad cared only for himself. You're lucky he didn't live long enough for you to work that out.'

This was Rosemary talking, not Ella, and any argument would be useless. There were times when Faith wished she could wash her hands of the whole family, but since Derek's death, she and Ella had formed a friendship of sorts and for as long as Faith remained in this house, she was the curator of Derek's legacy and his daughter was a part of that.

Faith tipped back her head and blinked hard before returning her gaze to Ella. 'I loved your father,' she whispered. 'Can you at least respect my feelings?'

Ella looked down at the sleeve of a dark suit reaching out from the open neck of a bin bag. She prodded it with her shoe. 'I'm sorry, but I hate to see you pining away for Dad. You deserve better,' she said, her voice softening. 'You know, moving to Spain might not be such a bad idea. Isn't it time for a fresh start?'

Faith considered her response, knowing it would be reported back word for word. Amongst Rosemary's many grievances was the terms of Derek's will, which had seen the lion's share of his estate left to Faith. What had they expected when Ella had effectively divorced her father in sympathy with her mother? The answer was obvious. They were waiting for a nice little handout should Faith sell up and move away. This was why Ella had been sent over. This was always why.

'If I do move, you'll be the first to know.'

'So you are thinking about it? Is that why you're emptying the rooms?'

Faith winced before she could disguise her feelings. She had expensive taste and in the last four years, money had been slipping through her fingers at an alarming rate. She had tried to cut back, going as far as taking a two-week cruise this year instead of the usual four, but it wasn't enough, and the proceeds from the sale of furniture was no more than a stopgap. Not that she'd ever admit as much to Ella or anyone else for that matter.

'Come on, let's go downstairs. I've missed lunch and I'm ravenous,' Faith said. 'I saw my friend Tara the other day and she sent me home with the most delicious cake.'

'I care about you, Faith,' Ella said, not easily distracted. 'You're still young. You need to move on.'

'Thank you for your concern,' Faith replied, 'but your efforts would be better spent helping Rosemary to move on. I'm happy where I am and as far as I'm concerned, the only way I'll be leaving here is in a box.'

As Faith approached the village hall, she caught a glimpse through the window of Steve and a couple of the others rearranging the chairs for their meeting. The foyer meanwhile was devoid of life, although someone had been busy setting out mugs on the trestle table and there was a tower of pre-packaged muffins sitting next to them. Following the sound of a running tap, she found Justine in the kitchen: undoubtedly the culprit responsible for the supermarket fare.

'Evening.'

'Oh, hi, Faith,' Justine said, her ponytail flicking like a horse's tail as she turned. 'Tara's running late, I'm afraid, so I offered to come in early. Thankfully, my mum's a godsend when it comes to childminding.'

'A relief, I'm sure, but I can't imagine it's something you want to be doing every time,' Faith replied.

Justine finished filling the kettle and set it to boil. 'It's no biggie. We all know Tara has her hands full at the moment,' she said as she rinsed out the flasks. She had yet to take a pause and the point Faith was attempting to make sailed over her head.

Faith was about to try again when a deep voice close to her ear gave her a start.

'Can I help with anything?'

She turned to find a stranger in their midst with dark brown hair and a sprinkling of grey at his temples. Dimples puckered his cheeks when he smiled, but it was his pale blue eyes that demanded Faith's attention.

'You came back then?' said Justine. She went to shake his hand, but water dripped from her fingers and she grabbed the first thing she could find to dry them on. It was the tote bag with its cheesy quote that Faith hated. 'Faith, this is Nick, one of our new members. Why don't you get to know each other and leave me to it?'

'Are you sure you can manage on your own?' Faith asked.

Justine almost dropped a flask. 'I'm fine,' she said. 'Honestly, go.'

Nick stepped back to allow Faith through the door and

placed his hand close to but not touching the small of her back as they returned to the foyer. 'Have you been involved with the group long?' he asked.

'About three years.'

They paused at a coat stand and Faith watched him slip out of his heavy woollen coat to reveal a dark grey suit that looked hand-stitched. 'And how was your initiation into our little enclave?' she asked.

'Just what I needed,' Nick confessed. 'For the first time, I feel like I can grieve properly.' He paused, momentarily distracted as he looked over Faith's shoulder. 'Ah, great. April's made it back too. Let's go over and I'll introduce you.'

'Not necessary,' Faith said, and as they went to greet April, it was Faith who placed her hand on Nick's back to guide him.

April appeared even more vulnerable than when they had first met, if that were at all possible. Her cheeks were hollow and her padded jacket made her look top heavy in comparison to her spindly legs wrapped in black Lycra. Faith didn't normally warm to people who looked ready to break rather than bend in a storm, but there was something about April that resonated.

Whilst there had been no other woman in Derek's life, Faith had felt betrayed by his death all the same. Derek had promised her a life of wedded bliss and she blamed him, in part, for making her a widow. Suing the car dealership had been her way of channelling that anger and frustration, but for April, they would need to find some other form of release.

Reaching her side, Faith went in for a hug just as April was slipping out of her jacket, and the embrace took her by surprise. When they untangled themselves, April was smiling.

'I bet you didn't expect to see me again.'

Faith spotted a damp autumn leaf stuck in April's hair and pulled it off. 'I would have hunted you down, if I hadn't.'

'Is Tara here yet?'

'No, but she will be,' Faith told her. 'I take it you've met Nick.'

April was swallowed up in a second hug and kept her shoulders hunched when she pulled away.

'I was wondering if I should have offered you a lift,' Nick said.

'Oh, no, it's fine. I live all the way over in Eastham.'

'It's a nice place,' said Nick. 'Have you lived there long?'

'Barring the time I lived with Jason, all my life. It's my parents' house,' April said. 'But I'm only staying there until I can afford to move out.'

'I'm surprised you can't. Didn't you say your husband worked for one of the councils? The Merseyside Pension Fund is a good investment . . .' His words tailed off and his mouth twisted. 'I'm so sorry, that was completely inappropriate. I used to be an investment banker and I was forgetting where I was.'

'Yes, you were,' admonished Faith.

'It's OK,' replied April, blushing on behalf of Nick. Her eyes narrowed when she added, 'Unfortunately Jason opted out of the pension scheme when he started work, not thinking through the consequences of his actions.'

'That's men for you,' added Faith.

'On behalf of all mankind, I'm sorry,' Nick said, holding Faith's gaze until she gave in and smiled.

It was April who filled the pause. 'I still haven't worked out what to wear to these things.' She pulled self-consciously at the hem of her man-sized Game of Thrones T-shirt, a

49

memento from her marriage if Faith wasn't mistaken. 'I feel completely underdressed next to you two.'

'Oh, don't let this fool you,' Nick said, loosening his tie. 'I had to come straight from work.'

'And what is it you do if you're no longer in finance?' asked Faith.

'I run a fleet of limousines. Basically, I'm a glorified chauffeur.'

'So you're a businessman,' Faith corrected. She didn't agree with people underselling themselves.

'Trying to be,' he replied. 'And what do you do, Faith?'

'I'm a biomedical scientist: I examine human tissue and pick out the cancer cells from the normal ones.' It was a skill she wished she could apply as easily to a person's character. She was still trying to work out Nick, who wasn't anything like she had imagined when Tara had described him. He didn't look the type to cry, but she would like to see it.

'And are you from the other side of the water too?' he asked.

'No, Woolton.'

'We're practically neighbours then. I'm from Hunt's Cross.'

They compared notes on favourite eateries until Faith spied Justine carrying two flasks of hot water over to the tables. 'About time too. Come on, let's get our drinks.'

The three were temporarily separated as more people arrived and wanted to chat. While Jodie and Nadiya made a fuss of April, Faith kept an eye on the door, but as seven o'clock approached, Tara failed to make an appearance. Nick had been pulled into a conversation with Steve and some of the other men, but he returned to April and Faith when Justine began directing them to their seats like a traffic cop.

Faith ignored Justine's instructions and laid claim to three chairs of her choice. She sat down on the first, but April and Nick became flustered when they both went to take the seat next to her.

'Sorry, you take it,' said Nick, the now familiar dimples appearing in his cheeks. 'I don't know why I'm so nervous.'

'Me neither,' April said.

In a show of chivalry, Nick took a step back and sat down on the third chair, leaving the gap next to Faith for April to fill, but before she could take it, she was distracted by the arrival of Tara and Iain. She turned to wave and by the time she turned back, Justine had claimed the much fought-after middle seat.

'Shall we get started?' Justine said loudly, seemingly unaware of April's displacement.

'Here, take my place,' Nick said.

Before he could stand, Justine placed a hand on his arm. 'It's probably best that you stay close to me for the first few sessions. April, you can sit over there next to Tara.'

'Apologies for being late, everyone,' Tara said once they were all settled. She was out of breath but didn't pause as she went on to open the meeting.

'It's good to see you back, Iain,' Justine said the moment they had dispensed with the introductions and updates. 'How are things?'

'Challenging.'

'Not because of me I should add,' Tara added, causing a ripple of laughter around the room.

'Definitely not you,' he replied, taking Tara's hand and giving it a squeeze. 'The good news is our solicitor doesn't see any reason why we can't complete the house move before Christmas.'

51

'Not that everyone will find that cause for celebration,' Tara warned.

'My in-laws aren't particularly happy with our plans. They think it's too soon,' Iain said. For Nick and April's benefit, he added, 'It's been three years since Joanna died and I'll admit, it still hurts like hell. I didn't plan to fall in love again, but I have and I'm ready to do this. Unfortunately my in-laws live in Newcastle so they don't see the difference Tara has made to our lives.'

'Has Lily come around to the idea yet?' asked Faith.

'She's quietly accepting – more quiet than accepting if I'm honest,' Iain said. 'I just hope her grandparents don't reverse what little progress we've made when she visits them over half-term.'

'It's funny how everyone has an opinion on how we should grieve,' Jodie said. 'First they're telling you to get out more, and the next thing they want you to slow down.'

Faith guessed Jodie had a story to tell. One comment could send the group off on a tangent, but Tara was there to make sure they kept their focus on one issue at a time. She was good at that. Better than Justine.

'Iain's going to have a word with them beforehand to make sure they don't give Lily mixed messages,' Tara said. 'With so much upheaval, what she needs from all of us is consistency. We're hoping they'll come around.'

'I hate to say it but they'll have to if they want to be a part of their granddaughter's life,' said Iain. 'I know they're grieving too, but Lily's welfare has to come first.'

There were mumbles of agreement and a couple of members went on to share their experiences of juggling relationships with their late partners' families, but once the subject had reached its natural conclusion, Tara turned to April and Nick.

'And how have you both been since the last meeting?'

Of the two, Faith expected Nick to speak up, but he simply nodded for April to go first. To Faith's surprise, his encouragement worked.

'I've been better,' April replied. 'I'm still trying to work out how I feel and how I want to feel, if that makes sense?'

'That's the one thing you learn fast here,' Nadiya said. 'What you're going through might sound confusing, alarming or downright weird to other people, but to us it's normal. You're not alone.'

'I'm starting to realise that,' April said. She glanced across to Faith when she added, 'It's a relief to know I don't have to keep all my thoughts locked away, although I'm not quite ready to tell everyone everything.'

'You can be selective,' Faith said. 'We all are.'

April pulled at her T-shirt. 'It's like when people ask if I've watched the final season of *Game of Thrones* yet and I feel stupid explaining why I can't. Jason and I always watched it together, and I'm so angry that he died before the finale aired. I can't watch it without him.'

The chair next to Faith squeaked as Justine straightened up. 'Anger is perfectly natural, April,' she said. 'It's one of the five stages of grief that we all process over time.'

'Oh, please, not this,' Faith muttered.

'Denial, anger, bargaining, depression and finally, acceptance,' Justine recited.

'Not that everyone experiences grief in such nice, neat stages,' Tara said diplomatically. Like Faith, she questioned the efficacy of applying that particular grief model like a Band-Aid.

'Of course not,' Justine said. 'Some people don't experience every stage, or not necessarily in that order, and it's perfectly normal to go back and forth between the stages.'

'Or to put it another way,' Faith said, 'you'll experience a lot of different emotions to greater or lesser degrees and at random times. Some days you might go through all five stages at once, or is it seven now, I lose track?'

'The stages are helpful to some people,' Justine insisted.

'I'm sure they are,' Faith said through gritted teeth, 'but for others it can be downright distressing, especially when someone with all the best intentions tells them that they should be at this particular stage or another. We are where we are. There's no road map.'

'Some of us seem to have become stuck on the anger stage,' Justine said, jutting out her chin.

'I have a lot to be angry about, Justine. Derek didn't need to die.'

'But at some point you have to move past that stage.'

'And move on to bargaining? Give me a break.'

Unlike Justine, Faith's understanding of the psychology of grief hadn't come from a Sunday magazine supplement; in fact, she had read extensively on the subject. Returning to April, she said, 'Did you know that the five-stage grief model was originally developed by Elisabeth Kubler-Ross after observing terminally ill patients? She expanded it later to include other types of loss but even she noted that popular culture had misunderstood her theory. The stages aren't supposed to be linear or predictable, if they exist at all.'

'I have heard quite a few people mention the stages I'm supposed to go through.'

'Yeah, Mrs Do-goody down the road and the bloke who delivers the newspapers,' Faith said.

She turned her head and was about to give Justine her best withering look when Nick caught her eye. She couldn't tell if the spark in his eyes was fear or admiration. After taking a breath, Faith released it with a sigh. 'Maybe I am holding on to my anger, but sometimes that's what gets me through the day. All I'm saying is that theories are made to be disproved and there are scientists better qualified than me to offer alternative grief models.'

'There's one based on continuing bonds,' Tara said, her soft voice adding balm to the discussion. 'It's where we redefine our relationship with our loved one, finding ways to keep them with us by allowing their influences to play a part in our new lives. There's no end stage, no point where we have to find closure and put the past behind us. I've been thinking about it a lot lately, wondering if there's a way for Lily and Molly to keep Joanna and Mike as a part of our new family.'

'I can understand how Lily must feel having to move home,' said Faith. 'My beautiful house is the strongest connection I have with Derek, but if we're talking about continuing bonds, his legacy goes far beyond the materialistic trappings of life. It broke my heart when I took the decision to withdraw his life support, but I made the right choice when I agreed to donate his organs. It comforts me to know four people are alive today because of him.'

'I talk to my wife's photo all the time and ask her advice,' Steve said. 'I can feel her pushing me out the door when all I want to do is lock myself away. It's why I managed to drag myself here in the first place.'

'And Justine and I would never have set up the group if it

55

wasn't for Mike and Lisa,' Tara added. 'Our paths have all taken a turn we never expected, but when we do something to challenge ourselves, it's nice to be able to glance over our shoulders and say thank you, I did that because of you.'

'Erin's death devastated me.' Nick was staring at the floor so he didn't see every face turn in his direction. 'After she died, I completely shut down,' he continued. 'I lost everything and that might have been her legacy, but she deserved better from me. She always did.' He tried to continue but his voice caught in his throat. 'Sorry.'

Justine reached over to touch his hand. 'I'm sure Erin would be proud of you for being here.'

Nick straightened up as Justine pulled her hand away. 'Actually, she'd probably tell me to man up. She said that a lot.'

'That won't do you any good here, mate,' Steve told him. 'It's the one place where you don't have to hide your feelings.'

'I think that was part of the problem, but I'm happy to report I've been turning things around,' Nick replied. 'After losing my job, I put on loads of weight to the point where people stopped recognising me. Then I realised it was the one part of my life I could control, so I hit the gym and literally worked out my frustrations.'

'I've tried working out,' April said, 'but I can't say it made me feel any better.'

'Give it time,' Nick said. 'I was lifting weights when I had this lightbulb moment about starting a limo business. I invested every last penny into it and, touch wood, it's going well.'

'As are you,' Jodie said.

'I have my moments. I can't tell you how many times I've had to pull over so I can bawl my eyes out. But just in case anyone's thinking of using my services, I don't usually break down when I have passengers in the back.'

'Letting loose my emotions while driving is my speciality,' Steve admitted. 'I have two teenage lads and the last thing they want to see is me snivelling.'

'Thankfully, I don't have kids,' replied Nick, 'but respect to those who have to deal with someone else's grief as well as their own.'

When Nick glanced at Faith, she felt compelled to respond. 'I have a grown-up stepdaughter, but I gave up trying to manage her feelings a long time ago.'

The comment was the perfect segue into the broader topic of difficult relationships, and nearly everyone had a contribution to make. By the time Iain returned to his problems with his in-laws, it felt like the conversation had come full circle and Tara suggested they break up early, leaving time for another coffee and Justine's untouched muffins.

While Tara was cornered by Jodie, Faith went to join April in the foyer and Nick followed. They chatted for a while, but when the discussion turned to fitness regimes, Faith saw it as the perfect opportunity to leave them to it. She had unfinished business.

Justine was understandably wary when she was pulled to one side, but Faith's expression was full of concern when she said, 'These meetings appear so seamless but I was thinking about what you said before about juggling childcare. It made me appreciate the extra effort you've taken tonight,' she said. 'How are things at home? It must be tough.'

'Oh, we manage.'

Faith leant forward. 'Only manage?'

'Well, let's just say it's not easy now that Isla's graduated to secondary school. Two school runs before work are a daily challenge, I can tell you.'

'No wonder the strain has been showing,' Faith said, placing a hand gently on Justine's arm. 'You spend so much time supporting the newer members, it's easy to forget that you need support too. I'm sorry if I was a tad harsh on you in the meeting.'

'Oh gosh, it's fine,' insisted Justine. 'If you can't be honest and open in the meeting, where can you?'

'The same applies to you, remember that,' Faith said, her tone one of sympathy. 'You must be worried about Tara. She's another one with her hands full, and I know she thinks we could carry on without her but how would we fill the void? She's been dropping hints about me taking over if she leaves. Can you imagine?'

Justine paled. 'No, not really.'

'Exactly, but I can't see you coping on your own either. We need to look after both of you. Don't suffer alone.'

'That's very kind of you, Faith, but I . . . I'm fine, honestly.'

Through the crowd, Faith spied Nick coming to join them. The timing was perfect. 'That's super,' she said, releasing her grip on Justine's arm. 'Here, I'll leave you two to it.'

She stepped away, but Nick pursued her.

'I'm heading off,' he explained, 'but it was a pleasure meeting you, Faith.'

'I'll see you next month then.'

'You couldn't keep me away,' he promised. 'But I was thinking it might be an idea to set up a WhatsApp group.'

Faith wrinkled her nose. 'We made a stab at using it at work, but all those pinging messages were so irritating. I muted all the conversations.'

'I hope you won't do that to me,' Nick said, tilting the phone in his hand.

'I can't promise,' Faith said. In the pause that followed, she realised he was waiting to take down her phone number. She reeled it out without thinking.

STATEMENT

The Widows' Club @thewidowsclub
We are saddened by the distasteful remarks on social media and in the tabloid press but are unable to respond to criticism whilst the police investigation is ongoing. The incident was a tragedy and we ask that people be respectful.

5

April lay on her back listening to the rattle of raindrops hitting her bedroom window. Darkness pressed against her closed lids and tried to push her back towards sleep as she struggled to work out if she had to get up for work. The sun hadn't risen, but that meant nothing. It was nearing the end of October and the days were getting shorter. Winter was on its way, which immediately laid a trail of languid thoughts towards Christmas.

They had bought a beautiful blue spruce last year and the memory of decorating the tree evoked the smell of woodland and the taste of mulled wine. Jason would recall only how he had picked pine needles out of his socks throughout January – except, April's weary brain told her, he wouldn't.

Pain stabbed at her heart, making April gasp, and she wrapped her arms tightly around her body. She stayed like that until she lost track of time and consciousness, but even as she slumbered, she was aware of the space in the bed next to her. When the duvet moved, she let out a whimper and was pulled into a dream not of her choosing.

Bright light flooded the room and April snapped her eyes

open to catch sight of Jason jumping out of bed. Wearing only shorts, his skin glowed a healthy pink. She could feel the warmth radiating from his body and everything about him felt real. She needed him to be real.

'You're here,' she said, her voice catching.

'Of course I am. Where else would I be?' he asked, looking around the flat they had shared together.

'I thought . . .' she began, raising herself on to her elbow. She didn't want to mention his death for fear of breaking the spell. 'I don't know. I'm just glad you're here.'

Jason's features twisted. 'You thought I was with another woman.'

'I didn't. I never—'

'Don't lie to me, April. Don't lie to yourself,' he warned. 'How could you think I'd cheat on you? I don't understand why you don't trust me. What did I do wrong?'

'You didn't do anything wrong. It's me. I'm being paranoid. I'm sorry,' she cried.

He fixed her with a stare. 'Why do you hate me so much?'

'I don't. I love you.'

'Liar,' he snarled.

'I'm not.'

'Go on, spit it out. Tell me why you hate me.'

April drew herself up so she was kneeling on the bed. She had longed to confront Jason, and this was her chance.

'Say it, April.'

'Fine then!' she yelled. 'I hate you because you died! You're dead, Jason! You lay down next to me and you just died. There was no goodbye. No warning.' Her voice grew weaker. 'You left me alone with your cold, dead body. It was horrible. It still is.' She clawed at the bedclothes, but her anger was spent and only the pain remained. 'The only person who could have helped me through something like that is gone. If you loved me so much, why do that to me? Why Jason?'

As quickly as it came, the vision dissolved and darkness filled the room. It filled April's lungs too and she struggled for breath. Panic consumed her as she fought her way out of the dream, and with one final, shuddering gasp, she opened her eyes. She was no longer kneeling but lying on her back. Above her head in the gloom, she could make out the limp paper lampshade that hung in her old bedroom at her parents' house.

Covering her face with her hands, April let the tears confined to her dream seep into the real world. She recalled her angry words and hoped she hadn't screamed them out loud. She held her breath and listened, but there was no sound except the thudding of her heart, which skipped a beat when she felt movement beside her again. Something cold touched her cheek.

'Oh, Jesus,' she whispered, recoiling until she remembered who was in bed with her. She allowed herself a smile as a wet tongue licked away her salty tears. She could hear the thud of a tail hitting the mattress as she turned to face her companion. 'You scared the shit out of me, Dexter.'

Since moving back home, her mum's cockapoo had been allowed to break the house rules and sleep upstairs. He was meant to guard against April's nightmares, but the dog's nocturnal movements had been responsible for the dark path her mind had just taken her down.

With Dexter's head resting on her chest, April threaded her fingers through curls of fur and sought to hold on to the silvery threads of the dream she ought to let go. She had told Jason she hated him and she had meant it. She did hate him, or at least she hated the dead Jason. He had every reason to be mad with her. She was doubting him, and she couldn't be sure he deserved it.

Joining the group had made April look at her grief with a more critical eye, and each member had offered a different perspective. She hadn't been sure what to make of Faith at first. She wasn't as warm or as open as Tara, but there were times when April caught a reflection of her own grief in Faith's eyes. The difference was that Faith didn't try to hide the kind of fury that April could only acknowledge in her dreams.

Whether it could be called a stage of grief or not, anger was a very real part of April's grieving process, as were the doubts she nurtured about Jason's character. She wanted to hate him, and convincing herself that he had been unfaithful was a neat way to validate that rage. She needed to be more like Faith and be honest about that. She had audited Jason's life and found nothing more than a handful of cash withdrawals. It was another change of behaviour that could be linked to what was going on in his brain. Doctors didn't know everything. It was time to let go of this idea that Jason wasn't worth breaking her heart over.

Turning onto her side, April snuggled up to Dexter, and the malleable mutt obliged by spooning with her. The soporific sound of the dog's snoring relaxed April's body and mind. She smiled, having finally worked out that it was Saturday and she could doze a little longer before paying a visit to the cemetery to make an overdue apology.

Taking the path around the side of the church, April filtered out the distant hum of traffic and the occasional bleat of a car horn, and concentrated only on the crunch of autumn

66

leaves underfoot. She and Jason hadn't been churchgoers, but his parents had wanted him buried here and it was one less decision for April to make when there had been so many others being forced upon her.

Eight months on, some decisions were yet to be made. Moving back home was meant to be a temporary arrangement and, whilst her parents were happy to keep her in the nest to rest her wings, April was no fledgling. Her so-called messiness clashed with their organised clutter, her binges on box sets were countered by daily doses of soap drama, and the rock music that got her moving in the morning chimed against the murmurings of Radio Four.

She envied her fellow group members who had a vision of what their new lives should look like, whether or not they were there yet. Even Nick had some idea of where he was going and what he wanted to achieve, and he had looked surprised and saddened when she had mentioned living with her parents. Every one of them was a survivor, while in contrast April remained a victim, trapped beneath the wreckage of a life that had collapsed around her. To escape, she had thought she needed to dismantle everything, including her marriage, but after her most recent nightmare, she realised she had gone too far.

April passed the ramshackle rows of headstones nearest the church without pausing to read the weather-worn names of the husbands and wives whose cherished memories had been eroded by time. The section of the graveyard reserved for its newest committals was hidden from view by a row of firs, but, as April approached, she felt the hairs on the back of her neck prickle.

Her pace slowed and the crunch of leaves became a whisper

lost to the soughing of the evergreens. No one would hear her approach and, as she dipped beneath the shade of a tree, she tensed, preparing for that first glimpse of Jason's imagined lover. Wisps of her dream floated through her mind until tears blurred her vision. She was looking for someone who didn't exist.

The white marble of Jason's headstone sparkled in the sunshine but offered no warmth as April trailed a finger across her husband's name. She knelt down in front of the patch of earth where his cremated remains had been interred, marked by a square of marble filled with pale frosted pebbles and a spray of white lilies. On another day, April might have questioned who had left them, but not today. They could only be from his mum, who made regular visits to tend his grave, although April doubted Jason would appreciate the flowers. He would much prefer the bottle of beer she took from her pocket and placed upright in front of the headstone.

'I don't know if you played any part in my dream this morning,' she whispered, 'but you need to know that I don't hate you. I hate that everything in my life has to be transformed into something other than us. I hate that you left me, Jay.'

April stroked the velvet petals of a lily and when her fingertip pricked on the calling card, she told herself that turning it so the writing faced her was accidental. The message was from a mother to her beloved son, as April knew it would be. The futile search for tokens left by another woman had to stop.

'I took what we had and tried to turn it into something I'd gladly throw away. I didn't want to think about how happy you made me,' she said as tears slipped down her face unchecked. 'But you did make me happy.'

April poked at the flower spray. The edges of the lilies were yellowing, and a couple had grown limp and brown. She suspected Jason's mum would return tomorrow with a fresh spray, but April didn't want to leave decaying flowers on his grave. Her shoulders shook as she picked out the dead blooms from the arrangement.

'I love you, Jason and I know you loved me. Please forgive me. I'm so sorry.'

April went to cover her face with her hands, but the movement unbalanced her and she fell forward. She grabbed hold of the marble border and stared downwards past the lilies, as though she could see through the earth to the small oak box containing ash and broken dreams.

'I miss you so much,' she cried over and over as her tears trickled down her nose and splashed onto the thinned-out spray of bruised petals. Still sobbing, she pushed the arrangement out of the way and sank her hands into the misshapen pieces of smooth glass mixed with dead leaves and the detritus of a summer Jason had never seen. She grabbed handfuls of the pebbles and watched helplessly as they slipped through her fingers.

As one particular stone dropped, she noticed it was whiter than the rest, and when she picked it up again, it didn't feel as cold. Wiping her eyes with the back of her hand, she realised the pebble wasn't glass at all. White and smooth, it appeared to be a flattened oval, but as April explored its circumference with her fingers, she noticed a dip in the centre of one of its longer edges. Turning it on its side, there was no mistaking the shape of a heart.

Squinting, April examined every millimetre of the stone. She rubbed her thumb over one side and felt a roughness that wasn't on the other. There was a scratched engraving so faint it was difficult, but not impossible to read with the naked eye: April stared at it long enough for her tears to dry.

Her nose was blocked and her throat hurt each time she attempted to swallow back the lump of dread. This token of love had not been dropped casually, or placed gently on her husband's grave. It had been buried out of sight. It was a gesture to be shared privately between the giver and the man whose remains lay beneath the dirt. April wasn't meant to see it.

After months of torturing herself with guilty thoughts of betrayal, April had visited the cemetery to bury her doubts, but instead she had unearthed a secret. The warm stone burned her palm and she was tempted to hurl it across the rows of headstones and into oblivion where it belonged, but instead she dropped it into her pocket.

Her breath came out in short, shallow gasps as she fought to contain the anger and the pain. She brushed off the mud clinging to her jeans and glared at Jason's headstone, too angry to speak. She was about to walk away when she caught sight of the bottle of beer she had left. She picked it up and in a move Jason had taught her, used the corner of the headstone and the side of her hand to knock off the bottle top. The beer tasted as bitter as her thoughts.

6

The fluffy dog sprinting across Pickering's Pasture towards Tara looked like a Steiff teddy brought to life, with its tongue lolling and ears flapping. At the end of a rapidly extending leash was April, one arm stretched forward and the other trailing behind. Tara made the mistake of bending forward to greet the dog and he ploughed straight into her.

'Oh Tara, I'm so sorry,' April panted as she caught sight of the muddy paw marks smeared over her caped coat. 'Dexter, will you sit still for one minute. I said *sit*!'

Dexter emitted an excited whine but otherwise ignored his mistress and continued to add streaks of ochre to the velvety blue of Tara's coat. 'It's fine, it's only second-hand,' Tara said, choosing not to use the word vintage.

April's cheeks burned as she pulled a bag of dog treats from her pocket. The cold breeze carried the scent, and with the next command, Dexter sat down and wriggled his bottom into the earth as he waited for his reward.

'He doesn't deserve this,' April muttered as she threw a treat into the air for Dexter to catch. 'He's good most of the time but he only really listens to Mum.'

'He's unbelievably cute. Molly would be beside herself.'

'I thought you might bring her with you.'

'It's half-term so she's spending a few days at Mum's while Lily's visiting her grandparents in Newcastle. They'll both be back for Halloween, but for now I'm enjoying some child-free time. And besides,' Tara added, 'I got the impression from your messages that you might prefer to talk without the interruptions of a squealing ten-year-old. So how are you?'

April yanked the lead to stop Dexter launching himself at Tara again and said, 'Maybe we should start walking.'

'OK, but let's stay within sight of the car park for now. Faith shouldn't be long.'

As they made their way down a sloping hill to the footpath that followed the banks of the Mersey, Tara expected April to explain what was behind her invitation to take a Sunday stroll, but instead she asked, 'How's the house move going?'

'We're on target to complete contracts by early December,' Tara replied, rubbing her jaw. It had been aching for days and she suspected she was grinding her teeth in her sleep. 'Six weeks and counting.'

'I'm so happy for you,' April said, but her voice cracked. Recovering quickly, she added, 'Are the girls excited yet?'

'We're making progress of sorts. Molly made me an offer the other night that I couldn't refuse.'

As April turned to Tara, she held up a hand to shield her face from the low sun. Dark shadows bruised her eyes. 'Why do you make it sound like that's a bad thing?'

'We had a bit of a conundrum with the new house,' Tara began. 'Of the two bedrooms for the girls, one is a double and the other a tiny box room. Iain suggested they draw straws and when Molly won, Lily said she didn't care, she would go and live with Joanna's parents. The whole thing was about to degenerate into a family meltdown when Molly quietly suggested that she didn't mind taking the smaller room if it meant Lily would stay . . . *and* if I agreed to get her a dog for Christmas.'

'Wow, she's some negotiator.'

'I've told her I'll only consider getting some sort of pet when we're settled, and she seems happy with that for now.'

'And Lily?' asked April.

'We'll see what happens.'

'It's the unknown that scares her.'

'It scares us all,' Tara replied as they reached the river's edge. 'What's wrong, April?'

Her friend looked across the water towards Ince Marshes where the brutal industrial landscape cut into the horizon. 'Maybe we should wait for Faith.'

'Did someone mention my name?'

Dexter had been digging up sods of earth on the embankment, but stopped at the sound of a new voice. His hindquarters tensed as he prepared to launch himself at Faith, who was wearing a full-length woollen coat in a beautiful shade of olive green.

Faith peered at the dog over the rim of her sunglasses. 'Down!' she said in a low growl.

Dexter pressed his body to the ground while April's jaw dropped. 'Here, you take him,' she said, offering the leash.

'Good grief, no. I can't stand dogs. I'm more of a cat person.'

'I didn't know you had any pets,' April said.

'I don't, but if I had to choose, it would be a cat. They seem less needy.'

'You make a good point,' Tara said as she watched Dexter slink away from Faith to hide behind April. His lower half was caked in mud and he no longer looked like a teddy bear that anyone would want to cuddle. Perhaps she *should* have brought Molly with her.

'Which way should we go?' asked April when Dexter resumed tugging on his leash.

They had the option of walking upriver for a closer view of the bridges spanning the Mersey at Runcorn, but Tara turned her back on the sun, and they set off on the path that skirted the edge of the pasture and led to an ancient duck decoy cut out of the salt marshes to attract water fowl. 'We might be able to spot Hale lighthouse across the marshes.'

'I imagine this would be quite a nice route for a jog,' said Faith.

'You're taking up running?' asked April.

'No, I meant for you,' Faith replied. 'You seemed very interested in Nick's fitness regime. I thought you two might have formulated a plan by now.'

Faith's comment sounded innocent, but Tara picked up an undertone. Did she think there was something developing between the group's newest members? Tara had seen April and Nick talking after the last meeting, but when she had gone over to join them, April had looked relieved to have the extra company. If there was any interest, it was one-sided.

'He hasn't been pestering you, has he?' asked Tara.

April's laugh held no mirth. 'No. And how could he? He doesn't have my number.'

'But he—' Faith snapped her mouth shut before she could finish her sentence.

'What?' demanded Tara. 'You didn't give it to him, did you?'

'Of course not,' she said. It wasn't often that Faith was wrong-footed, but she sounded unsure when she added, 'He mentioned setting up a WhatsApp group, that's all, and I presumed you'd all swapped numbers.'

'He never mentioned it to me. Do you think he needs more support than a monthly meet-up?' asked Tara. 'According to Justine, his only family is one sister. Could he be reaching out?'

'He's not shown any interest in going over to the pub whenever Steve's asked,' April said. 'I get the impression he's the type who prefers women's company.'

Tara was inclined to agree. Nick did appear more at ease talking to the female members of the group, in fact she could remember him making a point of saying goodbye to Faith. She could see Nick with his phone in his hand. 'Did he ask you for your number, Faith?'

She huffed rather than give an answer. 'Was there a point to coming out today? I thought you had some news for us, April.'

When April dug her hand into her pocket, Dexter's ears pricked at the rustle of the treat bag, but the object she pulled out was smooth and white.

'I found this on Jason's grave,' she said, unfurling her fingers.

The three women stopped to gather around April's open palm. Her hand shook, not least because Dexter had lost interest in them and was straining on his leash again.

'Here give me that,' Faith said, taking the leash and yanking it hard. 'Hey, you!'

Dexter froze immediately. The leash relaxed.

'Come here, sit down, and be quiet.'

The dog crept towards her, tail between his legs.

'I said sit!'

White crescent moons rimmed the dog's eyes as he sat down and gazed up at Faith. For the moment at least, they could concentrate on the object in April's trembling hand.

'What is it?' asked Tara.

April lifted the stone between her finger and thumb and turned it from side to side so it caught the light. 'It's a heart,' she said. 'I found it on Jason's grave. Someone had hidden it there.'

'Can I?' asked Faith. She pushed her sunglasses to the top of her head and held the stone inches from her nose. Her eyes narrowed. 'Are those random scratches, or could it be writing?'

'I've been staring at that bloody thing all night,' admitted April. 'I can make out a J and what might be a T for Jason's initials, but it's in the middle, so maybe it's a plus sign.'

'I think it's a plus sign,' agreed Faith, 'and there are more scratches to the left of it, but that's harder to read. Is it an S?'

'It could be,' April said with a shrug.

Taking back the stone and the leash from Faith, April set off again and the others followed. Dexter kept checking for Faith's approval. He was no longer leading the pack.

'It doesn't matter what the scratchings say, at least not completely. It's what they represent. Jason plus someone else – someone who isn't me,' April said. 'I'd almost convinced myself I was being paranoid and the cash withdrawals meant nothing. What an idiot am I? Totally trusting while he was alive and still ignoring what my subconscious has been screaming at me for the best part of a year.'

'I'm so sorry, April,' said Tara. She wanted to put an arm around her, but Faith was between them and as yet, she hadn't realised that April needed the human touch.

'I notice neither of you has said there's some other explanation.'

'It's possible the stone ended up on Jason's grave by accident,' Faith said, digging her hands into her pockets. 'A child could have picked it up from another grave and discarded it in the wrong place. But, when you consider the coincidence that the inscription includes the letter J, together with the bank account evidence and the doubts you had before Jason died, it does make for a compelling case.'

'What about you, Tara? What do you think?'

Tara walked in silence for a while. She wanted nothing more than for April to find some form of resolution and the simplest and least painful way for that to happen was to give up on the idea that Jason had secrets. Unfortunately, the heart-shaped stone pointed down a rockier path. 'No amount of talking is going to convince you one way or the other,' she said. 'You claim the letter that might be an S doesn't matter, but is there a name that springs to mind?'

'I don't know everyone in Jason's life, particularly his working life,' April said. 'I never audited the Highways Section because of the conflict of interest. I've met some of the staff, and I'm friends with a few, but Jason was on site a lot of the time and he dealt with all kinds of contractors.'

The tone of April's voice was off. Faith picked up on it too. 'But is there someone you do know?'

'I could list a dozen,' said April. 'There's a Sophie and a Siobhan, two Staceys, a Suzanne. Shall I go on?'

There was one name Tara noticed was missing. On the day

she had visited April's office, she had spoken to one of her colleagues. The woman had apologised on April's behalf for nearly knocking a couple of cake boxes out of Tara's hand, and had appeared desperately concerned – or had it been a severe case of guilt? Her name was Sara, and she had been heavily pregnant. Little wonder April wouldn't want to consider her a suspect.

As their pace quickened, April looked out across the river. The milky sunlight gave the water a pearlescent quality, while the land on the other side was painted in layers of varying shades of grey. There were church spires and other signs that the industrial landscape they were following had given way to gentler scenes. 'I think that's Eastham over there,' she said.

Tara remained quiet, as did Faith.

'There are some lovely places to visit. I could take you to Eastham Country Park some time. Jason and I were always borrowing Dexter so we could go for long walks and have brunch in the Mimosa Tea Garden,' she said, a wavering smile on her face.

'It sounds lovely,' Faith said with a heavy dose of cynicism.

'We were happy,' she replied, her steps faltering. 'And I don't understand why he would risk that for someone else. Yes, I could go through his phone and pick out women's names beginning with S, or any other letter you care to choose, but pretty much all of them are in my contacts list too. It doesn't make sense. Not one of them would be worth risking what we had. Not one.' She pursed her lips together and they trembled.

Tara willed Faith to put an arm around April or do something, anything, to let her know that she wasn't alone. When it became apparent this wasn't going to happen, she moved behind Faith and pushed her out of the way so she could slip an arm around April's waist.

'It's a lot to take in and you'll need time to process how you feel and plan what to do next,' Tara said.

'But where do I go from here?'

'You're the auditor,' Faith piped up. 'Do some more digging.'

Tara gave her a look, eyebrows raised. *You're not helping.* In response, she imagined eyes being rolled behind Faith's shades.

'You don't have to rush into anything,' Tara continued. 'Take it slowly. And keep talking to us.'

'I will,' April replied. They had reached the westerly edge of the pasture and were close to the hide where they could look out over the duck decoy, but April was already glancing back in the direction of the car park. 'But I've kept you long enough. I don't mind heading back.'

Tara had a million and one other things to do, but she wasn't going to pack April off home if she still needed them. 'I don't mind,' she said, withdrawing her arm so her friend could decide which path to take.

April did an about turn and her friends followed suit. Dexter was the last to notice, and hurried to catch up. He almost tripped Tara up as he wove through a forest of legs to be at Faith's heel.

'I think he likes you,' April said as she untangled the leash.

'I have a knack of attracting unwelcome attention,' she mumbled.

RESPONSES

Alex Butterworth @AlBut4550
Replying to @thewidowsclub
Your group has something to hide, no wonder you don't want anyone talking. From what I've read, there were a lot of arguments.

Jodie @iamJPriestly
Replying to @AlBut4550 @thewidowsclub
The papers are making it up. You have no idea what you're talking about.

Alex Butterworth @AlBut4550
Replying to @iamJPriestly @thewidowsclub
They're not making up a murder though, are they love?

7

Jason had been dead nine months, which perversely was the time it took to create a life; unless you were a widow; unless you had discovered your marriage was a sham. April's life could only be described as barren, although she hid it well. She ate when she wasn't hungry, slept although sleep was never peaceful, and rationed her display of emotions so as not to alarm anyone. The hardest part of her performance was in front of Jason's parents. She kept in regular contact, and whenever she spoke to his mum, her feelings became confused. They cried together and shared the sense of loss that April otherwise denied herself since discovering the stone on Jason's grave.

With the November support group meeting still over a week away, work was April's only refuge from troubled thoughts, but apparently not today. There was a cooing sound coming from the other side of the office that April studiously ignored. She had been over to say hello to Sara and smiled pleasantly at the six-week-old baby being passed from one clucking colleague to the next. It was only when the youngest member of the team, Georgie, was about to hand it to April that she had bolted back to her desk.

April had a lot of work to do. For months she had been assisting rather than leading reviews, but it was time for the team to stop carrying her. She had convinced her manager she was ready to tackle one of the departmental reviews that had slipped in the last year and she had been disappointed not to be given the Highways Section – it wasn't as if Jason worked there any more – but she was looking forward to losing herself in an audit of the staff attendance system.

Choosing a cross-section of employees to sample for her review was proving difficult, and the arrival of Sara and the baby had made it doubly hard. Her assignment was simply to confirm that time adjustments had been authorised, but an opportunity had presented itself. Faith had told her to keep digging, and that was what she would do.

April blocked out the background noise and stared at her screen. She had gathered a few names on her list so far and most were random selections, but not all. She needed to know what Jason had been doing behind her back and how he had found the time to get up to no good. They went to work together and they went out as a couple. There were only a handful of occasions she could recall in those last months when Jason had socialised without her, but if any of those nights had been a cover story, he had been thorough. There had been his team's Christmas meal and a few nights out with the lads, but all were documented on Facebook with photos as evidence. April had checked.

The only conclusion she could reach was that his illicit affair had taken place during the working week, which meant the council's attendance system must hold a vital clue. That was why Jason Thorpe's name was top of her sample list, but she didn't have to stop there. It was entirely possible that Jason had sneaked off work to see someone completely unconnected with the council, but since she was looking anyway, why not add a scattering of female employees whose first name began with S? What harm could it do?

The baby had started to cry and the sound played on every one of April's nerves. Its mother, however, was less perturbed. Sara handed a soother to Georgie and left her holding the baby while she made her way over to April.

'I hope we're not disturbing you,' she said.

'Don't worry, I can work through anything.'

Georgie glanced over at them. She was rocking the baby with a growing sense of panic. It – he – was still crying. Sara had called him Fred. She was anything but conventional.

'That's not what I meant,' Sara said. 'If this is upsetting for you, we can go.'

April's hands were splayed over the keyboard and one finger sought out the letter S. 'Can I ask you something, Sara?'

'Sure,' she said, drawing closer. Her hand came to rest on a stack of print-outs piled up on the corner of April's desk. On top of the pile was a white stone.

'How well did you know Jason?'

When Sara's fingertips sought out the curves of the love token, April's pulse throbbed against her ears.

'I knew him well enough to know not to be left at the bar whenever he ordered a round of shots,' Sara said, recalling one of their notorious nights out.

'He did pay you back, didn't he?'

'With interest,' Sara said as she spun the stone 360 degrees. 'What's this about, April? Is there something particular you're after?'

April held her friend's gaze. 'I sometimes wonder how well I knew him, that's all. There are definite gaps.'

'I'm no expert on grief, but maybe now that you can't make new memories with Jason, you want to hear ones you haven't heard before from other people.'

When Sara glanced down at the stone, April's heart skipped a beat, but there was no flicker of recognition on her friend's face. Sara was oblivious to the object's meaning.

'Yeah, something like that,' April agreed, resting her back against her chair and allowing her shoulders to relax.

'Have you talked to any of his mates? What about Callum? I'm sure he could tell a story or two, and Bree worked with Jason.'

'No,' April said, rejecting the idea with a shake of the head. It was possible that the pair had tales to tell, but Callum and his wife Bree had been Jason's friends more than hers and would never break his confidence. They would think they were protecting her. 'We've let our friendship drift and besides, going out with them was always a couples thing.' Forcing her tone to lighten, she added, 'I don't think it would look good if I suggested a threesome!'

'Never say never,' Sara said. 'Not that I'd know. There's only one person interested in these boobs.'

'He is beautiful,' April said, glancing over at the baby in Georgie's arms. She was tempted to take a closer look, no longer fearing the prospect of finding a reflection of Jason staring back at her. How awful was she to think that Sara would betray her like that?

But Jason had betrayed her, April reminded herself. And he hadn't done it alone.

'Do you want a hold?' Sara asked. She had that proud

mother expression when she added, 'He's quite cute when you get used to him.'

'I'd love to but . . .'

'You don't have to explain,' Sara said. 'And if you ever need to talk, I'm always at the end of the phone.'

'I don't deserve friends like you,' April said, her bottom lip quivering. 'You've had your own troubles this past year and I haven't even asked you about Connor. Has he made an appearance yet?'

'He's seen Fred and he'll be a part of his son's life whether he wants it or not. We're fine. Don't worry about us.'

'I will try harder to be a better friend,' April promised.

To prove her commitment, April returned to her computer once Sara had left her alone, and deleted her friend's name from the list. There were people she could still trust, and she prayed she was making the right choices.

8

The buzz of the hedge trimmer set Faith's teeth on edge as she set about cutting back the leylandii conifers that had grown at least another foot since her gardener, Leon, had tackled it earlier in the year. The hedge divided the land at the rear of the property from that of the neighbours, and she liked it to be high enough to shield her from prying eyes without leaving the rest of the garden in shade. Leon had made the job look easy.

It was Derek who had employed him, and Faith had continued with Leon's services for as long as she could, but sacrifices had to be made and she had taken the difficult decision to cut back his hours. For appearances' sake, Leon continued to maintain the front gardens, but Faith was no stranger to hard work and could take care of the rest. If by chance Mr Newton caught a glimpse of her cutting back the conifers, he would see only a figure dressed in black, wearing a baseball cap. He would never presume it was the second Mrs Cavendish.

If anything, pruning the hedge was a novel form of exercise, and Faith had convinced herself it was fun until the rotating blades of the trimmers snagged on a gnarled branch and she lost her balance. She stretched out her arms instinctively to stop herself from falling off the stepladder, and her grip on the trimmers loosened. With her finger still on the trigger, it arced forward and the whirring blades narrowly missed slicing into her thigh. She held back the cry for fear of being overheard, but the near miss left her shaken. She wept angry tears as she hacked at branches that she would not allow to defeat her.

When the job was done and the cuttings cleared away, Faith returned to the house, grabbed a bottle of Chablis from the kitchen, and dragged herself upstairs. She filled a deep bath and added a generous measure of her prized Jo Malone bath oil, because today she deserved it. Stripping off the cheap supermarket clothes she had been wearing, Faith sank beneath the suds and felt her old self return.

With Brahms playing in the background and her wine within easy reach, Faith leafed through a travel brochure. For as long as she cared to remember, planning a holiday was her way of surviving the pre-Christmas frenzy, and a couple of travel reps had been in touch already, having noticed their most loyal customer had yet to book her next trip. Faith had kept them dangling and there was no suggestion that she might forgo a holiday next year. It was something Faith had yet to admit to herself.

A two-week cruise around the Norwegian fjords took her fancy and as she folded the corner of the page, her phone rang. Her thumb hovered over the red decline button as she took a sip of wine. With an exasperated sigh, she accepted the call.

'Hello, Ella,' she said affably.

Faith's stepdaughter had made numerous attempts to call her over the weekend but irritatingly hadn't left a voicemail. Her persistence, combined with Faith's curiosity, had finally paid off.

'I'm glad I caught you at last. I was getting worried.'

'Ah, sorry about that. I treated myself to a little pamper weekend with friends,' Faith said as she put down her glass and flexed her hand. Her attack on the garden had cost her a couple of broken nails, and her skin had acquired a roughness she didn't like. With the money she had saved today, maybe she could afford a spa.

'I hope you had a good time,' Ella replied after a slight hesitation, as if she detected the lie.

Faith wouldn't be surprised if Mr Bloody Newton had a telescope trained on the house, but no matter. A fib told with confidence was far more compelling than whispering truths.

'Who knew a few days' relaxation would be so exhausting?' Faith said with a yawn. She lifted a leg out of the water and watched rivulets of scented oil glide over her skin and caress her tired muscles. 'It's probably my body's reaction to all that pummelling and prodding. Those Swedish massages are brutal.'

'I can imagine,' Ella said, possibly convinced. Possibly not. 'As long as you're looking after yourself.'

If Faith didn't do it, who would? Derek was gone.

She closed her eyes to staunch unexpected tears; she was stronger than this. She was a survivor and could face whatever life threw at her, even if it was getting harder. Only this week she had discovered that her department would face yet another reorganisation. It was an occupational hazard and, whilst Faith was good at defending her corner, it would invariably mean more duties being heaped upon her. She had no interest in acquiring new skills, she had adapted enough in her life.

Faith took another sip of wine and painted a smile on her lips loud enough for Ella to hear. 'So what can I do for you?'

'I have some news. Jack and I have set a date for our wedding. It's next July.'

'Oh, how lovely,' Faith said. It was a brave step for Ella, considering that her mother was testament to how a marriage could fail, and Faith wasn't exactly a good advert either. She wished her well.

'It's only going to be a small affair, but we would love it if you would come.'

'I wouldn't miss it.'

'I'll hold you to that,' said Ella.

Faith couldn't think of anything worse than an intimate wedding breakfast where Rosemary would deliver the speech in the stead of the father of the bride. Glancing at the travel brochure resting on the edge of the bath, she wondered if the wedding was the justification she needed for one last escape.

She yawned again. 'Sorry.'

'Before I let you go, there's something else I wanted to run past you.'

Reaching for her wine, Faith had an inkling she was going to need it. She should have known there was an ulterior motive for the call. 'Shoot,' she said.

'Last time I saw you, when you were having a clear-out, we talked about you making a fresh start,' Ella said. She paused for her stepmother to agree, but Faith remained tight-lipped. Only one of them had mentioned a fresh start. 'I know it's a difficult decision, but I was talking to Jack, and we wondered if it would be less of a wrench if I was the buyer?'

'Why on earth would you want to come back here, Ella? You hated your father,' Faith said, suspecting Rosemary was the true architect of this plan. She wanted the house back, and she had no qualms about using Ella as her puppet.

'I don't hate him,' Ella said softly.

Despite her annoyance, Faith smiled at the lie that had been delivered without conviction. Ella would have to do some serious backtracking to explain away the years of scorn she had poured over her father's memory.

'I had a happy childhood there before I went off to uni,' she said. 'And up until he dumped Mum, I thought Dad was a good dad. Who knows? Being back home might help me remember him in a better light.'

Faith almost choked on her wine. Rosemary would turn in her grave, if only she had one. 'Anything's possible.'

'And wouldn't it make life easier for you? Why pay for the upkeep of a house when you use only a fraction of it?'

Faith could almost admire Rosemary. She hadn't missed a trick. She had heard about the furniture sale and now the gardening, not to mention the car that hadn't been updated in over a year. She had picked up on all the signs that money was tight, and this was the argument she had told her daughter to use.

'And you think you can afford a house like this?'

'Not if we had to pay the full market value,' Ella said cautiously, 'but if we came to a private arrangement, there would be savings for both of us in terms of fees.'

Faith sat up, the water having lost its warmth. 'You have thought this through.'

'And will you?' asked Ella. 'Imagine a life full of new beginnings rather than living with empty rooms that remind you of what you've lost.'

To the untrained ear, the arguments were reasonable and persuasive, but not to Faith. How dare they discard her feelings so casually. She was well aware of the empty rooms. They were like open wounds, and Derek's family was ready as always to stick the knife in.

'Jack and I hope to have kids one day, Dad's grandchildren,' Ella continued. 'Don't you think he'd want us to bring the house back into the family?'

Faith forced down the corners of her mouth. 'I thought I was family, Ella.'

She imagined Ella kicking herself in the pregnant pause that followed. 'You're right, you are family. And you'd always be welcome.'

'I appreciate your concern and, as I've told you before, you'll be the first to know if I do decide to sell, but I'm not there yet.' Through gritted teeth, she added, 'I won't be pushed.'

'That wasn't my intention,' Ella said. 'I just wanted to float the idea past you as something you might want to consider. I'll be honest, I was in two minds whether to say anything at all, but I thought it was worth you knowing that there's another option on the table.'

'And that's very kind of you,' Faith managed to reply. 'But if you don't mind, I don't want to think about it right now. I'm tired.'

The call ended amicably enough and as Faith drained the bath, she attempted to put her words into action by not thinking about Ella's *kind* offer. Wrapping herself in a fluffy towelling dressing gown, she picked up her wine and travel

93

brochure and made her way downstairs. She paused in the palatial hallway and shuddered as an image came unbidden of Ella's offspring running through the house with Rosemary holding up the rear.

Faith could tell herself that the house was simply bricks and mortar, but it meant so much more to her than that. It represented the last vestiges of the dreams she had shared with Derek, and she would rather live with empty rooms than in some tiny apartment. She didn't want to downsize. Her parents had lived in a dingy flat above her dad's workshop, and the place she had rented before marrying Derek hadn't been much better. She loved this house. She would never surrender it, especially not to Rosemary.

Setting down her wine on a side table in the living room, Faith rolled up the travel brochure into a tight cylinder and fed it to the log burner that had been left ready to light. Faith would fight with all she had to keep Derek's legacy, and if that meant chipping more fingernails and sacrificing more luxuries, so be it. She flicked a match and as she watched flames lick at the glossy paper, her phone rang.

Faith was in no mood to continue her discussion with Ella, but when she realised it was an unknown number, she felt no relief.

'Hello?' the caller asked when Faith offered no greeting. 'Is that you, Faith?'

'Who is this?' she asked, feigning ignorance.

'Erm, it's Nick,' he said. 'I hope you don't mind me disturbing you.'

'What can I do for you?' she asked, leaving him to decide if she approved of him disturbing her or not. In fairness, his guess would be as good as hers.

After realising Nick had tricked her into giving him her number, Faith had been more annoyed at herself than him. She had let her guard down, having assumed she was in safe company in the support group, and Nick had taken advantage of that.

'It's our next meeting on Tuesday and since we're practically neighbours, I wondered if you wanted a lift,' he said. 'Steve keeps inviting me over to the pub and I thought you might be tempted if we can go in one car. I don't mind not drinking.'

Nick had gone from offering a lift to inviting her out for a drink in one deft move. Though she was quietly impressed, his efforts were wasted. 'I never go to the pub, which makes me think we'd be better travelling separately,' she said. 'Some of us have work the next day.'

'Oh, that's right. You're a bio-something scientist,' he replied, his tongue tripping over the syllables, a telltale sign that he didn't always pass on the opportunity for a drink. 'Maybe you could tell me more about it when I pick you up – as long as you use small words. I was never good at science.'

'I think you're cleverer than you let on.'

Nick let out a groan and Faith could hear the scrape of a palm rubbing against stubble. 'I used to think so,' he admitted. 'And I'm hoping the group will help me regain my confidence. I felt so much better after the last meeting. A lot of what you said about grief being a random mix of emotion struck a nerve.'

After a poor start to their conversation, Faith felt she was finally speaking to the Nick who had opened his heart to the group and not the bullish persona he used to impress his clients. Derek had been the same, but her husband had

95

eventually learnt that he couldn't win her heart the same way he won his contracts.

Realising where her thoughts had led, Faith stepped away from the flames she had been fanning. She didn't need nor want another man in her life. Romance was overrated, as poor April was in the process of discovering. Jason had cheated on her and, dead or alive, April needed to settle the score. That was where Faith could help. What her friend needed was some good old-fashioned revenge sex.

'If you're that keen on becoming a part of the group,' she told Nick, 'you can pick me up on the condition that you make an effort to get to know everyone. We all have something different to contribute, each with our own unique experience and perspective. What you can't get from me, you'll find from someone else.'

Faith was applying a final layer of mascara when the doorbell rang. She grabbed a silk blouse and buttoned it over her skin-tight jeans as she padded barefoot downstairs. Pausing halfway, she watched the dark silhouette of a man waiting for her. His tall, broad frame filled the leaded windows in the front door and she saw him reach up to ring the bell again, only to hesitate. His hand dropped and his silhouette shifted as he moved from one foot to the other. There was the flash of silver as he checked his watch. Nick was fifteen minutes early.

With a smile spreading across her face, Faith opened the door and put Nick out of his misery. 'What time do you call this?' she demanded.

He returned her smile. 'Sorry, in my line of business, it's better to be early than late.'

'You'd better come in,' she said, pushing the door open with her elbow as she continued to fasten the last of her buttons.

Nick's footfalls echoed down the hallway. 'It's an amazing place you have here,' he said, sneaking a furtive glance into the first reception room. The door was slightly ajar, revealing a stack of boxes atop the dining table. 'Have you just moved in?'

'I've been here ten years, the first six of which I spent with Derek,' Faith explained, closing over the dining room door. She was in fresh negotiations with the antique dealer to sell more of the furniture and had gathered up smaller items to auction on eBay. Every little helped.

'My husband had more traditional tastes and was loathe to make changes,' she continued. 'I've modernised here and there since he died, but it's a work in progress.'

'Preparing for a new phase in your life?'

'Something like that,' she replied, feeling no urge to explain her current dilemma. 'You can wait in the sitting room while I finish dressing. Did you want a drink?'

'I think I had more than my fair share the other night,' he said with a sheepish grin. 'I'm sorry if I was out of turn phoning you. I hope I didn't make you feel awkward.'

'If anyone was feeling awkward, it wasn't me,' she said. 'I take it you don't feel the need for Dutch courage tonight.'

'I don't touch the stuff if I'm driving and not only because my livelihood depends on a clean licence. It's devastating what damage drink-driving can do,' he said. 'Ah, sorry. I guess you already know that.'

'Derek's accident had nothing to do with alcohol.'

'Can I ask what happened?'

'You can ask, but you'll have to wait until we're in the car before you get an answer.'

Faith left Nick to wonder, but within ten minutes, she was setting the alarm and locking the front door. Nick had parked his car in front of her drive. The night was damp and drizzly and the haze from the street lamp picked out the black BMW's sleek lines and elegant curves.

When Nick opened the passenger door, a waft of polished leather filled Faith's nostrils. 'The limo business must be good.'

'What can I say, it's a dream job.'

'My husband loved his car,' she began as they pulled out of the drive. 'He locked it away in the garage without fail, and in the winter he was known to cover the engine in a blanket. Not that he knew much about the inner workings. Derek didn't know a spark plug from a crankshaft, but he was fastidious about keeping it properly maintained. He'd take it to a garage for something as simple as changing a wiper blade.'

'Most people are the same these days, even me. The problem is a lot of it's computerised.'

'That was part of the problem,' Faith said. 'Some kind of ABS warning light came on and when Derek explained that it was the brakes, I made sure he had it looked at straight away.'

'The brakes failed?'

'Not then. The car dealer couldn't find anything wrong with the car,' she explained. 'And the second time it happened, they claimed the fault was with the sensors and simply replaced them.'

'Easier than taking the car apart.'

'Exactly,' Faith agreed. It had been one of the strengths of the case she had brought against the dealership. 'A week later, the warning light was back on. It was a busy time for us. I was going away on a spa break and Derek had a lot of work pressures. It was me who suggested he ignore it. It was my fault.' Faith turned her head away from Nick and squeezed her eyes shut.

'Are you OK?'

'I should have made him get it checked again or cautioned him about driving too fast. I don't know. I could have done something . . .'

'You don't have to go on if you don't want to.'

'No, I'm fine,' Faith said, facing front again. 'Typical of Derek, he had been speeding down the M60 when the accident happened. From CCTV footage, it looks like the ABS failed while he was in the fast lane approaching slow-moving traffic. He clipped a couple of cars as he veered towards the hard shoulder and smashed into a barrier.'

'I guess he didn't stand a chance.'

'But Derek almost did survive. He was halfway out of the car when it went up in flames.' She had watched the recording, and it was scorched into her memory. 'It was a miracle there were no other fatalities. I suppose I should be thankful for that, but one fatality was one too many.' She could feel a familiar anger rise up through her body. 'It shouldn't have happened.'

'Christ, I'm so sorry. I hope you sued the garage for every penny they had.'

Faith didn't answer. It was none of his business and she had grown tired of crowing about money she no longer had.

'Something like that has to make you stronger,' Nick continued awkwardly.

'All adversity changes us.'

'And you've had more than your fair share,' Nick replied, taking his eye off the road to scrutinise her face.

Faith found herself laughing. 'I'll save my stories about my alcoholic father for another time.'

'You're an incredible woman, Faith,' he said before tearing his gaze from her. When Faith refused to respond, he squirmed in his seat. 'What I mean is, the whole group is inspiring. However sad the circumstances, it's been humbling to hear other people's journeys.'

'You've had a journey of your own.'

'I suppose I have,' he said, rubbing his knitted brow. 'It's just that I listen to stories like yours, or the others who had families to take care of, and . . . I don't know, I feel like I don't have a right to complain.'

Faith examined him as she might a specimen under a microscope. 'Oh, the group is going to have a field day with you.'

His features softened. 'You can't scare me. They're a great bunch.'

'I bet you were expecting a group of wailing weirdos.'

It was Nick's turn to laugh. 'Not at all.'

'Liar,' she said. 'I know I was.'

They were approaching Hale Village and, as they passed the hall, Faith noticed the Christmas decorations. 'Has Justine mentioned the Christmas party to you yet?' she asked. 'It's in a few weeks.'

'Yes, and I'm fully paid up. I hope you'll be going.'

'I think it's important that we all make the effort,' Faith replied as Nick drove into Ivy Farm Court car park. April's Corsa was in front of Tara's shop. 'And I was wondering if you might do me a small favour.'

100

Nick killed the engine and the internal lights lit up his face as he turned towards her. Faith was dazzled by his violet eyes. They were incredibly trusting. 'Anything,' he said.

'I need your help persuading April to come to the Christmas party.'

9

The group took their positions in the circle and, in a repeat of previous meetings, April found herself by Tara's side. She would have liked to be closer to Faith too, but they had become separated in the melee and she was on the opposite side of the circle, with Nick. April had seen them arrive together, and it was Nick who had made a beeline for her, hugging her like an old friend. He seemed about to ask her something when Justine closed down the chatter and corralled everyone into the meeting room.

'No Iain again?' Justine asked Tara.

'I'm afraid not. We complete in less than two weeks and Iain's making sure Lily's involved in deciding what to bring with them and what to let go. As you can imagine, it's been a long and painful process.'

'The important thing is you're here,' Faith said. She turned to Justine expectantly.

'Exactly,' Justine agreed.

'I hope you'll be letting Iain out for the Christmas do,' Steve said.

'It's literally four days before we move, and it did cross my mind that we should give it a miss.' There were mutterings around the room until she added, 'But we couldn't let you lot down. We'll both be there.'

'Is Lily still finding it hard?' asked Nadiya.

'It hasn't helped that her grandparents filled her head with all kinds of ridiculous ideas while she was away at half-term, like not being allowed to put up photos of her mum in the new house,' Tara said with an uncharacteristic growl in her voice. 'We've tried so hard to include her in every stage, but Joanna's parents have reinforced her fears and she's been having pretty bad nightmares. She's not interested in planning her new bedroom, even though Molly gave up the biggest room just to please her. I don't know what else we can do.'

'Have you thought about buying her a display case to put some of her mum's things in?' suggested Steve. 'Or a shelf would do. Our Jack has a "Mum" shelf, although he kept that quiet for a while. One day I noticed Bella's house keys were missing from the bowl in the kitchen where she'd left them. I felt sick because the boys had bought her the keyring one Christmas. Lo and behold, I found it, and her keys, on his shelf along with some other mementoes he'd appropriated.'

'That's not a bad idea. Thanks, Steve,' said Tara, nodding thoughtfully. 'So how is everyone else doing?'

Tara looked to April, but she shook her head. If they were talking about keepsakes, she didn't think anyone wanted to hear about the time sheets she had gathered to track Jason's last known movements. She had put a lot of hours into her latest audit and had even taken work home with her. She could see the sheets laid out across her duvet as she sat cross-legged on her bed. In her lap had been two phones, hers and Jason's.

April had gone back as far as September the year before, checking both their phone diaries against her husband's logged hours. Her heartbeat was thumping against her eardrums like a drumroll by the time she reached November, but when she spotted an afternoon Jason had booked as leave while she was at work, an eerie calm had descended. Within minutes she had found another clandestine afternoon off, and then another, right up to the week before he died. Clasping a time sheet in her hand, she had released a silent, tortured scream and, when it was over, the bed was littered with confetti.

They never took days off separately unless it was for something mundane like a repair in the flat or the delivery of a new appliance, but the only thing special about these dates were that they matched, or were close to, the dates of the cash withdrawals. In each case, Jason had claimed flexi leave – using accrued hours despite telling April that he never made up enough credit to take leave. All lies. So many lies, and only one undeniable truth. Jason had been having an affair.

April had tried not to think about who the other person might be, but of course she had. She had taken her time picking and choosing her sample list of employees, and she wasn't sure how she felt when her investigation drew a blank. No one she had targeted with her suspicions had been on leave at the same time as Jason. She ought to have felt some relief, but if anything, she was beset with frustration, and shame. Jason had turned her into someone she no longer recognised.

'I don't know that you ever get over it,' Steve was saying to a comment Nick had made, although April wasn't sure what it had been. The chatter from the group had floated over her head for the last five minutes, possibly longer.

I know how you get over it, April imagined herself saying. *You discover the person who wrenched your heart from your chest wasn't the person you thought they were. You realise that all that time you were loving them, you should have been hating them. You question whether the future you thought you had lost was ever yours.*

'But it does get easier,' Jodie said with a smile that grew broader as the group waited for the news she clearly wanted to share. 'I've been on a date. Two actually. I've finally reached the point where I don't want to be celibate for the rest of my life. And OK, it was nice thinking that the last person to kiss these lips was Ryan, but I have to get past that.'

'And you did by the sounds of it,' Faith said.

Jodie nodded. 'It was only a kiss, mind.'

April's pulse raced. 'Did it make you feel better?'

Jodie scrunched her nose. 'There was a brief moment of relief followed by all kinds of guilt –and not only because I knew I'd just let go of another piece of Ryan. The truth is, I didn't particularly like this bloke. He was a means to an end.'

'It broke the spell,' Faith said, glancing towards April, who blushed as if her friend had read her thoughts.

There was more chatter that faded in and out of April's consciousness and she didn't realise the meeting was over until Tara stood and touched her shoulder. 'Let's have a cuppa and a piece of cake before we leave,' she said.

By the time Tara had pushed a plate into April's hand, Faith and Nick had joined them. 'I was about to get our coffees,' Tara said. 'Do you want anything?'

'I'll help,' Faith said, tugging Tara away from their little group and leaving April with Nick.

'How are—' April began.

'The cake looks—' Nick said at the same time. 'Sorry, you first.'

'I was wondering how you were settling in.'

'It's been so much easier than I was expecting. How about you?'

April pushed the cake around her plate. 'It's weird. I don't know half the people here, but at the same time, I know them so well. I'm pretty sure I've made friends for life.'

'And it's good that we can do things outside of the group too. Are you going to the Christmas party?'

April's chin was pressed against her chest. 'I still don't know if I'm ready.'

'Rubbish, I can't be the only newbie there. Please say you'll come.'

The room felt suddenly hot, or was it the heat radiating from Nick's body? She could smell his aftershave, an unknown scent that wasn't Jason's. Daring to lift her head, she looked around the room rather than returning Nick's gaze, and spotted Jodie laughing at something Nadiya had said. Were they talking about Jodie's date? Had she wanted it to go further? Was that what Nadiya was asking? Why was the room so warm?

'It's probably too late,' she mumbled.

'Too late for what?' Faith asked, appearing at her side with two steaming mugs of coffee. Nick took one and Faith kept the other. 'You're not talking about the party, are you?'

'As a matter of fact we were,' said Nick. 'Is it too late to add April to the booking?'

'Ooh, have you changed your mind?' Tara asked as she squeezed between Nick and April with two more coffees.

'Well I . . . It doesn't matter.'

'Of course it matters,' Tara said. 'If you want to go then we'll make it happen. Justine won't mind.'

Faith snorted but said nothing.

'Thank you,' said April, hoping she wouldn't regret it.

When she moved to take one of the mugs from Tara, her friend twisted away. 'Eat your cake first. You'll need to build up your strength if you're going to keep up with me and Faith on the dance floor. The Macarena is our speciality.'

Nick laughed until Faith shot him a look. 'She's not joking, so you'd better brush up on your dance moves too.'

April scooped up a blob of buttercream from her plate and licked her finger. Her stomach was in knots and she could barely swallow, but was it due to fear or excitement? She looked over at Jodie again. She didn't want to spend the rest of her life knowing that the last man to taste her lips was Jason.

10

The Widows' Club Christmas Party was a dinner-dance at the Hilton in Liverpool city centre, and April's dad dropped her off as if she were a teenager at her school prom. In some ways she hadn't moved forward in her life since then, except this evening she wouldn't be stealing a kiss from Jason, and there was no curfew. As she got out of the car, her dad promised to pick her up at whatever time she liked, as long as it wasn't too early.

Her parents were visibly relieved that their daughter was showing some interest in the festive season and life in general. They didn't know that the spark in April's eyes was consuming fire rather than returning light, and April wasn't going to correct them. Her dad told her to have a good time and when he added awkwardly that she shouldn't feel guilty, April had given him a dutiful smile.

Making her way through the hotel, the last thing April felt was guilt, although there was some trepidation. She followed the throng until she reached the entrance to a dimly lit reception room containing a horde of partygoers that had consumed their small group of members. Above the chatter, George

Michael was singing 'Last Christmas' and April hummed along as she grabbed a flute of sparkling wine from one of the waiting staff before stepping deeper into the room.

As she scanned the faces in the crowd, April smoothed out the material on her new lace dress. She had bought it specially, wanting to feel beautiful in something that hadn't been sullied by Jason's touch, and she received some admiring glances before her attention was caught by the red of Tara's satin dress glinting beneath the lights of a chandelier.

'You made it then,' Tara said, unable to disguise her relief.

'Sounds like you weren't expecting me to.'

Iain was standing next to Tara and leant forward, 'If I had a beer for every time she's said, "I hope April comes tonight", I'd be drunk by now,' he said.

'You have gone very quiet on us,' Tara added in her defence.

April sipped her drink to give her time to form a response. She had swapped a few messages with Tara, but had offered no information other than to say she was fine. 'I didn't want to disturb you. You must be incredibly busy with the move.'

'Not to mention all the Christmas orders,' Tara admitted. 'But I'd always make time if you needed someone to talk to.'

Iain drained his glass of bubbly. 'Anyone want a proper drink? I'm getting a pint.'

'I'll have an espresso martini,' Tara said. 'Do you want something, April?'

Following Iain's example, April drained her glass. 'Actually, I'd love a G&T.'

'You look stunning by the way,' said Tara when Iain left.

'You don't think it's too much, do you?' asked April as she

109

adjusted her plunging neckline. 'I'm wearing a push-up bra and I'm scared they're going to pop out. Tell me if they do.'

'I'd say the reaction from half the blokes in the room would tell you if you had a wardrobe malfunction.'

Aware that her fidgeting had drawn furtive glances, April crossed her arms. 'You look lovely too,' she said. She was used to Tara nailing the vintage look, but she had excelled herself tonight. Her eyeliner flicks were perfectly Parisian, and her crimson red lipstick matched her full circle dress with its Bardot neckline.

'I picked this up in a vintage market when I was in college and always imagined wearing it on midnight walks along the Seine,' Tara explained. 'It never made it further than Chester when Mike took me to the races.'

'It's good that you're comfortable mixing old memories with new,' April said, but her features darkened when she added, 'I couldn't do it.'

Tara moved closer. 'What's going on, April? And don't say you're fine. Have you found out any more about the initials on the stone?'

'No.'

'But there is something.'

April nodded. She regretted downing the fizz. It had gone straight to her head and relaxed the muscles that had been holding back her tears these last weeks. 'I found out Jason was taking an afternoon off here and there. He worked on site a lot of the time, so it wasn't exactly difficult to fool me into thinking he was still in work.'

Tara pursed her lips but before she could say anything, Faith's hand touched April's shoulder. 'Don't you two look gorgeous.'

In the time it took the three women to hug each other, April had blinked away her tears. 'And as usual, you've outdone us all.'

Faith had teased her blonde hair into soft curls and was wearing a sapphire blue jumpsuit that accentuated her curves and included touches of chiffon that gave an alluring hint of bare skin beneath. 'No, I'm pretty sure everyone's looking at you,' she said to April.

There was a flutter of nerves in April's chest, exactly where she imagined everyone was looking. She needed a drink, or maybe she should leave; she couldn't decide. This was her first social event since Jason had died and she was aware of the space he would normally occupy. She needed him by her side. Damn him for dying. Damn him for betraying her.

'April's been telling me the latest news,' Tara said to Faith. 'Jason was taking afternoons off without her.'

'The sneaky bastard,' Faith said. 'How did you find that out?'

'I have access to the attendance systems at work.'

Faith's eyes narrowed. 'Have you checked if anyone else took leave at the same time?'

April's cheeks burned. 'I couldn't exactly go through every single employee's movements, but I did check out a few names, and I hated myself for it. They were friends who deserved better of me because nothing came up. I don't think this person does work for the council. Jason worked with a lot of contractors and sales reps, so I may never find out.'

'But there was definitely a someone,' Faith said, shaking her head in disgust.

'Yes, I think so,' April said with a finality that made her

111

legs wobble. 'Now, can we change the subject? I don't want to think about Jason tonight.'

'Fair enough,' Tara said. 'Let's enjoy ourselves, ladies.'

Iain's approach was slow and careful as he returned from the bar with three glasses perched on a tray. April grabbed hers first and took a large gulp.

'Go easy on that,' Tara warned.

'Nonsense,' Faith said. 'Start as you mean to go on. I've already had a couple of sly glasses at home.'

'Sorry, Faith,' Iain said, noticing she didn't have a drink in her hand. 'Can I get you something?'

'You stay there. I'll go,' she insisted.

Faith was turning away when April caught a glimpse of Nick pushing his way through the throng. When he caught her eye, he looked pleased to see her. He wasn't necessarily April's type, but in his favour, he was nothing like Jason. Nick was older, taller, and darker, and it didn't matter that there had been no immediate chemistry. Nick's greatest appeal was that he had shown an interest in her. He had wanted her to be here tonight, and April's pulse raced as he drew closer. One kiss. That was all she was after.

'Hello, everyone,' he said. 'Looks like we're in for a good night.'

Tara and Iain raised their glasses in welcome, but Nick appeared more interested in April. His now familiar aftershave grew stronger as he leant over her. She closed her eyes and lifted her cheek, but the kiss never came. Her eyes fluttered open in surprise and embarrassment. Nick was reaching past her to grab hold of Faith's shoulder before she could slip away.

'Here, do you want to be in charge of this?' he said, offering her a cloakroom ticket.

When Faith took it, Tara asked, 'Did you two come together?'

'It didn't make sense booking two taxis when we live so close,' replied Nick.

Faith shrugged. 'I'm off to the bar. Did you want another red wine, Nick?'

'Actually, I might switch to pints for now,' he said. 'And I'll get them. You stay here.'

'No, *you* stay here,' Faith replied brusquely. Nick had yet to learn that no one told Faith what to do. 'Tell April how beautiful she looks.'

April took another swig of her gin. 'Sorry about that,' she said after watching Faith part the crowd to reach the bar.

'No, I'm suitably chastised. You do look beautiful,' Nick told her as he kissed her cheek. 'I hope you're glad you came.'

'Ask me at the end of the night,' April said.

The group had been allocated one long table, and when they entered the dining room, April held back, positioning herself close to Nick while Justine took out what appeared to be a seating plan from her clutch bag. When Tara made a tactical move to distract her, there was a bit of a scrum as everyone grabbed their seats. April was edged towards the end of the table opposite Jodie and Iain. She intended Nick to have the spare seat next to her, but he insisted Tara take it.

Despite losing her preferred seating partner, April was happy to be next to Tara, and the conversation and drinks flowed. They pulled Christmas crackers and told jokes, and at one point between courses, Justine gathered them into a huddle for a group photo. They had all been laughing when it was

113

taken, not the sort of snap you'd expect from a bereavement group, but it felt good. April had started to relax, but when the dessert plates were cleared and the lights dimmed, her nerves returned. She didn't know how or if she should go through with her plan to get back at her dead husband, and as she pondered her options, Iain followed her gaze and shouted over to Nick.

'We're going to prop up the bar for a bit. Care to join us?'

'Maybe later,' Nick called back. He was further along the table, next to Faith.

April had been given a reprieve and she was still struggling to build up courage when Jodie got to her feet, urging the rest of the group to hit the dance floor. An Aretha Franklin song was playing.

'I wouldn't dare in this dress,' April said, pressing her back to her chair. Some of the others were more willing, but notably Nick wasn't one of them. An empty space had opened up next to him. This was her chance to make her move.

'Are you OK?' Tara asked, having also avoided being pulled onto the dance floor.

April beamed a smile. 'I'm fine,' she said.

Tara looked about to call out the lie, but Justine plonked herself down on Tara's right and tugged at her shoulder. 'Do you think we should do a roll call at the end of the night?' she bellowed above the thrum of music. 'There's one or two who are drinking way too much, and we need to make sure everyone gets home safely.'

Tara was forced to turn her back to reply to Justine, releasing April to find company elsewhere. She picked up her bag but remained seated, unsure if she had the courage to join Nick or should retreat to the Ladies to fix her make-up.

Another option was to slope off home. Her dad would be disappointed that she hadn't made it past midnight, but it would mean he could clock off from chauffeur duties earlier than expected.

'Come on, you,' Faith said, sweeping past Tara and holding out her hand to April. 'We can't have you sitting there by yourself. How about a boogie?'

'It's all right, Jodie asked me before,' April said, but Faith wouldn't take no for an answer.

It looked like Faith was going to pick Nick up on their way past and April surreptitiously adjusted her dress to make sure everything was secure.

'Actually, I need to nip to the loo first,' Faith said as they reached Nick's side.

'I'll come with you,' said April.

'And leave Nick by himself? No, you stay here. I won't be long.'

Nick pulled out a chair and turned his so he could face April as she sat down. They were dangerously close and she had to keep her knees to the side to avoid brushing against his leg.

'I'm glad I came,' Nick said, resting an elbow on the table and leaning forward to talk into April's ear. 'This lot are such an inspiration and it's been humbling to hear their experiences.'

She could feel his breath on her neck. 'I know what you mean. I'm nowhere near as together as some of the others, but at least they make me believe I can get there,' she said with more hope than conviction.

'Exactly. It's not like they don't suffer the same heartache, they're just better at carrying it.'

'You seem to have your life together,' April said as she picked at the diamanté edging of her bag.

'It's more of a work in progress. How about you?'

April's eyes flicked up to Nick's face. 'Maybe I'll tell you about it some time.'

He smiled. 'You sound like Faith. Now she's someone who's got it together. I gather you've become good friends.'

'It's hard to believe I've only known her a few months,' replied April. 'I didn't think she liked me at first.'

Nick's eyes sparkled. 'Well that fills me with hope. I thought she just liked giving me a hard time,' he said. 'She loved her husband very much from what I gather and I don't suppose anyone else would come up to scratch. I suppose it's the same for all of us.'

'That's the theory,' April said under her breath. 'So what about Erin? Was she as perfect as I imagine?'

For a second, Nick's eyes glazed over. 'She was beautiful, funny, kind-hearted, forgiving,' he said. 'She was the love of my life.'

'Do you have any photos?'

Nick hesitated for a moment, seemingly unwilling to bring his lost love into the new life he was ploughing. When he pulled his phone from his pocket, he took a while finding a photo to share. Erin was dressed in waterproofs and hiking boots, standing beneath the shade of a sprawling oak tree with dappled sunlight catching in her fiery curls. Her eyes sparkled as she laughed at the person behind the camera.

'She's beautiful,' April said. 'She looks so young.'

'And healthy,' Nick added. 'That was taken in Delamere Forest, just before her first diagnosis. Little did we know.'

'Ignorance is bliss,' April admitted as she let her body be drawn to his.

When April's knee brushed against Nick's, the thudding of her heart was as loud as the music. She could feel a tingling sensation running through her veins, but the heat turned to one of embarrassment when Nick moved his leg away. The rejection was twofold when he glanced over his shoulder. He was looking for Faith.

How had April not seen it before? Faith was older than Nick, and her friend had made it clear she wasn't interested in a relationship, but these were barriers Nick thought he could overcome. April consoled herself with the thought that she wasn't the only idiot. Nick didn't stand a chance.

She straightened up, needing to get away before Nick worked out why she was flustered. Had he noticed how she had turned her cheek for a kiss when he arrived, or registered the touch of her knee, not to mention the cleavage she flaunted? It was bad enough to realise her own foolishness without being found out. She was scrambling for an excuse to leave when Tara tapped her shoulder.

'Come on you two, this is our song.'

'This?' asked Nick, giving her a puzzled look. The DJ was playing, 'I Predict a Riot', by the Kaiser Chiefs.

'It's our group song,' she explained. 'No soppy ballads or simpering love songs for us. This is three minutes of shaking your fists at life. Now get up before I drag you up.'

The last comment was directed at April and she found herself doing as she was told. Tossing her bag on the table, she let Tara take her hand. Other members of the group appeared from nowhere and they all began leaping across the dance floor. It was exhilarating and liberating and just what

117

April needed. She caught a glimpse of Faith prising Nick from his seat, but she no longer cared if he joined them. She had had a lucky escape and decided there were less humiliating ways of exorcising Jason's ghost. Creating new playlists and binge-watching the last season of *Game of Thrones* might be a good start.

STATEMENT

The Widows' Club @thewidowsclub
We did not give permission for the use of photos from this account. We have deleted them and request media outlets and individuals do the same. They have been taken out of context and comments made are unnecessary and hurtful.

11

Tinsel twinkled around April's screen as she read through comments on her audit report, which had been out for consultation. It was late on Wednesday and she had until the end of the week to make the final amendments. Once the report was issued, her unrestricted access to the attendance system would be revoked.

April told herself that was a good thing. She had found out all she needed to know and it was time to move on. It was also time to go home but as she closed the file on her computer, the icon for the attendance system came into view. When she looked away, her gaze fell on the white stone she was still using as a paperweight, but she stopped herself from picking it up. She didn't want to re-examine the letters scratched into its surface or imagine who had scrawled them. She wanted to leave the office, but temptation held her prisoner. She had to remind herself that the names she had chosen not to include in her sample list had been left off for a reason. She trusted her friends. But she had trusted Jason too.

Turning away from her computer, April reached for her phone. It was moving day for Tara so she tried Faith first but there was no reply. She bit her lip and looked back at the icon on the screen. The office was deserted and she could delve into a witch-hunt without interruption. Someone might see the access log and query what she had been doing, but there were worse consequences to face. She might just find what she was looking for.

In desperate need of a distraction, April dialled Tara's number, but when the call connected, she could hear a little girl's sobs in the background. 'Sorry, is this a bad time?'

There was the creak of a door and the noise faded. 'No, it's fine,' Tara said. She let out a sigh and April imagined her collapsing into a chair.

'Was that Lily I heard crying?'

'Iain's mum has brought her home – well, I say home, but Lily's refusing to take off her coat. I'd made her a lemon drizzle cake especially, but you'd think I was trying to poison her,' Tara said, her voice straining despite the lightness in her tone. 'Apparently it's not like her mum's. I can only hope Molly's reaction when she gets here will be better. She's had her tea at Justine's and they should be here soon.'

'In that case I won't keep you. I just wanted . . .' What could April say? That she had decided to interrupt Tara on what must be an incredibly stressful day simply because she didn't have the wherewithal to take control of her own life? 'I wanted to wish you well in your new home, that's all. I'm sure Lily will be fine.'

'I really wasn't expecting it to be this emotional, for all of us,' Tara said. 'Iain hasn't said anything, but I could tell by his face that it killed him handing over his old house keys to the estate agent.'

'And are you OK?' April asked. She heard a gulp. 'Tara?'

'What if it all goes horribly wrong?'

'It won't,' April said, surprised that she should be the one required to give the pep talk. It reinforced how self-absorbed she had been lately. She could be a better friend than that, she told herself as she reached for her mouse and closed down her computer. 'You can do this, Tara.'

'Can I? I was never cut out to be a mother, and now I'm responsible for two kids. How did that happen?'

'You're the most motherly person I know. We all look to you for guidance in the group, me especially.'

'But isn't that the point? I'm only six years older than you,' Tara said. 'It was Mike who persuaded me to keep the baby and, as much as I love Molly, as much as I want to make Iain and Lily happy, I've been wondering lately if I'm in the right life. I don't know if I can do this.'

'You might not have chosen to be a mother, or a widow, but it was your choice to set up the support group. You did it because it's in your nature to take care of other people.'

'Faith's worried I'm going to quit.'

'And are you?'

'I might need to put a lot more effort into my family than I was anticipating. They have to come first. I definitely won't be at next week's meeting, and we'll have to see after that.'

April closed her eyes. As tempted as she was, she wouldn't pressurise Tara to stay. 'Then I should let you go,' she said at last.

'But how are you? Were you OK after the Christmas party?'

'I had a really good time, all things considered,' April replied. She could happily forget how close she came to making a fool of herself.

'All things considered?'

123

'See what I mean about you being a natural? I'm fine,' April insisted. 'You don't have to worry about me.'

Before Tara could respond, there was the sound of a doorbell in the background and April listened to her friend heaving herself up. The door creaked again. 'Are you sure you're OK, April? You haven't found out anything else about Jason, have you?'

April picked up the heart-shaped stone and weighed it in her hand. 'All of that's behind me now,' she said. Putting her words into action, she opened a drawer and threw the stone to the very back.

'Well, I'm here if you need me.'

'No, I'm here if *you* need me,' April said. She was about to say goodbye, but Tara must have opened the front door because there was a gasp that sounded like a child's.

'Wow, we have stairs!' came a voice that April presumed was Molly's.

'I'll leave you to it,' April said, and she could hear the smile in Tara's voice when they ended the call.

April hoped Tara was suffering from nothing more than moving day jitters, but it had felt good offering support instead of drawing upon it. Their conversation wasn't quite enough to chase away all of April's demons, but it gave her the strength to carry her home.

Concern for her friend was a distraction that saw April through Thursday too. She tried to phone Faith several times to update her, but without success. Tara, meanwhile, sent a message apologising for her minor meltdown and told April not to worry. The crisis seemed to have passed and typically, Tara was more concerned for April's welfare. Again, April told her she was fine: if she repeated it enough times, one day it might be true.

By Friday, April was within touching distance of the relief she knew she would feel once her audit review was closed. As she sat at her desk, she told herself that discovering Jason's secret afternoons was as much as she could endure. She wouldn't be able to cope if she discovered the other woman was someone she knew, someone who was still in her life. She was protecting herself. That was why she had added certain names to her sample list only to remove them when her courage failed.

But with only hours left before her access to the attendance system would be revoked, the temptation to take one last look and inflict more pain became all-consuming and April locked her computer screen and pushed back her chair to create some distance. It was lunchtime and she needed a break. The rest of the team were out on site visits, all except Georgie, who had taken the afternoon off to go Christmas shopping. April had a vague recollection she had done the same the previous year.

That thought led to another, and another, until April was caught in the trap of her deepest insecurities. With dread in her heart, she opened her desk drawer and took out the stone. What if she had misread the second letter? Squinting, she wondered if the lines were a crude attempt to form the letter G rather than an S. Should she check Georgie's leave records?

But if April did that, what about Sara? What if April had seen what she had wanted to see the day her friend had picked up the stone?

April grabbed her bag and headed out of the building before she did something she might regret. She planned nothing more than a brisk lunchtime walk, but soon found herself standing in the rain outside a pub that she and Jason had frequented. His best friend Callum worked around the corner and made a pilgrimage to his favourite watering hole every Friday at one o'clock without fail, whether his friends, or his wife, chose to join him or not. It was five to one. April had put off seeing him and Bree for months. She remained convinced that neither would tell tales on Jason but still, a catch-up was well overdue.

The rain showed no mercy and Callum would have sailed straight past the woman hiding beneath her umbrella if April hadn't grabbed his arm.

'Hey, April,' he said, not quick enough to hide his alarm. 'I've been meaning to call. How are you?'

'Fine,' she said. 'How are you?'

'Yeah, good,' he said. 'Good.' His voice trailed off. 'So, I hear you're back at work. How's it going?'

'Oh, same as usual.'

Callum looked longingly towards the pub. He wore no hood and had so far refused to take shelter under the umbrella April held out for him. 'I should get going,' he said. 'Unless . . . Did you want to join me?'

April shook her head. The idea of going inside without Jason was too much. There she was, missing him again.

'We haven't been out together since, you know,' said Callum. 'Maybe we should . . .' There was that weakening in his voice once more as he reached another dead-end in their conversation. They had always gone out as two couples. That was never going to happen again.

'Can I ask you something, Callum?'

'Anything.'

'Did Jason have secrets?'

Callum wiped rain from his face. 'What sort of secrets?'

126

'The kind he wouldn't want me to know about. Is there anything, *anything* at all you want to tell me?'

There was a hesitation, as if Callum were searching his memory for whatever it was that April needed. The sickly wave of disappointment hit her before he opened his mouth. He didn't know.

'Jay spent twice as much on his last pair of trainers than he let on, but that's about it. What is it, April?'

She took a breath. She could share Jason's dirty secret and destroy Callum's faith in his friend as hers had been destroyed, but what good would that do? Callum couldn't explain what Jason had done, or more importantly, why. And if Callum didn't know, then neither did Bree. They were the kind of couple who told each other everything, and if Bree had picked up on something at work with Jason, Callum would be looking decidedly uncomfortable about now. He wasn't. They couldn't help her. 'It's nothing,' she said.

'I can't begin to imagine how hard it must be for you.'

'I expect you and Bree miss him too.'

Callum looked relieved to share his pain. 'I still can't believe he's gone. And Bree's been in bits.'

It came as no surprise. Bree had known Jason almost as long as April. She had been an apprentice on the same scheme Jason had applied for when April was away at university. It was through Bree that he'd met Callum a year or two later and they had been best man at each other's weddings. Unlike their husbands' close attachment, April's relationship with Bree was more a matter of circumstance, and they had rarely met separately from the boys. Jason was the one thing that connected them all, and once they had lost him, their friendship had fizzled out. That feeling was never more pronounced than now.

'Bree says you don't want to come to our New Year's Eve party,' Callum continued. 'I completely understand. I can't say it's my idea of fun turfing drunks out of the house on New Year's Day but we felt like we had to do something different. Anyway, if you do change your mind, you'd be very welcome.'

April tried to speak but couldn't. There had been no invitation.

'I don't know what else to say, April. We'll be guided by you and what you want, but please know that we both miss you, Bree especially. She says she's going to keep calling, and she hopes that one of these days, you'll answer.'

April's breaths were shallow and she thought she might faint. With each inhalation, her chest expanded a little more. She had tracked Callum down in the hope that he would break some vow he had made to Jason, but he wasn't even aware of the truths he was revealing.

Bree hadn't tried to phone April. It had been Callum who made those first calls to check on her after Jason had died. Bree had sent a couple of messages with the vague promise of meeting up, but there had been no definitive invites – certainly not to a New Year's Eve party.

She was going to great lengths to avoid April, and not only that, she was lying to Callum about it. Why would she do that? Did she know about Jason's affair? But if that were the case, why hadn't Callum been brought into their little circle of trust? Why had Bree – or to use her full name, Sabrina with a fucking S – deceived her husband as Jason had deceived April?

No! screamed a voice inside April's head.

'I should go,' she said, turning away for fear Callum would read her thoughts.

April's heart clenched when she thought how she had suspected her friends – her real friends. At least now her search was almost over. She would return to the office and check the system one last time, but she already knew what she would find. Bree was as guilty as Jason.

12

There was a hold-up on Queens Drive exacerbated by fading light, heavy rain, and overeager drivers vying for position in the usual end-of-week crush. Cursing the other motorists, Faith debated whether to abandon the ring road and cut through Childwall when her phone rang. April's name appeared on the dashboard's hands-free display.

'Hey, April,' Faith said. 'How's it going?'

'I've been . . . I tried to phone you . . .'

Faith winced. This wasn't April's first attempt to speak to her that week or even that day. 'I know, but it's been hectic at work. There's a big hoo-ha over this bloody reorganisation. Can you believe they're asking us to apply for our own jobs? We're being consulted about the changes, and I'm tempted to tell them to stuff it. I was expecting a promotion, but oh no, they're offering the same pay for more work, and they expect me to beg for it! I'd love to see them try to manage without me.'

She spoke loudly to disguise the guilt she felt for ignoring her friend's calls, which surprised Faith because she wasn't used to her conscience being pricked. Running out of things to say, she waited for April's response, but only sobs echoed down the line.

'April? What's wrong? Where are you?'

More sobs. 'Pick— Pick–er,' she tried, her words punctuated with hiccups.

'Pickering's Pasture?' Faith asked. There followed a mixture of garbled sounds that was as close to a confirmation as she was likely to receive. 'What are you doing there?'

'I – I don't know.'

Seeing a rash of brake lights up ahead, Faith nudged the car into the nearside lane and took the next turn-off. She was no longer heading home.

'OK, I'm on my way, but it's going to take me fifteen minutes,' Faith said. She was being optimistic. 'Can you tell me what's happened?'

'I tried to phone . . .'

'I know, you said,' Faith replied sharply.

'I meant – I tried to phone Tara,' April explained.

'Oh,' Faith said.

She was a little put out at not being the preferred choice, but it was only to be expected. Faith had been avoiding April on purpose and it had nothing to do with distractions at work and everything to do with the man she had tried to set up April with. Nick was kind, generous, thoughtful, and ever so slightly enigmatic – everything a young widow needed to spice up her life – and Faith had done her best to make something happen between the two of them. It had looked promising at one stage at the Christmas party, but April wasn't as good as Faith at taking what she wanted.

'She's not answering her phone,' April continued. She took a breath that caught several times at the back of her throat.

'I wasn't expecting you to pick up either, but I had to keep trying. I don't know what to do.'

Faith had thought she couldn't feel any worse. It didn't help that April wouldn't stop crying. 'Are you going to tell me what's going on?' she asked, resisting the urge to add, 'Or do I have to shake it out of you?'

'I couldn't just let it go. I had to keep looking,' April said. She lowered her voice to a whisper when she added, 'I've found her. The dates match.'

'What dates?'

'Jason's secret afternoons off.'

Faith had a vague recollection of April telling her about it at the party, but if she were honest, it wasn't her take-away memory of the evening. Wrestling with a fresh wave of guilt, she focused on the matter in hand. 'You know who he was seeing?'

'B— Bree,' April said, gulping for air. 'It was Bree.'

There wasn't much more Faith could glean from April's sobs. 'Hang in there,' she said, her gloved hands tightening around the steering wheel. 'I'm on my way.'

The rain beat against the windshield and the arch of the wiper blades smeared red tail lights across Faith's vision until eventually the traffic thinned out and she picked up speed. Eager to reach April and find some way of making up for being a terrible friend, she was only five minutes away when her phone rang again.

'Hi,' she said.

'I was just checking to see if you're still OK for tonight?' said Nick.

'Expecting me to get cold feet?'

'I've stopped trying to predict anything you do, Faith.'

Nick was learning fast. He had made the mistake of second guessing her at the party. They had left the dance floor breathless, and Faith had made her excuses to visit the Ladies. Nick followed, and she had felt his hand on the small of her back. When she turned, he had kissed her. She had kissed him back, but only long enough for him to have a taste of what she was about to refuse.

'You ask before you do something like that,' she had hissed, shoving him hard enough to make him stumble.

Nick had looked momentarily shocked and then embarrassed. 'Sorry, I thought you wanted me to follow you.'

'Why?'

He had held her gaze, and she thawed just a little when he said, 'Because you keep looking at me like *that*. I thought—'

'Don't make any presumptions about me,' Faith warned.

She had arrived that night determined to light a spark between Nick and April, but despite engineering time for them to be alone together, it had failed to materialise. It was only when they were all up dancing and Faith felt Nick's body brush against hers that feelings were stirred. It wasn't exactly the result Faith had been expecting.

'Shall I go?' Nick had asked.

She should have said yes, but April wasn't the only one in need of a little light to brighten her life. The details of the reorganisation at work had just been released and Faith needed a diversion. She had grabbed hold of Nick's collar and pulled him closer. 'Only when I say.'

As Faith drove to meet her friend, the roar of the car's engine grew louder, or was it the storm she was heading towards?

'I've booked a table for eight,' Nick said.

Faith glanced at the time display. 'Ah, that might be a problem.'

'Hmm, I see,' he replied.

'I'm on my way to Hale and I don't know how long I'll be.'

'To see Tara?'

'I can't say,' replied Faith, determined to keep April's confidence and prove her loyalties remained with her friends.

'Do you want to cancel our date?'

Faith didn't know. She hadn't seen Nick since they had shared a taxi home from the Hilton. There had been a brief, drunken moment when she had considered inviting him in for a nightcap, but she had held back and Nick, having been told off once already, asked for no more than a goodnight peck on the cheek.

He had phoned the next day, however, and after a lengthy but surprisingly comfortable conversation, Faith had found herself agreeing to go out for dinner. Since then, she had avoided speaking to him, as she had April. She didn't know how April felt about Nick, and needed time to contemplate her next move. Almost a week later, she was still no clearer about what she should do.

This wasn't like Faith. She prided herself in being in control of her own destiny. When she had married Derek, it had been on her terms, and following his death, she had quickly adapted to the new turn her life had taken. It was what she did, and it was what she would do again – because of her finances, because of the uncertainty of her job, because change was necessary. Nick could alleviate some of her stress points, if only temporarily, but didn't that smack of desperation? Could this crisis of April's be a blessing in disguise?

'Unless you have alternative plans, I could ring you as soon as I know what's happening,' Faith said, postponing any decision she might want to make.

'I'll take a maybe rather than an outright no,' said Nick.

Pleased to have left him dangling, Faith ended the call and focused on April. She sped past the village hall and slowed slightly as she turned the corner at the war memorial. She was about to accelerate past Ivy Farm Court when she spied light coming from the back of Tara's shop.

Faith hadn't spoken to Tara, but she had sent a large John Lewis hamper on the day of the house move and they had swapped messages. Tara had been more concerned about April than the stresses of moving and Faith had promised she would look after her.

Presuming that Tara was working overtime to catch up with orders, Faith drove on. She could handle this on her own, and within a couple of minutes she was driving into Pickering's Pasture and past the sign warning visitors that the gates would be locked at 7 p.m. It was ten past six. If Faith could help April bring her emotions under control in the next fifty minutes, there would be time to retrieve her plans with Nick.

As Faith's headlights swept across the deserted car park, she could hear a horn blaring above the thrum of rain on the windshield. Guided by its continuous wail, she scanned the area more closely and spotted April's car tucked away in a far corner. Pulling up alongside, she peered through the Corsa's steamed-up windows and spotted a ghost-like form bent over the steering wheel.

Faith flung open the Range Rover's door and pulled up the hood of her rain jacket. It took only a few seconds to climb into April's car, but Faith's jacket was sodden by the time she closed the door.

'Can't you turn that thing off?' Faith shouted above the ear-splitting shriek of the horn.

April lifted up her hands. 'It's not me. I was hitting the steering wheel with my fists and now it won't stop.'

'Fuck,' Faith muttered under her breath. It was one more complication she could do without. 'How do you lift the bonnet?'

'I've no idea,' April said before her face creased up. 'Jason always looked after it.'

'Never mind,' Faith said, searching around the foot well until her fingers made contact with the lever. The clunk of the bonnet releasing was felt rather than heard above the deafening noise of the rain and the horn. Faith pulled up her hood again and jumped out of the car.

Lifting the bonnet and using her phone as a torch, Faith searched until she found what she thought was the connector to the horn. Needing two hands to disconnect it, she gave up holding her hood over her head and seconds later the wailing stopped.

'You'll have to take it to a garage and get it fixed properly,' Faith said, peeling away the locks of damp hair sticking to her face when she returned to April. She was soaked through and her lambskin gloves were covered in dirt and grease.

'Are they ruined?' asked April.

Faith rolled the gloves inside each other before the grease could get anywhere else. They were a recent acquisition from a little trip she had made to a selection of charity shops along the Cheshire belt. She had been on the hunt for designer cast-offs from soap stars and WAGs at a fraction of the original price. It was where she had found her outfit for the Christmas party.

'At least I haven't damaged my manicure,' she said as she inspected her wet and wrinkled fingers. She had spent the last few days having every part of her body pampered and preened. It could all be for nothing if she spent the evening with April.

'Sorry.'

Faith twisted in her seat so they were facing each other. Her friend's face was ashen and whatever make-up she had been wearing had left her red eyes muddy. The tears, however, had dried. 'Right then, tell me about this Bree.'

April nodded and took a deep breath. 'OK,' she said, although it took her some time to corral the emotions that had stolen her voice earlier. 'She worked with Jason, but we were friends too.'

'Or you thought you were.'

'Jason met her while I was away at uni,' she said. 'I was a bit jealous at the time but Jason treated her as he would any mate, and I've always thought that if something was going to happen, it would have happened then. And once Bree met Callum and they got married, I stopped seeing her as a threat. Jason and Callum became best mates, for God's sake.'

'And how did Bree react when Jason died?'

'Probably in shock like everyone else, but I was in too much of a state to notice. Before today, I'd say I'd been the one keeping my distance, but I realise now that she had too. The cow told Callum I wasn't returning her calls, like she wasn't sick of all the lies she'd already told,' April said, her words acquiring an edge.

'But what about the stone with their initials? Could it have been a B?'

'Bree is short for Sabrina, not that she ever uses her full name unless it's something official.'

'Or when she wants to hide her identity.'

'I remember seeing her name on the attendance system, but I was too preoccupied with all the other women I suspected.' She let out a wail before adding, 'God, the things I've been thinking about people who didn't deserve it.'

'You're not the one who did anything wrong,' Faith assured her.

April rubbed her hands over her eyes, scraping fingers against chapped and puffy skin. 'This feels like the worst betrayal, and I have no idea where to go with it. I could confront Bree and that might make me feel differently, but it's not going to make me feel better, is it? I knew I shouldn't have kept looking, and now I have to live with this, but I don't know if I can. The past can't be changed. It's hopeless.'

Faith was reminded of the tote bag Justine insisted on carrying. 'Listen to me, April. It's going to be tough and despite what some might say, hope doesn't have bloody wings. It has sharp teeth and claws, and you'd better learn to use them if you want to climb out of that dark place you're in right now,' she said. 'Fight back, and take no prisoners.'

'But who am I fighting? Bree?'

'Yourself,' Faith replied. 'You think you can't change the past, but you can. All you have to do is switch the narrative.'

'I don't understand.'

'There are two versions of Jason's life. There's the one you thought you had where you were happily married, where your last night together was filled with love and passion,' Faith said. 'And then there's the secret life where Jason's passions

138

were shared elsewhere. At the moment, both those realities exist in your mind, but they don't have to. You can decide to mourn the loss of your soul-mate, or you can say goodbye to someone who, in all likelihood, was never going to be your life partner.'

'You make it sound like a simple choice, but I can't ignore the fact that Jason cheated on me any more than I can forget how much I loved him.'

'Oh, everyone edits the past,' Faith explained. 'I lost both my parents before I was twenty, and I would never have come to terms with it if I thought only the best of them. Yes, there were good times, but Dad was a bastard, especially to Mum. He wore her down to a shadow of herself and when he died, that shadow dissolved into nothing. Weak and broken, that's how I choose to remember them, because it pushed me to be stronger. That was *my* choice.'

'I don't know if I can do it, Faith. I'm not you,' April said. She had dropped her hands and was playing with the white mark on her finger where her wedding band had been.

'Maybe you need to find out exactly how much you should be hating Jason before you decide.'

'Talk to Bree? What if she denies it?'

'You could always ask her husband. He might have his own suspicions.'

'No, no he doesn't have a clue, and I can't tell him,' April said, brow furrowing. 'It's bad enough dealing with my own feelings.'

Faith shrugged. 'The threat of telling him might be enough. Use it as a bargaining tool.'

The silence that followed was broken only by Faith's teeth chattering. The rain had stopped, but the temperature was dropping and the damp hair on the back of her neck felt like icy fingers.

'I should let you get home to dry off,' April said.

Checking the time on her phone, Faith said, 'Yes, and we'll be locked in if we don't move soon. Are you going to be OK?'

'I think so.'

'This might be your fight, but you're not on your own.'

'Thank you,' April replied. 'I don't know what I'd do without you and Tara. There's no one else I can talk to.'

'What about other members of the support group? You seemed to be getting on well with Nick,' Faith suggested casually.

April groaned. 'I know you were trying to set me up with him, but please don't,' she said. 'You do realise he's more interested in you than he is in me?'

'Do you think?'

April's eyes narrowed. 'Don't act daft, Faith. It doesn't suit you,' she said. 'Just promise me you'll let him down gently.'

Faith smiled. 'I promise.'

After climbing into her Range Rover, Faith peeled off her wet jacket and switched the heating to the highest setting. As she waited for the windows to demist, she dialled Nick's number.

'So is it a yes or a no?' he asked.

Checking the rear-view mirror, Faith raked her shrivelled fingers through her hair. 'I'm drenched right through and all I want to do right now is soak in a hot bath.'

'Sounds like you've had an eventful evening,' Nick said. 'I could put our booking back to eight thirty, or nine if it helps.'

April had pulled out of her parking space and as Faith watched her drive off she put the Range Rover into reverse.

'I don't think I'll want to face going out again once I'm home. I might just order a takeaway and have an early night.'

'I understand.'

'We could always try again another time,' she suggested, her body suddenly craving more than simply warmth.

'No pressure,' Nick said. 'And if nothing else, I'll pick you up next Tuesday for the group meeting. Drive carefully, Faith.'

'I will,' she replied, feeling slightly deflated that he hadn't tried harder.

Faith put her foot down as she drove out of Pickering's Pasture, zipping down Hale's country lanes and on through the densely populated housing estates in Speke. She crossed Speke Boulevard and carried on through Hunt's Cross where she imagined Nick was either relaxing in front of the TV with a bottle of beer, or shrugging into his coat to set off to meet someone who wasn't so difficult to please. Her yearnings only increased as she sped past.

Faith liked Nick, more so now that she knew April held no competing interest, but could her heart stand it? She had learnt at an early age not to rely on anyone else for her future happiness, and if anything, her marriage to Derek had reinforced her resolve to guard her independence. As she neared home, Faith told herself not to do anything stupid, but then she saw Nick's car outside her house and her insides twisted.

13

The gurgle of the central heating as it fired up pulled Faith from a deep sleep, and she opened her eyes to find her bedroom awash with the languorous glow of a wintry dawn. A mournful wind howled through the eaves and, as she snuggled under the duvet, the weight that had been pressing against her bare back moved. She smiled.

When she had arrived home the night before to find Nick waiting, her immediate reaction had been annoyance. She had dismissed him on the phone so he had no right to be there, but then Nick had emerged from his BMW with takeaway bags and a very good bottle of Argentinian Malbec. Someone wanted to look after her.

To all appearances, Nick had had no intention of staying, but Faith hadn't wanted to eat alone, and then she hadn't wanted to spend the night alone, and now here they were. She listened to him stirring next to her and felt a draught of cool air as the duvet was lifted to expose her shoulder. Warm lips kissed her skin.

'Morning,' Nick whispered.

Faith turned onto her back and Nick manoeuvred himself

over her. It wasn't a position she favoured. How had she let this happen? 'My head hurts,' she said, regretting that she had drunk so much.

'Can I get you anything?'

She was ready with a retort about a bed to herself, but the touch of Nick's warm skin against hers felt too good. 'I can take care of myself,' she replied, letting her hands explore his arms, his chest, his neck. She stroked a thumb across his smiling mouth before covering his face with the palm of her hand. In one quick move, she had pushed Nick over and climbed on top so their positions were reversed.

The mattress shook as Nick laughed, but he didn't laugh for long as she kissed the breath out of him. He groaned as she explored his body, making it fit hers, forcing his movements to match her own until she was satisfied.

Sliding off him, Faith propped herself up on her elbow and looked down at Nick.

'How's your head now?' he asked.

'Better.'

'You're one amazing woman, Faith,' Nick said. 'I've never met anyone like you.'

'I'm not like Erin?'

'No, not at all. Erin was . . .'

'Go on,' Faith encouraged. 'I want to hear.'

Nick's eyes narrowed as he gave the question some consideration. 'She was easy-going, thoughtful, forgiving. Without doubt she was the kindest soul I ever had the privilege to know,' he said. Seeing Faith raise an eyebrow, he added quickly, 'I'm not saying you don't have those qualities. You were ready to set aside our plans last night and go to whoever it was that needed you. You're kind, and you're loyal.'

Faith was proud of the fact that she had refused to share the sordid details of April's predicament despite Nick's probing the evening before. 'You didn't mention easy-going,' she said.

Dimples appeared in Nick's cheeks. 'I'm sure Justine would agree that you can be quite . . . forthright?'

'I don't suffer fools.'

'I'll take that as a warning,' he said, lifting his hand to cup her cheek. 'I like you, Faith, and although you're trying hard to disguise it, I suspect you like me too. It could do us both good to get to know each other better.'

'We'll see.'

Letting his arm drop back onto the pillow behind him, Nick's supplicant pose was deliberate. 'I'll take that as progress,' he said. 'Now, as I recall, I was told I could only stay over if I left early. Have you done with me? Do you want me to leave?'

He was testing her and she didn't know how to respond. 'Don't you have work to do?'

'I need to confirm the schedule with my drivers, and I have my first pick up at five, but I'm otherwise free. I was planning to go for a long run if you fancied joining me?'

'If you're looking for a running partner, you've come to the wrong place,' she said, recalling she had once thought April a better match.

'Are you sure I can't tempt you?'

'I'm too old,' she said. It was her turn to test him.

'Forty-six is not old,' he replied.

'Older than thirty-eight,' she said. 'And besides, I've had all the exercise I need for one day.'

'So what do you have planned?'

'Christmas shopping,' Faith replied. 'From the comfort of my sitting room.'

'Do you have a big family, or is it just your stepdaughter?'

'I'm closest to Ella, or at least I try to be. We have what you might call a love–hate relationship. I love her and she hates her father,' Faith explained. 'And as for blood relatives, I have a scattering of cousins and a slightly neurotic aunt on my mother's side who I visit dutifully every Christmas.'

'No parents?' he asked. 'You never did tell me about your father.'

Faith sank back onto her pillows to stare up at the ceiling. 'My father drank himself to death, although unfortunately for Mum, not nearly soon enough,' she said simply.

'What was he like as a father?'

'A strict disciplinarian. I was expected to do as I was told, helping with the household chores and plenty of other jobs to earn my keep. He taught me how to be self-sufficient, I'll give him that. I know how to fix a leaking tap and I'm a whiz with power tools.'

'It sounds like he wasn't a complete failure, despite what you say.'

That wasn't the narrative Faith would choose and if anything, her most important life lessons had come from her mother. Faith had learnt never to depend on a man.

'Dad was an angry drunk,' she said, turning her head to meet Nick's gaze. 'My mother tolerated it because he worked hard and she thought he was a good father. He never laid a hand on me, but I saw him lash out at her often enough, mostly with words but occasionally with his fists. His temper became worse after he injured his back. He was self-employed, so there was no sick pay and he literally crawled back to his workshop with booze being his painkiller of choice. I helped as much as I could and eventually left school without a qualification to my name.'

'But you have a good job now, I presume this story gets better.'

'You could say that,' Faith replied. 'My dad died of liver failure when I was eighteen. It should have meant a new life for us, Mum especially. I went back to college, but a week after my final exams, she had a massive stroke and died. She was younger than I am now.'

Faith didn't like the look of sympathy on Nick's face. Her childhood had prepared her for life's many challenges. 'What about you? Do you have family?'

'I'm an orphan like you. My mum died a few years back and I never knew my dad. It's just me and my sister, Liv.'

'I'll have to meet her so I can unearth all your childhood secrets,' Faith teased.

'I don't see as much of her as I'd like,' he replied. When Faith tipped her head, he added, 'She moved to Canada years ago.'

'Then it must have been hard not having her around when you lost Erin. What about her family? Do you keep in touch with them?'

His mouth twisted. 'We didn't exactly see eye to eye.'

'I know how that feels,' Faith sympathised. 'There were arguments galore after Derek died, starting with the funeral arrangements and going on from there.'

'Over the will?'

There was the briefest of pauses, but enough time for Nick to realise he had overstepped the mark.

'Sorry,' he said, 'I didn't mean to pry.'

'You can ask what you like, just don't expect me to always answer,' Faith said honestly. 'I do believe we were talking about you. Why did you and Erin's family fall out?'

'When she became ill, her family took over and I had to take a step back.'

'You mean you were pushed away?' When Nick didn't answer, Faith lifted his hand and threaded her fingers through his so she could scrutinise the bare flesh of his wedding finger. 'Did you not consider getting married? It might have put you in a stronger position.'

'We had talked about it, but it never happened.'

'You could have tied the knot on her deathbed,' insisted Faith. If he had loved Erin as much as he claimed, how could he allow an overbearing family to confine him to the sidelines?

'We wanted our wedding to be when she was full of life, not when she was sick and dying,' he whispered. It was his turn to look up at the ceiling. 'The important thing is she was with people she loved. She knew how I felt. That was enough for me.'

'Wait, are you saying you weren't there when she died?'

When he shook his head, Faith unknotted their hands. She knew when something didn't feel right.

Nick propped himself up onto his elbow and Faith found she was looking up at him again. 'Like you, I've learnt some hard life lessons that have made me stronger,' he said. 'Losing Erin changed me.'

'How?'

'My priorities for one thing,' he said. 'I like to work hard, but it shouldn't be all-consuming. I admire everything you've achieved, Faith, but your reward shouldn't be to spend the rest of your life locked away in a lab.'

'Who says I'm locked away? I've been on more cruises and visited more countries than I could possibly remember.' She could add that with every trip came a holiday romance that was severed the moment the liner returned to port, but she wasn't sure if that made her sound less like a lonely widow or more so.

'And what about when you're not counting down to your next holiday? Wouldn't you like to take a risk once in a while?'

'I do take risks. Calculated ones.'

Nick leant in closer, his lips hovering over hers. 'Will you take a risk on me?' he asked.

Faith considered her options. She was under pressure to make some serious decisions about her life, but she was no fool. Nick was trying too hard to impress her. 'Only when I know I can trust you,' she said. 'I want to know what it is you're not telling me.'

RESPONSES

Alex Butterworth @AlBut4550
Replying to @thewidowsclub
If you were so worried about privacy, maybe you should have been more careful about how you selected your members.

Dan Faye @DannyPeeps
Replying to @thewidowsclub
Have you seen the photo where they're all out partying? Looks like they're dancing on someone's grave – and we all know whose.

Petersj @Petersjhome
Replying to Dan Faye @DannyPeeps
I hate to agree with anything this group says but the use of that photo and the headlines about a Valentine's Day Massacre have been in poor taste. Show some respect. There's a family in mourning.

14

There were lots of empty chairs at the final group session before Christmas, making April wonder if the effort to leave the house had been worth it. She had locked herself away in her bedroom all weekend watching *Game of Thrones*, and her self-confinement had continued into the working week.

April had told her boss that she had a virus, but her parents were not so easily fooled. They had wanted her to open up, but how could she do that when they remained so close to Jason's parents? It was bad enough that April had to put on an act in front of them, she didn't want her Mum and Dad being forced to take part in the charade too. Her mother-in-law didn't know that her beloved boy was a cheat and a liar, and she would never hear it from April. Deciding how much Jason should be loved or loathed was April's agony alone.

Faith's idea of editing the past was a tempting proposition, but before April could begin to compartmentalise her feelings, she needed more information. Only one source was left to plunder, but before she confronted Bree, April wanted to talk it through with Faith again – except she hadn't shown up, and Justine was eager to open the meeting.

'Shall we make a start?' Justine suggested. 'It doesn't look like anyone else is coming tonight.'

'What about Tara?' asked Nadiya.

'She's asked me to pass on her apologies. The move went smoothly, but it's going to take time for them to settle in.'

'From the last message I had, they still had lots of unpacking to do,' said April. 'She mentioned they'd put up lots of family photos, but they're still having a debate over where everything else should go.' She missed Tara, but she was glad she wasn't there. She didn't need April adding to her woes.

'Ah, they'll be fine,' said Steve.

'I'm sure you're right, but we shouldn't expect too much of her in the coming months,' Justine replied. 'And I'm happy to muddle through on my own if you can all bear with me. I know I'm no Tara.'

'You can say that again,' Faith said under her breath as she joined the group.

She winked at April, who gave her a curious look. Faith's hair was tousled rather than tamed, and her complexion was glowing. The most marked difference, however, was her demeanour. She appeared relaxed as she nodded hellos and took a seat in an empty section of the circle. No sooner had she dropped her bag on the floor than Nick made an appearance.

'Sorry we're late,' he said, taking the seat next to Faith.

'If Tara isn't coming,' Nadiya said, 'perhaps you can pass on our appreciation. Here, there's one for each of you.' From a large shopping bag, she pulled out two identical gift bags. 'Apologies for the wrapping, the kids insisted on helping.'

'Oh, Nadiya, you shouldn't have,' Justine gushed.

'They're from all of us,' she explained, having organised

an impromptu collection at the Christmas party. 'You both work so hard and the group wouldn't exist without you.'

'*Both* of you,' Faith emphasised.

Justine's eyes glistened. 'Oh, I've taken as much from the group as I've put in over the last six years, and Tara would say the same.'

Faith rolled her eyes and nudged her shoulder against Nick's. They looked exceptionally comfortable in each other's company.

The last time April had seen Nick was when she had flirted with him at the Christmas party. The heat of embarrassment rose through her body as she returned to the moment she had realised Nick had set his sights elsewhere. April had assumed Faith would slap him down and she had felt sorry for Nick, but seeing them now, it was clear Faith was enjoying the attention. April's embarrassment deepened when she recalled telling her friend to let him down gently. Faith was full of surprises.

'Who wants to go first?' Justine asked.

April made the mistake of lowering her head, immediately drawing Justine's attention.

'Are you OK, April?'

'I've had better weeks,' she admitted.

There was a pause as she considered telling the group about her discovery, but the moment was lost when Justine said, 'We take small steps every day, but grief isn't a straight path. There will be times when we hit a bump in the road and it might seem like we're right back where we started, but you will make up ground again.'

April could explain that rather than hitting a bump in the road, she had fallen into a sinkhole, but one look at Justine's tote bag propped up next to her chair made her hold her tongue. She could do without Justine's advice. 'I'll be fine,' she said.

'And how about you, Jodie?' Justine continued. 'Have you been on any more dates?'

Jodie pursed her lips. Her eyes glistened. 'No.'

'Could it be you weren't ready?' Justine probed. 'Or is it that you haven't found the right person?'

Jodie's legs were crossed and her foot jiggled in mid-air as she attempted to form words. Nadiya moved up a few seats and took hold of her hand. 'It's the wrong time of year for her to be thinking of anyone else,' she said on Jodie's behalf. 'It's coming up to her wedding anniversary.'

'Sorry, of course it is,' Justine said, shaking her head and silently admonishing herself. She sounded less confident when she added, 'You were married on Christmas Eve, weren't you?'

'Ryan said marrying me was like the excitement you get in the run-up to Christmas, all that anticipation of what was to come,' Jodie managed. 'Which wasn't supposed to include a heart attack a year later at twenty-fucking-seven.'

'Have you made any special plans for your anniversary?' Justine asked.

'Same as the last two. Sitting on his grave and slugging back a bottle of champagne. That is until Mum drags me home so everyone can tell me how much Ryan would want me to move on, be happy, fuck someone else, have someone else's children,' she said, her voice growing stronger. She swiped angrily at the tears trickling down her cheeks. 'How the hell do they know what he'd want? I'm pretty sure it never crossed Ryan's mind what I should do if he died. It was never supposed to happen, for God's sake.' Her eyes followed the circle of faces until her gaze settled on Steve. 'Would it have made any difference? Did you have that conversation?'

'We did talk, though I'm not sure it helped,' Steve answered. 'Bella didn't want me to be alone for the rest of my life, but we had the added complication of the boys. I was told that if I did find someone, she wasn't to be introduced to them until I knew she was the one. Bella bent the boys' ears too, telling them to accept whoever I chose. Needless to say, we haven't put that to the test yet. It's not easy finding someone who would meet the approval of two grubby teenagers, and live up to Bella's expectations too.'

'And what's been your experience, Nick?' Justine asked. 'Did you and your wife talk about afterwards?'

'No, we didn't,' he said. 'And we weren't married.'

As Faith rested a hand on Nick's back, Steve said, 'She was the woman you loved, mate. Same difference.'

'See,' Jodie said. 'Not everyone wants to think about their partner copping off with someone else after they're gone. Ryan hated me mentioning my exes, so I doubt very much he'd be wishing me well with some other bloke. No one has the right to put words in his mouth. They only do it because they don't want miserable me spoiling their Christmas. Well, I'm sorry if I'm upsetting their perfect little lives. Shit happens, and it happened to me.'

Jodie's lips trembled and, as her body curled into itself, Nadiya pulled her close.

'Does anyone else have anything to share?' Justine said loudly. 'I'm sure Jodie's not the only one dreading Christmas.' When she darted nervous glances around the room, no one expected Faith to come to her rescue.

'How about you, Justine?' she asked, her tone softer than

155

usual. 'I know you've been finding it tough lately, tougher still without Tara.'

'Oh, it's not too bad. We'll get there.'

'I'm sure you will,' Faith replied. 'But won't you have some pressure points at Christmas?'

'Actually, I have Lisa's parents coming over on Boxing Day,' she said. 'We're not particularly close, they took time getting used to their daughter's life choices, but in their defence they accepted both of their grandchildren equally, even if Lisa was technically only birth mother to one. We've made the effort over the years for the sake of the children, but it's not always easy. They say they don't blame me for failing to get Lisa to the hospital sooner, but I would if I were them. I didn't know about sepsis back then. I kept telling Lisa she was a malingerer and that the NHS had enough to deal with.'

'Like you said, you didn't know about sepsis,' Faith replied. 'You need to forgive yourself before you can accept the forgiveness of others.'

Justine's mouth fell open and when she found her voice, it trembled. 'Thank you, Faith.'

The conversation limped on and it was a relief when Nadiya asked if they should call it a night. It had been impossible to concentrate on anything except Jodie's sobbing.

'If ever we needed proof that Tara is not allowed to leave the group, that was it,' Faith muttered to April as they gathered in the foyer. Nick had gone to fetch Faith's coat, but had been sidetracked by the group flocking around Jodie. 'Justine simply can't manage on her own.'

'Have you spoken to Tara lately?' asked April as she watched Nick put an arm around Jodie's shoulder. He was the first to tempt a smile from her.

'I've been so busy. How about you?'

'I haven't told her about my little meltdown yet, but I will. She's suggested I pop over while I'm off between Christmas and New Year.'

'Any progress to report?'

April spotted Nick approaching and lowered her voice. 'I've decided I will speak to Bree. It's time to be brave,' she said. 'Don't you think?'

'You do whatever it takes to make peace with yourself. Take other people's feelings out of it.'

'I'll try.'

'Here you go, m'lady,' Nick said, holding out Faith's coat for her to slip into.

April rummaged in her oversized handbag and took out a neatly-wrapped parcel tied with a shiny red ribbon.

'What's this?' Faith asked. 'No one told me we were doing Christmas presents.'

'It's more of a thank-you,' April explained. 'Open it.'

Faith tore the paper to reveal a pair of lambskin gloves not dissimilar to the ones she had ruined disabling April's car horn.

'Oh, you sweetheart,' Faith said, pulling April into a hug.

'I did try cleaning her last pair, but engine oil is tough to get out,' Nick said, sounding far more familiar with Faith and her laundry than he should. Had he been told whose car she had been fixing? Had he been told why?

If Faith registered the look of suspicion on April's face, it didn't stop her smiling broadly. 'I'm hoping I won't need these where I'm going. I've booked a holiday for early January,' she said. 'I was tempted to make it a Christmas break, but I couldn't get the time off work. The joys of being indispensable.'

'Are you going alone?' April asked.

Before Faith could answer, Justine joined them, and for once, Faith looked pleased to have her interruption.

'How are we all?' Justine said, wrapping an arm around April's waist and ever so subtly turning her towards the door where the last of their fellow members were filing out. 'Can you believe another year is almost over?'

'This time last year, I never dreamt I'd need a group like this,' April said, forced momentarily to remember what she had lost, forced to feel it.

Justine gave April a tight squeeze. 'The first Christmas and New Year are always the hardest, if only because you don't know what to expect,' she told her, smoothing over what was hopefully the last faux pas of the night. 'But don't forget you have my number if you need someone to talk to.'

'Thanks, Justine,' April said, trying not to wince. She gave her a hug and wished her a peaceful Christmas before following Faith and Nick out of the hall and into the cold. Faith was putting on her gloves when April caught up with them. 'Where are you parked?'

'Over in the Childe of Hale car park,' Nick said.

'I'm going this way,' April said, pointing over her shoulder to the path that would take her the shortest route to Ivy Farm Court.

'Right, I'll see you in the New Year then,' replied Faith.

'Wait,' April said, not ready to say goodbye. 'What about this holiday of yours? Will you be back in time for the next meeting?'

'We wouldn't miss it,' Nick said before adding an, 'ouch,' when Faith gave him a sharp dig with her elbow.

April's mouth moved, but it took a couple of attempts for her to speak. 'You're going together?'

'Do *not* tell anyone,' Faith instructed. 'God forbid, Justine should find out. She'll have us banished like Tara and Iain.'

'But . . .' April started, only to find herself lost for words. She was just getting her head around the possibility that they were a thing, but this took it to a whole new level. Wasn't it too soon to go away together? And what had caused Faith's sudden change of heart about relationships? The answer to that question was obvious. They looked happy. Setting aside her worries, April offered a smile. 'Didn't you tell me two minutes ago not to worry about other people's feelings? I hope you have a wonderful time.'

'We will,' Faith said with a note of surprise, as if she too were stunned by the sudden change of direction her life was taking.

15

Tara watched from a distance as the girls pressed their foreheads against the wrought-iron railings marking the grave of John Middleton. Molly was regaling Lily with stories about the Childe of Hale, not all of them true, and Tara caught the occasional giggle. This wasn't Lily's first visit to St Mary's church, but it was her first trip out without her father. Tara tried not to get too excited. It was only the prospect of walking a dog that had clinched the deal.

Tara heard a car's engine, but didn't pull her eyes from the girls until she heard a door slam and the excited whines of a cockapoo dragging April across the road. She was ready for Dexter this time and wore Iain's waterproof jacket, and jeans that were torn by age rather than design. The dog could splatter her with as much mud as he liked.

'Oh, my God! Oh, my God! Oh, my God!' Molly cried, her voice growing louder. She thumped against her mum in her haste to get to the dog. 'He's like a teddy bear.'

'An evil teddy bear,' April warned as she gave Tara the biggest hug.

'How was Christmas?' asked Tara.

'Stupidly weepy,' April said. 'But it's over now and I'm determined not to cry again until at least January.'

'It was the same for me that first Christmas, and New Year's Eve was tough too. Be warned, it can be hard stepping out of the last year you shared together and into one they'll never know.'

'I'm prepared,' April added. She looked about to say more, but both girls were circling.

'Did you want to stroke him, Lily?' asked Tara.

Lily's furtive approach alerted the dog to new prey. He wriggled free from Molly's clutches and would have launched himself at the new arrival if April hadn't kept him on a short leash. Emboldened, Lily came within pouncing distance and Dexter took advantage. The little girl shrieked as the dog jumped up, and as she did, Dexter stuck his tongue in her mouth, causing her to gag.

'Sorry!' yelped April, pulling him off her. 'He doesn't bite, but he might lick you to death.'

Molly was in fits of laughter, but panic wrapped itself tightly around Tara's chest. She wasn't equipped to deal with Lily's tears without Iain.

Lily wiped her tongue with her gloved hand and continued to make retching noises until she caught sight of the tears of laughter rolling down Molly's face. To everyone's relief, she started laughing too.

'Can we take him to Dad's grave?' Molly asked when they had calmed down.

Mike was buried at the back of the church and they had visited his grave only two days earlier on Christmas Day before making a similar pilgrimage to Widnes. Fearing that a return visit might trigger Lily, Tara said, 'Maybe not today. Let's head up to the lighthouse.'

161

Molly was sullen as they left the church, but April turned her mood around by suggesting she take charge of Dexter.

After giving Molly instructions on how to control the leash if not the dog, April turned to Tara. Her expression clouded with concern as she took in Tara's minimal make-up and hair scraped back into a ponytail. 'How was your Christmas?'

Tara tried to smile. 'Not as bad as I'd expected, although the bar had been set considerably low,' she admitted. 'Lily's moods have been up and down, mostly down if I'm honest, and her last day at school was particularly traumatising. She's starting the new term in Hale Primary, so she had to say goodbye to all her friends. It's been a while since I've dreaded Christmas as much as I did this year.'

When the last order had been sent off for delivery before Christmas, Tara had sobbed with a mixture of relief and trepidation. It had been late afternoon, the shop was closed, and the only item left on her list was to make a perfect Christmas for her new family: but there was no recipe for that.

'I was expecting it to go horribly wrong,' she continued, 'but on Christmas Eve I persuaded Lily to show me and Molly how to make her mum's lemon drizzle cake using the Mary Berry recipe Joanna had sworn by according to Iain's mum. Apparently it was close – nothing is ever going to be as good as her mum's – but the two of them tucked into the cake while they wrote letters to Mike and Joanna. We set them alight in the garden and let their messages float off to heaven.'

'That's so lovely.'

'It was,' Tara said, still surprised. 'And I'd wrapped up some books as little Christmas Eve gifts. Someone mentioned it's an Icelandic tradition, and it did the trick. The girls hurried off to bed to read and, apart from the odd scurrying of feet and a few giggles, we didn't hear a peep out of them for the rest of the night.'

'Sounds like you've made a new tradition of your own.'

'That's the plan, although next year I might dispense with the bottle of wine I demolished when the kids were in bed.'

'It must have been a tense time.'

Tara rubbed the side of her face unconsciously. She continued to grind her teeth in the night, and the queasiness she had attributed to a hangover on Christmas Day persisted. 'It still is.'

'How's Molly been?'

'A superstar,' Tara said, watching her daughter skip down the road. Dexter had found a water bowl that one of the residents had left out for dog walkers and was splashing the girls as he shook his dripping mouth. 'Although she was disappointed that there wasn't a puppy waiting for her on Christmas morning, despite me telling her time and again that it's too soon to think about pets. To be honest, I'm holding out hope that Dexter will send Molly flying into a muddy puddle and she'll go off the idea.'

'It's very possible she's going to end up muddy,' April said as they watched Dexter run rings around the girls, 'but I'm not sure it would put her off.'

As they continued their walk, Tara said, 'Now tell me everything that's happening with you. Faith phoned yesterday and mentioned you'd worked out who Jason was seeing. I'm so sorry I wasn't there for you that night. I was working late at the shop and I didn't notice the calls until it was too late. I feel awful about it.'

'You shouldn't. Faith was there, and she was brilliant,' April insisted. 'With everything else you've been dealing with, I'm glad you didn't answer. The last thing you needed was me ugly crying.'

Tara couldn't look at her friend. She was embarrassed to be the subject of her concern. She was meant to be stronger than this. Pulling back her shoulders, she asked, 'And how are you feeling now?'

'I'm fi—' April began only to stop before the lie had fully formed. She lifted her face to the bright sun and her breath caught on the chill wind. 'Actually, I feel like crap, but I'm working through it.'

'Tell me what I can do, just name it,' Tara said, desperate to make up for her absence. 'I can go and beat this woman up if you want, or how about I hire a hit man?'

Her threat had the desired effect and April laughed. 'And there I was thinking my plan was extreme.'

The playfulness disappeared from Tara's voice when she asked, 'And what would that be?'

'I'm going to a party on New Year's Eve.'

'Oh, right,' Tara said, immediately wondering if April's plan involved taking revenge on Jason by spending the night with someone else. It was the kind of advice Faith would have offered.

She wanted to ask April outright if the invitation had come from Nick. Tara had been watching him closely at the Christmas party, convinced that he had one of her friends in his sights and worried that he would choose the one least equipped to deal with the attention. It looked at one point as if April had been drawn like a moth to his flame, but they had drifted apart by the end of the night. Or had that been a smoke screen?

'Will you be going with anyone?' she asked.

'I'll be on my own, but it's a house party with people I know,' said April with a note of bitterness. 'Actually, they're more Jason's friends than mine.'

Ahead of them, Molly and Lily had reached the end of the road and were starting down the path that led across the headland fields to Hale Head. Neither of them looked back.

'It can be a bit of a minefield mixing with a bunch of drunks who want to reminisce,' Tara warned. It was why she and Iain had opted to stay at home with the girls this year. 'Make sure you have an exit plan in case it gets too much.'

'Come what may, I'm staying until midnight,' April said, her expression grim. 'But don't worry, I'm driving, so I'll have a getaway car.'

'Sounds like you're on a mission,' Tara said, then the revelation hit her like a beacon from the lighthouse they were walking towards. 'Oh, no, April. Has this got something to do with the woman Jason was seeing?'

April hunched her shoulders as if she knew what she was contemplating was wrong, but there was a glint in her eye when she said, 'It's Bree's party, and apparently she wanted me there, so who am I to refuse? I can't wait to tell her that I know exactly which old acquaintance she'll be thinking about when they start singing "Auld Lang Syne".'

'Are you sure you should be doing this? If you need to talk to Bree, fine, but do it in a controlled environment when you're both sober. If she's been drinking, she might say more than you're prepared to hear.'

'Or her husband.'

'She's married?'

April walked on without replying and they closed the gap

on the girls. Molly and Lily had reached the lighthouse and were veering east along the path that followed the curve of the river upstream. Dexter heard their approach and bounded towards Tara. He had been splashing in puddles and his paws left muddy trails across Iain's jacket.

'Dexter, get down!' April shouted. When the dog ignored her, she took a deep breath. 'Sit!'

The dog backed away and pressed his bottom to the ground.

'Can it be my turn to hold his lead, please?' Lily asked.

Before April answered, she turned to Tara, who nodded her approval. 'As long as you keep tight hold.'

Lily beamed a smile at April and then Tara. 'Thank you.'

Molly was reluctant to hand over the dog until she realised he would chase after her if she raced ahead. As the two women followed the squeals of laughter, April shaded her eyes with her hand and scanned the horizon where the river curved out of sight. 'Can we reach Pickering's Pasture from here?'

'Not by following the riverbank. The path detours back to Hale to avoid the salt marshes and the farmers' fields,' Tara said, though she refused to be sidetracked. 'April . . .'

'I'm not going to change my mind.'

'In that case I'll expect a full update from you on New Year's Day,' Tara said. 'In fact, I'll be opening up the shop for a few hours if you want to come over for a late brunch. I could invite Faith too.'

April laughed. 'I imagine she'll be otherwise engaged.'

'Why? What have I missed?'

'I thought you said you'd spoken to her?'

'We had a quick chat, no more,' Tara said. 'She was expecting a visit from Ella so we didn't have long. She mostly talked about the last group meeting. She said it was a bit of a disaster.'

'Jodie was a mess by the end of it.'

Tara had hoped Faith was being overly critical. Justine had said the meeting had been particularly productive. 'I should have been there.'

'Oh, you missed quite a bit.'

'Why?' Tara said. There was a warning in April's voice that she didn't like. 'Did Faith give Justine a hard time?'

'Not at all. If anything she was supportive,' April explained. 'I hadn't appreciated how much Justine has been wrestling with her own problems lately. Faith really got her to open up.'

'Our Faith?' asked Tara, dismissing any concern she might have for Justine. She had seen her over Christmas, and Justine was fine.

'Our Faith,' confirmed April, suppressing a smile. 'She was in a great mood. It was almost as if someone had put a spring in her step.'

The pause lasted a heartbeat. 'Wait, are you suggesting she's seeing someone? *Faith*?' Tara asked. She didn't like to gossip, especially about someone in the group, but this was their friend, and Tara needed to know. 'Please don't say it's Nick.'

Faith and Nick had been a double act towards the end of the Christmas party, downing tequila slammers with some of the others, matching each other drink for drink. To the casual observer, they made a nice couple, but this was Faith. She had made it clear that she didn't need another half to make her life whole.

'They're going on holiday together in a few days,' April said, her voice low.

'No way,' Tara replied. 'How the hell did that happen?'

'You know Faith better than I.'

'I thought I did,' Tara conceded as the queasiness she had been struggling with since Christmas intensified.

16

Every single person that April encountered at Bree's party insisted on giving her a hug, whether she knew them or not. She felt like the odd one out, the young widow in the corner dressed in black, but as the evening wended its way towards midnight, her resolve to stay didn't waver.

'Can I just say, your husband was one of the best,' a colleague of Jason's insisted on telling her. Keith had his hand curled around the neck of a beer bottle and pointed a finger to jab the message home. 'A class act.'

'I can agree with you there,' April said, raising her glass of lime and soda in salute. In her other hand was a small heart-shaped object that had become damp with sweat in her grip.

'He's sorely missed, but I don't suppose I have to tell you that.'

April was only half-listening. Her interest lay on the other side of the room where Bree topped up glasses to ensure her guests were ready to raise a toast at midnight.

They had spoken earlier, and the hostess had handled April's surprise arrival with the skill of an accomplished liar. Bree gushed over how well April looked and how much she had been missed before sloping off on the pretext of greeting other guests. The only genuine conversation April had had so far had been with Callum.

'We're so glad you're here,' he had said.

'I couldn't not come,' April replied, although her arrival had been deliberately late to minimise the time spent mingling before the showstopper. 'If Jason were alive, he'd be here. No doubt about it.'

Callum rubbed his face. 'If Jason were alive, April, we wouldn't be having this party. You know what Bree's like, she'd rather have a night in with a takeaway than do something like this.'

'And Jason would have happily joined her,' she replied. 'I imagine his death has affected her more than most.' She wanted to see a flicker of suspicion on Callum's face, something that might make her feel less alone, but there was nothing.

Callum put a hand on April's arm and squeezed. 'I can't believe you're thinking of others. We're fine,' he said. 'If anything, it's made us appreciate what we have more than ever, and we're determined to make every moment count. Hence the party, although fingers crossed it's something we'll be too busy to repeat next year.'

April tilted her head. 'What do you mean?'

Shifting uncomfortably, Callum turned the bottle in his hand. 'Too many beers,' he said. 'It's given me a loose tongue.' When April continued to stare, he added, 'We're going to try for a baby, but Bree didn't want to say anything, especially to you.'

'Why especially to me?'

'You know,' Callum said, looking anywhere except April's

face. 'It was no secret you and Jay were coming close to that decision too.'

It should have floored April, but instead she gave Callum the biggest hug. She had once been as naïve as he was to think that choice was ever a simple one for either couple.

Their conversation had settled one matter at least: she wouldn't be dragging Callum into the mess Jason had left behind, not if she could help it. Bree was another matter entirely, and her shrill laughter grew closer as she worked the room, filling glasses and making small talk. She was shorter than April, with an athletic frame that gave the impression she worked out regularly. She didn't. Bree could give masterclasses on how to pretend to be something you're not.

She could see Bree's appeal. She was a good listener, and made you believe you could trust her with your deepest fears, or your most beloved husband. She fooled you into thinking she wasn't a threat, but as she approached, April's heart beat a little faster.

'And how are you two for drinks?' she asked, having left April and Keith's corner until last. 'We're about to make our way outside to let in the New Year. Thank goodness it's stopped raining.'

'I'm fine with this,' said Keith. April had let his inane chatter float over her and he appeared relieved to have the opportunity to make his excuses and leave.

Spotting the empty glass April had drained deliberately, Bree said, 'Ah, we can't have that. Do you fancy a drop of champagne?'

'I'll stick to lime and soda.'

'Then why don't you head outside while I top up your

171

glass? I won't be a minute,' she said. She checked her watch and laughed. 'I'd better not be, it's almost twelve.'

As April followed Bree to the empty kitchen, her body shook, but she wouldn't allow her nerve to fail. She clenched and unclenched her fist over the stone and kept her breathing steady as she watched her one-time friend splash soda water and lime carelessly into a glass. When Bree turned, she was surprised to find April blocking the doorway.

Bree handed her the drink and was confused when April didn't move. 'Shall we go?'

'Not yet.'

From the street, they could hear people counting down to midnight. 'April, we're going to miss it.'

'Who wants to see in a new fucking year when the man you loved died in the old one? I don't. Do you?'

Refusing to acknowledge what April had implied, Bree said, 'I know it's hard, but we have to try.'

April didn't budge. 'Aren't you sick of all this pretending?' she asked. It sounded too much like a plea.

A cheer rose up and Bree glanced over April's shoulder. 'I'm sorry, but Callum's going to be looking for me. If you want to sit this out, fine, but I have to go,' she said, more in desperation.

'Do I have to ask you outright?' April said, cursing her voice for trembling. 'Couldn't you at least spare me that?'

The singing had started, although it took a few bars before the tune resembled anything close to 'Auld Lang Syne'. It was almost too much, and April wanted to run, or scream, or smash her fist into Bree's face, but instead she planted her feet firmly to the floor. She wouldn't give Bree the excuse to dismiss her suspicions as the histrionics of a grieving widow.

'What's going on? I don't understand,' said Bree, eyes darting around the kitchen, anywhere but at April.

'I need to know if my husband was worth all those tears. Mine, and yours.'

'He loved you, April,' she tried. 'He loved you so much.'

'I don't need you to explain his feelings for me. I want you to explain his feelings for you,' hissed April. She stretched out her arm and unfurled her fingers to reveal the heart-shaped stone.

Bree took a stumbling step back. 'I can't . . .'

'Do you want me to ask Callum?'

'No, please. Please don't do this.'

Bree's hazel eyes were wide, and April fed off her fear. 'Then tell me. It's not like you'd be destroying my marriage, just the memory of it.'

Bree retreated further into the kitchen. She couldn't face April, but neither would she turn her back. She settled for a sideways position and her knuckles turned white as she gripped the edge of the countertop. 'It wasn't something we planned,' she whispered.

'That's original.'

'I mean it,' Bree insisted. It was her turn for her voice to shake. 'We were out for drinks with the team last Christmas. We were drunk; we shared a taxi home; Callum was away overnight . . .'

April's shoulder knocked against the doorjamb. They had been here. In this house. Together. 'That wasn't the first time,' she said. 'You took afternoons off, the first was in November – or was it? For all I know, this has been going on forever. I was worried when you and Jason first became friends. He said there was nothing going on, but it was the perfect opportunity, wasn't it? I was at uni, and you were still single.'

'No, no,' Bree said. She took a glass from the drainer and filled it from the nearest bottle. Her face twisted as she knocked back a slug of vodka. 'We didn't . . . When I met Jason, he made it clear that he loved you. We had one drunken kiss, that was all, but he wouldn't let it go further, and I accepted that.'

'But you spent ten years trying to tempt him away.'

'No I didn't,' she said. 'Jason was my best friend, and yes, I loved him, but I never tried to break you up. Those afternoons together, it was when Callum and I were going through a rough patch and I needed a shoulder to cry on. Jason took me out so we could talk, but nothing happened then. It wasn't meant to be what it became.'

'If it were so innocent, why didn't I know any of this?'

Daring to look at April, Bree's quivering smile pleaded with her to stop, but April remained unmoved, forcing her to continue. 'Jason and I were comfortable with each other, and when he started sending me daft messages to cheer me up, I responded. I don't know how they became more explicit.'

'Sexting?'

'Neither of us imagined it was going to lead somewhere.'

'But it did.'

'We didn't touch each other until Christmas, I swear.'

'That's hardly a comfort,' April said. 'You might have been going through a rough patch, Bree, but stupid me, I thought my relationship with Jason was solid – until you kicked the foundations from under us.'

'It shouldn't have happened, but it was over as soon as it started.'

'Obviously. He died.'

'No, before then.'

April's face twisted into a sneer. Jason's last secret afternoon off had been less than a week before his death. 'If there was any justice in the world, it should have been you waking up next to his dead body, not me.'

'Please, don't,' begged Bree.

'How could you both do that to me?'

'I wish I had an answer. Maybe that first kiss all those years ago was unfinished business,' she said, closing her eyes briefly. 'Things hadn't been allowed to run their course, and I was left wondering if it had meant anything to Jason. I can tell you now that it hadn't.' Seeing April flinch, she added, 'If you want to hate someone, hate me. I made the first move, but I promise you, it was Jason who made the last. When he realised what he'd risked, he was crushed. You were the one he wanted to spend the rest of his life with.'

'Who says it was his choice? Didn't I have a say in whether I wanted to take him back? Doesn't Callum have a say?'

Bree spun around to face her. 'April, I swear, it was the biggest mistake of my life. Callum and I had a bit of a wobble, but we're making a go of it now.'

'He told me. Should you be drinking so much if you're trying for a baby?'

Bree put down the glass. 'What do you want? What can I do to make this right?'

It was a question that April had been asking herself for weeks, and she was hoping the answer would become apparent now, but inspiration failed to strike. Bree was a poor substitution for the person who should be answering her questions, and April hated her for not being Jason. She *hated* her. Anger flared and she felt the weight of the stone in her hand. Before she could stop herself, she pulled back her arm and threw the missile at Bree. The bitch caught it.

'I never want to speak to you again,' April said. 'Don't try to contact me, and if our paths have to cross at work, don't expect anything beyond professional courtesy.'

'And Callum?'

'That's for your conscience, not mine.'

April wasn't sure her legs would carry her as she left the kitchen, but she wouldn't stay a moment longer in the house where Jason had cheated on her. Her coat was by the front door, left in readiness for a hasty departure, and she didn't bother putting it on as she stumbled outside. She pushed through the throng of partygoers, but a few insisted on wishing her a happy New Year. After a couple of refusals, she gave in. Tara had warned her that it might feel overwhelming stepping out of the old year, but if this was her chance to leave Jason, so be it. Her marriage was over. Happy New Year.

17

'You look well,' Tara said as she watched April rip apart a croissant.

It was New Year's Day and the shop was otherwise empty. Tara had opened up only long enough for the village's hungover residents and visitors to refuel on coffee and carbs before sending Michelle home and hanging the closed sign on the door.

'I didn't get up until eleven,' April said with her mouth full. 'I had the best sleep ever. How about you? Late night?'

'Would you believe we were all in bed by twelve thirty?' Tara said, sweeping a finger under a gritty eye, conscious that she looked as tired as she felt.

Having left the house early that morning, she hadn't looked in the mirror until she had arrived at work. Horrified by her reflection, she had rooted out an old mascara from the flat, but the trip upstairs did nothing to improve her spirits. She was yet to advertise for a tenant, and the detritus of her previous life remained scattered in the empty rooms as if it expected her return.

'Does that mean it was quiet or uneventful?' asked April.

Tara wrapped her hands around a steaming cup of coffee. 'It started off promising enough. Lily and Molly wanted to write more letters to send to heaven, but unlike Christmas Eve, it was teeming down. Iain used a golf umbrella as a makeshift shelter, but there was no way I could get the burning pages to float away and they fell into a puddle.'

'Hardly your fault.'

'You think?' Tara replied. 'Lily was in tears when she FaceTimed Joanna's parents, and by the end of the call, I was the villain with a long list of offences, from stealing her mother's cake recipe to breaking promises to Molly about getting a dog. My introduction to the new year was Lily telling me she hated me.'

'You shouldn't take it to heart.'

'It's bloody hard not to,' admitted Tara. 'Iain keeps telling me she was a stroppy madam when Joanna was alive, but at least her mum could push back when Lily tested the boundaries. I can't and I don't want to. Behind that moody exterior is a lost and frightened little girl and I wish I could reach her.'

'Give it time.'

'I don't suppose I have any choice,' Tara said, and before her mind could consider other options she added, 'So how was your night? Quiet? Uneventful?'

As April launched into a blow by blow account of her confrontation with Bree, Tara was impressed. The vulnerable and broken widow Tara had met back in September was a pale reflection of the woman sitting before her.

'I know I should feel angry,' April said, 'and don't get me wrong, I aimed that bloody stone straight at Bree's head, but I came away feeling relieved more than anything. Can you imagine how I would have felt if she'd given me some rational, non-adulterous explanation for what happened? At least now I have permission to hate Jason.'

'And do you?'

April wiped flakes of pastry from her chin. 'Not only did he cheat on me, he died thinking he'd wiped the slate clean. On that last night, there was no hint of a dirty secret eating away at his conscience. He didn't think to ask for my forgiveness because he thought he'd got away with it.'

Tara blew the warm foam on her cappuccino before taking a sip. 'And if he had told you, would you have forgiven him?'

'In another reality where Jason hadn't died, my guess is I would have ended up back at Mum and Dad's one way or another, working out my options.'

'And is that what you're doing?'

'I can't switch off my emotions, but I'm not going to play the broken-hearted wife who lost her happily ever after. It was already slipping through my fingers and I have to let go of it.'

'Easier said than done,' Tara warned.

'Just you watch,' April said with unnerving confidence.

'You're beginning to sound a lot like Faith,' Tara said.

'I'd say I'm beginning to act a lot like her too, planning a future where I don't need or want a man,' April said, popping another long ribbon of puff pastry into her mouth. With her cheeks bulging, she raised an eyebrow, swallowed, and said, 'Except, of course, that would make me more like Faith than Faith.'

'I did invite her over, but she texted this morning to say she couldn't make it.'

'They're flying off to Las Vegas tomorrow.'

'Then you know more than I,' Tara said. 'She's ignored my calls, and her messages have been short on content. She must realise I know about Nick, but she's avoiding any discussion. That worries me.'

April pushed her plate away and swigged a mouthful of coffee. 'You've known her longer than I have, maybe she expects more of a grilling from you.'

'And she'd be right,' Tara confessed. 'It doesn't make sense. She wasn't interested in Nick when he joined, or at least not for herself.'

'She tried to set him up with me.'

'You noticed?'

'Faith wasn't exactly subtle,' April admitted. 'But I don't think Nick was ever going to be interested in a thirty-year-old hysteric living back home with Mummy and Daddy.'

Tara's turning thoughts made her insides twist. 'No one was in the running once he set his sights on Faith and you can't argue they're a good match when it comes to expensive tastes. He made sure he left with her number that first time they met. He moved quickly, I'll give him that.'

'You make it sound mercenary,' April said. She wasn't smiling any more.

'I do, don't I?'

'Now you mention it, he was quite interested in hearing about my financial situation, although he did apologise for prying. He used to be an investment banker.'

'That might explain it,' Tara said, but her thoughts refused to settle. 'And I'm sure I'm overthinking things, but Justine sent me the photos from the party the other day. In the few that included Nick, he had his head down, and he wasn't in the group photo because he offered to take it. Is he camera shy, or does he have something to hide?'

'It sounds like you have a dose of my paranoia.'

'But look where that led you.' They both fell silent for a moment. 'Oh, I don't know, maybe I'm just feeling like this because he's a fair bit younger than Faith,' Tara said, searching for a less worrisome explanation for her unease. 'I know it shouldn't matter, and if Faith were here and we were talking about you flying off with Nick, I'm pretty sure we wouldn't be talking about your eight-year age difference.'

'But you are worried?'

'I don't doubt that Faith can look after herself, but I'd feel better if she wasn't being evasive. In all the time I've known her, she's never felt it necessary to justify herself to anyone. She doesn't care who judges her, so why not be open with me?'

'Could it be guilt?' asked April. 'She was devoted to Derek, so she must have mixed emotions right now. She claims to embrace her independence, but what if she's simply been too scared to give herself to someone else?'

'You obviously haven't heard about her exploits on holiday,' Tara said with a smile. 'That said, I wonder if she sees this as another holiday romance. She could be avoiding me because she knows I'll give her a hard time for playing with Nick's emotions. Running the group is difficult enough, but it would be a disaster if Faith dumps him the minute the plane lands and we're left to pick up the pieces.'

'So why do you sound as if you'd prefer that to happen?'

Tara stared into her coffee cup, where foam clung to the sides. 'I want whatever's best for Faith and I wish I believed that was Nick. I don't know enough about him, I suppose.'

Her disquiet over the photographs was proving difficult to shake. 'Maybe our interview process ought to be more thorough.'

Pulling a face, April asked, 'What interview process?'

'We vet all new members before we introduce them to the group. That's why I arranged to meet you beforehand, and Justine did the same with Nick,' Tara explained. 'We like to go through what's expected, particularly around confidentiality and mutual respect, but mostly it's about making sure you're genuinely interested and that you'll fit in with the others.'

'It's a bit of a stretch calling it vetting if you're taking everything you're told on trust. Nick wouldn't have found it difficult if he did have something to hide,' April said, focusing on Tara's doubts.

'When we were setting up the group, Justine suggested we ask for death certificates to prove a member was widowed, and birth certificates too, but I thought she was being overly bureaucratic. We've never had an issue before, and there's nothing to say we have one now.'

'Isn't there?'

'It's a gut feeling, that's all,' Tara said, and true enough it was making her nauseous.

'There's nothing to stop us doing some checks now,' April said, looking into the distance as her mind whirred. 'Social media would be a good start.'

'Facebook?' asked Tara. 'There was talk of setting up a closed group for members, but it was another of Justine's suggestions I wasn't comfortable with. You can't trust who might be accessing the information, and I leave it to Iain to run my business page. I can't remember the last time I looked at my account.'

'I noticed,' April said. 'I sent you a friend request ages ago and you ignored it!'

'Did you send one to Nick?'

'No, and I'm not sure I would now. He'd know we were checking up on him,' she said. 'But I could take a look on Twitter and Instagram to see if he or Erin had accounts. It's a shame they weren't married. I don't suppose he's ever mentioned her surname.'

'Sorry.'

April put her cup to her mouth, but hesitated. 'You know, he did take his time finding a photo of her when I asked to see one.'

'Was he in it?'

'No,' April said, only to shrug it off. 'Don't look so worried. I'll take a look online, and I bet we don't find anything.'

That possibility didn't fill Tara with hope. An online presence might give them some insight, good or bad, but what if April could find no trace of Nick or his dead girlfriend? Was it possible that Nick had joined the group under a false pretext?

STATEMENT

The Widows' Club @thewidowsclub
Again we feel obliged to respond to certain criticism. We would like to point out that we have always welcomed new members and the admins interview everyone before admission to the group. We accept we have a duty of care but we are not fortune tellers.

18

April had her earphones in to seal herself off from the house that was yet to wake. She was in bed listening to a playlist that had neither been borrowed nor shared with Jason. All the songs were new releases and not a single riff was tainted by his memory. There was only one man April had on her mind, and it wasn't her husband.

Conjuring an image of Nick, April recalled his confused expression that time she had told him she couldn't afford a place of her own. It had been only their second meeting, but Nick had already noted that Jason had been a council worker and presumed she had been left with a decent pension. Was that when he had lost interest? It was the same night that he had met Faith, and Tara was right to say he moved fast; he had pursued her from that moment on.

What did they really know about Nick? He was charming, charismatic, and appeared to be a genuinely nice guy, but, as April had discovered to her cost, not every man was as he seemed, and the interview process for the group wasn't exactly robust. April had been asked to complete a form to provide her contact details, but she hadn't been required to prove who she was. Neither had Nick.

When April rubbed her tired eyes, Dexter crawled up from the foot of the bed to rest his chin on her lap. He licked at her hand as she tapped her phone, his deep brown eyes glinting in the soft glow of the screen. A new George Ezra song was playing and she remembered that time Jason had been singing along to 'Budapest' in the car. The window was down and a passer-by had laughed at his misquoted lyrics. April caught herself before she could smile.

If she had to resurrect memories, they ought to be taken from those last months when Jason's behaviour had altered. April had known something was off. She should have tripped him up on his lies, but love had blinded her. Lust could do the same. Was that why Jason had thought he could get away with it? Was that why Faith was acting so out of character?

Faith was on holiday for another week and, unsurprisingly, there had been no word from her. She was probably having the time of her life, and where was the harm in that? She had looked radiant at the last meeting, and April had been happy for her. It was only after speaking to Tara that she had thought to question Nick's motives. Trusting people was a habit she needed to break. She had ignored the warning signs with Jason, buried any lingering doubts she had about Bree, and all for fear of what she might find. This time, it was a friend who risked being hurt, and April needed to be brave. When her instincts told her to dig deeper, she listened. She opened up the web browser on her phone.

After twenty minutes of checking out Nick's business credentials, April had found nothing sinister. His profile on LinkedIn backed up what he had told them about working for an investment bank, and the end date for his employment tied in with his claim that he had lost his job because he had been grief-stricken. His current job role was as a businessman and, although his limousine hire service had been in operation for less than a year, all the reviews so far were positive.

Turning to social media, April could find no trace of Nick on any platform except the Facebook page for his business. That didn't mean he was hiding something. There were lots of people who weren't interested in sharing every facet of their lives online. Tara was one of them, and only the other week, April had been tempted to delete her Facebook account too, having been confronted with one of those annoying videos capturing her 'best moments' of the year.

April didn't like reaching a dead-end so soon, but as she slumped against her pillow, she felt defeated. If only she knew Erin's surname. Dexter nudged her hand with his wet nose. It wasn't much encouragement, but it was enough. She rubbed the dog's floppy ears before resuming her search, this time putting as much information as she knew about Erin into the search engine, which wasn't much. After a couple of attempts with different combinations of where she had lived, the year she died, and her illness, April found a fundraising page. It had been set up to raise money for the hospice where a young woman called Erin Peters had been cared for in her last weeks. There was a collection of photos that confirmed April had found the right person. Her heart sank.

The page had been set up by Erin's husband and he was in some of the photos. He most definitely wasn't Nick.

April pulled out her earphones and dropped her phone as she jumped out of bed. She needed to do something, but what?

She paced the room to shake off the shock before picking her mobile up again and sending the link to Tara. Despite the early hour, Tara responded immediately.

What's this? X

It's Nick's girlfriend x

As she waited for the next response, April pictured Tara skimming through the page's updates. Her phone lit up and she answered the call before it could ring out.

'Are you sure it's her?' asked Tara.

'Nick showed me a picture of Erin,' April whispered in reply. 'It's definitely the same woman, and the description of her illness and everything she went through ties in with what Nick told us.'

'Except the bit about her being married to someone else. Do you think he knew her at all?' asked Tara. 'I can't see him in any of the photos.'

'And Nick wasn't in the photo he showed me of Erin,' April reminded her.

'Shit,' hissed Tara. 'Who the hell is he?'

'Not the grieving husband, that's for sure. We need to let Faith know.'

April's phone picked up thuds and bangs coming from the other end of the line until Tara was able to speak. 'She's thousands of miles away, in another country with a man who's been lying to us all,' Tara said at last. 'If we show her this, she'll want to confront him there and then and there's no telling how he'll react because we don't know him – at – all. We're going to have to wait until she's home.'

There were more thumps and crashes. 'Tara, where are you?'

'I'm in the shop.'

190

'It's . . .' April paused to check the time. 'It's four thirty. I know you start early, but I didn't realise it was this early.'

'It isn't usually, but I couldn't sleep. It's the girls' first day back at school today and I've decided it's safest if I stay out of Lily's way,' she said. 'So what's your excuse?'

'I was worrying about Faith,' April said, if only because Tara must be sick of hearing her complain about her unresolved feelings for her husband. Jason was consigned to the past. Her friends weren't. 'Do you want me to speak to her when she gets back? I don't imagine you need this right now.'

'Possibly not, but Faith's always been there for me, and besides, this is a support group matter as much as it is a private one. I'll talk to Justine and find out exactly what Nick said to her when he joined. There's a chance we have our wires crossed.'

'Do you think?'

Tara released a sigh. 'No, not really.'

19

Contained in her sanctuary at the back of the shop, Tara filled the delicate macaron shells baked before dawn with hazelnut ganache. It was all she could do to stop her hand shaking. Michelle was posted out front and Tara would join her when the herds of school-run mums arrived to graze on pastries and coffee, and not before. She had ventured to the front of the shop only once so far, and it hadn't been by choice.

Iain had arrived unexpectedly with the girls to let her know that she had been missed at home. He claimed it was Lily's idea to come in and show off her new uniform, but his daughter had been as sullen as Molly, who was upset that she had to make do with clothes from last term. Tara had drawn on every ounce of strength she had left to offer a warm, reassuring smile, and she had felt some relief when the girls had rushed outside to greet Molly's school friends. As she watched on, it became clear that their frowns had been reserved for Tara alone.

Retreating back to the kitchen, Tara had resumed her wait for what would be another difficult meeting. She had sent Justine a message asking if she could drop by between school runs and her race to work. It would be a push, but this was a conversation that couldn't wait.

When the bell above the shop door jangled, the macaron shell in Tara's hand turned to dust. Michelle's friendly greeting confirmed the wait was over and Tara wiped her hands before going out to greet her fellow administrator.

'I wasn't sure you'd have time,' Tara said.

'Isla's convinced me she's old enough to get the bus to school,' Justine said. She clutched her mobile and glanced at the screen. 'I've told her to message me when she gets there, and I'm not going to relax until she does.'

'It's going to make life so much easier for you,' Tara said, recalling Faith's concerns. Justine liked to project an image of being in control, but life would have become more complicated since her eldest daughter started secondary school. Tara and Iain would have the same issue next year when Molly graduated, but these were tangible problems that required practical solutions. It was nothing compared to the issue at hand.

'It gives me a bit more time, but I do need to set off in ten minutes,' Justine warned.

'I'm sorry, I shouldn't be adding to your stress.'

'It sounded urgent.'

Tara glanced at the group of mothers who had slipped into the shop behind Justine and were placing orders with Michelle. 'Come through to the back. I'll be as quick as I can,' she said as she pulled out her phone and opened up the link April had sent earlier. Safely ensconced in the kitchen, she turned the screen towards Justine. 'Do you recognise this woman?'

'Should I?'

'Did Nick ever show you a photo of his girlfriend?'

'Yes, he did,' Justine said, taking the phone from Tara. Skimming through the online photos, she added, 'That does look like her but oh . . .' Her eyes widened. 'Oh, my goodness. This is Nick's Erin?'

'We think so.'

'We?' Justine asked without looking up. She was devouring the information onscreen.

'April found the site. She was worried about Faith.'

'What does Faith have to do with any of this?'

Tara steeled herself. She didn't want to pass on information that Faith had yet to share directly with her, but what choice did she have? 'She and Nick have gone on holiday together.'

Justine pulled her gaze from the screen. '*Together* together?'

Tara nodded as she took back her phone. 'According to this site, Erin's husband was with her to the end. There's no mention of Nick anywhere.'

'But he told me about the conversations they'd had when she knew she was dying. It doesn't make sense.'

Fear pulled taut every nerve in Tara's body, making her shoulders hunch. 'Nick's been lying to us,' she said. 'It's the only explanation.'

'But why would he do that?'

'That's what I intend to find out.'

'No,' Justine said. 'I accepted him into the group. I should be the one to speak to him.'

'This isn't your fault, it's mine,' admitted Tara. 'We wouldn't be in this mess if I'd listened to you about checking members' backgrounds.'

'If this is anyone's fault, it's Nick's,' Justine countered. 'How about we speak to him together?'

'Sure,' replied Tara, grateful for her friend's support. 'And I think it would be safest if we meet here, in a public place.'

'Should we be that concerned? I can't imagine him turning nasty.'

'Neither can I,' Tara said, 'but if he's been putting on an act, who knows what the real Nick Malford is capable of?'

'Fair point, but if you ask me, it's Nick who should be worried,' said Justine. 'I'd hate to be in his shoes when Faith finds out. Exactly how involved are they?'

'I honestly don't know,' Tara admitted. 'She's been very quiet since Christmas, and that's something else that worries me.'

20

Faith peeled open her eyes and surveyed the pre-dawn landscape shaped by teetering bags and mounds of clothes strewn across her bedroom floor. It would all need to be sifted through and put away before she went back to work on Monday, but not yet. It was Saturday morning and the post-holiday realities could be postponed for a little while longer.

Judging by the arm that snaked around her travel-weary body, Nick was of a similar mind. He kissed her shoulder, her neck, and followed the curve of her jawline until his lips found hers. She grabbed a clump of his hair to pull his head back.

'Morning,' he said, giving her a lazy smile.

'Aren't you exhausted after yesterday?' she asked.

'No,' he said, still smiling.

Faith grinned back at him. 'In that case, how about making some coffee?'

'Are you sure that's what you need?' he asked as he resumed his exploration of her body with his mouth.

'Yes,' she groaned.

He didn't dare argue a second time, and crawled out of

bed. Picking up his mobile, he navigated his way across the darkened bedroom, stopping at a pile of clothes to find a dark navy dressing gown. He took his time to slip it on, aware that she was watching his naked silhouette. She waited silently for him to leave.

As Nick's humming grew faint, Faith turned on the bedside lamp and reached for her phone. There was a long list of messages she had been ignoring for the last two weeks and she was touched that her absence had been noticed by so many. Ella was top of that list.

Her stepdaughter had visited on Boxing Day for the obligatory swapping of gifts, but Faith couldn't give her what she really wanted. Ella's offer to unburden Faith of the responsibilities of running a large family home hadn't been repeated, but neither had it been withdrawn. Faith might be putting off the inevitable, but as she listened to the clink of a spoon echoing through the cavernous house that Derek had bequeathed to her, she thought not. Her circumstances were about to change.

Thumbing past Ella's unacknowledged messages, Faith wasn't surprised to see April and Tara's names appear, although she hadn't expected quite so many occurrences. The texts from April were initially updates regarding her set-to with Bree, and Faith felt a swell of pride. April was coming into her own and despite the inevitable pain, she would be a stronger person because of it.

Over the last couple of days, however, April had fallen silent, and Tara had taken over as most persistent. Her earlier messages had been simple hellos, followed by questions that changed in nuance, confirming Faith's suspicion that April had been telling tales. The last cluster of messages were more intriguing. Tara beseeched Faith to get in touch, each repetition more desperate than the last.

'Have you had a text from Justine?' Nick asked when he returned carrying a tray.

'No. Have you?' Faith replied, propping herself up in bed to take a cup from Nick.

Remaining on top of the duvet, Nick settled down next to Faith. She could feel the solid weight of him filling the cold empty space that had been her bedfellow for over four years now.

'She wants to arrange a meeting,' he said. 'Says she needs to speak to me before the group meets next week.'

'I suspect that's why I've had so many messages from Tara,' Faith said, glancing back at her phone. Her skin prickled. She didn't like being caught in a pincer movement 'Something's going on.'

Faith had known there would be questions. She couldn't be sure if Tara would approve, but there had been no doubt in Faith's mind that Justine would take umbrage at another intergroup relationship. 'See if Justine can meet you this afternoon.'

'I thought we were going to sort all of this out,' Nick replied, tipping his head at the scattered clothes and assortment of belongings they had transferred from Nick's flat within hours of landing.

Like the holiday, it was another rash decision, but in Faith's mind, it was also rational. Others might not see it that way. 'We might as well get the inquisition out of the way first,' she said.

'You think it'll be about our relationship?'

'Oh, I'm certain of it.'

Nick was quiet for a moment. 'Should we tell them we're living together?' he asked. 'Your friends are going to be worried we're moving too fast, and maybe we are. If you need a cooling off period . . .'

The idea of Nick living with her had come about one drunken evening in Las Vegas when he made a comment about going back to an empty flat that had never felt like home. Apparently, he had taken out the lease without much thought, explaining that he had no enthusiasm for spending his hard-earned money on himself and had reinvested everything in his business, which was expanding at a rate of knots. Now the foundations were established, he wanted someone to share in his success, hence the holiday, and it didn't have to end there. He had been the one to make a tentative suggestion about moving in, but Faith would like to think she had led him to that conclusion. And naturally, she had added conditions to their arrangement.

'You're staying,' Faith said. 'And if anyone asks, you can show them your rent book. You're my lodger, that's all.'

'That's all?' he asked. They locked eyes and his expression became serious. 'I can't believe this is happening.'

'Do *you* need a cooling off period?'

'It's too late. I don't know how it happened, but I've fallen madly and deeply in love with you, Faith.'

The declaration of love took Faith by surprise and, instinctively, she moved her body a fraction away from his. She liked Nick. He was kind, generous, and he was good company. Together they made the perfect partnership and that was why she was doing what she was doing. Love was a different game entirely. It meant giving up something of herself, and she couldn't do that.

'I'd better text Justine,' Nick said when he received no response.

Faith sipped her coffee as Nick sent the message. He was about to say something else when Justine pinged a reply.

'That was quick,' remarked Faith, her jaw tightening.

'I'm meeting her at two.'

'No, *we're* meeting her at two,' Faith corrected. When Nick gave her a puzzled look, she added, 'You're going to need backup.'

'Why?' Reading her thoughts, he added, 'Do you think they know what I did?'

'There's only one way to find out.'

When Faith and Nick arrived at Tee's Cakes, Michelle and another girl were behind the counter. It was busy and all of the tables were occupied by customers apart from the booth in the furthest corner that had been reserved for support group business. Tara sat with her back to the door, so Justine spotted their arrival first. Her paling expression made Tara look over her shoulder. Clearly, she hadn't expected to see Faith, and the smile she offered was tight. She looked tired and a little worn around the edges.

'I've been trying to get hold of you,' Tara said, standing up to give Faith a hug. 'We need to talk.'

'Well, I'm here now.'

Glancing at Nick, Tara's cheeriness was forced when she asked, 'Did you have a good holiday?'

'Vegas was amazing,' he said. 'But a word of warning, don't play cards with this one. She has a lethal poker face.'

Justine turned to Tara. 'Why don't you catch up with Faith out the back while I talk to Nick?'

Before she could respond, Faith stole Tara's place at the table opposite Justine, and Nick slotted in beside her. 'No, let's all have a catch-up here,' she said. 'What's this about? Have we broken one of your golden rules, Justine?'

'No,' she said, bristling.

Tara slumped into the remaining seat next to Justine. 'OK, let's get started,' she said, only to pause. She fiddled with the phone she had placed on the table, seemingly unsure how to proceed. 'There's no easy way to do this.'

'There are questions we need answering if you're to remain in the group, Nick,' Justine interjected. 'It's about your past.'

Faith sniffed. 'And what does his past have to do with you?'

'It's rather the point of the group, wouldn't you say?' retorted Justine.

'Please, Faith,' said Tara.

Faith pressed her back against the padded backrest and folded her arms. She didn't like that Tara had picked a side and it wasn't hers.

'What do you want to know?' Nick asked, his eye twitching.

Tara turned her phone and nudged it towards him. 'Is this Erin?'

After glancing down briefly, he released a sigh. 'Yes.'

The glimpse of Erin's smiling face as Nick slid the phone back to Tara was an image Faith had seen before. When he had mentioned not being at his girlfriend's deathbed, Faith had recognised a half-truth. She had unearthed Erin's fund-raising page too, and had asked the same question Justine asked now.

'Did you even know this woman?'

Faith was about to respond, but Nick held up his hand. It

was for him to explain and, begrudgingly, Faith accepted that Tara and Justine were right to expect an answer.

'Yes, of course I knew her,' Nick said. 'She was the love of my life.'

'According to this website, she married the love of her life. It wasn't you,' said Tara, surprisingly kindly, although it wouldn't be Nick's feelings she was trying to protect but Faith's.

'Erin and I had . . . a complicated relationship,' he began. 'Yes, she was married to someone else, but that doesn't take away how we felt about each other. I wasn't her husband, but I loved her to the very end, and she loved me.'

'So you were having an affair?'

Nick cast his eyes down. 'Yes.'

Tara looked to Faith, as shocked by her friend's lack of reaction as she was by Nick's answer.

When Faith had prised this information from Nick, her emotions had been conflicted. She had witnessed the pain April had suffered for a similar betrayal, but in Faith's mind, it was Erin who had broken her wedding vows, not Nick. He was by no means blameless, but wasn't it better to know a man's faults before getting involved?

'Satisfied?' asked Faith.

'Well, I don't know,' Justine said. 'We've never had anyone in the group who—'

'I wish you could have forewarned me, Faith,' said Tara. 'You must have known this would cause complications if ever it got out.'

'I've been away,' she said, but Tara's hard stare was enough to break even her. Faith needed to recruit her friend back to the right side. 'OK, OK. I didn't want to tell you. I know this isn't ideal, but Nick's still grieving like the rest of us. He has as much right to be in the group as anyone.'

'In that case, I'm sure the others will understand,' Justine said to Nick. 'Assuming you're willing to explain your circumstances.'

'No,' Tara said, jumping in before Nick could relax. 'The others won't understand. Not all of them.'

'I'm sorry, Tara,' Nick replied. 'I'm not proud of my past, or how I've kept things from the group, so if you have an issue with me remaining a member, I'm happy to leave.'

'It's not me who'll take issue,' she replied. Her jaw was set as she looked again to Faith. They both knew they were talking about April even if Justine and Nick didn't.

'This is different,' Faith replied. 'Nick wasn't the one who was married.'

'You know it's not that simple.'

'Then I'll tell you what is,' Faith said. 'If you expel Nick from the group, I'm leaving too.'

'Please, Faith,' Tara said.

'Would you stay if Iain were asked to leave, or would you make a stand?' replied Faith. When Tara didn't answer, she added, 'Nick is part of my life, Tara. We're living together.'

Tara's mouth fell open, but it was Justine who gasped. 'When did this happen? Oh, my gosh.'

'I'm only moving in as a lodger,' Nick added. 'In case you were worried that we're rushing into things.'

When Faith glared at Tara, they locked eyes. Tara was the first to blink.

'I'm not saying Nick has to go. I just think we need to consider how some of the others might react. At the very least, we need to prepare them.'

'Prepare who?' demanded Justine. 'Is someone going to explain what's going on?'

Tara held her breath before releasing it with a sigh. 'I can do that,' she promised. She glanced at Nick before adding, 'Later.'

'So what's your decision?'

Tara thought hard before she answered Faith. 'Can you leave it with me?'

Faith pursed her lips, but then her mouth softened into a smile. 'Our fate lies in your hands, Tara.'

21

It was the first group meeting of the year and the foyer walls echoed with chatter and the occasional burst of laughter, not that April was laughing. She held her body tense, with her gaze fixed on her phone. The message had been received the day before and she knew it by heart.

I know this doesn't help but I'm glad you know. I felt awful keeping it a secret and I can't tell you how sorry I am for the pain I've caused. I don't expect you to forgive me or ever understand but I hope we can be friends again one day. I'm here if you want to talk xx

The text was from Bree, but it could so easily have been from Nick. Both had had affairs and were brazen enough to think they could relax now their secret was out. April was yet to provide a response to either.

'I was hoping they'd be here by now,' Tara said. 'Are you feeling OK?'

'No,' replied April, slipping her phone into her pocket. 'I thought confronting Bree was bad enough.'

'This doesn't have to be a confrontation, April. I know it's bad, but it could have been so much worse. For a moment there I thought Nick was a conman out to rip off a rich widow. For Faith's sake, I'm glad he isn't.'

'That's a matter of opinion.'

'You have a right to be upset, and Nick is going to have to work hard to justify why he should stay,' Tara said, 'but we should hear him out.'

'He lied to us,' said April, bringing into tight focus the one thing she didn't think she could forgive. 'He tricked us into feeling sorry for him and I don't understand how Faith can be blind to that.'

As the entrance door swung open, April took a step back reflexively and almost bumped into Justine who had hurried to be at her side.

'They're here,' Justine whispered.

The three women watched in silence as Faith and Nick were ambushed by group members wishing them a happy New Year. A few commented on their post-holiday glow, but Faith side-stepped the comments and pulled Nick along with her.

'I've been trying to phone you,' she said when she reached April.

There had been precisely one missed call from Faith and it had been when April was in a meeting. Neither of them had attempted to call back. 'We seem to have a problem connecting lately.'

'That's something I intend to rectify,' Faith promised.

The taut muscles in April's arms and shoulders began to tremble at the sound of Faith's gentle words. This was the friend who had raced through rain and rush-hour traffic to be by her side on the second worst day of April's life. She didn't want to lose her, but she wasn't sure she could stomach hearing her friend defend Nick.

206

'We're due to start in five minutes,' Justine said, 'but we can put it back if you need more time?'

'I don't know that I have anything to say,' April replied. She was yet to look at Nick, who was standing behind Faith's shoulder. She had tried to picture this moment, but each and every time, Nick's face had morphed into Jason's.

'Why don't you try?' Faith said.

When April shook her head, Nick said, 'The last thing I want to do is upset you, April. I know you don't think I belong here, and there have been times when I've felt like a fraud too, but my relationship with Erin was complex. It wasn't a fling. Our circumstances were very different to what happened with your husband.'

'You told him?' April asked Faith.

'He needed to know.'

Finally, April looked to Nick. 'And what about Erin's husband? Does he need to know about you? Shouldn't he be here in your stead?'

'You're right,' he said. 'And if I'd known how much this would hurt you, I'd never have joined.' To Faith he added, 'It was a mistake coming. I should go.'

Neither Faith nor Nick had taken off their coats, and Nick could simply turn and walk out the door. But if he left, Faith would follow, and April didn't want that.

'No,' she said quickly. 'You came here to explain yourself, so let's hear it.'

Not wanting to let Nick off with a private confession, April turned her back and went to join the group. Most of the others had taken their seats, but thankfully Iain had saved a couple for her and Tara. Faith, Nick and Justine had to settle for being scattered amongst the others.

When Tara opened the meeting, there was only one topic on the agenda.

'There's an important matter we need to discuss tonight,' she began. 'Justine and I have become aware of an issue with one of our members that some of you might find challenging.'

There was a wave of restlessness and chairs squeaked as members scanned the faces that made up the circle. Faith stared straight ahead, and Nick, a few seats further along, kept his gaze to the floor.

'I would ask that you listen to what he has to say,' Tara continued, 'and that you consider your thoughts before speaking out. This is not a place for judgement, but we appreciate that some of you may find it difficult to offer the support we've come to expect from each other. We can talk more about that afterwards, but first, I'd appreciate it if you kept any questions until Nick has finished.'

Heads snapped in Nick's direction. He cleared his throat and leant forward, spreading his legs and resting his elbows on his knees. He looked up and as he began to talk, he met the gaze of each member in turn, including April.

'I'd like to start off by offering an apology. I haven't been completely honest with you all.'

April huffed. Nick hadn't been honest full stop. There were no half measures. He had deceived them.

'As you know, Erin and I weren't married, but what I failed to mention was that she was married to someone else,' he said, pausing to acknowledge a couple of gasps. 'We were ill-fated lovers in many ways. When we met, I knew straight away that I wanted to spend the rest of my life with her and she felt the same. If things had been different, if she hadn't become ill, we'd be married by now, I'm sure of it.'

'It wasn't a simple matter of you choosing to marry her, Nick,' April said coldly, ignoring Tara's request not to interrupt. 'She had a husband.'

Nick glanced towards Faith, but she was out of reach, wedged between Jodie and Steve. 'We stopped seeing each other when she found out she had breast cancer. The initial prognosis was good, and I was going to be a distraction she could do without. She needed stability to get her through her treatment.'

'Oh, it gets better,' April interjected again. 'So you ducked out when it got tough and let her husband look after her. I suppose you thought you'd pick up where you left off when the hard work was done.'

Nick held her gaze. 'I wish I had stepped up,' he said. 'You look at me and you see a bastard, but believe me, I do too. My only defence is that I was rooting for Erin to get better and make a go of it with Josh. Erin wanted that too, but when she realised she was dying, she got in touch. Time was running out and we couldn't ignore our feelings for each other any longer.' Nick hung his head down and played with the cuff of his shirt until he had composed himself. He coughed. 'I don't want to use Erin's cancer as an excuse, but neither do I want you to think badly of her. She died keeping her love for me a secret because she didn't want to hurt her husband, and I had to do the same. I wasn't allowed to grieve. That's why I was such a mess. That's why I'm here.'

The room fell silent, and even April couldn't think of a smart retort. She refused to feel sorry for Nick, however. He was still a liar and so was his dead girlfriend.

'We thought it best that Nick was open with the group,' Tara said. 'And as I mentioned before, this is not about judging

209

the rights or wrongs of what Nick and Erin did, this is about whether we as a group can continue to offer support. We all have our own stories and not everyone's experiences are the same, but we have a certain commonality. The question is, are there enough commonalities between Nick and the rest of us to allow him to remain in the group.' She gave nothing away about her own feelings on the matter.

'It makes no odds to me,' Steve said, sitting back in his seat with his arms folded. 'We both lost the women we loved to cancer. I feel bad for the husband, but it's Nick who came to us. His loss might be slightly different, but that doesn't mean it's any less. It wasn't an easy job to nurse Bella at the end, but at least I was there. I'm guessing you weren't.'

The tears welling in Nick's eyes threatened to spill as he shook his head.

'I can't say I'm as comfortable with this as Steve,' said Nadiya. 'There are things the rest of us will have experienced as long-term partners that Nick won't . . . That said, I'm willing to give it a try.'

A few of the others echoed Nadiya's reservations, but no one was willing to step forward and say that Nick hadn't earned his place. April was on her own and she had to speak up.

'I know Tara said we shouldn't judge, but I'm sorry, there's an elephant in the room we're all ignoring,' she said. Addressing Nick directly, she added, 'What you and Erin did was wrong, especially Erin. If she loved you like you say she did, she wasn't only betraying her husband, she was using him as a sop to nurse her to the bitter end. How could she do that? You only have to speak to Steve or Tara to know how awful it must have been for him.'

210

'She has a point. It was a shitty thing to do,' said Jodie.

'Thank you,' April said, relieved that someone else was finally getting it. Emboldened, she turned back to Nick. 'Erin's husband is the one who has to wrestle with the memory of watching her die. Not you.'

'No, Nick was forced to keep away,' Faith said, defiance sparking in her eyes. 'How awful must that have been?'

'There are worse things,' April assured her as her mind made an involuntary leap to the last morning she had woken up next to Jason. Her fingertips turned to ice at the memory and the cold reached her heart.

'We appreciate this is difficult for you, April,' Justine replied. 'And it's right and proper that you should discuss your feelings rather than let them fester. I'm sure Nick feels better for having shared.'

Nick didn't look nearly as comfortable as Justine suggested, but she was going somewhere with the conversation. April could sense it and so could Tara, who sat bolt upright.

'Why don't we leave it there for now,' she said, reaching for April's hand. 'Justine and I can stay behind later and chat to anyone who needs to talk it through.'

'I'm not sure we're finished,' Justine persisted. 'The group is most effective when people are open, and, as has been proven tonight, there's nothing to be gained from keeping things bottled up.' She looked directly at April when she added, 'This is a safe environment.'

'Seriously?' Faith interrupted. 'You think now is a good time for this? If you ask me, there's been enough oversharing for one night.'

'I disagree. Now would be the perfect time.'

'No, Justine, it wouldn't,' Tara said.

April pulled her hand free of Tara's grip. It was nice to know her friends had her back – especially Faith, given how April had behaved towards Nick – but it was time to stand up for herself. She took a breath. She opened her mouth, but before she could speak, Nick stood up.

'I should go,' he said. 'This is my fault.'

Tellingly, no one said it wasn't, not even Faith, although she did stand up too.

'You don't have to go,' Justine offered.

'No, it's probably better if you continue this conversation without me,' Nick replied. 'I'll come back if you'll have me, but I'll understand if you won't. And, April, I'm sorry.'

As April watched Nick head out of the room, she was happy to see him go, but her feelings were mixed when Faith followed. She tried to tell herself that if her friend was leaving for good, the group would carry on regardless, but it wasn't the group that had seen April through the last few difficult months: it was Tara and Faith, especially Faith. Before she could stop herself, April leapt up from her seat.

'Stop, please,' she called out when she reached the foyer.

Nick was handing Faith her coat and they both froze. Faith's mouth cut a thin line across her face and her eyes were blazing. 'In case you didn't notice, I stood up for you in there, April. It's a shame you didn't extend the same courtesy to me.'

'This isn't about you.'

'But it is,' Faith replied while Nick stood mutely beside her. 'You're not simply challenging him, you're challenging me and the choices I've made.'

April was at a loss for words. She couldn't and wouldn't row back on what she had said in the meeting. Faith shook

212

her head in disappointment and was turning to leave when Tara appeared.

'Please Faith,' she said. 'Justine has a point. We shouldn't let our feelings fester. If you leave now, we all know there's a good chance you won't come back.'

'Then you don't know me at all,' Faith said. 'I don't back down from a fight.'

'This was never meant to be a fight,' Tara replied.

'So it's my fault?'

'No, it isn't,' April said, deliberately choosing not to look at Nick as she spoke. She inched closer to Faith. 'If I've upset you, I'm sorry.'

'It's not me you should be saying sorry to.'

April knew an apology to Nick was beyond her. He was a charmer and, unlike Faith, April didn't like that in a man. He had spun his stories from that first group session and his omissions were as good as lies. She wasn't going to apologise for calling him out.

'April doesn't need to apologise,' Nick said. 'I deserved it.'

'I can't condone what you did . . . but perhaps I could have handled it better in there. I'm sorry for that,' April conceded through gritted teeth.

It was enough to appease Faith and she relaxed as Nick helped her into her coat. 'The last few months have been a testing time for all of us,' she said, 'but at least that disaster of a group session has allowed us to vent our anger.'

'I can't promise I'm going to be OK with this going forward,' April warned, 'but I care about you Faith. I don't want to argue.'

'Then learn to bite your tongue,' Faith suggested.

Tara laughed, breaking the tension. 'Like you do?'

Faith smiled. 'Come what may, I think we all have a great year to look forward to.'

Tara noticed April wince. 'Isn't it Jason's anniversary soon?'

'The beginning of February.'

'Then we need to be there for you,' Faith said. 'And for goodness' sake, stop worrying about me. Let me be happy, with Nick.'

To his credit, Nick blushed. 'I appreciate you have no reason to take my word for anything,' he added, 'but I promise you I want only what's best for Faith.'

'We all do,' April said, hoping Faith would open her arms as she stepped forward. She did, and they hugged fiercely.

'Why don't you two come over for a girls' night?' Faith asked. 'How about this coming Saturday?' She turned to Nick and added, 'You can make yourself scarce, can't you?'

'I'll be working anyway,' he replied. 'I won't be home until the early hours.'

'Perfect. Is that a date?' she asked her friends.

April had to take a moment. After dating for barely a month, Nick was calling Faith's house his home. How could they all pretend to be comfortable with that? How could they not be worried? April would be happy never to see Nick again, but if tonight had proven one thing, it was that they needed to keep him in their sights.

'I wouldn't miss it,' she replied.

22

The mounting pressure in the group had found a temporary release during the last meeting, but the underlying cause was unresolved as far as Tara was concerned. Her friendship with Faith was being tested and she was grateful for April's offer to pick her up en route to Faith's on Saturday evening.

'I wasn't looking forward to arriving on my own,' Tara said, gathering up the folds of her black satin skirt so she could close the car door.

'Me neither,' said April as she drove out of Pepper Street. 'I have this image of Nick wearing a smoking jacket as he welcomes us into *his* home.'

'It does feel odd, doesn't it?'

'Very.'

As they drove past the village hall with its lightless windows, Tara said, 'I've known Faith for over three years and compared to anyone else in the group, her life has been the most constant and predictable. She was heartbroken over Derek's death, but she had embraced her new life.'

'I've never met anyone more self-assured and proud of their independence. That's why I wanted to be more like her.'

Tara smiled. 'Judging by your performance the other day, I'd say your mission is complete.'

'Nick deserved it. He's never had to face the consequences of what he did,' April said, taking a bend a little too fast. As she overcorrected, Tara's shoulder thumped against the passenger door. 'Sorry.'

When the car slowed to within the speed limit, Tara said, 'We can at least rest assured that he'll pay for his mistakes if he dares hurt Faith. I know he's moved in with indecent haste, but Faith would kick him out just as quickly if she had to.'

'Hmm,' April said, not filling Tara with hope. 'But what damage could he do in the meantime? Maybe I'm being cynical, but we went snooping into Nick's past for a reason. Something still doesn't feel right.'

Not wanting to feed each other's fears, they fell silent and Tara spoke only to give April directions to Woolton. There were no easy solutions, or at least none that would be met without resistance. Faith had been aware of Nick's past long before April and Tara made their discovery, and she had reached her own conclusions. She would have cross-examined Nick over every detail before allowing him to take up residence in her home. Faith wasn't stupid.

'Wow, I gathered Faith had a nice place, but this is something else,' April said as they pulled up outside a large detached house set on a rising slope and surrounded by mature hedgerows and trees. The gated entrance was peppered with spotlights that highlighted the white stucco and black fascia to show off the house to its best advantage. Tara had visited before, but it never failed to impress.

'Maybe you should park away from the gate,' Tara said, having spotted Nick's BMW on the drive.

They took their time getting out of the car and wasted a few more seconds on the doorstep, straightening their clothes in the reflection of the black glossed door before Tara rang the bell. As April had foretold, Nick was the one to greet them, although he was wearing a white shirt rather than a smoking jacket.

'Come in, make yourselves at home. Faith's upstairs, but she won't be long.'

Nick took their coats and ushered them towards the tantalising aroma of garlic and herbs. Tara wasn't sure what she had expected, but the kitchen appeared unaffected by the addition of Nick to the household. The oak benches and breakfast table that claimed the kitchen nook looked cosy and inviting, with flickering candles and plump scatter cushions.

Seeing the bottle of wine in a cooler on the table, Tara said, 'We can look after ourselves if you're busy?'

Nick cast a glance at his socked feet. 'Actually, I was in the middle of getting ready. I'll be out of your hair in five minutes.'

'And then we can talk about you to our hearts' content,' Faith said.

She had appeared behind Nick, wearing a peacock blue wrap-over dress. Her hair fell loosely on her shoulders and despite her jibe, she appeared relaxed. She was happy, and that happiness shone when Nick's hand followed the curve of her hips. His lips glanced briefly off hers as he slipped past.

'Have fun, ladies,' he said, smiling confidently as he left the room.

The display of affection did nothing to warm Tara's feelings for Nick. She wished she could like him again, but the last group meeting had served only to prove how adept he was at getting out of tricky situations. She had secretly hoped that the group would reject him, but having stayed around to hear members' views, she had been surprised how many had admired Nick for having the courage to stand up and admit his past failings.

'Right, who's ready for a drink?'

'I'm driving,' April said as she looked longingly at the bottle Faith had picked up from the table.

'I'd love one,' replied Tara. 'Is there anything I can do?'

Faith followed her gaze to the discarded plates, pots, and knives scattered across almost every work surface. There was a large focaccia smothered in garlic butter and pricked with rosemary waiting to be baked, and judging from the dusting of flour and discarded herbs on a chopping board, it was homemade.

'God, he has left a mess, hasn't he?'

'Nick made dinner?' asked April.

Still holding the wine bottle, Faith edged towards the range cooker as if approaching an open furnace. 'He certainly did. The lasagne's on a timer apparently and there's a salad prepped in the fridge.' She pulled a face as they heard the front door slam. 'Does anyone know how long the bread needs?'

Tara grabbed a discarded apron lying on the counter and rolled up her sleeves. 'Right, Faith. You sort out the drinks and I'll do the rest. Make mine a large one.'

'You don't have to,' Faith said, already on the retreat back to the table.

'Honestly, I'll feel better once I see those counters gleaming.'

'What should I do?' asked April.

'There's some elderflower pressé chilling in the fridge if you'd like something cold,' Faith suggested as she snuggled amongst the scattering of cushions. When April returned after pouring her own drink, Faith handed her a glass of wine. 'Can you pass this to Tara for me?'

April did as she was instructed and remained with Tara. 'Don't you like cooking, Faith?' she asked as she began filling the dishwasher.

'I fell out of the habit,' she called over. 'And if I'm being perfectly honest, I used to hire caterers for the big dinner parties Derek and I held. I would have ordered something in from Marks and Sparks, but Nick insisted on helping. See, he does have his uses.'

Tara shared a look with April, but neither replied. And what was there to say? Nick was going all out to impress his new landlady.

'I'm so glad to see you both,' Faith continued. 'We haven't had a proper catch-up in ages and I didn't stay long enough at the last meeting to listen to everyone's updates. I want to hear how you two are doing. April, tell me everything that's happened between you and Bree.'

'I said what needed to be said,' April explained.

'Oh, this sounds good. Go on.'

As April retold her story, she helped Tara clear away the detritus Nick had left behind until the black granite countertops shone.

'And what happens now?' asked Faith. 'Do you need more from her?'

'She sent me a message the other day. Another apology and a suggestion we could be friends again. I wasn't going to dignify it with a response, but with Jason's anniversary coming up, I thought I'd warn her to keep away from his grave, just in case she was tempted.'

Faith leant forward. 'And will you go to the cemetery?'

'I don't know,' April said as she stood in the middle of the kitchen wringing a tea towel. 'I try so hard to stay angry with him, but it's not easy. If he were alive and I'd found out about Bree, I imagine at this stage we'd be talking about a reconciliation. Is it bad that I still love him?'

'There are no rules for something like this,' Tara said softly. 'Go with how you feel, even if how you feel changes by the day or by the hour.'

April's eyes glistened. It was possible she was about to crumble, but Tara didn't think so. Handing her friend a stack of plates from the plate warmer, there was no crash of crockery onto the porcelain tiles. 'Take these over and have a seat,' she said. 'Everything's pretty much ready.'

It took a few trips to bring the food to the table, but once it was done, Tara sank down onto the bench and mopped the sweat from her brow with a napkin.

'You really didn't have to,' Faith said as she refilled the glass Tara had drained.

Tara laughed. 'Now you tell me.'

Faith drove her mad at times, but her attitude made a refreshing change to most people she knew. If Faith didn't want to do something, she didn't do it. Tara had to keep reminding herself of that.

'It could have been worse,' Tara continued. 'We could have arrived and found nothing but ingredients. I hope Nick's cooking tastes as good as it smells.'

'I can vouch that it does,' Faith said confidently. She could see Tara was about to ask a follow-up question and quickly added, 'Tell me your news. Have you all settled in yet?'

While Faith took over the hostess duties and served up the

lasagne, Tara sipped her wine. 'There are still a few sticking points, one being the argument over getting a pet,' she said. 'I would have liked to wait a bit longer, but Iain persuaded me the time was right, and we found a gorgeous Ragdoll kitten for sale. It's not ready to leave its mum yet, but we took the girls to see it after school yesterday. It was supposed to be a nice surprise.'

'Why do I get the feeling this doesn't have a happy ending?' Faith said.

Tara took another gulp of wine. 'The kitten was grey and white with the most beautiful blue eyes, and Lily literally gasped when she saw it. For once it was Molly who was the fly in the ointment, but I was expecting that because she was holding out for a dog. I was hoping she'd come around – she'd do anything for Lily, and the kitten is adorable. It was meant to be something that could unite us. It doesn't come with a history and has no claim on one side of our misfit family or the other.'

'You're hardly misfits,' said Faith. 'And you'll come together eventually, with or without the kitten.'

'At the moment it looks like it's without. Molly and I had a flaming row this morning,' Tara said. She winced at the memory. She'd found her daughter skulking in the utility room. 'I thought she was up to no good when I caught her up so early. She'd assumed I'd gone to work, but knowing tonight would be a late one, I'd treated myself to a lie-in. Molly was messing around with the washing machine and . . .' She covered her eyes with a hand as shame scorched her cheeks. 'I was already angry with her for being so truculent over the kitten and I let rip. We woke the rest of the house up, and it was Lily who came to her rescue. She admitted she'd wet the bed and Molly was only trying to hide the evidence.'

'And I presume wetting the bed is a sign that Lily's still troubled,' said April.

'The arguments over the kitten must have been another tipping point. Iain had mentioned she went through a phase of bed-wetting when her mum died, and there's a protective sheet on her bed just in case. Anyway, so much for the kitten bringing us together,' Tara said, raising her glass as if in a toast.

'I am so glad I never had kids,' Faith muttered.

'I could be living in Paris, running my own patisserie by now if things had been different,' Tara rued.

Mike had been her undoing. 'Come work for me and you'll have enough money to go to Paris within the year,' he had promised her. A year later and it was, 'Keep the baby and let's build new dreams together.' And his last words to her, 'Let me go, and I promise you'll be happy again.'

Coming out of her reverie, Tara realised her friends were watching her. She blushed. 'Not that I'm wishing Molly away,' she said quickly. 'But she has no idea of the sacrifices I made when I found out I was pregnant.'

'I doubt I'll ever get the chance to be a mother,' April added. She tore off a piece of focaccia and picked at the warm dough. 'Did I tell you Bree and Callum are trying for a baby?'

'How nice for them to be able to pick up and carry on as if nothing happened,' said Faith.

'As far as Callum's concerned, it didn't,' April replied. 'If you were me, would you tell him?'

Unfazed by April's hard stare, Faith said, 'I can understand how someone in your position would want to know the extent of their partner's betrayal, but if there are no suspicions, why inflict unnecessary pain on an innocent party?'

When April's scowl persisted, Faith rolled her eyes. 'I do

know you're talking about Nick here. And in his circumstances, no I don't think it would serve any purpose to expose the affair. Erin isn't going to be punished for her sins, is she? The family seems to have placed her on a pedestal, and they're raising a lot of money in her name. I'd say keeping quiet is the charitable thing to do.'

'You seem well informed,' said Tara.

'I know you must think I've lost the plot, but I haven't gone into this with my eyes closed.'

'But why go into it at all?' asked April. 'I thought you liked your independence.'

'I'm allowed to change my mind,' she said, 'and Nick reminds me so much of Derek.'

'In what way?'

Faith swallowed a forkful of lasagne before replying to Tara. 'For one thing, they both look good in a suit.'

'You like the successful businessman types,' April surmised.

'There are worse vices in the world,' admitted Faith. 'But I'd say what links them most is their persistence. Nick knew I wasn't interested, but that made him all the more determined to win me over. Derek was the same. The less interest I showed, the more he pursued me. It took my darling husband almost two years before I was ready to give in.'

'Then why did it take Nick less than two months?' demanded Tara.

April put down her fork. 'Wait. Was Derek still married when you met him? Is that why you rejected him at first?'

Faith shrugged.

'Oh, my God,' said Tara. 'I've heard that story a million times but it never crossed my mind that he wasn't divorced when you met. Why didn't I ever think of that?'

Faith gave April a withering look, but she was smiling when she said, 'Because you're not a cynic like our friend here. I'll have to be more careful around you, April.'

'You met on a cruise. Does that mean he was with his wife back then?' asked Tara, needing to hear the unabridged version of Faith's love story.

'My holiday romances are only ever with men who are unattached, or at least ones who claim to be unattached. Either way, when the holiday is over, that's the end of it – normally. My dalliance with Derek was different,' Faith said. 'I'd met him on the coach transfer to Portsmouth, so I knew he was married and turned down his advances throughout the holiday. When we arrived back in Liverpool, he and his wife insisted we share a taxi. That's how he tracked me down later, and the rest is history.'

'He did all of that under his wife's nose?' Tara asked. She had imagined Derek as the perfect gentleman, but she was seeing him in a different light.

'When I said that we didn't start dating until after he was divorced, that was true. We did *not* have an affair,' Faith insisted. 'Derek wasn't a philanderer. He told me he didn't expect his marriage to last the year, and he asked me to wait.'

'At least he was open with you,' April said. 'It's a shame you can't say the same about Nick.'

'April's right,' Tara said before Faith could come back with her rebuttal. 'I'm not saying Nick isn't making you happy . . .'

'But?'

Tara smiled at her friend. 'Do I need to point it out?' she asked, taking a long swig of wine before adding, 'The fact that you've looked into his past means you know you should

224

be cautious. The only thing we can be absolutely sure of, apart from the fact that Nick makes great lasagne, is that he knows how to deceive. Are you sure it's you he's interested in, or is it this?' She waved a hand around the kitchen and tipped her head to the rest of the house.

'It's not like that. And in case you've been wondering, he paid for the holiday, not me.'

'All of it?' asked April.

'For the sake of my own conscience, I found his bank details and transferred what was a small contribution to the cost, but Nick sent it straight back.'

'By sneaking a look at your bank details in return?' April said.

Tara wanted to pat April on the back. Her friend was much better at this than Tara would be, even if she were sober. Faith was less impressed.

'This is ridiculous. May I remind you that Nick has his own business? And before you ask, he's doing really well. He's using my home office, and I'll admit, I've had a sneaky peek. The calendar on the wall is bursting with bookings.'

'But have you seen his accounts, his balance sheet?' asked April.

'I've not hacked into his computer if that's what you're asking, but I've seen some paperwork. He sent out some hefty invoices the other day, so he is making money.'

'Assuming those invoices get paid in full and on time,' April replied. 'And what's to say he isn't deliberately leaving out paperwork to give you a false impression?'

'Oh, please. Nick is a savvy businessman. He doesn't need my money, and thank goodness for that.' Faith eyed her friends over the rim of her wine glass. 'Would it get you two off my back if I said I'm not nearly as wealthy as you suspect?'

'Yes,' April and Tara said in unison.

Faith set down her glass. 'This house is a money pit and, for the record, Ella has a vested interest, which means it wouldn't be my decision alone should I be coerced into selling up,' she said. 'To add to my woes, there are issues at work that I won't bore you with, but suffice to say I would have struggled to pay for a holiday this year if Nick hadn't offered.' She put both hands on the table. 'Look ladies, I'm not looking for love or a life partner. My arrangement with Nick is as much a financial arrangement as anything.'

'How do you mean?' April asked, leaning forward.

'Nick is a lodger with benefits. His rent gives me a safety net and means I can stay here indefinitely. I don't know why I didn't think of it before.'

April eyed her with suspicion. 'And was it your idea?'

'This works to both our advantages,' Faith said. 'Neither of us could afford a place like this on our own.'

April refused to back down. 'And does Nick know you're not the rich widow people presume you to be?'

'It would make no difference.'

'I'll take that as a no then.'

'Are we going to fall out again, April?' asked Faith.

Tara could see the conversation degenerating. 'We're just worried about you, that's all.'

Faith's voice was clear and confident. 'Then don't make me choose between our friendship and my relationship with Nick. You won't like the outcome.'

23

The sleeves of Faith's silk dressing gown slid down her arm as she stowed away the crystal glasses from her little dinner party. She had drunk far too much and had no recollection of who had cleared away the plates; it was just a shame she had to unload the dishwasher herself. She wasn't expecting Nick to help. He had arrived home at an ungodly hour and was snoring softly when she rolled out of bed.

Faith had hoped Nick would be more domesticated, but despite his prowess in the kitchen, he was oblivious to the mess he created. He was as bad as Derek and their similarities kept Faith smiling as she finished her chores and made a strong coffee to wash down some painkillers. Her head throbbed, but in all other respects she felt good. She hadn't been able to allay all of April and Tara's fears, but she had made a start. Nick was a good thing in her life, they would come to see that.

The second cup of coffee was for Nick and she placed it on the bedside table before sitting on the edge of the bed to watch him sleep. She imagined how the dark stubble on his chin would rasp against her cheek if she leant over and kissed him, but before she could give in to the urge, dimples appeared in his cheeks.

'I'm not sure if this is a weird or nice way to be woken up,' he said, opening an eye.

She leant over and kissed him. 'I'd say weirdly nice.'

He pushed back her hair so he could see her face. 'I would too.'

'I love you,' she whispered, feeling a warmth flood her body as Nick grabbed a handful of her hair to pull her closer. He kissed her hard and the stubble against her soft skin hurt.

When the doorbell rang, Nick wasn't ready to release Faith, but she wriggled from his grasp. 'If I don't answer it now, she'll probably camp outside until I do,' she said.

'You're expecting someone?'

Faith stood up and stretched her spine. 'In a fashion,' she said. She was only surprised it had taken Ella this long to investigate why a BMW had been parking overnight on her drive. 'It'll be my stepdaughter. Stay up here and keep quiet.'

'I'm going to have to meet her at some point, or are you ashamed of me?'

'Oh, I can't wait to tell her about you,' Faith said, 'but it's a sensitive issue. I need to do this on my own.'

The doorbell chimed again as Faith checked herself in the dressing-table mirror. She carefully applied her lipstick and tamed her hair before closing the bedroom door and padding barefoot down the stairs. She opened the front door to find Ella clad in Lycra and stretching out her leg muscles.

'Have you been for a run?' asked Faith.

Ella wiped the faintest hint of perspiration from her brow. 'I'm trying to get back in shape after Christmas and thought I'd drop by to wish you a happy New Year.'

228

'And a happy New Year to you too,' Faith said despite the fact it was practically February.

In Faith's view, there should be an amnesty on the requirement to repeat this nonsensical mantra beyond January the first. Change of fortune didn't happen with the turn of page on a calendar; it happened without ceremony, and often without warning. The best anyone could hope for was that they chose the fork in the road and it didn't choose them.

Faith allowed Ella to lead the way to the kitchen and watched her crane her neck as she passed the sitting room. Nick had abandoned his shoes in front of the chair where he'd taken them off the night before.

'I've made coffee if you'd like one.'

'Water's fine,' Ella said, taking a glass from the cupboard and filling it with filtered water from a jug in the fridge. 'You kept it quiet about the holiday. Where did you go?'

Faith closed the kitchen door and sat down at the breakfast table to face her second cross-examination in as many days. 'Las Vegas.'

'Not a cruise then?' Ella asked pleasantly. She remained standing with her back resting against the counter. One foot was crossed casually over the other, but her stance was hardly relaxed. She tried again. 'Did you go with anyone?'

'Yes, I did.'

They smiled at each other.

'OK, I have to ask. Is that someone else's car parked outside?'

'Yes.'

Ella really wasn't any good at this, but then she didn't need to be. She had already been fed some of the answers. Faith hadn't told Ella about the holiday, but she had asked Mr Newton to watch over the house while she was away, and presumably his beady little eye had remained trained on her property ever since. He would have seen not only the car but the driver too, and Faith wouldn't be surprised if photographs had been bundled into a brown envelope and passed to Derek's embittered ex-wife and thence to Ella.

As amusing as the game was, Faith was hungover and she had no interest in shooting the messenger. 'His name's Nick,' she said. 'I'll have to invite you over to dinner some time so you can meet him.'

'Gosh, it must be serious if you're ready to introduce him to the family. That's wonderful news.'

Faith pulled her cup of coffee towards her. 'We're living together.'

'Here?'

'Naturally. You were right about this house being too big for one person.'

'But I thought . . .' Ella pursed her lips and checked her emotions. 'Does this mean you're not selling?'

'Your father wanted me to live here for the rest of my life and I intend to honour his wishes.'

Ella frowned. 'Do you honestly think you'd be here now if he were still alive? You know what he was like, Faith. At some point he would have tossed you on the scrapheap and taken everything, just like he did with Mum.'

'You can hardly claim Rosemary was left with nothing,' Faith challenged. 'Your mother had a healthy payout from the divorce. I should know, things could have been very different for me if Derek hadn't been forced to cash in his pension.'

Ella straightened up and set down her glass. 'Mum got a fraction of what she deserved, Dad saw to that. He was a manipulator of the worst kind.'

'According to Rosemary.'

'You know it's true.'

'I don't disagree that's what your mother wants you to believe,' Faith replied. 'But I'm worried that you've become as fixated on this house as she is. Let it go, Ella. This is my home.'

'Technically, it's only half yours.'

Faith tipped back her head. They were usually too polite to mention the true reason why they continued to suffer each other's company. For all of Derek's alleged faults, he had left his estranged daughter with a generous inheritance. Ella was entitled to half the proceeds should the house be sold, but Derek's first concern had been for his wife. Faith had been granted a life-interest in the property, which meant Ella wouldn't receive a penny until Faith sold up or dropped dead.

'This is my home until I or my maker dictate otherwise.'

'Dad wouldn't be too pleased about someone else moving in,' Ella said churlishly. Derek had always said she was a whiny child.

'If your father's feelings came into it, neither would he want Rosemary sneaking in through the back door. I know it wasn't your idea to buy me out of my share,' Faith said. 'Your mother might be fool enough to let her life be dictated by a dead man, but I'm not. For once, I'm putting myself first. I've made my decision, Ella, and woe betide anyone who tries to stand in my way.'

RESPONSES

Evie Chadwick @EvieandChad
Replying to @thewidowsclub
It was a disaster waiting to happen. There should have been proper background checks. Why aren't these so-called admins being charged with negligence?

Nora Pendle @NoraPen77
Replying to @thewidowsclub
Too right. They have to accept some responsibility for what that poor woman went through.

Petersj @Petersjhome
Replying to @thewidowsclub
You're missing the point. It's not about who was allowed to join, it's about what went on in their inner circle. From what I've read, there was too much focus on negative emotions which led to negative outcomes. It shouldn't have happened.

24

When April awoke in the early hours, she was transported back to that moment a year before when she had sought out the warmth of her husband only to find his dead body. The coroner had been unable to give a precise time of death and the only thing April could be sure of was that she had gone to bed a wife and woken up a widow.

Clinging to Dexter's warmth as she waited for dawn, April kept her mind off the ticking clock inside her head by browsing the Internet on her phone. She was drawn to the photograph Justine had posted on Twitter from the Christmas party. She was glad Nick wasn't in the group photo, but there was someone she wished had been there. Erin's husband plagued her thoughts.

She wondered how he would feel if he knew that when he had held his wife's hand and listened to her take her last breath, it was another man who held her heart? It was entirely possible that Erin had made some deathbed confession, and April's feelings of injustice on her husband's behalf were misplaced, but when she looked up the fundraising page, she didn't think so. Josh was organising a charity gala dinner in her memory a few days before Valentine's Day. What better expression of love and devotion? He had no idea what she had done to him.

April's eyes grew heavier as she looked up the details of the fundraiser. It was to be held in a hotel on the edges of Sefton Park in Liverpool and there were tickets still available. She knew the area fairly well because she had been to several festivals held in the park. Her last visit had been for the Liverpool International Music Festival, and Jason had been the designated driver, leaving April to drink far more than was good for her.

Tempted into the memory by tiredness, April closed her eyes and Jason stayed with her until a tap on the door from her mum startled her.

'Did you want me to bring you up a cuppa and some toast?' she said.

April rubbed sleep from her eyes. The room was full of morning light that hadn't been there moments ago. 'What? No, no, I'll have a shower and come down,' she said.

'How are you feeling, love?'

It was a question April was going to be asked a lot, making her wonder if taking the day off work had been the best idea. 'I'm fine, Mum. I just want it to be over if I'm honest.'

Her mum paused, torn between leaving April in peace or sitting down on the edge of the bed to wait for the tears she expected to follow. She stayed by the door. 'Sue phoned. She's invited us out to lunch.'

April felt sorry for Jason's mum, but she couldn't give her what she wanted, not today. 'I can't. I'm going to see Tara,' she replied. It was Wednesday, which meant half-day closing at the shop and hopefully Tara hadn't made plans that couldn't accommodate a runaway.

Trying not to show her disappointment, her mum said, 'We've said we'll join them at the cemetery before going for a meal. Could you at least meet them there? You wouldn't have to stay long. Please, April.'

April had yet to decide if she would visit Jason's grave, but she supposed going as a group and reflecting their pain rather than attempting to define her own was a compromise she could make. 'You're right, I should go,' she said. 'Just don't expect too much from me, Mum.'

'We'll follow your lead,' she said.

Jason's parents were waiting outside the cemetery when April arrived with her mum and dad, and after the trembling embraces, they all held back for April to lead their sad little procession.

April felt numb inside and her feet dragged across the damp grass as they neared Jason's grave. Someone squeezed her arm to remind her that she wasn't alone, but it offered no comfort. She was alone. She didn't share their sorrow, she wouldn't allow it, even as she leant forward and touched the name etched into the marble. It was as cold as she expected.

Sue knelt down to replace the flowers on her son's grave with a new spray of lilies, and Jason's dad had to help her up again. April's parents had brought a wreath too and sweet scents briefly masked the smell of rotting earth.

'Do you want to do it?' her mum asked, offering April the wreath.

April took a step back and shook her head. She told herself not give in to the tears threatening to spill, or the bile that churned her stomach. She bent her head and encouraged the

237

others to join her in a moment of quiet reflection, but when she looked up again, Sue began to speak.

'I remember one Mother's Day when Jason was about seven, he gave me the biggest bunch of tulips and daffodils. I knew straight away he'd sneaked into Mrs Johnson's garden two doors down and I didn't know whether to be pleased or horrified. I sent him around later to give her an apology and a box of chocolates.'

'He brought me flowers the first time I met him,' April's mum added. 'I'm pretty sure they were from a florist though.'

There were awkward smiles and suddenly everyone wanted to reminisce, everyone except April. They talked about school days and holidays, weddings and job interviews, and when the anecdotes dried up, April realised they were waiting for her.

She didn't think her parents or her in-laws would appreciate the story of that time Jason pretended to be in work when he was actually fucking one of their friends. Digging her hand into her pocket, she pulled out the bottle of beer she had brought, hoping that the act of leaving it on the grave would signal the end of this tormented ceremony, but as she stared at the label, the memory she had revisited earlier that morning came back to her.

'The other year we went to a music festival in Sefton Park,' she began as she recalled the heat of that summer and the warmth of her husband's touch. 'Jason was driving so I got really, really drunk and literally couldn't walk in a straight line when it was time to go. He gave up trying to keep me up and flung me over his shoulder. I remember laughing so hard I'm surprised I wasn't sick down his back.'

She felt sick now and put a hand to her mouth.

Sue rushed forward and wrapped her in her arms. 'Oh, my love, I know how you feel. I miss him too,' she sobbed. 'It's so unfair. The last time I spoke to him he was so excited for the future. He wanted to make you happy more than anything. He'd be devastated that he's caused all this pain. We have to carry on, for him. We have to.'

April squeezed her eyes shut and held on to Jason's mum. They were both shaking, but the noise April released was more of a howl than a sob.

'Why don't we go to the restaurant and get you a stiff drink?' April's dad offered when the two women pulled apart.

Seeing the look of panic on April's ruddy face, Sue said, 'It's all right, your mum said you had other plans.' She blew her nose and tried to smile when she added, 'I think you'd like some time on your own, wouldn't you, love? Shall we leave you to it?'

When April nodded gratefully, they slowly filed away, leaving her alone with the man she hated now as much as she had loved him then. Her jaw clenched as she opened the bottle of beer, but as she poured it out on a patch of grass next to Jason's grave, the smell hit her. The memory of the music festival wasn't ready to release her and she was hit by a fresh wave of grief. After Jason had flung her over his shoulder, and in between her fits of giggles, she had kept telling him off for tugging at her dress. She had been oblivious to the fact that her knickers were on show and Jason had simply been trying to protect her dignity.

As the cold February air stole her breath, April wanted to run, but her legs were as unsteady as they had been on that lost summer's day. Jason wasn't there to sweep her up, so she dropped to the ground and when her body shook, it wasn't with laughter. 'When did you stop trying to protect me, Jason?' she demanded. 'When did you think it was OK to hurt me like this?'

25

'Have you been to the cemetery?' asked Tara when she unlocked the shop door to find April on her doorstep. She had been thinking about her all morning.

'Yes, and I'm glad it's out of the way now,' April replied. Her eyes were bright and defiant but the mask almost slipped when she noticed Tara's apron dusted with flour. 'Sorry, I should have phoned. If you're busy, I won't stay.'

'Nonsense,' Tara told her, trying not to wince. 'Do you want a coffee?'

'No, I'm fine,' she said. 'Honestly, carry on doing what you need to do and I'll just watch.'

Tara didn't argue and led April through to the back. Iain was waiting for her to call so he could go out on deliveries, and she hoped that while she completed her stack of orders, April would relax enough to open up about how she really felt.

Picking up a piping bag, she said, 'You can help boxing up the finished cupcakes if you like.'

April fetched a large cardboard cake box and began lining it with careful rows of pretty cupcakes topped with delicate pink petals and green leaves. They worked in silence until Tara heard a sniff.

'Jason didn't like buttercream.'

'How was it this morning, really?'

'They made me remember him,' April said, jabbing a finger into the next cupcake she picked up. 'They made me remember the nice Jason.'

'You're allowed to miss him, April.'

'But I don't want to,' she said, keeping her voice firm. She was in the process of adding the spoiled cake to the box when Tara stopped her. April stared at the mashed-up petals and the smears of buttercream on her trembling finger. 'I'm so sorry. Have I messed up your order?'

'Not at all,' Tara said with a waft of her hand. 'I have some spares. It can be fixed.'

'Can you fix me too?'

'No, but you can fix yourself, and you will. The first anniversary is a tough one, but it's here, and you're doing fine.'

'I've been dreading it for weeks,' April admitted. 'I had no idea how I was going to feel.'

'And how do you feel?'

'Bloody frustrated,' April said, swiping away a tear with the back of her hand. 'His mum says he was excited for the future, *our* future, but what if that was just words? It doesn't exactly match his actions, does it? I need Jason to tell me how he felt. He's the only one who can convince me that we had something worth breaking my heart over.'

'Your love for him was real whether he deserved it or not. Your pain is real.'

April shook her head, but when she pressed her lips tightly together, a tiny sob escaped. She pushed crumbs of cake into her mouth to muffle the sound, but to no avail. The sobs grew louder, and other than pressing a piece of kitchen towel into her hand, Tara left her friend to weep uninterrupted, but not alone. By the time Tara had sent a message to Iain to collect the orders, April had cried herself dry.

'Thank you,' she said, wiping buttercream from her face.

'Feeling better?'

'I think so,' she said with a hiccup. 'It's a relief knowing that today's almost over. Now I can start focusing on what I want to do with the rest of my life.'

'And what will you do?'

'I can't stay at Mum and Dad's for much longer, it would drive us all insane.'

'There's an empty flat upstairs if you're interested,' Tara said before she could stop herself.

She had been wondering about April's current living arrangements since Faith's girls' night, although her first preference was that April replace Nick as Faith's lodger, assuming they could persuade the current tenant to leave. Realistically, that wasn't going to happen. Faith was enjoying more than Nick's money, which left April in need of a place of her own and Tara with an empty flat.

'The plan was always to rent it out and I don't know why I've been holding off,' Tara said. 'Actually I do. I liked the idea of having a bolt hole.'

'You can't be frightened off by an eight-year-old.'

Tara laughed. 'Oh, I can.' More seriously, she added, 'But we are making progress. I've been checking Lily's bedding and her night clothes, and there have been no more accidents. And yesterday she dropped a hint that she's making a Valentine's Day card in school for me and her dad. We can

243

be happy.' After a pause and a deep breath she added, 'We will be happy.'

'And if it helps, you could tell Molly that she can give me a hand looking after Dexter whenever my parents go on holiday,' April said. She glanced up at the ceiling. 'Would I be allowed pets?'

'Are you seriously considering taking the flat?'

April checked the crumpled cupcake wrapper in her hand. 'Who wouldn't want to live above a cake shop?' she said. 'And it wouldn't be such a trek to the group meetings, or to see you. Unless you think I'd be a pain . . .'

'Well, there is that,' Tara said before coming over to give her a hug. 'It would be lovely to have you near. You're as much a support to me as I am to you, but let's not get ahead of ourselves. You haven't seen it yet, and you might want to think about your commute to work. You'd have to cross the river, which means tunnel or bridge tolls every day.'

'That might not be an issue for much longer,' replied April. 'I've been looking for another job. I may not work in the same office or even the same building as Bree, but I can't avoid her completely, and I need to if I'm going to come to terms with what happened.'

'Would you like a viewing?'

It was the first time Tara had seen April smile since she arrived and, as she took her up to the flat, she hoped her initial excitement wasn't about to be extinguished. It was fair to say the place wasn't in the best of shape. There were ghostly imprints on the lavender walls where pictures had hung, bright cream patches on the carpet where furniture had been removed, darker patches where the pile had been worn down, and what pieces of furniture remained were in disrepair.

244

'I know I talk about missed opportunities, but Mike and I were happy here,' Tara admitted as she picked up a discarded coat hanger. 'I wouldn't have missed it for anything.' When April didn't respond, she asked, 'What do you think?'

'This could be the start of it,' April said, her eyes catching a spark as she looked past the mess, the murk, and the memories. 'My new life.'

'And it comes partly furnished,' Tara said with a note of apology.

'Some of the furniture Jason and I bought is in storage, everything except the bed,' April explained. 'I've often wondered if I should throw it all away, but I don't know. I can imagine some pieces here.' She bit her lip. 'I could make it work.'

'Is that a yes?' asked Tara.

'Would you mind if I gave the walls a coat of paint?'

'Not a chance,' Tara said. 'Iain and I will do all of that and lay new carpets too, but you can choose the colour scheme if you want.'

'Deal,' April said. She placed her hand on her chest. 'This is the first time I've had something to look forward to in ages – twelve months to be exact.'

'Well, that was easy,' said Tara. 'It's good to know I can stop worrying about one of my friends.'

'The other being Faith?'

'I keep telling myself Nick's done nothing wrong, but I can't shake the feeling this isn't going to end well,' she said, wishing she felt differently – and not only for Faith's sake. How could she consider giving up the group while all of this was going on?

'He may not have done anything wrong as far as Faith's

concerned, but what about the affair?' asked April. 'It takes some gall turning up to a group of widowed spouses expecting a shoulder to cry on, especially after we caught him out. What about Erin's husband? Aren't we supporting the wrong person?'

'You're not suggesting we invite him to the group, are you?'

April hunched her shoulders. 'All I'm saying is I'd feel better offering sympathy to the person who actually deserved it,' she said. 'Aren't you just a little bit curious about him?'

'Why? Are you?'

'I might have revisited Erin's fundraiser page. She obviously meant a lot to him.'

'I imagine she did,' Tara said cautiously. 'But he's found a way of dealing with his grief by creating the charity, and we should let him be. Faith had a point when she said we'd be saving him from unnecessary pain.'

'But what if that pain is necessary? Finding out about Jason and Bree almost destroyed me but I'm glad I found out.'

Tara wasn't so sure. April couldn't know how that knowledge would affect her in the future, particularly with new relationships. Neither could she know how the truth would affect Erin's husband. 'April, it's not your decision to make,' she warned.

'There's going to be a Valentine's Day fundraiser this weekend and I was thinking of going,' April said. When Tara spluttered, she quickly added, 'Not to talk to him or anything.'

'Then why go at all?'

'I want to hear what he says about his wife. You're probably right about him finding his own way to grieve, but if I have to pretend to feel sorry for Nick, I need to know that Josh is OK. I have to see it for myself.'

'You really shouldn't.'

'But I will,' April said, locking eyes with her friend. She would not be dissuaded.

Tara muttered a collection of expletives under her breath. 'Well, I suppose if you're going, I'll have to go too.'

April's face lit up. 'I was hoping you'd say that.'

26

Nick stared at Faith across the table, the flickering candlelight adding fire to his eyes. 'You look amazing,' he mouthed, although there was no one close enough to overhear.

The Holdi wasn't a restaurant Faith had been to before despite it being practically on her doorstep. She wasn't a fan of Indian food, but it was relatively busy for a Thursday evening so she surmised it must be good. It was Nick's choice and she had left it to him to order from the menu. They served Liverpool Gin; that was all she needed to know.

'So what are you after?' she asked.

'Who said I was after anything? I simply wanted to do something nice for you after all the grief I've given you lately.'

'You're not the one who's been giving me grief. They should rename the support group, the interference group,' she said, smashing a poppadom into smaller pieces. 'Justine can be a bit overzealous, but she knows better than to argue with me.'

'And what about April and Tara?'

Faith was surprised it had taken Nick this long to ask what had gone on at their little dinner party. 'They're protective, that's all,' she said as she scooped up some lime pickle with a poppadom shard and took a mouthful. Spice burned her tongue. 'Don't expect them to give you an easy time, Nick.'

'I know they're not impressed with my track record, and if I could go back and do things differently with Erin, I would,' he said, 'but I did love her.'

'No one doubts that,' she replied, although she was growing a little weary of Erin's spectre. 'It's what you do going forward that concerns them most.'

'I only want the best for you,' he assured her. 'And whatever assumptions your friends have made about me, I'm happy to prove them wrong. The same goes for your stepdaughter. If I'm allowed to meet her.'

Faith's eyes narrowed. Nick had remained upstairs for the duration of Ella's visit and Faith had kept her voice deliberately low. Unfortunately the same couldn't be said for Ella. Had Nick overheard their discussion?

'I did invite her for dinner, but she's not interested,' Faith said.

'And why is that?' asked Nick, not reacting to the lie. 'Did you give her the story about me being your lodger?'

'I don't think I specified. Is that how you want to be introduced?'

Nick held her gaze. 'No,' he said softly.

'I didn't think so,' she said with a satisfied smile. 'And what about you introducing me to your family? Have you told your sister about me yet?'

'I don't get to speak to Liv nearly as often as I should, but I will tell her,' he promised as the waiter appeared with their starters.

Nick had ordered lamb chops because he liked to watch her eat with her fingers. Faith preferred silver service, but she could adapt to some of Nick's proclivities, on the understanding that he would come to appreciate her finer tastes. He had suggested the holiday in Las Vegas, and it had been as loud and vulgar as she had feared. They would do better next time.

'There are some lovely cruises around Canada and Alaska,' she said, picking up a lamb chop and snapping the bone. 'We could combine a holiday with a trip to meet her.'

'I like that you see us having a future together.'

Was that what she was doing? For so long Faith had told herself that she would never again rely on a man for her future happiness, but a happy future was a tempting proposition. 'And what about you?' she asked.

Nick was transfixed as he watched her lick her lips. 'I have plans that most definitely include you,' he admitted.

'Will I like them?'

'I hope so.'

As she scrutinised his face, there was no hint of deceit. 'I hope so too,' she said. 'The only other man I ever said I love you to was Derek, and he broke my heart. I won't let that happen again.'

'You have nothing to fear from me. But we could have an amazing future together, Faith.'

She picked up a serviette and wiped her fingers. The oils from the meat had made the gold band on the third finger of her right hand glisten. 'Tell me your plans.'

Nick played with his food. 'I don't want to scare you off.'

'Nothing scares me,' she promised. 'Tell.'

He pushed his plate away and took a deep breath. 'We make a good team, don't you think? We both like to work hard and play hard.'

'I'd agree with that.'

'I see us living the life we want,' he said, his gaze fixed on a point Faith couldn't see. If he were looking forward in time, he was excited by what he saw. 'If I'm honest, I don't imagine us staying in the suburbs rattling around in a house that was built for a growing family. I'm not interested in having kids, never have been.'

He was very good. They had talked about their age difference before, but not in the context of having children. He would know it was too late for her, even if she had wanted them. Whether his disinterest in fatherhood was genuine or not, he had raised the matter to allay her fears. He was adapting to her needs.

'I imagine us dividing our time between a swish apartment in the city and a villa in Spain,' he continued.

'I'd prefer Italy,' she said, drawn into his imaginary world.

'Whatever you want,' he promised. 'I need you, Faith. What's the point of making my fortune if I can't enjoy it with someone?'

'You could do that without me.'

'But I don't want to,' he said, holding her gaze until a frown formed on his brow. 'Sorry, I'm getting carried away. I know how much you value your independence. It's you who doesn't need me. You have your house, your incredible career as a scientific . . .'

'A biomedical scientist.'

'Exactly. And I can't expect you to give that up.'

No, he couldn't, thought Faith, but the choice wasn't entirely hers either. 'The reorganisation at work isn't going the way I'd like. There's an offer of redundancy . . .'

'Then take it,' Nick said, leaning forward. 'Start with a clean slate. With me. We'd make an incredible partnership.'

Oh, how Faith was tempted, but her friends' warnings hadn't fallen on deaf ears. 'So I sell the house and take redundancy. Then what? Are you expecting me to invest in your company?'

'No, I didn't mean it like that.'

Unfortunately, Nick didn't expand on what he did mean. Was there another form of partnership on offer? Faith's imagination went into overdrive. 'I won't be a kept woman. I need to make my own living.'

'Then work for me, I mean *with* me,' he said, correcting himself when he saw Faith stiffen. 'At the moment, I'm turning down bookings when I could easily double the fleet and still not meet demand. Finding investment isn't going to be a problem. No one wants to put their money in savings accounts these days and the property market is stagnant.'

'But you'd expect me to help you build up your company for no return?'

'I'd pay you a wage. I don't need your money, Faith, if that's what you're thinking.'

'If we were to join forces, it would have to be on an equal footing. An employee has no voice. An investor on the other hand would have a say in how you operate,' she said, willing to consider making an offer now that she knew it wasn't being demanded of her. 'If I did put my money into the business, what kind of surety would you provide?'

Dimples appeared in Nick's cheeks. 'I can't believe I'm even considering this,' he said. 'But OK, if you insisted on investing, naturally there would be a form of contract agreed by both parties. If you're serious about it.'

The arrival of the main course gave Faith time to consider what else was being placed on the table. She had always suspected Nick had an agenda and now that she knew the details, she could make an informed decision. In her previous marriage, she had never become involved in Derek's business ventures and that had left her vulnerable. If she were to join forces with Nick, she wouldn't be a sleeping partner. The terms would have to be right and there was only one form of contract that would interest her. She played with her wedding band and waited for Nick to notice.

27

Tara had agreed to meet April at the venue, but she wasn't familiar with Sefton Park and almost missed the hotel sign partly obscured by shrubbery. If she had driven past, she wasn't sure she would have turned back. Tracking down Josh Peters was a bad idea. It was hard enough knowing that the wrong man had been welcomed into their group without coming face to face with the person they should be supporting.

Once in the car park, Tara grabbed one of the few remaining spaces before manoeuvring herself out of the car. It wasn't an easy process in her tight dress. She had been worried that one of her vintage outfits would draw too much attention and had ordered what she thought was a simple black number online. It was meant to be understated, but it hugged her curves in all the right places and, to Tara's surprise, it made her feel good about herself in a way she hadn't felt in months. Lily had helped with her make-up and announced she looked beautiful, which was another reason Tara yearned to be home with her family. They had reached a turning point.

As she waited for April, Tara took in her surroundings. With only a few days until Valentine's Day, the hotel was decorated with heart-shaped balloons and banners. Love was in the air and it was concentrated on one woman whose photo shone out on the bitterly cold evening. Aware of the other guests milling around, Tara wondered how many had known Erin personally, and if they had ever been introduced to Nick. As fresh doubt assailed her, headlights swept across the car park. The car slowed and there was the hum of an electric window.

'You look stunning,' April said.

'I'm bloody freezing,' replied Tara, teeth chattering. 'Can we hurry up and go inside, please?'

April reversed into the last parking space and wrapped a blue pashmina over her bare shoulders as she hurried towards Tara.

'You look amazing too,' Tara said.

'My heart is thumping through my chest,' April admitted.

'I don't know why. We're only here to observe.'

'Obviously,' April replied. 'Shall we go in? Do we have our stories straight?'

'I'm playing the widow, so not much change there.'

After some discussion, it had been decided that Tara's experience of nursing her husband in his final months offered a valid justification for supporting a fundraiser for a hospice. The same couldn't be said of April and declaring that she was also a widow might raise too many questions. 'Are you happy not to mention Jason?'

'More than happy,' April said. 'Come on, I thought you said you were cold.'

There were drinks on arrival, and April and Tara picked up fruit juices without enthusiasm before heading over to a flipchart that displayed the seating plan. Their tickets had been amongst the last sold so it was no surprise to find they had been allocated seats on a table tucked away at the back of the room. They had been slotted in with eight other miscellaneous guests who weren't part of the core group of supporters.

Blending in wasn't going to be as difficult as Tara had feared, and she was about to relax when a name on the chart caught her attention. She considered not mentioning it to April, but her eagle-eyed friend had spotted it too.

'Do you think it's a coincidence that there's another Malford here?' April said, pointing to the table next to theirs.

'It's not as common as a Smith or a Jones, but I'm sure Nick said he didn't have family nearby.'

'Just because he said it, doesn't make it true,' said April.

As they stepped away from the seating plan, April's body froze and Tara followed her gaze to the man they had come to see. Josh Peters was taller and wirier than he appeared in the photos on the fundraiser page. He didn't fill out his suit in the way that Nick did, nor were his blue eyes as piercing, but they were kinder than his rival's.

'Can we go over and say hello?' April asked, already on the move.

There was a tight circle of guests around Josh, all eager for his attention, but none was as determined as April. She squeezed between two gentlemen who were obliged to make way for the young lady with sharp elbows. One was about to say something to her, but Tara nudged into the gap between them.

April shot out her arm to shake Josh's hand. 'Hello, we've not met, but my friend and I think the work you're doing here is just wonderful.'

It was Tara's turn next. 'I lost my husband too,' she said, squeezing his hand.

'Was he at the hospice?'

'We tried to keep Mike at home for as long as we could, but unfortunately he had to be admitted into hospital. We were waiting for a bed in a hospice, but he died before we could move him.'

'I'm sorry to hear that.'

'Saying goodbye isn't easy, wherever you are. You don't just lose a life-partner, you lose all those plans you'd made together,' she replied, still holding his hand. Thinking of all the other widows and widowers Tara had brought under her wing, it was a wrench when she let Josh slip from her grasp.

'I sort of knew what I was getting into with Erin. She was going through her first round of chemo when we met and by the time I convinced her to marry me, we knew we wouldn't have long together. That didn't mean I was prepared to let her go and it's why I keep her with me now,' Josh said, looking about him. There were pictures of Erin everywhere.

'She was so beautiful,' April said, pointing to one photo in particular. Erin's face was dappled by sunlight as she stood in waterproofs beneath an oak tree. 'Where was that taken?'

'I'm not too sure. It was before we met, but I do know it was special to her. It was the last photo taken before she found the lump in her breast. How quickly life can change,' he said. 'But I count myself fortunate to have had Erin in mine, even if it was for a short while.'

'How long were you married?' asked April.

Tara was tempted to nudge her. It was beginning to sound like an interrogation.

'Not long enough. Erin wanted to wait until she was cancer-free and when she found out that was never going to happen, she said I was a fool for insisting. This fool was her husband for ten months and twenty-three days and I treasure every minute.' He turned to Tara. 'How about you?'

'Mike and I were married for three years, and I've been a widow for more than eight.'

'Do you have children?'

'My daughter was two when Mike died.'

The crowd had swelled around them and an older woman tugged at Josh's sleeve to draw his attention away from the group.

'Sorry,' he said to Tara, 'but I have duties to perform I'm afraid. It was nice meeting you though.' Ignoring the next tug, he added, 'It's always good to talk to someone who's been through something similar. It's like you don't have to explain things, they just know.'

Tara remained frozen to the spot as Josh was pulled away. 'He wanted to talk,' she said. 'If it had been anyone else, I would have invited him to the group. He'd fit in well.'

'Better than Nick?'

Rather than answer, Tara backed away, heading across the room to buy raffle tickets. April pursued her.

'That photo I pointed to,' she said. 'It was the one Nick showed me. He knew it was taken at Delamere Forest.'

'And?'

'It was the last photo of Erin before she realised she was ill. You don't get it, do you?'

'Get what?' She had been too concerned about Josh to give a thought to Nick.

April kept her voice low when she said, 'Think back to

what Nick told us about his relationship with Erin. They were involved and then she found out she had cancer. He took a step back while she had treatment, and their alleged affair only resumed when they realised there wasn't much time left. Does that sound about right?'

'Well, yes, but . . .' Tara felt a rush of horror as she realised the implications. 'That would mean Erin was involved with Nick before she had even met Josh.'

'So why did Nick take a step back if there was no husband standing in his way? And why did Erin find someone else if Nick was her one true love? With only months left to live, Erin chose to marry Josh. He was the one she wanted to be with, not Nick. There was no extramarital affair, Tara. There was barely a relationship.'

'Or none at all,' Tara replied, her voice hollow. 'Nick could be lying about everything.'

'No, the best liars start with a grain of truth,' April said, glancing at the photo of Erin again. 'I haven't come across that particular image online, so I'm guessing the reason Nick had it was because he took it. It's entirely possible he was her boyfriend back then.'

'But not the kind of boyfriend she wanted around while she battled her illness.'

April rubbed her arms as if she too felt the unease that made Tara's skin crawl. 'It's hardly the tragic love story Nick would have us believe, is it?'

'If Nick is nothing more than an ex-boyfriend, why did he join the group? What does he want from us, April? Is he some kind of sick grief tourist?'

Before she could respond, the guests were asked to make their way to the dining room. There were at least twenty round tables, and Tara found some momentary relief from troubled thoughts as she searched for their seats. She was only vaguely aware that April had wandered off.

'We're over here,' Tara called to her, pulling out a chair.

April pretended not to hear as she circled the neighbouring table, scrutinising name cards as she went. People were taking their seats and there was one woman in particular who had caught April's attention. She was in her forties with dark brown hair cut into a severe bob that framed her angular features. Her eyes were a striking shade of blue not dissimilar to Nick's.

'That's Olivia Malford,' April said when she returned. 'Don't you think there's a family resemblance? Could she be Nick's sister?'

Tara wrinkled her nose. 'Possibly, but I don't see how we can find out more. We're not going to have much of an opportunity to mingle,' she said, picking up her serviette and twisting it. She had lost her appetite. 'I think I've heard as much as I can stomach. We should go home.'

'It's too late now,' April replied as the sound of a fork tapping against a glass brought the room to order.

Josh stood behind a lectern on a small stage. 'My honoured guests, on behalf of my wife and myself, I'd like to welcome you all here tonight.' He paused until the round of applause had died down. 'With your help, we've done some incredible work over the last year and it's not going to stop there. I warn you there will be speeches, auctions, and perhaps some tears later, but all in a good cause. I'll be asking you to dig deep into your pockets again, but first I'd like you to enjoy your food and relax with a few glasses of whatever takes your fancy. We'll speak later.'

As the starters were served, April and Tara did their best to make small talk with the other guests on their table. Most were colleagues or casual acquaintances of Josh, but none had known Erin particularly well. Tara's heart wasn't in it, but when she mentioned being a widow, the conversation picked up a pace. Her fellow diners were eager for her to share her experience so they could better understand what Josh was going through and for the first time that night, Tara was back on familiar ground.

'The best advice I can give is not to pre-empt what might or might not be in Josh's best interest,' Tara said. 'Don't assume he doesn't want Erin's name coming up in conversation, for example. He wouldn't be here tonight if he'd rather pretend she never existed.'

'But how do we know when it's the right time to talk?' asked a woman sitting opposite.

'Ask him,' Tara said simply. 'Say you want to know more about Erin and ask if he could tell you about her. You won't always get the timing right, but it can't be any worse than the awkward pauses that replace the questions he's waiting to be asked. And can I just say, you're doing pretty well so far tonight.'

'In that case, would you mind telling us what happened to your husband?'

Tara relaxed into the conversation and occasionally directed questions to April. It felt awkward introducing her as simply a supportive friend, but they quickly settled into the roles they had agreed. It was surprisingly easy to become a fraud.

As the main course was being cleared away, Tara noticed movement out of the corner of her eye. Olivia Malford was on the move. April grabbed her bag.

'I'm just popping to the Ladies,' she said, pausing long enough for Tara to realise she was expected to follow.

They hurried out of the dining room and followed the signs. Tara was about to turn left when April grabbed her arm.

'She's gone that way,' she said, pointing in the opposite direction. There was a glimpse of Olivia striding towards the main entrance. 'Probably a cigarette break. Shall we join her?'

Tara didn't relish the idea of going out into the cold again, but April wasn't about to be persuaded back to her seat. 'Could I stop you?' she asked as April stalked after Olivia.

28

As they left the warmth of the hotel, the air was cold enough to make April gasp, but there was no time to go back for her pashmina. She gritted her teeth and walked down a short set of steps as if it were a balmy summer's evening. Tara was less nimble, but that had as much to do with her dress as it did the drop in temperature.

There was a small group of smokers lighting up and Olivia was amongst them. If she was Nick's sister, there was no knowing where her loyalties might lie, but April had loyalties of her own. She hadn't been as surprised as Tara to discover a new layer of deceit tonight. As much as she had wanted to meet Josh, it was Nick's life she continued to hold under the microscope. This was for Faith.

April and Tara exchanged glances with Olivia as they approached and when they smiled at her, she smiled back. Her curiosity must have been piqued when neither of them lit up a cigarette.

'Want one?' she asked, offering the new arrivals an open packet.

'That's kind of you,' Tara said, taking a cigarette and at

the same time, positioning herself so that the three women split off from the main group. 'I packed in smoking years ago, but old habits die hard.'

April couldn't hide her shock. 'Are you sure you want to?' she asked. 'We only came out for a bit of fresh air.'

'Sorry, it's my fault. I shouldn't have offered,' Olivia said.

Tara took a long drag of the unlit cigarette and exhaled no more than vapour. 'Don't worry. I won't light up.'

'Do you mind if I do?' asked Olivia.

She flicked her lighter and her hand swayed in front of her face until the flame found the cigarette. As she took her first draw, its tip glowed orange and dimples appeared in her cheeks. She turned and made to blow the smoke over her shoulder, but the wind carried it straight back towards April and Tara.

'It's not ideal, is it? Sneaking out for a ciggie when we're here to remember someone who died from cancer,' Olivia said, her words ever so slightly slurred.

'Did you know Erin?' Tara asked, playing with the cancer stick in her hand but making no further attempt to pretend-smoke.

'We worked together years ago,' Olivia said. 'We were good friends for a while, but you know how it is, life took over. Did you know her?'

'I'm afraid not,' April said before Tara could respond with the practised explanation of why they wanted to support the hospice. Now was not the time to be sidetracked by someone else's story. They needed to hear Olivia's and they only had the time it would take for her cigarette to burn down, or for one of them to die of hypothermia, whichever came first.

'We're simply here to support the hospice, but Erin sounds like she made a big impression on a lot of people. Josh in particular.'

Olivia smiled drunkenly. 'You can say that again. I can't claim to know Josh particularly well, but she was lucky to find him.'

'They sound like they were soul mates,' said April.

This time Olivia hesitated. She took a long drag of her cigarette. 'I managed to go in and see her before she died and it was heartbreaking to watch them together. She couldn't have asked for anyone better by her side.'

The conversation had reached a natural, if somewhat premature conclusion. April's frozen fingers and toes stung with pain, but panic forced heat to her chest. 'We're glad we came,' she said quickly. 'It was an old friend of Erin's who told us about the fundraiser. Nick.'

Other than the smoke swirling in front of Olivia's face, she remained utterly still. 'Nick Malford?'

'Yes, although we don't know him very well,' Tara said, her eyes flicking a warning towards April.

'He would have liked to be here tonight,' April said, 'but he couldn't make it.'

'I bet he couldn't,' Olivia replied coldly.

'You know him?'

'He's my brother.'

April adjusted her expression to one of surprise. 'From what he's told us, he cared a lot about Erin.'

Olivia's laugh was closer to a snarl. 'You could say that,' she said as she clamped a finger and thumb over the end of her cigarette, pinching off the glowing embers. 'I should get back.'

Before she could walk away, April said, 'He's dating a friend of ours.'

Olivia swayed. Pressing her hand to her forehead, she said, 'I refuse to be drawn into another of my brother's messes. Good luck to them. I hope he treats her better than he treated Erin.'

'What do you mean?' Tara asked. She was no longer there simply to humour her friend. 'What did he do?'

'Didn't he tell you? They were engaged,' Olivia said. 'Erin was planning their wedding when she found out she had breast cancer, and while none of us were surprised when they postponed their plans, we didn't realise it was Nick who pushed back the date and not Erin's treatment plan. Apparently, my brother wasn't prepared to take on someone in sickness and in health. They split up.'

'But why would he do that?' insisted Tara.

'Because Nick always puts himself first,' Olivia said, only to shake her head. 'He's family so, fool that I am, I have to see it from his perspective. He worked really hard, and at the time, he was being headhunted for a dream job in a new firm. He couldn't pursue his career *and* look after a sick fiancée at the same time. In some ways, it was a blessing in disguise for Erin. She found Josh and he became her rock, which was far better than Nick's shifting sands.'

'Did Nick keep in touch with her?' April asked.

'Nooo. Although she did ask to meet him just before she went into the hospice. To clear the air, I suppose.'

April cringed as she recalled the awful things she had said about Erin in the last group session. It had been totally unde-served, whereas there was more reason than ever to despise Nick. The story of the affair had been a lie from start to finish. How could he smear Erin's memory like that, especially after everything else he had done to her? Feeling sick to her stomach, April saw an echoing look of contempt on Olivia's face. She pulled herself together to ask one more question. 'If Erin had forgiven Nick, why haven't you?'

Olivia's head had a distinct wobble as she glanced up to the hotel entrance, seeking escape. 'I thought I had. When Erin died, Nick lost all interest in himself. It was probably what convinced me that he might have actually cared for her, and I felt sorry for him.'

'Are you suggesting his feelings weren't genuine?' Tara asked.

'Maybe. I'm not sure. Sorry, I've drunk too much, too fast,' Olivia said. 'I came here because I wanted to honour Erin's memory, but I also carry my brother's shame. You would think dumping a seriously ill woman as if she were unnecessary baggage was as low as he could sink, but after some of the things I've heard tonight, apparently not. I almost wish he had dared to show up. He needs to see that there are good people in the world, although he'd probably be working out whose pockets he can pick.'

Tara sucked in her breath. 'Are you saying he cons people out of their money?'

'I don't know, am I?' Olivia asked. She blinked hard, and it looked like her vision had suddenly cleared. 'Ignore me. I'm drunk.'

She was ready to stagger away, but Tara placed a hand gently on her arm. 'Should we be worried about our friend?'

'You should worry about anyone who tries to help him,' she said. 'Nick's better at taking than he is at giving.'

'How do you mean?' asked April.

'He told me he gave up his job because he was depressed and couldn't work,' she said, giving in to the pressure to confess. 'I've just found out from one of the fundraisers that he was fired. She thought I knew.'

Olivia seemed to have finished, but Tara gave her the merest nod of encouragement. 'What did he do?' she asked gently.

Taking a deep breath, Olivia said, 'When Erin died, Nick hadn't been with this new investment bank for long so his colleagues didn't know their history.' She paused and looked over her shoulder. The other smokers had drifted back into the hotel, but nevertheless, she leant in close as if sharing the worst of secrets. 'When Josh set up Erin's memorial fund, Nick used it as a smokescreen to start his own little fundraiser. I imagine he had some pretty wealthy clients who didn't realise he was out to line his own pocket.'

'My god. Were the police involved?' asked April.

'Oh, no, it was all handled very quietly, so quietly even his own bloody sister didn't know about it. My brother could get away with murder.'

'Is it possible he never intended to take the proceeds?'

April admired Tara's optimism, but Olivia's sneer snuffed it out. 'He's never been what I would call responsible with his finances,' she said. 'Even in the days when he had more money than most of us would know how to spend, Nick somehow managed to get through it all. And, as I've found out to my cost, when he runs out of funds, he expects others to bankroll him.'

'That includes you?' asked April.

'I was happy to take him in when he lost his job, but I don't like being taken for a mug,' Olivia said. 'When he was ready to move out and lease a flat, he convinced me to be

guarantor. He'd overstretched himself setting up his business
– you know about that, right?'

'Yes,' April replied. 'He says it's going well.'

'Not well enough to pay his bloody rent. There's my savings
gone while he, apparently, jets off on a holiday. I can always
tell when he's up to no good – he goes off the radar. I don't
imagine I'll see that money again. Final demands have been
appearing at the flat and it looks like he hasn't kept up with
the lease payments for his limos either.'

April's teeth chattered and it was loud enough for Olivia
to notice.

'Anyway, I've said more than I should, and I really, really
hope Nick treats your friend better than he has everyone else
he's supposed to care about,' Olivia said, inching towards the
steps that would take her back to the hotel. 'And next time
you see him, tell him to remember he has a sister.' Her eyes
welled with tears. 'In spite of everything, I do love my brother.
He's weak, that's all.'

When Olivia left, April was still shivering, but she was also
numb. 'He might be weak but someone that ruthless can't be
harmless,' she said.

'At least now we know why he joined the group,' Tara said,
returning to the unanswered question she had posed earlier.
'And it has nothing to do with grief.'

STATEMENT

The Widows' Club @thewidowsclub
The accusations levelled against us are undeserved and
we strenuously deny any suggestion that we did
anything other than provide our members with a safe
place to heal. We cannot legislate for people who enter
the group under a false pretext. Nick Malford lied to us.

29

The windowless room smelled musty and one of the fluorescent tubes running along the centre of the ceiling flickered. This was some comedown for Faith, after a weekend of being cosseted by her new tenant. It had been years since she had helped with the annual stocktake, but things were changing at work and not for the better. Of the three junior members of staff who should be doing this, two were being retrained and the third had been promoted. Technically, the latter had become Faith's supervisor, but not for much longer. Faith didn't like being managed at the best of times.

Pulling an unwieldy cardboard box from a shelf, Faith let it drop to the floor with a clatter. The seal was broken, which meant there would be less than the five hundred plastic pipettes stated on the box and as she pulled back the lid, she found a range of discarded Post-it notes and tissues littering the contents. She wouldn't have used the box as a bin if she'd known she would be the one sifting through the mess. Without touching a thing, she judged the box to be half full and noted the figure on the inventory list.

Faith used to enjoy her job, but she had worked at the

hospital for almost twenty years and it was time to go. She liked the idea of running a business, and having a fleet of limousines at her disposal would be an added bonus. She wasn't too keen on dealing with the drunken shenanigans of stag and hen parties, but in time she would cultivate a more sophisticated clientele.

As Faith reimagined her future, she was distracted by the fluorescent light sizzling above her head. The sound grated on her nerves and it was hard to say whether she or the tube would explode first. She could wait for maintenance to fix the fault, but she wasn't known for her patience. She fetched the set of fixed ladders from the next aisle and wheeled it directly beneath the offending light fitting. Muttering to herself, she climbed up and removed the cover to expose two tubes, one of which had a blackened connector.

Having identified the source of her irritation, Faith climbed down to switch off the lights and used the torch on her phone to guide her back through the racks of supplies. It took seconds to disconnect the faulty tube and she was on her way down the ladder when her phone rang.

The stock room plunged into darkness as Faith pressed her phone to her ear and smothered the only light source. 'Hi, Tara, what's up?' she asked, resting her body against the steps, her elbow on the top rung.

'I tried phoning you yesterday.'

Faith had developed a bit of a habit of ignoring her friends' calls, but there were days when she could do without the dramas April and Tara seemed to thrive upon, and Sunday with Nick had been one of them. 'Sorry about that,' she said with a shrug.

'So anyway, April has some leave she needs to use up this week and we thought we'd have a catch-up on Wednesday afternoon if you fancy it?'

She was slightly out of breath as if she had been exerting herself, but the hairs on the back of Faith's neck had pricked. It was nerves that made Tara's voice shake.

'I've already booked Wednesday off,' said Faith. 'You do realise it's Valentine's Day?'

'I know, but I thought . . . Do you have plans for the whole day? Could you come over for an hour at least?'

Faith's eyes bored through the gloom, picking out the shapes of boxes and gallon-sized poly bottles lining the shelves. 'Nick's going to be busy with work in the evening so we wanted to spend some quality time together in the day,' she explained. 'I think he's planning something special.'

'Oh, I see.'

Faith was disappointed by the response. Did Tara assume his plan was something as mundane as sex? What would she say if Faith told her she expected Nick to propose?

'What if we made it earlier in the day?' Tara suggested. 'If I can get someone in to help Michelle, we could go for a walk in Pickering's Pasture.'

'Does that mean April will bring that stupid dog of hers?'

'You know you love Dexter,' Tara said, her voice no longer straining. She thought she was winning Faith over. 'And if we met at say, ten o'clock, you'd have the rest of the day to yourself.'

'What if I wanted a lie-in?'

There was a pause. Cogs turned. 'I'm sure Nick wouldn't mind getting you out of the way for a couple of hours if he's preparing something special. And April could really do with you as a sounding board. She survived Jason's anniversary, but she needs our help finding a new direction.'

'You're not going to take no for an answer, are you?'

'Please come.'

Tara's persistence was aggravating. Faith wasn't being summoned to help April. Her friends were interfering again and she was minded to refuse, but if this battle must continue, she wouldn't shy away from it.

'Fine, I'll be there, but only for an hour. Then I go back to Nick.'

'An hour is all we need.'

When she finished the call, Faith switched off her phone and let the darkness wrap around her. The faulty light had been silenced, but a new sound had become Faith's irritant. It was the echo of Tara's voice. 'An hour is all we need,' she had said. An hour to do what? Spoil the best chance Faith had in years of finding happiness?

Anger swelled inside her chest and with a sweep of her arm, she shoved a box off the nearest shelf. It smashed on impact and there was the tinkling of broken glass scattering across the floor. She couldn't see what had fallen, but guessed she would have to cross a box of petri dishes off the stock list. Never mind. She had bigger problems to worry about.

At what point had she given her friends the impression that she needed looking after? *Never*. Faith knew what she was doing. Admittedly, she didn't know Nick nearly as well as she had known Derek, but whatever the risks, she was in control. Not Nick, and certainly not Tara or April.

30

A hand appeared in front of Tara's face. 'Earth to Tara,' said Iain.

They were in the kitchen clearing up after their evening meal. It must have been good because Lily had asked for extra meatballs, although it was a miracle the child had been able to eat anything while talking non-stop about her day at school. There was a suggestion she preferred Hale Primary to her old school, but this little victory wasn't enough to settle Tara's nerves.

'Sorry,' she said, coming out of her fugue and handing Iain an empty plate after scraping her untouched meal into the bin.

'Dare I ask who you're fretting over most? Molly or Faith?'

'I'm dreading tomorrow,' she admitted. 'I don't know what I'll do if Faith doesn't turn up, but I'm just as scared about what will happen if she does.'

Tara had gone through countless imaginary conversations with her friend and none of them had ended well. She would have gone straight over to Faith's house on Sunday morning to give Nick his marching orders if April hadn't persuaded her to take a more considered approach. It was Faith they had to convince, and they stood a better chance if she was as far away from the house and Nick's influence as possible. Thank goodness Faith had eventually answered her calls and agreed to meet them.

'Faith will see sense,' Iain said.

'I wish I could be so sure,' Tara replied. 'She's fiercely protective of the people she cares about most, and right now that's Nick. You only have to read the stories of women being seduced out of their life savings to know it's never easy. They don't want the spell broken and God help anyone who tries to make them see reason,' she said. 'And you can bet Nick will have more lies and promises to counter anything we say. He joined the group looking for a rich, vulnerable widow and that's exactly what he thinks he's found.'

'Faith is neither of those things,' Iain insisted, having heard about Faith's claim that she wasn't as rich as people assumed.

'Maybe she hasn't got cash in the bank, maybe Ella does have some say over what happens with the house, but it's still an asset for Nick to plunder.'

'However charming and persuasive he might be, Faith wouldn't be that gullible.'

'Wouldn't she? I have this horrible feeling Nick's about to propose and Faith sounded excited by the prospect. A few months ago, she would have laughed at the idea, but Nick's blindsided her.'

'You have to trust that Faith will see through him, but if she doesn't, there's nothing more you can do.'

'Don't be so sure. I could expel Nick from the group for a start,' Tara promised. 'If he has the gall to think he's still welcome, I'm going to take great pleasure in putting him right.'

'Do not confront him, Tara.'

'Rather him than Faith,' she replied, only half joking.

'You might think you have the measure of Nick, but you can't know how he'll react,' Iain warned. 'We've only seen his charming side. He won't appreciate you snatching away his chance to make some easy money.'

'I know.'

'You're not responsible for what Faith decides tomorrow,' Iain persisted.

'But Faith would never have met Nick if we hadn't invited him to join the support group. That makes it my responsibility.'

'And Justine's,' he reminded her. 'Shouldn't she be involved?'

'Faith would walk away if Justine was there. It's going to be hard enough persuading her to listen to me, and if I get this wrong, it won't be Nick she cuts out of her life.'

The sense of foreboding lay heavily on Tara's chest and pressed down harder when she picked up the last plate to be scraped clean. It was another untouched meal, only this one belonged to Molly. 'Do you think I should be worried about Molly too?' she asked, registering Iain's earlier comment.

'She didn't say a word when I picked her up from school today. Considering she's the one who usually keeps us buoyed, I don't like to see her down.'

'Me neither,' Tara said, biting her lip. Since the fundraiser, she hadn't given her family much thought, having been on the phone to April every chance she could get. So much for making Iain and the girls her priority.

'Here, I'll take that,' Iain said, pulling the plate from Tara's hand. 'You go and sort things out.'

There was laughter coming from the living room, but Lily was on her own watching cartoons so Tara continued her search upstairs. She knocked once on Molly's bedroom door before stepping inside to find her daughter lying on her stomach with her head pressed into her pillow.

'What?' Molly demanded, voice muffled.

Tara's heart clenched when she saw her daughter rub her eyes against the pillowcase before looking up. She had seen Molly cry before, but it was the first time she had tried to hide her tears.

Sitting down on the edge of the bed, Tara went to touch Molly's leg but her daughter scrambled backwards and wedged herself into a corner.

'You can't escape me,' Tara said.

Molly glared. 'I know I can't. The room's too small.'

'Is that what this is about?' asked Tara, feeling the first stirrings of frustration. 'Look, sweet pea—'

'I'm not your sweet pea any more. Lily is!'

The term of affection had once been reserved exclusively for Molly, but Tara had started using it with Lily too. She had seen it as progress. 'Molly, you're my daughter. You mean more to me than anything.'

'Not enough to get me a dog.'

'That's unfair,' Tara said. 'I was ready to get a pet and if you hadn't been so stroppy, we could have been bringing a kitten home soon.'

'A kitten,' Molly repeated. 'Because that was what Lily wanted. Everyone treats her like she's special because she lost her mum, but I lost my dad too.'

Tara scooted along the bed and took hold of Molly's hand whether she liked it or not. 'I know it must look as if she's getting special treatment, but you've seen how hard it's been for her, and we couldn't have got this far without you.'

'So get me a dog.'

Tara's body tensed, or was it her heart hardening? 'No, Molly. It's too much effort.'

'Obviously!'

When Molly tugged her hand away, Tara let her go. 'I really don't have time for this,' she said, rising to her feet. 'I don't want to hear another thing about a flipping dog.'

'Fine, I won't say anything to you – ever – again!' Molly called back as her mum left the room.

Tara stood on the landing shaking, already regretting losing her temper. This wasn't like Molly, and her sullenness was a symptom of a problem Tara was only beginning to grasp. It was a period of adjustment for all of them and they had made allowances for Lily but not Molly. That had to change.

She inhaled deeply to shift the weight against her chest but it refused to move. If she couldn't negotiate the feelings of a ten-year-old, what chance would she stand with Faith?

31

Cold and bright, the day was a stark contrast to the last time April had visited Pickering's Pasture. It was hard to believe she had been that broken woman sobbing in a deserted car park with the horn blaring. At the time, April thought that final blow had knocked her down for good, but she had been wrong. She had survived and come back stronger, which was fortunate because she was going to need all her strength today.

There was no doubt that Faith would be angry, but the question was who would feel the force of that anger the most. As April considered the difficult conversation ahead, Dexter whined in sympathy. He was impatient to leave the relative warmth of the car, but April needed more time to brace herself.

She had arranged to meet Tara ten minutes early to ensure that neither of them faced Faith alone, but her friend was already five minutes late. She checked her phone, but there was no message and, as April glanced up, she spied Faith's white Range Rover entering the car park.

April was about to put her phone away when a message flashed up.

So sorry cant make it can u manage without me? X

'Don't do this to me, Tara,' April said out loud, keeping her head down so that Faith wouldn't see the horror on her face.

The shadow of the Range Rover passed over April as she continued to stare at her phone, trapped by indecision. Faith displayed no such hesitation, and when she tapped on the window, April jumped. Faith's bright yellow rain jacket dazzled in the sunshine, making April squint as she offered a weak smile.

Climbing out of the car, April spent longer than was entirely necessary seeing to Dexter. After she had attached his leash and double-checked it, she stole more time adjusting her scarf and bobble hat. She had yet to decide what to do. Could she manage without Tara? She doubted it. She couldn't even zip up her jacket.

'Here, let me take the dog,' Faith said, assuming control. Dexter settled at her side within seconds and they both watched April zip up her jacket. 'So what's so important that you had to drag me out into the freezing cold when I could be snuggled up in bed?'

'Nothing,' April replied.

'According to Tara's message just now, it's something more than nothing,' Faith said. 'I'm under instruction to hear you out.'

April's mouth was dry. Tara's question about her managing on her own had been rhetorical; she thought April could handle Faith without her. But why did she have to? What emergency had kept Tara away? April would have to worry about that later. She could only deal with one crisis at a time.

'Let's start walking,' April said, heading down the hill.

Unlike her previous walk with Tara and Faith, she chose to go against the flow of the river and turned east. Her eyes stung from the glare of the low winter sun.

'I'm still waiting for an answer,' Faith said, slipping on a pair of sunglasses.

'You're not going to like it.'

'I'd worked that out for myself.'

April took a lungful of air that was so cold it hurt and yet beads of sweat pricked her brow. 'OK,' she said. 'It's about Nick.'

'Again, no surprise.'

'He's been lying to you,' April said, forcing out her words in a rush. 'Tara and I have spoken to his sister.'

'What? How the hell did you track her down?'

Faith's tone was enough to make April flinch and her pace quickened. She kept her gaze fixed on the curve of Runcorn Bridge poking through a layer of low-lying mist when she said, 'We were at a fundraiser at the weekend. It was being held in memory of Erin.'

'And what were you doing there?'

'It was my idea.'

April could feel Faith's eyes boring into her from behind her sunglasses. Her friend was waiting for a proper answer.

'I just wanted to see how Erin's husband was doing,' she said. 'I felt guilty that Nick was in the group and he wasn't.'

'And you saw Nick's sister?'

'Yes, and she told us what happened between him and Erin. It wasn't an affair, Faith. They didn't begin a relationship when she was married, it was the exact opposite. They were the ones who were engaged first, but when she was diagnosed, Nick dumped her. He didn't want her illness getting in the

284

way of his career. She met Josh later, while she was having treatment.'

There was no snappish response this time and they walked on in silence. That was good, April told herself. Faith needed time to digest the information before being assaulted with more damning evidence.

'Nick mentioned being a commitment-phobe in his youth,' Faith said eventually, having examined the yawning holes April had picked in Nick's story. She was trying to knit it back together. 'And I can see why he would want us to think he kept away because Erin was married, not because she was ill, but that doesn't mean the affair was a lie,' Faith said. 'He said all along that he didn't know how much Erin meant to him until he found out she was dying.'

'Look at it from Erin's perspective. Nick had dumped her when – no, *because* – she got sick. Would you want him back after that? And the fact is she married Josh around the time Nick claims the affair resumed. Why would she cheat on the man who stood by her with the one who ran away when she needed him most?' asked April. Offering some balm to ease the pain she was inflicting, she added, 'I'm not saying Nick doesn't have genuine issues over what happened, but their so-called affair just isn't believable – he made that bit of it up so we'd stop asking questions. He doesn't deserve our sympathy, he really doesn't.'

As they crossed a narrow footbridge that crossed Ditton Brook where it joined the river, Dexter kept close to Faith's heel. Ahead of them was a formidable set of wooden steps that zigzagged up the sheer face of a cliff. April wasn't sure she cared enough about the view to justify the climb, but Faith was leading the way.

'Whatever the timing of his relationship, Nick loved Erin in his own way,' Faith said with a shrug. 'And if I were in his position, I think I'd gloss over the details too.'

'That's not all we found out, Faith. Nick's sister was very open with us when we told her he was dating a friend of ours.'

Faith raised her hand, ready to deflect the next assault. 'No, that's enough, April. I appreciate you and Tara mean well, but I know as much as I want to know about Nick. It's Valentine's Day for God's sake. It's the first time in years I've woken up next to someone who's told me they love me. Nick's at home right now preparing a special lunch for us and I intend to share it with him – unfortunately we couldn't enjoy breakfast in bed this morning because my meddlesome friends needed to ruin my day,' she said as she stomped up the wooden steps.

April hurried after her and when she reached the first turn in the zigzag, Faith was on the next flight. They paused to face each other, but only Faith found the breath to speak.

'I won't stand for interference from you or from Tara, whenever she dares to show her face,' she said. She pushed her sunglasses up the bridge of her nose and April felt the full force of her scrutiny. 'Please don't say you're the decoy to get me out of the house. Has Tara gone to see Nick?'

It hadn't crossed April's mind, but it made more sense than she would like. She wasn't wholly convinced when she replied, 'She wouldn't do that.'

'None of us know what we're capable of until we're tested,' Faith said, glancing in the direction of the car park.

While Faith considered whether to go back or carry on, April stretched out her arms to grip the wooden handrails, effectively blocking Faith's path should she decide to head back to the car. Faith smiled, seemingly impressed, before tugging on Dexter's leash and continuing the climb.

'Olivia told us that Nick didn't lose his job because of grief,' April called after her. 'He was trying to make a profit from Erin's death, taking money off colleagues and clients. They sacked him when they found out he had nothing to do with Josh's memorial fund.'

There was another wave of a hand. 'Was it in the papers? Did he get arrested?'

'No, but—'

'Then it's hearsay. I don't know who's been filling your head with all of this nonsense, but I don't believe it was Nick's sister. She lives in Canada and I seriously doubt she'd come all this way for an event held in memory of the girl her brother dumped – allegedly.'

'There was no mention of Canada. I got the impression she lives here,' April said. Her lungs burned and she was out of breath, but Faith hadn't slowed and neither would she. 'It sounds like another lie.'

'But whose lie? Who's to say the woman you spoke to wasn't some mischief-maker wanting to get back at Nick for whatever reason? Think about it.'

'I'd take her word before believing another word Nick says.'

April was panting as she reached the final turn where Faith was taking in the view. With the sun on their backs, the western sky was a milky blue and the river had slipped free of the last tendrils of mist as it snaked its way out to sea. April spied Hale lighthouse, but her eyes were drawn to the opposite shore; Eastham, and home. Faith wasn't the only one who wished she had stayed in bed.

Gripping the rail, April turned to face Faith one last time. 'Please, listen to me.'

'I know you mean well,' Faith began, 'but if Nick asks me to marry him, and I think he will, I'm going to say yes. I appreciate you have your own reasons for wanting to punish past misdemeanours, but I'm looking to the future, and Nick is fundamental to my plans.'

To April's dismay, there was no hesitation in Faith's voice. 'But he's a con man, Faith. He'll do anything for money. Why do you think he dumped Erin? Olivia said he was being headhunted – he didn't want to risk a sick girlfriend distracting him from earning those fat bonuses. And now the money's dried up, he's looking for someone to bankroll him.'

'Nick's not exactly short of funds,' Faith said. 'Our holiday cost thousands.'

'It was a confidence trick to reel you in, and it worked, didn't it?'

As Faith turned to April, her breath curled into a cloud of vapour that floated over the handrail and across the flowing river a hundred feet below. Dexter was by Faith's side, watching her expectantly.

'Nick couldn't afford to pay for the holiday *and* his rent,' April continued. 'Olivia was his guarantor, and she had to use her savings to clear his debts when he abandoned his flat and stopped paying rent. Think about it. What do you know about his business other than the information he left out conveniently for you to see? There are no assets. His fleet of limos are on lease hire and he's behind with those payments as well. I bet that BMW of his is leased too.'

'It's not true,' Faith said, but her voice had weakened.

288

'I wish it wasn't,' April said. 'Has he tried to get money out of you, or asked you to invest in his company?'

'No,' whispered Faith.

It wasn't clear if Faith was refuting the question or denying the possibility that Nick was a fraudster. Her jaw tensed and she balled a hand into a fist as she looked for something to strike.

'It can't be,' she hissed.

'I'm sorry, Faith. He's not who you think he is.'

Faith leant over the handrail and released a moan through gritted teeth, a sound echoed as a whimper from Dexter.

When her friend straightened up, April asked, 'What are you going to do?'

'I have to go home,' she said, thrusting Dexter's leash into April's hands.

'You can't go now,' April said, hurrying down the steps after Faith. 'We need to talk. You need a plan.'

'I have a plan,' Faith called over her shoulder. 'I'm going to get that bastard out of my house.'

Olivia Malford @LivM584
Replying to @thewidowsclub
I'm sorry.

The Widows' Club @thewidowsclub
Replying to @LivM584
You shouldn't have to apologise. Your brother destroyed lives and he alone is responsible.

32

At around the time April was waiting for Tara to arrive at Pickering's Pasture, Tara was sitting in her car outside Tee's Cakes with the engine running. She had made an exceptionally early start so that she could hand over to Michelle when it was time to go, but as the sun rose, her confidence had dipped. She had spent the night replaying her argument with Molly and cringed at how badly she had handled it. Iain had taken the girls to school, but Tara would be waiting for her daughter at home time so she could try again. With Faith, however, there would be only one chance.

With a heavy heart, Tara put the car in reverse, but as she checked her rear-view mirror, she caught a glimpse of Faith's car speeding towards Pickering's Pasture. Tara needed to catch her up, but instead she drummed her fingers on the steering wheel. Would Faith think it unfair if two friends ganged up on her? Would it be better if Tara spoke to her alone, or should she let April try? Would anyone be able to convince Faith that Nick wasn't worth the risk?

She was still of the mind that persuading Nick to disappear might be the easier option. Now that she knew for certain that Faith was out of the way, she could drive straight to Woolton. Iain had warned her to be wary, but wasn't it possible that Nick was as weak as his sister believed? She could convince him of Faith's likely reaction without having to rely on Faith's actual response. He could be out of her life before she came home.

A decision was within Tara's grasp when her phone rang. It was the school.

'Hello?'

'Hi there, it's Mrs Hollande,' said the school secretary. 'We were wondering if we should mark Molly as absent, or are you running late?'

Tara felt a sensation akin to being punched in the stomach. 'But Molly's already there,' she insisted. 'Iain dropped the girls off at the usual time. He came into the shop afterwards. There were no problems. She has to be in the school.'

The pause made Tara's heart stutter.

'Lily arrived, but Molly's been marked absent. I've been in her classroom. She's not there.'

'Have you asked Lily?'

'Not as yet. The procedure is to call you.'

'Then I don't . . . I don't know where she is.'

'Oh, goodness,' said Mrs Hollande, echoing the panic in Tara's voice. 'Could she have gone back home?'

'I'll check with Iain, but in the meantime, can you speak to Lily?' asked Tara as a search plan formed in her mind. She cut the engine and got out of the car.

'Do you think we should contact the police?'

'No,' Tara said as she glanced across the road to the school entrance and willed her daughter to appear. When she didn't, she added, 'I don't know . . . Can you speak to them?'

'Leave it with me. And I'll phone you straight back if I find out anything from Lily.'

Tara phoned Iain next and stayed on the line while he checked every room in the house. Molly hadn't gone home. Or had she? By the time Tara had issued Iain with instructions to check the bus stops and search the park, she was standing in the middle of the flat. They had made a start pulling up carpets and preparing the walls so April could move in, but for now the rooms were utterly devoid of life.

Pressing a clammy hand to her brow, Tara recalled Molly's parting shot the night before. 'I won't say anything to you – ever – again!'

'No,' whispered Tara. If a dog meant that much to Molly they would get a damn dog. She just wanted her baby back. She recalled their walk down to the lighthouse with Dexter pulling on his leash. Would she go back there? It was nearer than Pickering's Pasture and deserted enough for a schoolgirl not to be noticed playing truant.

As Tara turned to leave, she spotted the colour charts April had left. Realising she should be with her friends by now, she tapped out a quick message to April asking if she could manage on her own. As soon she sent it, Tara knew that postponing wasn't an option. Faith needed to be told and in an attempt to smooth the way, she sent a second message to Faith telling her to listen to what April had to say. It was all she could do, and she hoped it would be enough.

The police phoned while Tara was driving towards Hale Head. Apparently Mrs Hollande had been unable to glean any useful information from Lily and they were taking Molly's disappearance seriously. With a pounding heart, Tara gave them a detailed description and explained as much as she knew.

When the call ended, Tara was driving past St Mary's church and she said a silent prayer to Mike, asking him to look after their daughter, but she didn't slow until she reached the gates that blocked the footpath to the lighthouse. There was a spray of gravel as she came to a screeching halt and then she was running across the headland fields. She paused for breath when she reached the lighthouse and called out Molly's name before turning in circles. Eventually, she turned east and followed the route they had taken with Dexter.

The sun was in Tara's eyes as she forced her legs to move faster, but the figure of a little girl refused to materialise. Quickly running out of path, her gaze was drawn to a distant bend in the river. East of Pickering's Pasture, the land rose up and she could just make out the zigzag of steps that cut into the cliff face. She stopped in her tracks. Molly had overheard her making plans to meet April. Tara was on the wrong side of the salt marshes.

33

Faith's shadow stretched ahead of April's as they raced back to the car park.

'Slow down,' April said. 'Please, Faith. We need to talk calmly about this.'

'Calmly?' Faith said, turning on her. 'That bastard sold me a lie and I was ready to pay a premium for it. He's not paid any rent yet and I don't suppose he ever intended to! How did I fall for something so crass? When did I become that person, April? When?'

'You haven't fallen for anything,' April said. 'You see him for what he is now, that's the important thing.'

Faith bent forward and rested her hands on her knees. 'I've been such an idiot! What must everyone think of me?' she asked. Her shoulders shook.

April edged closer, but when she put a hand on Faith's back, her friend straightened up.

'I won't be made a fool of a second time,' she said, sniffing back tears. She adjusted her sunglasses. 'He leaves today.'

'Do you think he'll go quietly? Should I come with you?'

Faith took a deep breath and held it before letting it go. 'I'm not scared of him,' she said. 'He might talk hard, but I don't think it's anything other than a fantasy.'

'What do you mean? What fantasy?'

'Play-acting, that's all, to spice up our sex life. You know the sort of thing.'

'I don't think I do.'

'Nick . . . he likes the idea of holding me at knife point while we have sex,' she said. Raising a hand, she added, 'Don't worry, I have my limits. I don't indulge him.'

April's expression of horror was wasted on Faith who was on the move again, leaving April to catch up. 'What if he's dangerous, Faith?'

Faith's momentary show of weakness wasn't going to be repeated. She ignored all further pleas from April and strode towards her Range Rover. The car unlocked with a clunk and as Faith pulled open the driver's door, April hurried to the other side and opened the passenger door.

'What are you doing?' asked Faith.

'I'm coming with you.'

'No, you're not.'

It was April's turn to feign deafness as she pulled open the rear passenger door too. She picked up Dexter and was about to bundle him into the back seat when someone cried out his name. The dog fought to wriggle free

'Dexter!' the little voice called again.

Molly appeared from behind April's Corsa and, as she buried her face in the dog's fur, April heard the driver's door slam shut. Faith was behind the wheel.

'What are you doing here, Molly? Is your mum with you?' April asked as she scanned the car park.

Molly didn't reply and to April's growing frustration, Tara didn't appear.

'I need to go!' Faith yelled. 'April, close the doors!'

April's attention was fixed on Molly. 'What's going on? Shouldn't you be in school?'

'I ran away,' Molly said, head bowed, voice low. When she did glance up, April realised her eyes were red and crusted with tears. 'Isn't Mum here?'

'No. My guess is she's looking for you.'

'For Christ's sake, April! Close the fucking doors!'

They glared at each other. 'There's a child present.'

'I can see that! You said I should stay calm but I can tell you now, this is not helping! Take Molly back to Tara and leave me to deal with my own problems.'

'You're right, we need to get her back to her mum,' April said, her jaw set firm. 'Tara's going to be sick with worry. Get in the car, Molly.'

Still holding the squirming dog, April ushered Molly towards the back seat. Molly climbed in, and Dexter bounded onto her knee.

'I didn't mean come with me,' Faith hissed when April climbed into the front seat and closed the door.

'We can drop Molly off on the way,' April said as she took out her phone.

Faith was cursing under her breath as she reversed out of the car park space. Keeping her eye on the rear-view mirror, she said, 'Put your seat belt on.'

There was a click as Molly did as instructed. 'Sorry,' she whispered.

'There's nothing to be sorry for,' April said before Faith could respond with something less sympathetic.

April had her phone to her ear as Faith swerved out of the car park. Tara answered on the second ring.

'Oh, April, I'm so scared. Molly's missing,' she said, gasping for breath.

'No, she's not,' April replied. 'She's with me.'

Tara's throat sounded hoarse as she took a gulp of air, then another. Her voice was muffled and punctuated by sobs when she said, 'She's OK? She's safe?'

'She's safe,' April said as her shoulder thumped against the car door. Faith hadn't slowed as she turned onto the main road that would lead them directly to the village. 'We should be with you in a few minutes.'

'Wait, where are you?'

'We've just left Pickering's Pasture. Where are you?'

'Erm, I don't know,' Tara said, catching her breath. 'Somewhere on the coastal path, heading back to Hale Head.'

'We could meet you by the lighthouse,' April said, only to hear Faith huff. She wasn't going to make a detour. 'Or we could drop Molly off with Iain.'

'He's out looking for her too,' Tara said, her voice jolting over her words as she moved. 'I could make it back to the shop in fifteen minutes. Can you wait? Where's Faith?'

'She's driving,' April said.

'She knows?'

'Yes.'

'Tell her to drive carefully,' Tara said. 'Sorry, I need to call Iain, and the police.'

'Of course, I'll see you soon.'

'Tell Molly I love her. Tell her she's not in any trouble.'

'I will.'

'Is Mum mad with me?' asked Molly when the call ended.

300

'No, sweetheart. She's just relieved you're safe,' April said. For Faith's benefit, she added, 'We can wait for her in the shop and then everyone can catch their breath.'

There was no argument from Faith, which April took as a good sign until they approached Ivy Farm Court. The car didn't slow.

'Faith . . .'

'I can drop you off, but I'm not getting out,' she said.

'Then I won't get out either.'

'I thought as much,' said Faith. 'So when I get home, you can wait in the car with Molly while I sort things out with Nick. Tara can meet us there.'

'You can't—'

'Is that all right with you, Molly?' asked Faith. 'There's a nice park close to where I live. You could take Dexter for a walk when your mum catches you up.'

'If she'll let me,' Molly replied.

'After the stunt you've just pulled, your mum will let you do whatever you want, so make the most of it,' Faith said. To April, she added, 'There you go, you wanted a plan, and now we have one. Satisfied?'

'Fine, speak to Nick on your own, but if I don't see him coming out with his bags packed within ten minutes, I'm phoning the police,' April muttered. 'I'd better let Tara know.'

When she tried to phone Tara back, it went straight to voicemail so she tapped out a message. After a couple of minutes, Tara sent a reply. It was one word. 'Fuck!'

Faith's driving became less erratic as they drove through the suburbs of Liverpool, and April didn't interrupt her thoughts – there was only so much they could say with Molly in the car. Within a quarter of an hour, Faith was pulling up alongside Nick's car on the drive. She didn't say a word as she got out.

April released her seat belt and twisted in her seat. 'Here, phone your mum,' she said, handing Molly her phone. 'Let her know what's happening.'

Faith was on the doorstep with her keys in her hand when April caught up with her. 'Are you sure about this?' she whispered.

'You're not coming in with me.'

'But what if . . .' April began.

She didn't want to imagine the what-ifs, especially after hearing about Nick's sick fantasy. Glancing through the window panes in the door, she expected to catch a glimpse of him sneaking up on them, but the house appeared undisturbed by their arrival.

'He's spent a lot of money on you, Faith,' she continued, 'and he'll be expecting a return on his investment. He's not going to leave without something to show for his endeavours.'

'I told you, I have no spare cash and I guess now is the time to break the bad news,' Faith said, reaching to unlock the door. She hesitated. 'I really thought I'd found another Derek.'

'Oh, Faith, I'm so sorry.'

'It's not me you should feel sorry for.'

'Be careful,' April warned. 'And I meant what I said about phoning the police.'

'I tell you what,' Faith said. 'I'll open a window so you can hear me shout for help if something does go horribly wrong.' She sounded blasé about the whole thing. Her anger had dissipated and she appeared fearless, which was possibly more disquieting.

As Faith disappeared into the house, April's heart thudded beneath the padding of her jacket. Feeling hot and a little faint, she loosened her scarf and walked back to the car. Dexter jumped up and scratched at the window while Molly offered her a smile; she was on the phone to her mum. April mouthed for her to stay in the car, which was what she should do too, but how would she hear Faith's cries?

Telling herself that nothing bad was going happen, April crept around Nick's BMW. If he was making lunch, she guessed Faith would find him in the kitchen at the back of the house, but as April slipped around the side, she found her route barred by a high fence and a locked gate. She peered through a hollow knot of wood and spied the window she recalled being over the sink. Faith had been true to her word and opened it.

Holding her breath, April strained for the sound of voices, but her pulse was racing and all she could hear was the whoosh of blood pumping through her veins. She breathed in through her nose and out through her mouth, determined to regain her composure as Faith had done, but her pulse refused to slow and her blood pressure soared when she heard someone cry out.

'But I do love you!'

April took another look through the peephole, as if seeing the open window would improve her hearing. Pressing her forehead against the fence, she could hear something. Was it Faith sobbing?

'No! Keep away from me!' Faith cried out.

'For God's sake!' Nick yelled back. 'Will you just . . .'

'Stop! Leave me alone!'

April spun around, looking for something to use as a step to climb over the fence but there was nothing. She stood on tiptoe and curled her fingers over the top of the wooden panels, but she couldn't find a foothold and remained planted on the wrong side of the fence. She gave up with a grunt of frustration that transformed into a whimper when she heard Faith yell, 'No!'

The scream that followed was the most chilling sound April had ever heard, loud enough for Dexter to start yapping from the confines of the car. She fumbled in her pocket for her phone only to release a sob. It wasn't there. She had given it to Molly.

Stumbling back to the front of the house, April found Molly cowering in the back of Faith's car with a frantic Dexter, who launched himself at her when she opened the door. 'I need the phone, now!'

It was pressed to Molly's ear, but when April went to take it, Molly scrambled over to the other side of the car. The child was terrified and there was no time to coax the phone from her. Panting, April tried to keep her voice calm. 'OK, fine. Is that your mum?' Molly nodded. 'Tell her Faith is being attacked! Tell her to phone the police!'

April had the presence of mind to close the car door before Dexter could escape, but she couldn't lock Molly in. Faith had the keys. April felt powerless as she approached the house, at a loss for what to do next. Should she knock on the door? There was a risk that Nick would answer, but the interruption might just give Faith a fighting chance – although April hated to think what exactly was going on in there.

With nightmare images at the forefront of her mind, April

hammered a fist against the door. She pressed the doorbell and kept her finger on it for what felt like an eternity. She caught a glimpse of movement through the frosted window. A figure drew closer and a hand reached up to open the door.

34

When April had told Tara that Molly was safe, the relief had been intense, but it wasn't to last. After calling off the search, Tara was jogging back towards the lighthouse when she saw the message from April saying Faith hadn't stopped and was driving home.

Fuck!

Tara ran as fast as her aching legs would carry her back to the car, but it took more time than she would have liked. Sweat dripped off her face as she peeled off her jacket and threw it onto the passenger seat, and as she prepared to drive off, she heard the muffled sound of her ringtone.

'Shit, shit, shit,' Tara said as she searched through folds of material to find her jacket pocket. Her hands were clammy and when she found her phone, she couldn't connect the call. 'Shit,' she said again.

'Mum, is that you?' asked Molly.

Tara's lips trembled as she put the phone to her ear. 'Yes. Yes, it is, sweet pea. Are you OK?'

'Hmm-hmm.'

'Are you still in the car?'

'Yeah. We've just pulled up outside a big house. April and Faith are standing on the doorstep talking.'

'OK, I'm on my way and in the meantime, I need you to stay in the car,' Tara said as she wedged the phone under her chin and fumbled with her seat belt. Why was she so terrified? There would be arguments and there might be threats, but that didn't mean Molly would be drawn into them. Nick was weak, she reminded herself. But still. 'If anything happens that makes you scared, I want you to run to a neighbouring house.'

'Which one?'

'Any,' Tara said. The car lurched forward as she set off for Woolton at speed. 'Don't worry about April and Faith. You look after yourself, do you hear me?'

Tara hadn't meant to raise her voice.

'I'm s— I'm sorry,' Molly said.

The sound of her child weeping on the other end of the phone tore at Tara's heart. 'Don't be sorry,' she said. 'None of this is your fault.'

'But I've caused so much trouble.'

'If anyone's to blame, it's me,' Tara soothed. 'I lost my temper when I should have given you the time you needed to talk.' Her voice broke when she added, 'I'm listening now.'

There was a pause in which her daughter's attention was pulled elsewhere. 'Yeah, OK,' Molly said, replying to someone else.

'Who was that?'

'April. She's just told me to stay in the car and now she's sneaking around the side of the house. Faith's gone inside. What's going on, Mum?'

'Don't worry, it's something and nothing,' Tara said. 'Talk to me, Molly. Tell me what's wrong.'

There was a long pause. 'It's not about my bedroom, or a dog,' mumbled Molly.

'Is it about Lily?' asked Tara, recalling the flash of jealousy her daughter had revealed the night before.

Molly sniffed. 'Sort of,' she said. 'I hate that she can remember her mum but I can't remember Dad. Not one thing.'

'If you want to know more about him, we can make that happen,' Tara promised. 'I've made such a huge mistake, haven't I? I put all my energy into managing Lily's feelings when I should have been thinking of you too. You know, the only reason Lily started to feel at home with us is because of you. You're pretty damn amazing, Moll and I've taken you for granted.'

There was disturbance on the other end of the line as Molly grappled with the phone and the dog. Dexter was yapping. 'Mum—'

Tara's breathing slowed and she managed a smile. 'I told you dogs were hard work.'

'Mum—'

The sweat trickling down Tara's neck froze. There was fear in her daughter's voice as the dog's barks became frenzied.

'I need the phone, now!'

April's shout made Tara flinch, but it was Molly's panicked breaths that made her heart stutter.

'OK, fine. Is that your mum?' she heard April say. 'Tell her Faith is being attacked! Tell her to phone the police!'

'Molly, let me talk to April!' Tara said.

There was the thump of a car door slamming. 'She's gone,' Molly said.

'Where to?'

The pause was tortuous. 'She's at the front door. She's ringing the bell.'

'Molly, listen to me. You have to get out of there. You have to get out of there now!' Tara told her. She wouldn't cut the call to phone the police until she knew Molly was safe. 'Go to a neighbour.'

'Hold on, the front door's opening,' Molly replied. There was a gasp. 'Oh, my God. Oh, my God. It's Faith and there's blood pouring out of her neck.' She started to cry. 'You need to phone someone, Mum.'

'Run, now!' screamed Tara.

She heard the car door open and the resonance of Dexter's barks changed, suggesting the dog was now in open space.

'Molly, speak to me! Tell me you're running!'

'Wait, there's a man. It'll be all right, Mum. Phone the police.'

The line went dead.

STATEMENT

The Widows' Club @thewidowsclub
We very much appreciate all the messages of support.
Faith has been a valued member of our group for many
years and supported us as much as we supported her.
That has been the nature of the group and always will be.

Mike T @MikeTheRailway
Replying to @thewidowsclub
I knew Faith when she was a girl. She loved helping her
dad in the garage and we joked she could run it without
him. She doesn't deserve this.

Julie Delaney @JulieDel99
Replying to @thewidowsclub
This Faith sounds like a right character. She knew what
she was getting into when she found out this bloke had
had an affair with a married woman. She should have
known he was trouble.

35

The first thing April noticed when the front door opened was the blood. It was splattered across Faith's face and dripped from the sleeve of her rain jacket as she pressed a bloodied hand to her neck. She staggered onto the step.

'No!' April cried as her friend's knees buckled.

Faith's make-up was muddied and her features ashen. Her lips moved but she could manage only a series of guttural gasps. As April comforted her friend, she peered through the open door and down the hallway, following the trail of blood towards the kitchen. There was no sign of Nick, but April would feel better if she could hear the wail of a police siren above Dexter's fretful yaps. Had Tara made the call yet?

As she glanced over her shoulder to the car, a figure loomed over her. April shrank in horror when she saw the golf club in the man's hand, but this wasn't Nick. The man was grey-haired, with what looked like a century's worth of wrinkles that deepened as he shuffled towards her in his slippers.

'I'm Mr Newton from next door,' he said. 'The emergency services are on their way. What on earth happened?'

'We need to get her away from the house,' April said, aware

of the open door and the danger beyond. She pulled her scarf from her neck and prised her friend's hand from her throat. She expected a gush of blood, but the wound she glimpsed before pressing her scarf to Faith's neck didn't appear deep. Where had all that blood come from?

'Mrs Cavendish, can you walk?' asked Mr Newton. 'We need to get you to safety.'

'No,' she whispered. 'Too late.'

'What do you mean?' April asked. 'Where's Nick?'

Faith recoiled at the sound of his name. 'Dead. He's dead.'

A shudder ran down April's spine and rose up as bile in her throat. She wanted to feel relief, her friend was safe, but a man was dead. Nick was dead. She couldn't take it in. She didn't want to. Where the hell were the police?

'I heard her screams,' said Mr Newton, shaking his head.

As April glanced up at Faith's neighbour, she noticed Molly standing behind him. 'You should get back in the car, Molly. You don't want to see this.'

Molly didn't move. She was staring at Faith.

'He laughed at me,' Faith said. 'He said if I was stupid enough to believe the story about Erin, I only had myself to blame. He picked up a knife and told me he liked taking money from dead people. I thought he was going to kill me.'

'Oh Faith, it's OK, you're safe now,' April said.

Faith grasped April's arm. 'I couldn't believe the change in him. I told him I loved him, and I did, April. I did.'

April remembered hearing the distant shout. 'I know.'

'He said he wouldn't leave unless I paid him. I tried to explain that I didn't have that kind of cash, but he made me log into my bank account. I transferred what I could, but it wasn't enough. That's when he grabbed me and held the knife to my throat. He thought I had money squirrelled away somewhere, but I didn't and he was so angry. When I felt the blood trickling down my neck, I fought back. I had to.'

'I heard most of it,' said the neighbour. 'Help will be here shortly. You're safe now.'

'I should be the one who's dead,' Faith said as tears slipped down her face. 'I don't know where the strength came from, but I think my blood made his grip on the knife slippery. I got it off him and I . . .' She clenched a hand into a fist and made a single stabbing motion before letting her fingers unfurl. 'I had to do it. He gave me no choice.'

'No one could blame you for this,' April assured her, listening out for sirens but hearing only the distant hum of traffic. She glanced back into the hallway. 'Someone . . . I should check on Nick. He might still be alive.'

'All the more reason to stay out here,' Mr Newton said. He wasn't offering to go in her stead, they could both agree that he was no match for a man in his thirties, mortally wounded or not.

'Can you manage without me?' April asked Faith, taking hold of her hand and moving it to her throat so she could maintain pressure on the scarf pressed to her wound.

'April, you don't have to do this. He was definitely—' Faith began, only to be interrupted by the sound of a phone trilling.

'It's Mum,' Molly said. She was holding April's mobile.

'Let me take it,' April said. She didn't want to be alone when she stepped into the house.

'Take this too,' said the neighbour, handing April his golf club. 'In case he is alive.'

April's courage almost failed, but she kept moving. She connected the call as she stepped out of the bright sunlight and into the gloom.

'Molly?'

'No, it's April,' she whispered.

'What's happening? Where's Molly? Is she OK? Please, tell me she's OK.'

'Molly's fine,' April assured her as she followed the trail of bloodied footprints. 'She's outside.'

'What do you mean, outside? Where are you, April? Where's Faith? Is she . . . Molly said there was blood.'

As April neared the threshold to the kitchen, she could see Faith's crimson handprints smeared on the door. She tried to speak, but her breath caught in her throat. The air was heavy with the aroma of roasted herbs and spices, but there was something else too and it left a metallic taste in her mouth.

'Oh, my God, is Faith dead?' Tara said, her question wet with tears.

'No, she has a superficial cut, that's all,' April said. She didn't know if she could take a step further. The smell was overpowering. 'She stabbed Nick. She says he's dead.'

'Are you *inside* the house? Can you see him?'

'Not yet.'

'Then don't move,' Tara demanded. 'I'm driving through Hunt's Cross. I'll be with you in five minutes. Wait for me!'

'What if he's alive and needs help?' April asked, hoping for Faith's sake that she hadn't killed him. Whatever Nick's crimes, Faith didn't deserve his death on her conscience. 'I can't just leave him.'

'You bloody well can,' Tara said, raising her voice loud

316

enough to break the stillness of the house. 'Get out of there, April.'

There was a noise from inside the kitchen. A gurgling sound that might be a pot bubbling on the stove. She raised the golf club, ready to strike. 'I have to check, but stay on the line,' she said before slipping her phone into her pocket without cutting the call. She forced herself to move, stepping across Faith's footprints as she entered the kitchen. She dropped the golf club with a clatter.

April had seen a dead body before, but Jason's skin had been alabaster white and gave no clue to the bleed in his brain. What she faced in Faith's kitchen couldn't be more different, not least because Nick was still alive, though barely.

She was vaguely aware that the kitchen was in disarray, but no more so than when Nick had cooked lasagne for them. This time, however, the chef wasn't wearing a sharp suit or a convincing smile. He was slumped on the floor in a pool of blood. There was a blood-smeared iPad and a knife close by, but Nick's hand was clamped to his neck. Like Faith, the flow of blood was no more than a trickle, but April suspected that in Nick's case, it was because he had very little left to lose. His heart would be slowing and although he was semi-conscious, he seemed aware of April's presence. She grabbed a tea towel and almost slipped on the blood to reach him. Stemming the flow was futile, but she tried anyway.

'An ambulance is on its way,' she said.

The gurgling sound she had heard earlier came again. There was a large soup pan nearby, but the hob was unlit. The noise had come from Nick. He was trying to speak and she caught the sound of a syllable and tried to make sense of it.

'Water? Do you want water?' she asked in the hope that she could do something to help.

Nick fought to hold her gaze, imploring her to listen, but when his lips moved, April couldn't understand. His dying words were lost and would come to haunt her in the following days and weeks.

STATEMENT

The Widows' Club @thewidowsclub
We feel we must clarify one particular matter in relation
to suggestions that Nick was involved in an extramarital
relationship with Erin Peters. This was a lie told to the
group and we apologise unreservedly to her family for
any distress caused.

Petersj @Petersjhome
Replying to @thewidowsclub
And how did that gossip get into the public domain? If
your members are supposed to abide by confidentiality,
why are they repeating things they know nothing about?
Your group is toxic.

The Widows' Club @thewidowsclub
Replying to @Petersjhome
Our group is not toxic. If you were a widower, you would
know how isolating it can be. We thought we were
supporting Nick, but he betrayed us.

36

As Faith lay in the darkness, she wanted to imagine she was back home, but the mattress was narrow and hard and the blankets rough. There was an odious smell of disinfectant and body odour, and the thumps and clangs that kept her awake were not the gentle rattles of a temperamental heating system. She was being held on remand on suspicion of manslaughter and although the duty solicitor hoped to have her out in a day or two, the waiting was interminable.

Ella had been to see her and was the only visitor Faith had allowed. It would be too painful to see Tara or April, who would want to talk about feelings and emotions, and Faith wasn't there yet. Still in shock, she couldn't believe what had happened, or that it had happened so fast. That same sense of shock had been reflected on her stepdaughter's face.

'Why have they charged you?' Ella had demanded. 'Haven't you been through enough?'

'Apparently not,' Faith had replied, touching the dressing on her neck.

'Does it hurt?'

'Not as much as the thought of my home becoming a crime

scene. Have you been there? Are the police trampling through every bit of my life?'

'They'll be gone soon. What happened, Faith?'

As Ella had leant forward, Faith had leant back. 'Don't you think I'm tired of hearing that question?'

'But why are the police still holding you? Isn't it obvious that it was self-defence?' There had been an edge to Ella's question, sharpened no doubt by Rosemary.

'I would be out by now if I had a decent solicitor.'

'There'll be a public outcry if you're not released soon. All the papers are supporting you.'

Faith had been pleased to hear that. She was already planning to set up a GoFundMe page to procure better legal representation, and public sympathy could only help her cause. 'What are they saying?' she had asked. Hope dimmed when she noticed Ella's reticence. 'What?'

'I'm not sure you'd recognise yourself from what they're saying,' Ella had replied. 'They're making you out to be a poor, defenceless widow who was taken in by a charmer.'

'But I'm afraid that's exactly what I am.'

It was better that than being labelled a callous killer, which was what the Crown Prosecution Service might do if her plea of self-defence fell on deaf ears. Innocent people were locked up all the time, sometimes for years, and the fear of that happening was compounded by the darkness that wrapped around Faith as she lay in bed. Tears pricked the corner of her eyes. Why couldn't Nick have been who he said he was?

When she had woken up on Valentine's morning, he had told her that he loved her. She had believed it to be true. They could have had a future together, but he had lied about everything. Nick should be the one in a prison cell right now, not Faith. It wasn't her fault. Her conscience was clear, and if she had to prove her innocence in a court of law, she would.

Faith had told the police exactly what she had told April, except in a lot more detail and more than once. She had returned home to find Nick with his back to her as he prepared lunch. The kitchen was a mess and there was something bubbling on the stove – probably homemade carrot and coriander soup, because it was her favourite. She had no idea what was in the oven, but it had smelled mouth-watering. Nick had turned to greet her, but his smile had left her cold. He had fooled her for the last time.

Her clearest recollection was feelings of crushing humiliation and burning anger. She had seen the knife on the chopping board, but it had never crossed her mind, even fleetingly, that Nick would use it against her. She would prefer to block out what came next, but the police had pushed her for answers.

Explaining her financial predicament to the detectives had been particularly unpleasant, but necessary. They would be scrutinising her bank statements anyway, if only to confirm that she had been forced to transfer money into Nick's account whilst April and Molly waited outside. The few hundred pounds that Faith could ill afford wasn't what Nick was expecting. She would never forget the look of confusion on his face when she had shown him her account balance on her iPad.

She hadn't intended to do what she did. She had been defending herself, and anyone with half a brain would realise she had no choice.

37

'Can I move yet, Mum?'

'No,' Tara replied, pulling her daughter close so she could rest her chin on top of Molly's head. They had been curled up on the sofa all morning watching *Saturday Kitchen*. Michelle was running the shop with some extra help, and they had stopped taking online orders to lessen the burden. There was nowhere else Tara needed to be; nowhere else she wanted to be.

Her body was still recovering from her frantic race along the banks of the Mersey on Wednesday morning, not to mention the fraught journey to Faith's house. The police had been on the scene by the time she arrived and, after a tearful reunion with Molly, Tara had caught only a glimpse of Faith before being pulled away to give an initial statement, and she had been questioned several times since.

Of particular interest was the link between Faith, Nick, and the support group, and it wasn't only the police who wanted this information. The media was eager to sniff out a good story and, although Tara and Justine had agreed to ignore all press enquiries, it wasn't enough to keep them at bay. After decades of being overlooked, suddenly everyone knew their way to Hale Village.

Home was Tara's safe place and although Molly fidgeted, she made no attempt to escape her mother's clutches. They had agreed to spend more quality time together, just the two of them, and while this wasn't exactly what either had in mind, it was enough for now. Despite the challenges ahead, Tara felt at peace for the first time in months, and when a loud thud overhead made the ceiling shake, her pulse remained steady.

'I should go upstairs and help,' said Molly.

'We're fine here,' Tara insisted. 'Lily wants it to be a surprise.'

'But I already know what they're doing.'

'I know, but this is Lily's gift to you.'

'You know I was never angry with her, right?'

'Yes, I know,' Tara replied. 'You were angry with me and rightly so. I convinced myself you'd been spared the pain of losing your dad because you didn't remember him. I should have realised your loss was as real as Lily's, just different. You can't judge one person's grief against another's, I should have known that. I'm sorry.'

'That's OK,' Molly said with a shrug.

It wasn't Tara's first attempt at an apology and it wouldn't be her last. She would make amends by sharing memories of Mike with their daughter to help fill the void in her knowledge, but there was no rush. The biggest obstacle between them had already been overcome. Molly's grief had been acknowledged.

'Can I go now?' Molly asked again.

'At least wait until all the furniture has been moved and then the two of you can plan a proper makeover. It's going to take weeks to get it right, and Iain and I have to sort out April's flat first. There's no rush.'

'I like April.'

'Me too.'

Molly rubbed her cheek against Tara's dressing gown. 'I like her more than Faith.'

Tara stroked her daughter's hair. 'You do know she didn't mean to hurt that man, don't you?' she said, as guilt pricked her conscience. Faith might have held the knife, but April and Tara had played their part in Nick's demise. And so had Nick, she reminded herself. He was dead, but Faith was the victim. It was only a matter of time before the police dropped the charges.

Molly sat up to look at her mum, but she was hesitant when she spoke. 'But why did she smile?'

'Why did who smile, sweet pea?'

'Faith,' Molly said. 'When April came out and said he was dead, Faith smiled.'

Tara had on occasion told Faith she was heartless, but she didn't believe it, not really. 'She was in shock, that's all.'

Before the slithering sense of unease could unsettle her, the doorbell rang. There had been a steady stream of journalists calling at the shop, all eager to speak to one half of the support group's administration. Given how small the village was, it was entirely possible they had discovered where Tara lived. Was this the first call of many?

'I'll get it,' Iain shouted and was stomping down the stairs when the doorbell rang a second time.

Tara focused on her breathing. She didn't want anyone to invade her inner peace, but when she recognised the voice echoing down the hallway, she knew her defences had been breached.

'I saw that you weren't back at the shop and thought I'd check on you,' Justine said as she stepped into the living room and slipped out of her coat.

Iain was behind her, his expression offering a silent apology. 'Why don't you come and see what we've done upstairs, Moll?' he asked.

Molly jumped up and there was nothing her mother could do to stop her. Feeling exposed, Tara pulled her dressing gown a little tighter across her chest.

'Iain says you're reorganising the girls' rooms,' Justine said above the sound of hurried footsteps across the landing.

'It was unfair having Molly crammed into the box room while Lily had more space than she could possibly need. They've decided to share the big bedroom and convert the other into a walk-in wardrobe. It was Lily's idea and they're both thrilled.'

'They're almost like sisters.'

'We're getting there,' Tara said, daring to hope. 'Do you want a drink?'

'No, I won't stay,' Justine said as she took a seat. 'I just wanted to make sure you were OK. The shock must be wearing off by now and you're going to need support when the full impact of what happened hits you.'

'We're all going through the same.'

'I'll admit I haven't had a wink of sleep, but I can't compare my experience to yours. You're one of Faith's closest friends and it'll be you she leans on when she's released, assuming they do let her go.'

'Do you think they won't?' Despite her best efforts, Tara's pulse picked up the pace.

'I'm no expert, but the CPS can't ignore the fact that

someone died. Even with self-defence, you're only allowed to use reasonable force. The fact that she's been charged with manslaughter suggests the police aren't entirely convinced.'

'But she was threatened with a knife. How else was she supposed to protect herself?'

Justine's hands were resting in her lap. She picked at her fingernails. 'Let's hope the jury sees it that way.'

'It won't get to court. The public would be up in arms if it did.'

'Don't count on it,' Justine said. 'You know how fickle public opinion can be, and Faith has a habit of rubbing people up the wrong way. I have a horrible feeling she and the press are going to fall out, not that it should have a bearing on what the CPS decides to do, but you never know.'

'When she's ready, Faith will handle the press,' Tara said. 'I imagine she'd be quite good at it.'

'Hmm,' Justine said. 'She won't be happy reading how much of her private life has been published. Did you know she didn't own the house? Apparently her stepdaughter has a half share. Little wonder Faith complained so much about her.'

'Faith wasn't obliged to tell anyone about her financial affairs.'

'But she could have been more honest about her job,' Justine continued. 'I had the impression she was some high-flying scientist, but it turns out she was a junior lab assistant. And if today's papers are right, she was about to be made redundant. They're saying she was desperate to find a new man to look after her.'

'We know that's not true.'

'But it did look odd, didn't it? Nick was so much younger,'

Justine said. Her fingers continued to twitch. 'It's ironic when you think about it. They were both attracted to each other's false image. In some ways, they were as bad as each other.'

'No, Justine, they weren't,' Tara hit back. 'Faith might have overstated her position but she would have been happy enough on her own if Nick hadn't targeted her. It's only a matter of time before we find out what other skeletons were lurking in his past. Other victims.'

Tara was counting on it, for Faith's sake. There had to be something to explain how Nick had gone from being a spineless charmer to the kind of man who would cut a woman's throat.

'It's entirely possible. Social media has gone into overdrive,' said Justine. 'Actually, that's why I called around. It's not only Nick who's getting the blame for what happened. We're coming under fire too.'

'Who's we?'

'The group,' she replied. 'And I know we agreed not to make any statements, but we have to say something, Tara. If it goes on like this, our reputation will be destroyed and we could be forced to disband the group.'

'That's not such a bad idea,' Tara replied. 'What if we are to blame?'

'This was not our fault!' Justine said, her eyes widening in shock. 'Faith and Nick are responsible for their own actions and this can't overshadow all the good we've done over the years. Our members need us now more than ever, and I for one have every intention of going to the meeting next week.'

'With photographers staked outside?' Tara asked. 'It's too soon, Justine. I appreciate people need to talk about what happened, but is that wise, or even legal, while a police investigation is ongoing? Faith certainly couldn't attend, and I don't think April would be up to it either.'

'Or you?'

Tara's breathing had quickened. If she didn't feel so guilty she would wash her hands of the whole thing. She had mismanaged the group and she had mismanaged Molly. Something had to give and it wasn't going to be her family. 'Look, why don't we postpone the meeting until we know whether Faith is or isn't going to be released? In the meantime, we can issue a statement asking the press to respect the group's privacy.'

'We'd have to confirm that Nick was a member. At the moment it's only speculation.'

'Then we give them facts,' Tara snapped back.

Justine didn't flinch. Her voice was gentle when she said, 'Do you want me to do it? I could put a short message on Twitter.'

Tare could hear her girls' giggles floating from upstairs. The sweet sound calmed her. 'I'd appreciate that. I'm not sure I have the stomach to read what people are saying out there.'

'Leave it with me.'

38

April arrived in Hale earlier than she would have done if there had been a group meeting, but she still lost her race with the setting sun. The lighting wasn't ideal for painting walls a shade that matched the shadows, but she liked the honesty and simplicity of the grey. It had nothing to do with her mood.

'I could have managed on my own,' she told Tara, who greeted her at the flat in a pair of paint-splattered overalls and a headscarf tied in a knot at the top of her head.

'Nonsense,' Tara said. 'I want to help, and we need this finished before the new carpets are laid. I have a spare pair of overalls if you need them.'

April had brought some old clothes to change into. The Green Day T-shirt had been one of Jason's favourites and the gesture was meant to prove to herself how little she cared about him. She hesitated. 'I suppose overalls would be better.'

While April changed, Tara opened the paint tins and was pouring the darker shade into a tray when April reappeared in the living room. The label had described it as highland mist but when Tara loaded the roller, the white pile turned pewter.

'Are you sure you want this in here *and* the bedrooms?' she asked.

'Yep,' April replied, hoping the paint would dry a lighter shade. 'And the silver dawn is for the kitchen and bathroom.'

'Fair enough. Do you want to start in one of the other rooms so we're not bumping into each other? I've brought two of everything and we can take turns with the stepladder.'

'Oh, OK.'

April had assumed there was more to Tara's offer to stay than practicalities. It was less than a week after Nick's death and they needed to make sense of it all, but as April gathered up supplies, her friend turned her back on her and set to work.

Relegated to the bedroom next door, April listened to the slurp and swish of the roller gliding over the living room walls as she prepared her own work area. She chose a different approach to Tara and picked up an angled brush to paint a neat outline around the edges of the room before attempting to fill the gaps.

'I can't wait to move in,' April said, striking up a conversation whether Tara wanted it or not.

'Me neither.'

'I've applied for a couple of jobs on this side of the river.'

'That's good.'

April kept her hand steady as she painted a grey stripe that followed the outline of the door frame, crouching down as she neared the skirting board. It took all of her concentration to keep the bristles away from the woodwork but she refused to work in silence. 'When do you think we'll be able to resume the group meetings?'

'When the media lose interest.'

'That could be a while,' April warned. 'There's no guarantee Faith's going to be granted bail at tomorrow's hearing. It's a serious offence.'

'I was hoping the police would have dropped the charges by now.'

The rhythmic sweep of the roller was interrupted only long enough for Tara to soak up more paint from the tray. It was left to April to keep the conversation flowing.

'I don't imagine Faith is the best witness.'

The sound of movement next door slowed a fraction. 'Why do you say that?'

'You know what she's like. Faith might not be a scientist after all, but she has a very logical thought process that puts everything in black or white. There's no in-between,' April replied. She squinted at the sluggish trail of grey on the wall before adding, 'She sifts through information and discounts anything that doesn't match the judgement she's reached.'

'By lying,' Tara said. It could have been the echo of the room, but her voice sounded hollow.

'More like being selective with the truth,' April replied, although they both knew she was being generous. 'If you'd asked her about Nick a week ago, she would have extolled his virtues and glossed over his faults, but I doubt very much she'll tell the police anything that puts Nick in a favourable light now. Maybe he deserved it.' The pause lasted a heartbeat. 'Do you think he deserved it?'

The rhythm of the roller on the wall speeded up. 'It's not for us to decide.'

'We were quick enough to form our own judgement before he died,' April said, testing out recurring thoughts to see if they made better sense spoken aloud. 'I can't help wondering

333

what might have happened if their relationship had been allowed to run its course. Would there have been a crisis point, or would one or both of them have realised that they were lying to each other and called a truce?'

'You said Faith wasn't lying.'

'You know what I mean,' April said as paint dribbled onto the skirting board unchecked. 'I saw him, Tara. Nick didn't look like a cruel and ruthless criminal. He looked shocked, and scared.'

'He was dying.'

'But why did it happen? Did we create the situation?' April asked. When Tara didn't respond, she stood to stretch her spine. Dabbing paint onto the wall, she added, 'I know the danger felt real and it just kept building, but were we the architects of Nick's downfall? When Faith told me he had this fantasy about having sex with her at knife-point, it was like what happened next was already written.'

'*That* was his fantasy?' Tara asked.

'Faith said he talked about it but she wouldn't entertain the idea. People imagine doing all kinds of things, but they don't follow through with it, *normally*. I'm hoping someone out there knows more about Nick's dark side so everything doesn't have to rest on Faith's account,' she said, staring at the pattern of paint splodges. 'It's all so messy. Don't you think?'

The roller continued to be rolled.

'It's a telling sign that no one has come out publicly to defend Nick, not even Olivia. Did you see the torrent of abuse she received online once people realised who she was?' April asked. 'I was wondering if we should get in touch.'

'We've interfered too much,' Tara said. Her exertions were

making her breathless. 'And how bad will she feel when she realises it was her conversation with us that led directly to the events on Valentine's Day?'

'My guess is she's worked that out already,' April said. 'That photo of us all at Christmas has been splashed across every newspaper.'

'Maybe, but Olivia gave her statement saying she was sorry and if that's all she wants to say, we should leave her be.'

'A statement? Do you mean the tweet?'

'Is that what it was? I read it in the paper.'

April held her brush in mid-air. 'It was a reply to a tweet from the support group.'

'Justine's been taking care of that side of things. I saw the draft tweet asking the press to respect our privacy, but that's about it.'

'You should look at what's been said since, Tara. Justine's been fielding a lot of criticism directed at the group, including a suggestion we incited our members to react the way they did. The strongest accusations have come from someone with the twitter handle Peters J. It looks like the account was set up recently and there's no profile, but I think it's Josh Peters. Which begs the question, why would he want to wade in and defend Nick? I don't understand it. Should we be worried?'

No sound came from the next room. No sound at all.

'Tara?' April asked as the silence stretched between them. She put down her brush and returned to the living room. Three walls had been painted although there were gaps everywhere. 'Why don't you want to talk about this?'

Tara kept her back to April, her head bowed. 'We've all been through so much and I'm sick of this feeling of dread, right here,' she said, rubbing her palm against her chest. 'I

335

keep telling myself the worst has happened and it's over, but I wake up every morning and the pressure's worse than ever.'

'Do you think there's a chance Faith will have to face a trial?'

When Tara turned, her face was as grey as the walls. 'Faith is my friend and there's no one better I'd want fighting my corner. I love her like a sister,' she said. 'She can be brutally honest sometimes, but as it turns out, she can also be deceitful. I would never say this to anyone else, April, but I'm scared that I don't know her as well as I thought. She cut a man's throat for God's sake.'

'She was defending herself.'

'But was her reaction proportionate? I'm not saying she put the knife in Nick's hand, but holding a knife to someone's throat and using it are two very different things. What if the cut on Faith's neck was accidental? I'm not condoning what he did, but when Faith disarmed him, why couldn't she simply back away? Help was close at hand.'

'But her attack on him wasn't exactly frenzied,' replied April. 'Nick had one small stab wound to his neck as far as I could see; it just happened to be in the exact place where it could do most damage. And you can't blame Faith for expecting the worst when Nick had told her he liked making money out of dead people. She had a right to be scared.'

'But was she?'

The sense of dread Tara had described pressed down on April's chest. 'What do you mean?'

'The police could come to the conclusion that her fatal strike was controlled and measured,' she said, concentrating on the one aspect of the attack that ought to put their minds at ease. 'Did Faith look upset when she came out of the house?'

'Yes, of course.'

'And what about when you told her Nick was dead?'

April's discomfort intensified as she pictured the scene after leaving the kitchen. Faith had remained on the doorstep with Mr Newton crouching next to her and Molly standing nearby. When April told them Nick was dead, the old man had clutched his chest. Faith's reaction was slower.

'Faith had her back to me,' she said.

'Molly said she smiled.'

The icicles forming on April's spine made her shudder. They had all witnessed the events unfold from a slightly different angle, and only Faith had the complete picture. 'All I remember is that it took a moment for the news to sink in and then she sobbed.'

'You know, when Faith joined the group, it was months before I ever saw her cry. It was like she learnt how to grieve from us.'

'You're always telling us we find our own way to navigate our feelings,' April said. 'And if Faith smiled, it could be she was traumatised. It's hard to imagine what went on in that house.'

'But from what you saw and heard, did Faith's version match yours?'

Tara was searching for holes in their friend's statement and, as uncomfortable as that was, it would be better for Faith if they found them before the police. 'I didn't hear everything that passed between Faith and Nick,' April said, wishing she had been able to climb that damn fence and look into the kitchen. 'But the first thing I heard was someone saying I love you – as if they meant it.'

'Someone?'

'I told the police it was Faith,' April replied because Faith had told her as much after collapsing on the doorstep. 'But the voice in my head when I replay it belongs to a man. I couldn't swear one way or the other. I doubt it's important.'

'I hope you're right,' said Tara. 'What else?'

'Faith yelled at Nick to keep away,' April continued as her mind constructed the scene she hadn't been able to witness; she imagined Nick coming towards Faith with a knife in his hand. 'She'd transferred money, but it wasn't enough, and that's when he must have pressed the blade to her throat. I heard him shout at her as she struggled, she told him to stop and then she screamed. Maybe the cut to her throat *was* an accident.'

'Maybe.'

'I didn't hear anything after that. I raced to the front of the house.'

'And nothing struck you as odd?'

'I didn't see her smile,' April repeated.

'But when you saw Nick, he was shocked and scared.'

April was pulled back to the last moments of Nick's life. 'When I went into the kitchen, Nick tried to say something, but he was choking on his own blood,' she explained. Remembering that Tara had been on the other end of the phone at the time, she asked, 'Did you hear him?'

'I could barely hear what you were saying.'

'I wish I knew what he'd been trying to tell me.'

'Me too,' said Tara.

'You're worried, aren't you?'

'I'd feel better if I could think of a good reason why Josh Peters wants to blame us and not the man who diverted money from his charity and lied about having an affair with his wife.'

39

'I was about to phone you,' Tara said when Justine arrived in the shop. 'We need to talk.'

'Yes, we do,' Justine said, the glint in her eyes a counterpoint to Tara's scowl.

As Tara led the way to the furthest booth, she remained alert to her surroundings. The morning rush was over and of the scattering of customers who remained, all were known to her. For the time being, there would be no interruptions from journalists demanding a quote from the support group that had spawned the Black Widow, as the press had dubbed Faith.

'I've had some interesting conversations online,' Justine said.

Tara rubbed her chest. Conflicting emotions weighed her down; guilt, fear, and a selfish desire to dismiss her doubts and let the dead rest, whether that was in peace or otherwise. 'I know you have,' she said when they had taken their seats. 'I've been checking Twitter.'

'Have you seen the things people are saying about us? It's getting ridiculous.'

'I can agree with you there.'

Justine leant across the table and lowered her voice when

she said, 'I think one of us is going to have to have a word with Jodie. I know she's only trying to defend the group, but she's doing more harm than good.'

'I was about to say the same to you. We agreed to release one statement, Justine. One,' Tara repeated for emphasis. 'You can't become embroiled in arguments because people choose to believe all the rubbish being spread by the media. Too many lies have been spun already and it's getting to the point where none of us can see the truth. You have to stop.'

Justine sat back and folded her arms, saying nothing as Michelle brought over their coffees.

'I'm not certain,' Tara continued when they were alone again, 'but I think one of the people you've been arguing with is Erin's husband. He's on Twitter as Peters J.'

'I know,' Justine said, not looking directly at Tara.

'Then you should also know that whatever we say can't undo the harm Nick caused. It can only add to it,' Tara said. 'We used to be a good team, didn't we?'

'I thought we still were.'

Tara wanted to believe that too. 'It's painful to see our group being attacked and, depending what happens in court today, things are probably going to get worse before they get better,' she said softly. 'You were right about our members needing support. April's struggling and she won't be the only one. I imagine that's why Jodie has been hitting out on social media.'

'You think?' replied Justine.

Tara stretched her back to loosen her shoulders. 'If I'm honest, I was being selfish postponing the meeting. My heart isn't in it like it used to be, but it was unfair of me not to consider everyone else's needs. Maybe we should call a meeting soon.'

'Without waiting for Faith?'

'I have no idea what to do about Faith, I really don't.'

'Does that mean you've seen through her at last?' asked Justine. Finally, she met Tara's gaze. 'I know we're all supposed to feel sorry for her, but we can't blame Nick for all the fractures in the group. It was never the same after she joined. *You* weren't the same.'

Tara went to say something but found she couldn't defend Faith as once she might. She couldn't defend herself for that matter.

'Faith brought conflict to the group long before Nick walked through the door,' continued Justine. 'I doubt you noticed because Faith's passive aggression was an art form and it was never directed at you. She picked on me for some reason.'

Forced to consider Faith's behaviour from Justine's perspective, Tara was shocked by what she saw. She took a breath but couldn't quite fill her lungs. 'You're not suggesting . . . Do you think she's homophobic? Because I swear, I never picked up on anything like that. I would have done something if I had.'

'It wouldn't be the first time I'd faced that kind of prejudice, but no, I don't think her dislike of me has anything to do with my sexuality,' she replied, but her posture remained tense. 'Faith's bullying is indiscriminate. She has her favoured few and it's tough luck if you're not one of them. The worst thing for me was, I didn't always recognise when I was under attack. She'd make the odd comment about my abilities and wrap it up as concern, but suddenly everyone was believing her version of who I was, including me for a while. It's so much easier to pick someone off when they've become isolated.'

Tara winced. 'God, I'm so sorry, I didn't realise that was how you felt.'

'No, Tara, you didn't *care* how I felt.'

341

'I am sorry,' Tara repeated. Her cheeks blazed with shame as she thought back to all the times she and Faith had laughed behind Justine's back. She would reprimand Faith from time to time by telling her that Justine was her friend, but Tara hadn't acted like her friend. 'You were the first person I opened up to about Mike and I'd be lost without you. You deserved better from me.'

Justine uncrossed her arms and let her hands drop onto her lap. 'I'll forgive you, if you'll forgive me.'

A shared smile eased the tension, but it didn't disappear entirely. 'What do I have to forgive you for?'

'The Twitter storm I created.'

'It was natural that you'd want to defend us from attack,' Tara replied. It wasn't how she would have responded, but that was because she wasn't as invested in the group as Justine. It was a sobering thought, but not an issue she needed to tackle today. 'My main concern is that Erin's husband seems to have a problem with us – assuming I'm right and he is the one who's been replying to your tweets.'

Justine dipped a spoon into her coffee, cutting into the foam. 'And that's the other reason I need to apologise,' she confessed. 'For a split second there, I wasn't going to tell you what I came here to say.'

'Which is?'

'Josh Peters sent me a direct message yesterday.'

Tara's heart sank. 'And what did he say?'

'Not much. He wants to meet,' Justine explained. When Tara's mouth gaped open, she added, 'You're invited too.'

'OK. Right. Good. That's good,' Tara stuttered.

'Who knows? We might be able to convince him to join the group.'

Tara went to take a sip of coffee but the cup knocked against her teeth. 'He called us toxic, Justine,' she reminded her friend. 'He won't be interested in joining, but I'd love to know what he's after.'

'I imagine he wants to know what lies Nick spread about his wife. It can't have been easy seeing Erin's name dragged into the headlines for all the wrong reasons.'

'When are you meeting him?'

'Six thirty.'

'Today?'

'I said we could meet in the Childe of Hale, but it's a bit too public, don't you think?'

'He can come here. I'll make sure we've finished closing up so the place is empty,' Tara said without enthusiasm. Her pulse was racing and her heart skipped a beat when her phone rang. She held her mobile at arm's length, as if she had spotted a spider crawling across the screen. She didn't recognise the number, but she suspected she would know the caller.

'Are you going to answer it?'

Tara connected the call and placed the phone tentatively to her ear. 'Hello?'

'I bet you didn't expect to hear from me again,' replied Faith.

Tara could hear the smile in her friend's voice but she couldn't return it. A man's death was no smiling matter. 'What's happened?'

'The buggers have let me out is what's happened. I can't believe it's taken this long and I hope to God I never have to go back there,' she said above the hollow rumble of what sounded like a diesel engine.

'Have the police dropped the charges?'

'No such luck. They've given me conditional bail and I

have to jump through all kinds of hoops until they come to their senses, but they will. Have you seen all the messages of support? God, it's so moving, Tara,' Faith said, her voice trembling as if she had just remembered she was the victim.

Justine stared at Tara, desperate to know what was happening, but Tara's gaze was drawn to the shop window and the car park beyond. She expected to see a black cab pull up at any moment. 'Where are you going now?'

'I'm on my way home,' Faith said with real emotion.

'To the house?'

Justine mouthed the word, 'What???'

'Too right I am,' said Faith. 'I need to sleep in my own bed. It's been exhausting having the police crawl all over my life, and I'm hoping that now they've finished with the house it means their investigations are nearing completion and we can all go back to the way we were.'

'But are you sure you're ready to go back there?'

'I know what you're imagining, and it will be hard,' Faith said, letting her voice catch. 'But Ella has been a godsend. She organised specialist cleaners to get in there first thing this morning, and I expect everything to be spick and span when I get home.'

'Is Ella with you?' Tara asked. She wasn't used to Faith talking about her stepdaughter in such glowing terms, which meant she had to be close. Why had it taken Tara so long to realise how two-faced Faith could be?

'Yes, I'm using her phone. The police still have mine, *and* my iPad.'

'They'll have their reasons.'

'I'm going to need you, Tara,' Faith warned, picking up on her dull tone. 'I can't take up all of Ella's time. She said she'd feel better if she knew I wasn't going to be on my own this evening, so I hoped you and April might come over after work? Don't worry, we can order a takeaway and stay in the sitting room.'

Tara flinched. 'I'd love to come over,' she said, pulling a face at Justine. She and her oldest friend were back on the same page. 'But I have a meeting later and I don't know how long it will last.'

'A meeting? Can't you cancel, or let Iain take over for once? I know I'm being selfish, but it's so hard going back there, and my nerves are shot to pieces as it is.'

'I might be able to come over later depending on what happens,' Tara said, being as honest as she could. She had no idea if speaking to Josh would make her feel better or worse about what had happened.

There was a sigh loud enough to be heard down the phone. 'I understand. You have pressures of your own, what with Molly running away like that. I knew there must have been a good reason for you not to be there that day. God, I wish you had been, it could have ended so differently,' Faith said. More firmly she added, 'But I don't want you to feel guilty about it. You were right to put your daughter first. I'm sure I would have done the same.'

It was true, Tara did feel guilty for not being there, but she didn't like the way Faith pointed it out. Passive aggressive was how Justine might describe it, but Tara let the comment slide. 'Have you spoken to April?' she asked.

'Yes. She said straightaway that she'd be there. So will you come?'

'I'll do my best,' Tara said with more conviction this time.

345

40

When April pulled up outside Faith's house she could see light shining from the windows. A regiment of spotlights lined the driveway and disappeared behind the tall shrubbery to lead callers to the front door where Faith had collapsed a week ago. She couldn't believe Faith had wanted to come back here. April certainly didn't.

She had taken some persuading to accept Faith's invitation, so when Tara had phoned to suggest April stall her arrival until she could join her, she had quickly agreed. Tara was trying hard not to show it, but she was scared, and it had been most apparent the other night when she questioned April over her account and how it compared to Faith's. It was understandable, April supposed. Tara hadn't been there and she hadn't heard Faith's scream. April could recall it far too easily, and clung to the belief that Faith had been placed in an impossible position. She hadn't gone into the house intending to kill Nick.

It was Faith's smile that bothered them both. As much as it pained April, she could easily believe that their friend took some perverse satisfaction in knowing Nick had died for what he had tried to do to her.

As she waited for Tara to arrive, April opened the window a crack to stop the car steaming up. She could hear a siren in the distance, a sound that had been frustratingly absent when April had stood next to the pool of blood that cooled and congealed around Nick's dead body. Trapped in the memory, April jumped when she heard a door slam. There were footsteps coming from Faith's house and a figure appeared on the driveway. It took a heart-stopping second to realise the woman slipping through the gates wasn't Faith.

Whoever she was, she spotted April immediately. She was young, smartly dressed, and walked towards the car with a confidence that suggested she belonged there and April didn't. She bent down to take a better look at the driver.

'Can I help you?' she asked.

'Erm, no. I'm waiting for a friend,' April said as the two women sized each other up. There was a moment of mutual recognition.

'Are you April?'

'Yes, and I'm guessing you're Ella.'

Ella smiled. 'Sorry about that, you can't be too careful. I've already caught a handful of journalists snooping around, although I don't think anyone's twigged yet that Faith's back in the house.'

There was an awkward moment where neither knew what to do. They were talking through a tiny gap in the window and with the engine switched off, April couldn't lower it further. Seeing that Ella wasn't ready to continue on her way, April got out of the car and joined her on the pavement.

'How is she?' asked April.

'In a foul mood.'

'She's been through a lot.'

'So she keeps reminding me,' Ella said. 'I want to feel sorry for her, really I do, but I can't help thinking this mess is of her own creation. You would think age and experience would have hardened her.'

A chill breeze bit at April's neck and she wrapped her jacket around her. 'I'd say it had.'

'But it should never have come to this. I don't understand why she didn't see through this man straight away.'

'We did try to warn her.'

'But she wouldn't listen,' Ella finished for her. She shook her head. 'It was the same with Dad. Why does she fall for such utter bastards?'

'Your dad wasn't a bastard though,' April said with a nervous laugh, assuming she had misconstrued Ella's meaning.

'She didn't talk about him? I thought your group shared everything,' Ella said, but she could see from April's expression that she was wrong. 'Of course she didn't tell you. Faith won't admit to anyone what Dad was really like. It's probably why she's just kicked off. She hadn't realised the police would want a statement from me, and I'm guessing my recollection of their marriage isn't the same as the one she gave them.'

'We all want to help her, but if she isn't being honest with herself, how can anyone else believe what she says?' April said.

Ella looked back to the house before meeting April's eye again. 'You're a good friend, right?'

'I'm trying to be,' April admitted. 'Help me understand, Ella. What was your dad really like?'

'Ruthless,' Ella said simply. 'When he grew tired of Mum, he planned his escape meticulously so he could screw her over. He claimed the business was failing, and lo and behold, when it came to calculating the divorce settlement, his company was pretty much worthless – on paper. An accountancy sleight of hand. And our family home was registered as a company asset to be used to offset his alleged debts.'

'I did wonder why it was Derek who kept the house.'

'Strangely enough, the business picked up after Mum was forced to settle. Dad told me what he did. He was quite proud of it.'

Setting aside the image of the doting husband Faith had kept alive, April made a start at deconstructing what she had been told. 'Faith complained his company was worthless when he died. She said it was because she didn't know how to run it without him, but that wasn't the whole truth, was it?'

'It was worthless because he wanted it to appear worthless. Like I said, he was a careful planner.'

'He was going to divorce Faith too?'

'I wasn't speaking to Dad that much before he died, but I saw enough to pick up the signs. He was getting ready to dump her, no doubt about it.'

'Was there someone else?'

'That wasn't Dad's style. He preferred to stay squeaky clean,' she said. She bit her lip. 'Faith claims she didn't become involved with Dad until after his divorce, and I believe her, but they had met. Mum remembers her from a holiday long before there was any hint Dad wanted a divorce. He kept Faith dangling while he prepared the groundwork for shafting Mum.'

'Do you think Faith realised history was about to repeat itself?'

'It could be that she's living in denial, or maybe it's us she wants to fool,' Ella said, with a shrug. 'All I know is that it's me who has to deal with the messes my dad left behind. I'm guessing you're aware I have a legal interest in the house, but

I swear the only reason Dad put it in the will was to wind both of us up. It's a heavy burden sometimes because, as Faith has probably told you, Mum is bitter about losing the house, but I do my best to make both of them happy. I love Faith and her funny ways, but lately she's been bloody difficult to like. Someone needs to talk sense into her before she gets into more trouble.'

'That someone would be me then,' April said, wishing Tara would hurry up.

'I'm worried about her, April. We all know she has a temper, and if this goes to court, I don't think the jury will see her in her best light.'

'I'll see what I can do.'

When Ella pulled her into a hug, April shouldn't have been surprised. As with Derek, Faith's stepdaughter wasn't anything like April had been led to believe. She would have liked to continue their conversation, but Ella had to go and April had to stay.

She was about to return to her car when Ella's receding footsteps found an echo. Another figure appeared on the driveway. Faith opened the gate.

'I thought I heard voices,' she said, leaning out but not stepping onto the pavement. She glanced down the road at Ella's retreating form but made no comment.

April locked her car with a thud that reverberated through her body. 'How are you?' she asked.

'Let's get in first,' Faith whispered.

The front door had been left wide open and as Faith stepped into the welcoming light, she couldn't have been more different to the woman who had sat on the doorstep clasping a bloodied hand to her throat. Wearing a pair of linen trousers and a pink shirt, Faith's make-up gave her cheeks a bronzed glow that was reminiscent of a Mediterranean holiday rather than a spell in prison, and her smile was warm and relaxed. If she had been upset by her recent argument with Ella, or the events of Valentine's Day for that matter, it wasn't showing.

'Come in before you catch your death,' she said, pulling April inside.

It was a relief to be away from the doorstep, but the hallway held horrors of its own. 'I'm fine,' she said as Faith helped her out of her jacket.

'No you're not, you're shaking,' Faith replied. 'I felt exactly the same, but we'll settle you in the sitting room and you'll feel much better.'

April followed a trail of jasmine and sandalwood into a room immersed in the soft glow of candlelight. Faith was pulling out all the stops, but the scented candles couldn't disguise the smell of death that lingered in April's memory. Above the crackle of fire from the log burner, she could hear Nick's last gasps for air.

'Here,' Faith said, handing April a takeaway menu. 'Pick anything you want, and I'll put in our order once Tara arrives. Don't worry, we can eat on our knees. I don't intend going into the kitchen except to fetch our drinks.'

One look at the photos of pizza dripping melted cheese was enough to make April swallow hard. 'I don't think I could face food. Could I have a glass of water for now?'

Faith's bright smile faltered and her voice reflected some of April's anxiety when she said, 'You're right. I'm not sure I could eat anything either. I felt ill from the moment I stepped through the door.' She picked up a glass stained with bright red lipstick marks and drained what was left of her drink.

Tilting the glass towards April, she added, 'Are you sure you won't join me in something stronger?'

'I'm driving.'

April perched herself on the edge of an armchair as she waited for Faith to fetch the drinks.

'Are you sure you wouldn't like a little brandy to put some colour in your cheeks?' Faith called from the kitchen.

'No,' April tried to call back, but her voice was lost to an echo that floated across her mind. 'No!' Faith had yelled. 'Keep away from me!' Nick would have been crossing the kitchen towards her with the knife in his hand. Faith may not show it, but she had been through a traumatic experience. April had to keep reminding herself of that.

When Faith reappeared, she placed a tray on the side table next to April. There was a bowl of nuts, two tall glasses and a smaller one filled with a dark amber liquid. 'I couldn't hear you,' she said, 'so I brought you the brandy anyway. My God, you look like you need it.'

'Thanks,' April said, taking the shot glass Faith pressed into her hand.

Faith lifted up her gin and tonic. 'Cheers,' she said.

The brandy warmed April's tongue and loosened the muscles in her shoulders. She rubbed the back of her neck and noticed Faith do the same.

'How are you?' April asked.

'On the mend,' she replied as her hand moved to the scar on her neck. A newly painted fingertip followed a sharp, thin line about three inches long. Fortunately, she hadn't needed stitches. 'It's the mental scars that will take longest to heal.'

When Faith sat down on the overfilled sofa, she kicked off

her shoes and tucked her feet beneath her. April tried to relax too and took another sip of brandy.

'I hope Ella was polite,' Faith said. 'She can be a bit of a madam.'

'No, she was lovely.'

When Faith extended an arm towards her, April tried not to flinch. Faith was only reaching for the bowl of nuts and, after scooping up a handful, she popped one in her mouth. 'What did you talk about?'

'She said you're not happy with what she told the police about Derek.'

Faith scowled. 'That's an understatement.'

'She's worried about you, Faith.'

'Oh, don't be fooled. She might wrap it up as concern, but that child is determined to muddy the waters. Why my marriage should have anything to do with the police investigation is beyond me.'

'They'll want to understand your frame of mind at the time of the attack. Nick was trying to take Derek's place after all,' said April. 'And I'm sure Ella wasn't intending to cause trouble.'

'Take it from someone who's known her for ten years and not two minutes, the only thing Ella is worried about is this house.'

It was an odd thing, listening to Faith and not being able to trust what she said. Faith's stubborn determination to cling to her false beliefs was going to lead to a serious miscarriage of justice if she wasn't careful. April had to make her see sense, but she couldn't do it on her own. She wished Tara would hurry up.

'Ella thinks Derek was going to divorce you.'

'Rubbish.'

April brought the shot glass to her lips and was surprised

to find it empty. 'Faith,' she said, 'I know from experience how hard it is to admit your husband wasn't the man you thought you'd married – or thought you'd lost – but at least I can keep Jason's secrets to myself. You don't have that luxury. If the police can't believe what you tell them about Derek, how are they meant to believe what you say about Nick?'

'There was no proof that Derek was intending to leave me.'

'But you must have known how he tricked his first wife. Ella said he was quite proud of it. And when you checked his business accounts after he died, it would have been obvious what he had planned.'

Faith tutted. 'You and Ella did have a cosy chat, didn't you?'

'She's not the only one worried about you,' April said. 'Your judgement last week must have been affected by past experiences. Derek tried to take everything from you, and Nick was doing the same.'

'Nick assaulted me, remember,' she said, lifting her chin to expose her scar again.

'You'd survived one manipulative man only to be taken in by another. That must have hurt,' April said. 'Please, Faith. Talk to me.'

Faith stared into the fire. 'Derek never cheated on me,' she said as flickering flames cast shadows across her face. 'But he could be cruel. I didn't like how he boasted about the divorce, or how he made Ella squirm whenever she was forced to beg for handouts. But more fool her for coming to him if she hated him so much.'

'Maybe she was checking that you were OK.'

'Well, if Ella says that, it must be true,' Faith said. 'Everyone seems to have an opinion on my life these days. Have you seen the rubbish online?'

354

'The public's coming out in support, Faith.'

'And in the process they're grabbing their fifteen minutes of fame by claiming they knew me,' she snapped. 'It doesn't matter what I say or don't say to the police. They'll be reading that load of nonsense.'

'Are you upset by what some of your colleagues have said?' April asked, guessing that Faith wasn't too happy about being caught overstating her job and her qualifications.

'Why would work bother me?' Faith asked, either genuinely confused or not willing to acknowledge the specifics of her deceit. 'It's the principle of the matter, April. I have a right to my privacy.' Draining her glass, she added, 'Do you want another brandy?'

'I'll stick with water.'

'Any idea how long Tara will be?' Faith asked, rising to her feet.

'It's hard to tell.'

'I wonder if it's support group business. They've been coming under fire of late,' she said. 'And maybe they do have questions to answer.' She raised an eyebrow. 'Tara's not with the police now, is she?'

'No. Definitely not.'

Faith sighed. 'I know I shouldn't say this, but I can't believe she's letting me down again. What on earth can be so important for her not to be here?'

April picked up her water. Tara had told her not to mention the meeting with Josh. It could be something or nothing, and it made sense not to worry Faith unnecessarily. It wasn't that they didn't trust her. 'I'm sure she'll tell us when she gets here.'

'Fine,' Faith said with a waft of the hand. 'Everyone else can keep their secrets apparently.'

41

Tara took slow, mindful breaths as she wiped down the shop counters, but each time she inhaled, her chest remained stubbornly constricted.

'There's a car turning into the car park. I think it's him,' Justine said. She was on guard by the door, waiting for Josh while searching the shadows for any roving reporters on the hunt for a scoop; and their meeting would certainly qualify as that. 'Oh, hold on, he's with someone.'

Hoping Justine was mistaken, Tara joined her for a closer look. To her horror, she recognised both figures walking towards the shop. She took off her apron and stepped away as Justine opened the door and beckoned them in.

'You must be Josh,' Justine said, shaking his hand. 'I'm Justine.'

Josh turned to his companion. 'This is Olivia, Nick's sister.'

'Oh,' Justine said. 'Oh, I see.' Her eyes darted to Tara, who was making a good show of being preoccupied closing the blinds.

'I was the one who asked for the meeting,' Olivia confessed. She too was watching Tara. 'I didn't think you'd agree if you knew it was me.'

'Shall we sit down?' Justine asked. 'Would you like a drink, or something to eat perhaps? Tara makes the most amazing cakes.'

'Water is fine,' Olivia said. It was clear she was going to be the spokesperson.

While Tara fetched four glasses, Josh and Olivia were directed to the booth closest to the door. Neither took off their coats and, when Justine joined them, they all waited for Tara in silence.

'What is it you want?' Tara asked after setting down the glasses and taking her place next to Justine. It was the first time she had looked directly at Olivia and her heart wrenched. Her eyes were Nick's eyes, and they were jagged with raw grief.

Olivia gulped hard. 'I want to know what happened. What made her attack him? The police won't tell me, and the papers are making it up as they go along.'

The blood drained from Tara's face. She didn't want this conversation, and Olivia was right to presume she wouldn't have agreed to meet her. 'Nick was—' She paused and failed again to fill her lungs. 'He was trying to extort money from Faith. He attacked her and she defended herself.'

'I don't believe it. I won't believe it,' Olivia said, reaching for her glass. Without looking up, she asked, 'Was it my fault? Was she angry because of the things I told you?'

'I don't know,' Tara said, her voice hoarse as if her throat refused to be complicit with the lie.

'But you did tell her?'

'Yes.'

'I'm so sorry,' Olivia replied, repeating what she had said in her tweet. 'I shouldn't have said the things I said. I—' She couldn't go on and attempted to sip her water. It slopped in her hand as the first sob escaped.

Josh set the glass down for her, then squeezed her hand. 'We were expecting your other friend to be here,' he said. 'We saw the photo of the support group and recognised you both.'

'April is one of our members, but Justine and I run the group,' Tara replied. 'Although I should add, Justine wasn't aware that I'd gone to the fundraiser.'

'Why did you go?' Josh asked.

'Faith is a close friend of mine and I was worried that the attachment she was forming with Nick had happened too quickly. We – I was also concerned that the information Nick had disclosed to the group had been lacking.'

'I was the one who initially accepted Nick into the group,' Justine offered. 'He told me that he and Erin hadn't been married, but there was no suggestion of an illicit affair.' She blushed before adding quickly, 'Not that there was an affair. That was another lie Nick told us after we discovered Erin was married to someone else – you. And I'm so sorry that particular piece of misinformation has been leaked.'

'That's not why we're here,' Olivia said. She took a shuddering breath and pulled back her shoulders. 'Maybe Nick wasn't perfect but neither was he the monster being described in the papers. I was wrong to say what I did about him that night. I was drunk. My brother was a good man. A weak man, yes, but he had a good heart. Whatever happened in that house, I don't believe he'd attack a woman.'

'Faith has a knife wound to her neck,' Tara said, comfortable with some facts at least.

'What's she like?' Olivia asked. 'Could she have been hysterical?'

'No, I don't think so,' said Tara.

Josh leant forward. 'What we're struggling to understand is why Nick would turn to violence. What was he like in the group? Did he show his anger there? Was it encouraged?'

'Absolutely not,' Justine replied. 'If anyone showed anger it was—' She stopped before she could let Faith's name slip. 'It wasn't Nick. He was quiet and charming.'

'While he lied to us,' Tara added, needing to remind them all that even the dead had their faults. 'And he must have had a ruthless streak to do what he did to Erin.'

Olivia took the blow without flinching. 'You don't know him like I did. My brother was the kind of person who got what he wanted without even trying. God knows how he passed his exams, and when he landed a job investing other people's money, it was like a game to him,' she said. 'It was me who introduced him to Erin and when they announced their engagement, I took it as a sign that he was ready for the grown-up stuff, but it turns out he wasn't. When she got sick, he used his career as an excuse and ran away like a frightened child.'

Tara took in Josh's silence as much as Olivia's words. She could understand why Nick's sister would rush to defend her brother's name, but why was Josh there? 'Erin must have been devastated when they split up,' she said, to test his reaction. There was none.

'To be fair, they both were,' said Olivia. 'And I know Nick doesn't deserve any sympathy for what he did, but Erin forgave him eventually. Tell them, Josh.'

They all looked at him, and Josh was obliged to respond. 'Erin spent her last months getting her affairs in order and that included resolving her feelings about Nick's abandonment.

They met – but only the once,' he said. 'It definitely wasn't an affair – that was a complete fabrication. Nick may have declared his undying love, but Erin didn't reciprocate those feelings. All she wanted was to show him what it was like to be the better person.'

Talk of Erin's final months triggered Tara's memories of Mike. She had encouraged her husband to do all the things he had put off while building his business and making a family. He had suggested a holiday to Paris, wanting to fulfil a dream of hers rather than one of his own, but the journey would have killed him. She might have killed him herself if he'd suggested a catch-up with an ex-girlfriend.

'Why are you telling us this? It doesn't change what happened,' Tara said, wanting this torture to be over.

Olivia's jaw was set firm. 'Because that night at the fund-raiser, I was angry and I shouldn't have been. I got it wrong. If only Nick had returned my calls sooner.'

'Does that mean you spoke to him before he died?' asked Justine.

'I'd tried to phone him that Sunday, once the hangover was clear,' Olivia began. 'It took a few hours, but he did call back. He admitted he'd been avoiding me and said he was sorry. There'd been a cash flow problem, but he was about to settle all of his debts, and mine was top of the list.'

Like most things Tara had heard lately, her first response was to challenge. 'Did you believe him?'

'Not then, I suppose, but the money appeared in my account the next day.'

'He wasn't broke?' Tara asked.

'Not unless it was your friend who bailed him out.'

Tara shook her head. 'No, Faith wouldn't have done that.'

360

'Shouldn't you be telling this to the police?' asked Justine.

'I already have,' Olivia replied. 'I spent yesterday at the station, telling them what I'm telling you. Nick had money, and by all accounts, business was booming. My brother would never threaten a woman, for any reason, and especially not her. He spent half of our last conversation telling me how amazing she was and how much I'd like her.'

With a hand curled around her glass, Tara stared at her fingers through the water. How could something so transparent give such a warped view? 'I understand why you would want to believe what Nick told you, but the fact remains he forced Faith to transfer money to him, the police have evidence.'

'I don't know why Nick would do that,' Olivia said as a fresh wave of anguish twisted her features. 'I can't believe it. Maybe if I'd warned him about speaking to you he would have had time to think things through before Faith challenged him, but I didn't know who you were or if you'd tell her. And I was ashamed of what I'd said. Deep down, Nick was a good man.'

'Only if you ignore some serious character flaws,' said Tara as kindly as she could. 'What about the fraud at his old firm?' Looking directly at Josh, she added, 'He was callous enough to take money raised in Erin's memory.'

'That's not true!' Olivia said, raising her voice. 'I asked him about it and he admitted he'd been sacked, but he swore he didn't take a penny for himself, and was never going to. It was a vicious rumour. He wouldn't dishonour Erin like that. He loved her more than life itself and she died loving him too.' She took a couple of sharp gasps to contain her tears. 'Oh, God, this is killing me.'

Before Tara could respond, Josh rose quickly to his feet. 'Sorry, I need some air,' he said.

Olivia was too consumed with her own grief to notice Josh's distress, but Tara couldn't ignore it. Leaving Justine to console Nick's sister, she followed Josh out of the door. She checked the time. April would be waiting for her.

Josh stood with his head in his hands and his forehead resting against the wall. He didn't acknowledge Tara's approach.

'Are you OK?' she asked.

'She didn't love him,' he whispered. 'Not the way Nick believed. Erin always said he was a fantasist.'

'Why are you here, Josh?'

He straightened up. 'Olivia got in touch when she saw my comments about your group on Twitter. She thought I was coming out in support of Nick, and I haven't had the heart to tell her the real reason.'

'Will you tell me?'

'I needed somewhere to direct my anger,' he said simply. 'You were right to say Nick had some pretty serious character flaws. I never met him, but I've often wondered why people fell for his charm.'

'Including Erin?'

'She loved *me*,' he insisted, revealing a glimpse of his anger. 'I was her husband and I lost her, not Nick. It made me sick to think a group of people who'd suffered more than he could ever know had been fooled into supporting him. Nick threw Erin away, for fuck's sake. She should never have seen him that last time. It only fed his fantasy.'

'And I wish we'd expelled him from the group as soon as we found out he'd lied about their relationship,' Tara said.

'But in the end, we're not responsible for what happened. We didn't make Nick do what he did.'

'But we each played our part,' Josh said, holding her gaze.

At first Tara thought the comment was a dig at her but then she registered what he had said. 'Wait, are you saying you played a part too?'

'The one thing that kept me going after Erin died was raising money in her memory, so when I received an unexpected donation and tracked it back to Nick's little fundraiser, I was furious with him. I spoke to his bosses and made it clear that he wasn't acting on our behalf.'

'Because you thought he was misappropriating funds?'

Josh couldn't look at her. 'Because he had no right to be a part of the legacy I was building for her. His company investigated the matter thoroughly and I wasn't surprised when they came back and said there was no evidence of fraud. I knew he'd be innocent, but still,' he said. He took a breath. 'I threatened to go public if some form of action wasn't taken, and no investment bank wants that kind of publicity. That's why Nick was asked to leave.'

'Did he know it was you?'

'Yeah, but he didn't put up a fight. I guess he took the punches because he knew he deserved the punishment,' Josh said. 'I'm not proud of what I did.'

'Does Olivia know?'

Josh shook his head.

It was going to be a long night, Tara realised. She couldn't be in two places at once, but the choice was an easy one. She would phone April and ask her to abandon their evening with Faith. They would rearrange, but that prospect held fresh horrors. How was Faith going to react when she discovered the accusations they had made against Nick were false? He hadn't been in debt. He hadn't committed fraud.

'If I'm honest,' Josh continued. 'I've been trying to blame the group because I don't want to consider that it was my actions that led Nick down this dark path. He'd been labelled a fraud so maybe that's why he decided to act like one. Does that sound like the person you knew?'

'If you're asking if Nick was angry and embittered, no, he wasn't. If anything, he was as laid back as Olivia describes.'

With a sinking feeling, Tara realised that Olivia's view of her brother, however biased, couldn't be ignored. Nick wasn't the type to threaten a woman. This idea that he had a fantasy about knives had come from Faith, and Tara was learning not to take her word for anything.

Except there was the cut on Faith's neck, and proof that Nick had forced her to transfer money. The evidence was there, and yet Tara could feel the story Faith had woven coming undone. With a sudden jolt, Tara found the loose thread. 'Nick admitted to the fraud.'

'To you?'

'No, to Faith. He laughed at her and said he liked taking money from dead people.'

Josh kicked his shoe against the pavement. 'I'm not his greatest fan, but I don't see why he'd admit to something he didn't do.'

'I agree,' Tara said. 'I think you need to tell the police what you've just told me, and soon.'

Josh rubbed a hand across his face. 'I was hoping to keep the charity out of any scandal, but you're right. It was my mistake and I have to own up to it,' he said. 'But what about your friend? This isn't going to look good on her. Do you think she was confused?'

'I don't know. What other explanation is there?' Tara asked, but it wasn't a question for Josh. 'First things first. You need to go back in there and explain everything to Olivia. She deserves to hear it from you.'

With his head hung low, Josh made a move towards the door, but Tara didn't follow. He looked back. 'Are you coming?'

'I need to make a quick call first,' she said and was dialling April's number when Josh disappeared into the shop.

Her friend answered on the first ring. 'Hi, Tara. Are you on your way?' she asked.

'I don't think it's a good idea either of us seeing Faith tonight,' Tara said as she began pacing. 'Oh, April, I've had the worst evening. Olivia's here and Josh has just told me Nick wasn't trying to steal any of the money he raised in Erin's name. Josh made a false accusation because he was angry. But that doesn't make sense. Faith definitely told you Nick admitted it, didn't she?'

'Yep.'

Tara frowned. She was trying to work out why April sounded so chirpy, but then she heard Faith's voice in the background.

'I hope Tara's not bailing out again.'

'Oh, God. Are you with her?' Tara asked April.

'Yep.' Her voice was more of a squeak now.

'Can you get out of there?' Tara asked, but she already knew she couldn't leave April to deal with this alone, not again. 'Never mind. Hang in there and I'll be there as soon as I possibly can. If we do this, we do it together.'

42

Tara's arrival was taking longer than April would have liked and Faith was knocking back the G&Ts at an impressive rate. It was hard to know who Faith was anymore and, as she gave an account of her recent incarceration, April's attention drifted over to the bookshelves. She was looking for some hint of her friend's true identity, only to find a confusing collection of fiction and non-fiction titles. There were romance novels next to autobiographies, cookbooks rubbing shoulders with thrillers, and a wide selection of practical guides, including several on the subject of grief.

'I'm sorry if I'm boring you,' said Faith.

'You're not. I was just looking at your books.'

'Many of them were Derek's. I expect I'll have to throw them all out if I move.'

'I never looked back when I left my flat,' said April.

'Hardly a comparison,' Faith replied. 'I've fought so hard to stay here, but now that I have no tenant and no job, it's going to be tough. I only agreed to redundancy because I thought I was going into business with Nick.'

'The papers said the redundancy was compulsory.'

'Then who am I to argue?' Faith replied coldly. 'It's so annoying that they can make money out of printing my so-called life story without paying me a penny. Someone suggested I set up a GoFundMe page to cover my defence costs. If it goes well, I could use the remainder to cover my bills, in the short term at least. It would be foolish to sell the house now. It's not as if it would attract the full market value given recent events, and I don't want Ella cashing in,' she added. 'She must be rubbing her hands with glee, thinking she can take it off my hands for a fraction of its worth.'

'I don't think she'd do that.'

Faith smiled. 'She's a sly one,' she warned. 'Watch her.'

When April's skin crawled, she didn't immediately understand why. She had been looking at Faith's mouth, and the way she formed her words was hauntingly familiar. April was back in the kitchen, crouching down in front of Nick. He had looked shocked and frightened as he tried to speak. She had thought he was asking for water, but now she realised the syllable she had heard was more of a '*chuh*' sound. His lips had moved to form the words that Faith had just uttered: 'Watch her.'

Oblivious to the fear constricting April's throat, Faith said, 'I know what you're thinking. How can I possibly want to stay here? And you're right, it won't be easy, but what choice do I have?' Her voice quavered and she took a sip of her drink. 'Nick made me believe I had a future to look forward to but it's been stolen – again. Why the hell does this keep happening to me?'

April wondered the same thing, but before she could respond, someone rang the doorbell.

'About time,' Faith said with a roll of her eyes before slipping out to answer the door. Tara appeared moments later.

'I'm so glad you're here,' April whispered as they hugged.

'I don't suppose you're drinking either,' Faith said from behind them. She had grabbed another handful of nuts and was crunching as she spoke.

'A coffee would be good,' replied Tara.

'Have you eaten? I wanted to order a takeaway, but April isn't hungry. I could see what's in the freezer. Nick might have left some frozen pizza.'

Faith talked as if he had simply packed up and left. There was no sign of the emotion or regret she had expressed earlier. It was as if those emotions had never existed.

'Coffee is fine,' Tara repeated.

Faith sighed as she picked up the tray. 'In that case, I won't be long. Make yourself at home.'

When she left, Tara turned to April. 'How is she?' she asked, keeping her voice low.

'Scaring me if I'm honest. I bumped into Ella outside and she told me they'd argued about the statement she'd given the police. Apparently Derek was planning to divorce her.'

'You don't say,' replied Tara, sounding tired rather than surprised. 'I was told tonight that Nick was a bit of a fantasist and I don't think he was the only one.'

Tara went on to tell April as much as she could about her meeting with Josh and Olivia, and by the end of it, April's legs were weak. 'What's going on, Tara? Has Faith told the truth about anything?'

'And what are you two whispering about?'

Faith was at the doorway with two coffees and a fresh G&T.

'We were talking about the flat,' Tara said. 'April should be able to move in next week.'

'You didn't tell me,' Faith said, admonishingly. 'Come on, sit back down. I want to hear everything.'

The three women took their seats and for perhaps fifteen minutes, they talked as old friends might. But April and Tara were less practised at the art of performance, and Faith eyed them beadily.

'I wish you wouldn't worry about me,' she said after a pause. 'You know what I'm like. I can weather most storms.'

'But after everything you've been through,' Tara said, 'it must have taken its toll.'

'I expect it has.'

The mug April was holding didn't feel safe in her clammy hands. She put it down before she asked, 'Did you really have feelings for Nick, or was it a financial arrangement?'

Faith's head tilted. 'Just because the world in general is poking its nose into my life, doesn't mean my friends have to do the same.'

The note of warning was enough to provoke a reaction from Tara. 'But we're the ones who have to defend you,' she said. 'You need to be open with us, Faith.'

Faith appeared to consider her position, giving April the courage to press on. 'You say one thing, but there are people out there who are going to contradict you. You talk about an unhappy childhood, but others say what a great team you and your dad made. You want us to believe your marriage was perfect, but Ella and her mum will testify that wasn't entirely true. Things will come out about Nick too. Only you know the whole truth, the good and the bad, and if you don't correct people's assumptions, they'll begin to mistrust you.'

369

'It sounds like they already are,' Faith said. Her lip protruded before she added, 'I don't care what other people think.'

'Well you should,' Tara said, 'because the police won't be relying on your word alone.'

'Are you two ganging up on me?'

'If that's what it takes, yes,' Tara replied, which was more than April would have dared say. 'Please, Faith. You need to be honest about what happened.'

Faith looked at her empty glass. 'I need another drink.'

When Faith disappeared to the kitchen, April rose to her feet. 'Tara, I think we should go. I can't believe I'm saying this, but when Faith told me about Nick's fantasy with knives and I said it was as if the future were already written, I'm starting to believe that Faith was the one holding the pen, not Nick.'

43

Stepping into the kitchen, Faith resisted the urge to hurl her empty glass at the nearest wall. She reminded herself that her friends had her best interests at heart and if she could remove all doubt from their minds, she was halfway to convincing a jury. This was simply another test of nerve. Every move, every word uttered had to be controlled and calculated. It was what she was good at. It was what she had done when she confronted the last person to betray her.

Nick had had his back to Faith when she entered the kitchen and was unaware of her soundless return. He was wearing a grey T-shirt and sweats and whistling to himself as he stirred a pot on the stove. Taking a moment to admire his muscular frame, Faith wished she didn't have to do this, but she would keep to the plan she had perfected on the drive home from Pickering's Pasture. She had already done the groundwork, adding just the right amount of jeopardy by sharing Nick's knife fantasy with April, but nothing was guaranteed. There remained one variable. Nick's reaction.

Slipping behind him, she whispered into his ear, 'That smells nice.'

'Hello you,' he said, turning with a smile. He kissed her gently. 'When I'm done here, I was going to take a long soak in the bath if you'd care to join me? There's champagne on ice waiting for us.'

'Sounds perfect,' Faith said, feeling a pang of sadness as she pulled away for what would be the last time. Nick had seduced her with promises he knew he couldn't deliver. She couldn't respect a man like that.

Wafting a hand in front of her face, Faith appeared overcome by the heat. 'Could you open a window?' she asked, tipping her head to the one above the sink. She wasn't sure April would pick up her cries, but old Mr Newton next door had the hearing of a bat.

As Nick did as he was told, Faith fetched her iPad from the breakfast table.

'Did you have a nice walk?' Nick asked. 'Or was there another crisis for you to sort out?'

'After convincing me to go, Tara didn't even show up.'

Nick picked up the annoyance in her voice and gave her a curious look. 'Is everything OK?'

'It will be,' she said as she logged into her bank account.

As Faith listened to April and Tara's whisperings from the living room, she placed her empty glass carefully on the counter. Remaining calm and being consistent had seen her through endless interviews with the police, and it was how she must remain.

She opened the fridge and took out a bottle of Indian tonic water, the second of the evening. She was tempted to add a splash of gin this time, but it was enough for her friends to think she was drinking away her pain.

'How can you not be freaked out being in here?' asked April.

Faith turned to find her staring at the spot where she would have found Nick slumped on the floor. Tara was standing next to her. 'Just because I'm better at hiding my feelings doesn't mean they're not there,' Faith said, her voice catching perfectly. 'Do you think I don't replay what happened over and over and over again? It's there in my head now. It won't go away.'

Faith had been loath to transfer a single penny into Nick's account, but her plan would succeed or fail on the trail of evidence she left behind. Anger swelled in her chest and she used it to eviscerate any remaining doubt. Men like Nick were the cancers that blighted women's lives and they had to be removed. She began to cry.

Nick turned at the sound, holding a wooden spoon that dripped globs of soup onto the floor. 'My God, Faith. What's wrong?'

As Faith placed her iPad on the chopping board strewn with vegetable peelings, Nick discarded his spoon and moved towards her. 'Don't come near me,' she warned.

'What is it? What's happened?'

'April's spoken to your sister. She told her everything,' Faith said. Tears trickled down her cheeks but when she saw Nick's shoulders slump, she wiped them away. 'So it's true?'

'If this is about my relationship with Erin, I can explain.'

'Just like you can explain why your sister isn't in Canada?'

373

'OK, I made that up,' he said. 'I didn't want you two to meet. I didn't want you to think badly of me.'

'So you admit you're a liar?'

'Only about that, I swear. And maybe I let you think Erin and I had had an affair, but it wasn't a million miles from the truth. We split up when she got sick because I was under a lot of pressure at the time and I couldn't handle it. I'd been offered a new job and, if I'm being honest, I used it as an excuse. I didn't want to watch her suffer, and she had family who were better equipped to look after her than me. But later, after she married Josh and she knew she was dying, she was desperate to see me. After everything I'd done, she still loved me, Faith. And if there had been some miracle cure for her, we would have got back together. We were meant to be.'

Faith's jaw clenched as she watched Nick put down the spoon. He thought he could talk his way out of this.

Aware that the pair of frightened schoolgirls by the door were scrutinising her every move, Faith took a sip of tonic water. Her hand shook and the glass knocked against her teeth. It was something she had seen many of her fellow members do after oversharing an aspect of their lives. She had learnt a lot from them, so much more than she had gleaned from text-books on the subject of grief.

'Why did Nick threaten you with a knife?' Tara asked.

'Seriously?' asked Faith. 'You want to do this now? Here of all places?'

'Yes, here,' Tara said. 'Why did it descend into violence so quickly?'

'I've explained it all to the police, but fine, make me go through it again,' Faith said weakly. 'When Nick knew he

374

wasn't going to be able to talk his way out of it, he decided to take what he wanted by force.'

'And he picked up the knife first?' asked Tara.

Faith refused to follow Tara's gaze to the stainless steel knife block. There were five slots, but only four knives. The missing one had been on the chopping board amongst a scattering of peelings that Nick had made a half-hearted attempt to clear away. There had been more slivers of carrot and onion skins on the floor, tracing his path from chopping board to bin. At least Derek had been house proud, she had thought.

'I'm not interested in hearing your fairy tales,' Faith told Nick. 'You expect me to believe any woman would be interested in a heartless coward like you?'

'I'm not saying I deserved her forgiveness but—'

'And you don't deserve mine.'

'I know I don't, but that won't stop me trying,' he said, taking a step forward. 'I'll say whatever you want me to say to make you trust me again, Faith.'

'Then explain what kind of man makes money from a dead ex-girlfriend?' she asked as she rested her hand on the chopping board. She could feel the handle of the knife poking out beneath her iPad.

'That was a misunderstanding,' he said, raising both hands. 'I accept it looked bad at the time and I don't blame Josh for reporting me, but it was never my intention to take a penny of that money for myself.'

'Liar.'

'Please, Faith. Stop and listen to me,' he begged. 'I'm sorry, I should have been more honest with you, but that's what I'm doing now.'

375

'So are you or are you not up to your eyes in debt?'

Nick raked his fingers through his hair. 'Christ, is there anything Liv didn't say?'

'You tell me,' Faith said, but her heart was already sinking. Of all the things she had learnt about Nick, this was the one truth she couldn't overlook. 'How long would I have had to wait for you to pay any rent? As long as your last landlord?'

'Look, I was experiencing some cash flow problems after our holiday, but I've already paid Liv back. If I overstretched myself, it was only to make you happy.'

'No, you wanted me to believe you were something you're not. I'm surprised you didn't drag me off to some chapel in Vegas to marry me before I realised it was all a confidence trick.' It was what she had been expecting.

Nick's pained expression was almost believable. 'I chose Vegas because I was hoping you were my lucky charm and I'd win enough in the casinos to cover the holiday and more. I wouldn't dream of asking you to marry me, it's too soon for both of us, I know that.'

'So there isn't an engagement ring sitting in a champagne flute next to the bath?'

'No.'

For once, she believed him, and it peeved her. 'But marriage was your plan in the long term. We were going to have an "incredible partnership," you said.'

'A business partnership, yes,' he replied. 'And we could still make that work. With your self-discipline to keep me on track, I could double your investment in a year, easily.'

Faith laughed, although she wanted to cry. What a fool she had been. She had thought he loved her. She had been counting on it.

It had never been her intention to hook Nick, but he was a catch she couldn't ignore. At first, he was simply a means to solve her immediate financial difficulties, but the more he talked about involving her in his business, the more she wanted from him. There would be risks, but nothing that couldn't be managed. She would, if she had to, extricate herself from the marriage and take the business with her. Except Nick hadn't been offering her marriage, or a burgeoning wallet. He had humiliated her, and she couldn't forgive that.

Looking down at the chopping board, pure anger pumped through Faith's veins, but she was in control. She left the knife and picked up her iPad, logging back into her account before handing it to Nick.

'What am I looking at?'

'Call it payback.'

The confusion on Nick's face as he looked at the money transfer was imprinted on Faith's memory and had been the most compelling element of her account to the police. She caught herself before the memory could bring a smile to her lips. 'I told Nick the game was over and he admitted everything. He laughed at me, at all of us to be honest. I wasn't the only one he'd taken in.'

'Did he just admit to making up the affair, or was it the other stuff too?' asked Tara.

'I told her what he said,' she replied, narrowing her eyes at April who stood mutely beside her friend. 'He *liked* making money off dead people, and when he picked up the knife, I thought he was going to kill me. Why are you doing this to me? Would you rather I'd been the one lying in that spot April keeps staring at?'

'Just to be clear,' Tara said. 'You're saying Nick admitted he'd raised money in Erin's name for his own benefit.'

'Why is this such a shock when it was you two who passed on the information in the first place?' Faith asked, but the tone of Tara's voice was getting to her. Something was off.

'I've spoken to Nick's sister again,' Tara said. 'As you can imagine, Olivia's distraught. She told me that everything she'd said that night was wrong. She'd been angry with Nick for not telling her the real reason he'd lost his job, but she spoke to him just before he died. He was adamant that he never had any intention of keeping the money he raised, and I'm surprised he didn't tell you that.'

'And you're accepting the word of his sister? Seriously, Tara. Of course she'd claim his innocence. Like you say, the poor woman's distraught.'

'Erin's husband was there too. He was the one who made the allegations against Nick, and he admits it was out of spite,' Tara said. 'From what I've heard today, I don't doubt that Nick was weak and selfish, but he wasn't a thief. And he certainly wasn't violent.'

As April fidgeted next to Tara, Faith wondered which of her friends would burst into tears first. They were out of their depth, unlike Faith. She controlled her emotions, they didn't control her. 'You weren't there. You didn't see the way he looked at me,' she said, voice trembling.

'Two hundred pounds? I don't want this,' Nick said, lifting his gaze from her iPad. His eyes widened in shock. Faith had picked up the knife while he was distracted, and held it to her own throat.

'You said you loved me, but you lied.'

378

Nick had been immobilised by shock but Faith's wails forced him into action. He lurched forward. 'But I do love you!'

'No! Keep away from me!' she cried, pressing the blade against her skin.

'For God's sake! Will you just—' he said, edging closer.

'Stop! Leave me alone!'

Nick was within touching distance, but to Faith's relief, he didn't attempt to wrestle the knife from her grasp.

'No!' she cried out, following it up with a blood-curdling scream that had nothing to do with Nick's actions and everything to do with Faith's audience. She hoped to God someone was listening.

'OK, OK,' Nick said softly. 'Whatever you're about to do, don't. Please, Faith.'

'Admit it. When you joined the group, you were sniffing out the money. You picked the richest widow and you thought that was me,' she said, keeping her tone as low as his so only they could hear.

'Please, put down the knife.'

'Admit what you did.'

Nick's mouth fell open in horror as Faith scored the blade gently across her flesh. Blood trickled down her neck. 'Fine!' he said. 'I'll admit anything!'

Faith lowered the knife and allowed Nick to take it from her. She felt a sense of victory as she watched him place it on the counter. Her neck stung, but it had been a clean cut and would heal in time. Her work was done.

'It's easy for other people to judge, but you don't know what you're capable of until you're thrust into extreme situations,' Faith said to her friends. 'Nick was playing me and maybe he admitted what he did to intimidate me. I was defending myself, that's all. You know that.'

'Do we?' April said, having recovered her power of speech. She met Faith's gaze only briefly before looking towards the window that had been open that day. 'I never heard Nick laughing at you. I didn't hear him say much at all except that he loved you.'

'Shut up, April. You don't know what you're talking about.'

To Faith's indignation, April ignored her. 'Nick was still telling you he loved you, right up to the last.'

'You mean just before he held a knife to my throat?' Faith said, jabbing a finger at her scar. 'It wasn't Nick who screamed for me to get away from *him*, now was it?'

April frowned. The stupid girl was trying to dismantle the story that had been carefully crafted, and Faith couldn't let that happen.

'Whatever Nick did or didn't do in the past,' Faith continued, 'it's beyond doubt that he was after my money. How was I meant to protect myself, and not only me, but other women too? How would you have fared if Nick had come after you instead of me? Think about that, April!'

It was supposed to end there with the knife on the counter and Nick's fingerprints on the handle. From outside, Faith could hear Dexter yapping and if April had any sense, she would have phoned the police by now. When they arrived, Faith would explain how Nick had threatened her at knife-point, they would see the money taken from her account and they would lock him up. That was all she wanted, but when April hammered on the door, Faith was touched by her friend's selflessness. Shame and anger quickly followed and blazed in her cheeks as she recalled how she had tried to push Nick into April's path. If Jason had been a better husband and left his wife properly provided for, Nick might have chosen her as his victim.

As April pressed the doorbell, refusing to give up on her friend, Faith allowed her anger to overwhelm her and she grabbed the knife. She would protect April and women like her from this ever happening again. Before Nick could react, she plunged the knife into his neck. He clutched his throat as blood spurted far enough to splatter the walls, then dropped to his knees. It was going to be some cleaning job.

She waited as long as she could to ensure no one else would see Nick alive, but she took no pleasure in watching him as his convulsions slowed. He couldn't take his eyes from her as the blood pumped out from between his fingers, but Faith's attention drifted. Above the guttural sounds coming from his mouth and the persistent ringing of the doorbell, the pan of soup bubbled away. She stepped around Nick to turn off the hob and the oven. She didn't want the place burning down.

The more Faith thought about it, the more convinced she was that it was April's fault Nick was dead. Faith had done it for her, and she was annoyed that April couldn't see it.

'I'm sorry,' April began, 'but I think Nick's worst crime was maintaining a lifestyle he couldn't afford, just like you do. You were as guilty as each other, but he's the one who was killed for it.'

'Killed?' Faith asked. She took a sip of her drink and a slosh of tonic water dribbled down her shirt. 'I didn't plan any of this.'

'We know you didn't,' Tara said. 'But the truth is, Nick

wasn't the threat you thought he was. He had his faults, but he didn't deserve to die. Did he?'

The question was a plea from one friend to another. Tara wanted to believe Faith's version of events, but then so did Faith. She hadn't got it wrong. Nick was a threat. 'I loved him,' she whispered.

'Him, or the life he offered?' asked April.

'Am I being accused of something?'

'No,' April said, too quickly.

'Are you sure?'

April dared to hold her gaze. 'When I told you what Olivia had said about Nick, it was only when I mentioned his debts that you reacted.'

'And is that what you're doing now? Forcing me to react?'

Faith was good at facial expressions and the one she used with April was a gentle plea to stop overthinking everything. Thoughts like that could get someone killed.

'I watched Nick's life ebb away,' said April, reliving that day in all its gore. She was tougher than Faith gave her credit for. 'He wasn't angry or vengeful, he was scared, and not only for himself. He was scared for me, Faith. I thought he was asking for water, but he wasn't. He said, "Watch her", meaning you. Why would he think I was in danger?'

To give herself time, Faith turned back to the fridge. Her drink needed a slice of lemon. 'If this is where you're expecting me to confess all, I'm sorry to disappoint,' she said. 'You said yourself that Nick's words were incomprehensible.'

'Please, Faith,' Tara said. 'We know Nick didn't laugh in your face while admitting he'd lied to us. What else did you make up? It's time to tell the truth.'

'Is it really?' she demanded. 'Is Josh going to risk bringing

382

his charity into disrepute by admitting he had an innocent man sacked? I'm guessing not, otherwise he would have gone to the police, not to you. We use the little lies and half-truths to protect ourselves and those we love.'

When Tara shook her head, fresh anger rose through Faith's body like lava. 'Don't take the moral high ground, Tara,' she said. 'How would Molly feel if she knew you'd gone as far as booking into a clinic for an abortion? What would it do to her to know her first cries had snuffed out your Parisian dreams? And how much harder would it be for Lily if she knew you didn't want one, let alone two daughters? We all project the best images of ourselves.'

'She's a good mother,' April said as Tara's mouth gaped open.

'But are you a good friend?' When April looked to Tara, Faith smiled. 'I don't mean her. I was thinking of your other friends. Take Bree for example, or more to the point, her husband. Wouldn't he benefit from knowing the truth? And shouldn't Jason's parents know that their son was a lying cheat given how important you think it is to be honest?'

'Are you threatening us?' asked Tara.

Faith rounded on her. 'Do I need to?'

April and Tara gasped. From the corner of her eye, Faith could see the knife block, but there were only three knives there now. The fourth was in her hand and she was pointing it at her friends.

Faith could claim she had post-traumatic stress disorder. It was her first night back at the house and it would be under-standable if she were to suffer a flashback. She could tell the police she couldn't recall what happened. She had lost control and that part at least would be true. The knife felt good in

383

her hand, almost as good as watching the colour drain from April and Tara's faces. April was nearest the door to the hallway and her pale skin flickered blue from a light coming from outside the house.

'For fuck's sake, I was only cutting myself a slice of lemon,' Faith said, putting down the knife. She had recognised the flashing blue light for what it was. 'When did you call the police?'

'I didn't,' replied Tara. 'You were wrong about Josh. When I left him, he was on the phone to the detective running the investigation. Nick wasn't the man we thought he was.' There was more pain than fear in her voice when she added, 'And you're not the person I thought you were either.'

'I was defending myself,' Faith said, but as a single tear slipped down her cheek, even she didn't know if it were the truth or a lie.

Eight Months Later

Sharp heel taps on the pub's timbered floor made Tara turn in her seat, but it was only a young city worker who swept past their table to greet a friend. The place was busier than Tara expected for a midweek afternoon, but this was no quiet village. She was looking out onto Derby Square in Liverpool city centre with the Victoria Monument as its centrepiece. Close by but out of sight, was the monolithic concrete building that housed Liverpool Crown Courts.

'What time did she say she'd be here?' asked April.

'We've got ages yet. Did you want to order something to eat?'

'I'll just wait for my drink for now,' April replied, playing with the corners of the beer mat in front of her. 'Did she say what this is about?'

'I imagine she wants help processing everything that came out in the trial.'

When the waiter arrived with their drinks, April took a gulp of wine before placing it on the now-tattered beer mat while Tara sipped her lime and soda. She was glad it was over and thankful her stint in the witness box had been relatively painless considering she had appeared as a witness for the prosecution in a murder trial. The CPS had upgraded the manslaughter charge and rearrested Faith that last night at her house.

Fortunately for Tara, the majority of her evidence was undisputed. She had described the events leading up to Valentine's Day, and when it came to the small matter of Faith's frame of mind, what could she say? She hadn't seen Faith immediately before or after Nick's death and her testimony was mostly background noise. April, however, had been drawn into the battle between the defence and prosecution counsels.

'I made a complete mess of it, Tara.'

'You were as honest as you could be.'

'But I went in there thinking I was clear about what happened. The prosecution's theory that Faith had cried out to make it sound like she was under attack matched what I heard. And yes, I did think Faith capable of cutting her own neck. It wasn't exactly deep and there was more of Nick's blood on her than her own,' she said. She swallowed more wine. 'But the defence team really pushed this idea that Faith was a broken-hearted widow.'

'It was something she learnt to do well, thanks to us,' Tara said. 'It took me years to see through her lies and inventions. Imagine how difficult it's been for the jury to make sense of who she is. How many of Faith's character witnesses would go back and reconsider their testimonies if they knew how Faith had spoken about them behind their backs?' Tara was thinking of Ella in particular, but there was also Mr Newton, the neighbour Faith had blasted for his allegiance to the first Mrs Cavendish. He was a convert now, taking great pleasure in being Faith's hero of the hour.

'And meanwhile we're the treacherous friends,' April added.

'We took the stand and spoke the truth, that's as much as we could do.'

'Mine was more of a mumble between sobs. Molly did better than I did.'

'She was amazing, but then she didn't have to go into the court or face the same kind of brutal cross-examination you endured.'

'I wish I hadn't fallen apart, but the defence kept badgering me about my original statement. I should never have said it was Faith I heard telling Nick she loved him. If only Mr Newton had been listening in on that part of the conversation. Yes, I was confused about that bit, but not the rest – not about Faith claiming Nick confessed all.'

'He did love her, didn't he?' Tara said. 'It's so wrong that the trial has been more about his character than Faith's. If Nick were alive, I'd be having strong words with him right now about how selfish and irresponsible he was, but why the hell should a jury – or the nation for that matter – get to decide whether he deserved to die for it? He didn't. He really didn't.'

'Is there any doubt in your mind that she did it?'

The night Olivia had showed up at the shop with Josh, Tara had gone from worrying that Faith had overreacted to believing she was capable of premeditated murder, but even as the trial started, there had been lingering doubts. 'It was the forensic evidence that did it for me,' Tara said finally. 'Particularly the trail of Faith's footprints leading past Nick to the cooker. She had been more concerned about burning her dinner than the man dying on the floor.'

April rubbed her arms. 'Can we talk about something else? There's nothing any of us can do about it now.'

'You're right. It's over and it's time to look to the future.'

Despite Tara's optimism, neither woman could think of anything to say. April finished her drink.

'Iain's decided not to come back to the group,' Tara said at last.

'But you're going to stay involved, aren't you?'

'It feels like we've been limping along in the last few months and maybe it's time for a change of direction,' Tara said. She bit her lip. It wasn't going to be easy letting go, but hopefully her friends would make the process easier. 'Justine and I are organising a special meeting just so members can talk about the trial, but I want it to be my last one. I have a growing family and I keep telling myself they're my priority, but it's time I put my words into action.'

'Growing?'

Tara laughed. 'No, I'm not pregnant, although it's not beyond the realms of possibility,' she said. 'What Faith said about me not wanting kids wasn't a million miles from the truth. I've spent eleven years resenting being a mother simply because it was thrust upon me. Up until now, I never appreciated what I have. Mike didn't get the chance to see his daughter grow up, and it's the same with Joanna. That's my privilege, and I'm going to do my absolute best for them. I love my girls.' The swell in her heart washed over her and her smile broadened. 'And we're all going to love our new puppy.'

'Wow, you gave in?'

'And you can nip over to ours any time you like for some puppy time.'

'You won't be able to keep me away,' April said, although

she couldn't follow through with a smile of her own. 'How will the group go on without you?'

'You'll manage,' Tara said with a twinkle in her eye, but before she could say more, April straightened up. Her body stiffened.

'She's here.'

Tara had yet to meet Ella in person, but they hugged like fellow survivors. They ordered fresh drinks, but it was only when the small talk had fizzled into silence that Tara asked the question they needed to know. 'Has Faith sent you?'

'Good God, no,' Ella said. 'I'm sure if Faith wants to get in touch with you she will. They're expecting the jury to take a few days deliberating, but it's scary to think that she might be out soon.'

'Scary?' asked April.

'I'm as reluctant as you to see her again. My hope is they lock her up and throw away the key.'

After exchanging a look with April, Tara spoke first. 'But you defended her.'

'Believe me, I didn't want to, but I answered questions in court as truthfully as I could,' Ella said. She was quiet for a moment as the waiter arrived with their drinks. 'You're not the only ones who started to doubt Faith, but a lot of what I've discovered about her is still conjecture.'

'You think she set up the crime scene and killed Nick deliberately?' Tara asked, needing to be sure they were in complete agreement.

'Yes, I believe Faith is capable of murder.' Ella looked at April when she added, 'Your testimony was particularly compelling. I didn't know about Nick's alleged fantasy about knives.'

'Nor did anyone else,' said April. 'Obviously she made it

up. Literally minutes after me telling her Nick wasn't as rich as she assumed, she was planning his murder. I can't begin to understand how her mind works.'

'I can,' Ella said. 'That fantasy wasn't something plucked out of thin air.' She concentrated on turning the stem of her glass before continuing. 'This can go no further, and if it does, I'll deny it, and Mum most certainly will.'

April's jaw dropped. 'The fantasy wasn't Nick's, it was your dad's, wasn't it?'

'And not so much a fantasy,' Ella replied carefully. She flinched as if the thoughts she was about to share caused physical pain. 'Mum broke down after she heard you describe what Faith had said. That's when she told me Dad had attacked and raped her twice, once soon after he'd suggested a divorce and she'd refused, and again when she had the audacity to demand that she should keep the house and he should leave. She was too scared to go against anything he said after that. He held a knife to her throat, both times.'

'Shit,' April whispered.

Ella bent forward and covered her face with her hands. 'I knew he'd treated Mum badly, but I never realised how sick he was.'

Tara rubbed Ella's back and waited until she had straightened up before asking as gently as she could, 'Do you think he did the same to Faith?'

'From the way she talked about him, you would think he was a loving and devoted husband, but that was a lie, and I don't believe it's a coincidence that Faith described a fantasy that my dad liked to enact.'

'You have to say something,' said April. 'What if Faith is found not guilty?'

'It won't change Mum's mind, and our energies are better spent elsewhere.' Ella paused and took a breath, her composure returning. 'My doubts about Faith go back much further than what happened last February. She's always been a bit elusive about her past, and I was wondering if she ever spoke to you about her parents.'

'I know they died within a short space of time,' Tara said. 'I think Faith had lost them both by the time she was twenty.'

April gave a nervous laugh. 'You're not suggesting she killed them are you?'

'No, they both died from natural causes. I checked,' Ella added. 'Her mum had a stroke and her dad died from cirrhosis of the liver.'

'She told me her dad made her mum's life a misery,' said April. 'He was an alcoholic.'

Ella held her gaze. 'He was also a car mechanic.'

April and Tara reached for their glasses at the same time. If she hadn't been driving, Tara would have asked for something stronger. 'Faith mentioned he had a workshop and that she was expected to help out when he was too drunk to function,' she said. 'But until I saw comments on social media from people who remembered her working at the garage, I always presumed he was a carpenter or a joiner.'

'She fixed the horn on my car once,' April said. Like Tara, she was trying to join up the dots that had been laid in front of them. Her words were tight as if her throat had constricted. 'She rooted under the bonnet as if she knew her way around an engine, but I never questioned it.'

'If Faith was good at fixing cars,' Ella said, 'she'd have a good idea how to break them too.'

'You think she caused Derek's accident?' asked April, daring to voice what Tara had been thinking too.

'I didn't know Faith particularly well while Dad was alive,' Ella explained. 'But after he died, whenever she mentioned her parents and her dad's workshop, she was deliberately vague. I think there was a reason for that.'

'But she was away when the accident happened,' said Tara.

'Our theory is that she had been tampering with Dad's car in the weeks before it happened. The first two engine faults logged with the dealership would have been decoys. Faith could have loosened a connection to trip a sensor only to retighten it before a mechanic went anywhere near it. When the ABS warning light appeared the third time, she was about to go away on her spa weekend, and I imagine Dad had plans of his own. No doubt Faith convinced him that the fault was with the sensor, not the brakes.'

'She did,' Tara replied. 'She told the group how guilty she felt about it.'

'That's good,' Ella said. 'We'll need a statement from you.'

'We?' asked April. 'Who exactly is involved in this?'

'The car dealership have put me in contact with the insurers who settled the negligence claim. They're very interested in reviewing the case.'

'Do they still have the car? Might there be incriminating evidence?' asked April.

'No such luck, but I'm sure they gathered as much forensics as they could at the time. The car was a burned-out shell and I don't know how far we'll get making a case, but I have to try, not for Dad but for Mum.'

'Rosemary wants the house to go to you,' guessed Tara.

Faith would be stripped of her assets if it were proven that she had caused Derek's death.

'I can tell you now that I don't want it,' Ella said. She played with the wedding band on her finger. 'It's time I had a life of my own and if Faith comes out of this without a stain on her character, I'll happily give her my share of the house just to wash my hands of the whole thing.'

Tara reached over and picked up April's glass. With a nod of apology, she drained her friend's drink. 'Faith always did have the luck of the devil on her side.'

Movement outside the pub caught their attention. There were people milling around, excited reporters and cameras next to vans with satellite dishes. A news story was breaking.

'The jury didn't take long,' Ella said, checking her phone. 'Are you coming?'

'I'm not going back in there,' April said.

'I don't want to go either,' added Tara. She had no desire to hear the verdict. Her mind was already decided on the matter. Faith was guilty, and if by some chance she repented the actions that led to Nick's death, she wouldn't be the only one.

The meeting room bustled with nervous energy, although April noted that the circle wasn't as large as it had been at the beginning of the year. In addition to the gaps left by Faith and Nick, there were the spaces vacated by Tara and Iain, and Jodie was missing too. She hadn't taken kindly to Justine chastising her for her online comments, especially when Justine had been guilty of the same, but April expected her to return soon. The group would heal in time and there were already signs of new growth.

'How's everyone feeling after the meeting last week?' asked Justine.

'Stunned,' said Nadiya on behalf of them all.

Tara had kept to her promise of holding one last meeting to allow everyone to deal with the aftermath of Faith's trial. Unlike the courts, the group wasn't used to passing judgement, but they had reached a conclusion that fell somewhere between the verdict and the truth that Faith would never reveal.

'I know it's a big ask,' continued Justine, 'but I think going forward, we need to focus our attention on our own lives. It's natural that our thoughts will be pulled back to what happened from time to time, but we'll take it one meeting at a time.'

'We're going to miss Tara,' Steve admitted. 'She had a knack of keeping us in check. Sorry, that wasn't meant to be a reflection on you, Justine.'

'I fully accept that it's going to be tough without her, which is why I've enrolled some help,' Justine said, glancing to April. 'For those who don't know yet, I've managed to persuade April to share some of the administrative burden.'

April listened out for the mutters of dissent, but they didn't come. Other members had been canvassed, but no one else had been foolhardy enough to take on the role. 'I'm not trying to fill Tara's shoes,' she said.

'Except when it comes to supplying the cakes,' Nadiya replied.

'It's one of the benefits of living over a cake shop, and technically, they're still from Tara,' explained April. 'What I will be doing is taking over the accounts, so I'll be pestering you for subscriptions from now on, giving Justine more time to concentrate on the newsletter and organising events.'

'And on that note,' Justine added, 'I need to gauge opinion on whether or not we have a Christmas party this year.'

'Why wouldn't we?' asked Steve.

There were some nervous glances around their fragmented circle. No one wanted to point out the dangers of encouraging social interaction beyond the confines of the village hall.

'No decisions have to be made today,' Justine said when Steve's question remained unanswered. 'We're entering a new phase as far as the support group is concerned. None of us can ignore the past, we wouldn't be here if we could, but we can learn from it. We let go of what we can't change and nurture what makes us stronger.'

There was a spattering of applause around the room, something April had never seen before and it gave her the courage to pick up where Justine had left off. 'And if we're all ready to start the meeting, I'd like to introduce our newest member,' she said, offering a smile to the man sitting on her right. 'For those who haven't had a chance to say hello yet, this is Josh.'

The introduction wasn't entirely necessary. Josh had been unable to avoid the media attention surrounding Faith's trial. Some blamed him for setting Nick down a path of self-destruction, but Josh had weathered the storm, and for all the sponsors who had withdrawn support from his charity, there had been others to take their place.

'Hi,' Josh said with a nervous wave. He cleared his throat. 'I'd like to start with an apology. I said some unkind things about this group, but having spoken at length to Tara and Justine, and more recently with April, I've come to realise that it's too easy to judge from the outside. I was wrong to question the support you offer each other.'

'Good to hear it,' said Steve. His tone had an edge to it

and April knew he wouldn't be the only one with reservations. It was sad to witness, but the group wasn't as trusting as it had been when she had joined. Faith had left a festering wound and, although the last meeting had gone some way to excise the infection, it hadn't been removed completely.

Convincing Josh to join the group was part of the healing process and was as much for April's benefit as his. She needed to put things right where she could, and amongst her other challenges would be persuading Jodie back to the group, but there was something else more pressing. Faith had accused April of hiding unpleasant truths and she wouldn't let that stand. Faith would not have the last word.

'I'm sure we'll hear a lot from Josh in the coming months, but I thought we'd start by showing him how we, as a group, are committed to supporting each other. And the best way to do that is through example,' April said, only realising she'd run out of breath when her words caught in her throat. She took a breath. 'I want to show Josh that this is a safe place where we can share the most painful and difficult aspects of our grief without fear of judgement.'

There were a few nods, but no interruptions. It was April's time to talk. 'I haven't been entirely open with you about my relationship with Jason. I could blame Faith for making me believe I was better off editing my past, but I take responsibility for my own decisions,' she said as she cast a glance out of the window, expecting a shadowy figure to catch her eye. Faith continued to haunt her.

April still felt responsible for what had happened, not only that fateful day, but later in court. The case had come to rest almost exclusively on her testimony and that of Mr Newton. In April's opinion, Faith's implausible account of Nick's confession should have pointed to the right verdict. They had all been shocked when it hadn't.

Rather than dismiss April's claims, the defence had used Mr Newton's testimony to corroborate much of what April had heard pass between Faith and Nick, and some things she hadn't. When April had raced to the front of the house, Faith's neighbour had continued to eavesdrop as he made the call to the police. 'Fine! I'll admit anything!' he had heard Nick shout. Was that part of the confession Faith had referred to? The jury thought so and had returned a verdict of not guilty.

It was a shame that Ella's mum wasn't prepared to share what must be her deepest and darkest secret, but April held out hope that the historic case Ella was preparing would ensure Faith faced justice at some point.

For the time being, however, Faith was free, but that didn't mean she would be welcome if she dared to show her face. April may not have persuaded a jury that Nick was an innocent victim, but she had convinced her fellow members.

'If it's OK with you guys,' she said, returning her gaze to the lighted room. 'I'd like to share everything with you now.'

Justine reached over and squeezed her hand. 'Take your time,' she urged.

'After Jason died, I discovered he'd cheated on me with one of our friends. I thought I had two choices – to pretend it never happened and keep my memories unblemished, or to hate Jason for the pain he inflicted and tell myself he wasn't worthy of my grief. I can tell you now that neither of those options work.'

Her confession was met with initial silence and April wished Jodie was there with an expletive or two.

It was Josh who spoke up. 'I can't imagine how that must feel. It was bad enough that people thought Erin had been unfaithful.'

'It's been tough,' April said, 'and I wish I'd shared with the group sooner, but in some ways, it wasn't only my story to tell. Bree, the other woman, was and is married, and up until recently we worked for the same council. When I left, I expected to feel some relief, but that didn't come until Callum contacted me.'

'Is he her husband?' asked Nadiya.

'Yes,' April said. 'He wanted to meet me and I spent a sleepless night worrying about what he might say. Did he have suspicions of his own? Would I tell him about Bree and Jason if he asked? As it turned out, Bree had beaten me to it. They'd been trying for a baby without success and she must have decided that her conscience was getting in the way.'

'How did he take it?' asked Steve.

'He was a mess as you'd expect and wanted me to tell him what to do. I said he was lucky to have a choice of whether he and Bree had a future,' replied April. Her hands rested in her lap and she played with the wedding band on her right hand. She had come close to throwing it away after discovering the affair, but she was glad she hadn't. 'Knowing what I know now, I'd forgive Jason anything to have him back. Maybe not for good, but long enough to give him the chance to convince me we were worth fighting for. That's what Bree and Callum are trying to do, and I could tell that he still loves her. I told him I hope they'll stay together.'

'Is that really how you feel?' Steve asked.

April looked around the group. This was the one place where she could be honest. 'No, I'm bloody angry,' she said, but she was smiling because her anger was a normal reaction, as was the relief she felt washing over her. The wound was clean. It was time to heal.

The low sun peeked over the conifers in the back garden to bathe the kitchen in early morning light. Faith was sitting at the breakfast table with a freshly brewed cup of coffee and a warm croissant smothered in butter and a smear of jam. The deep red of the raspberries was enough to give her flash-backs to that terrible day, if she had a mind to, which she didn't. She wiped a blob of jam from the corner of her mouth and sucked her finger clean before picking up the papers scattered on the table.

Her future remained an evolving beast, but it was nice to see there were so many opportunities coming her way. There were requests for exclusive interviews, which she had initially declined only to receive new and improved offers. There was even an approach from a publisher to write a book, but Faith wasn't sure how any of this would be received by her growing army of supporters. The money raised in her name was more than enough to keep Faith comfortable for the time being and she didn't want to appear mercenary. She wasn't merce-nary. She simply had a strong belief that she deserved her fair share of life after too many years of suffering.

Faith had grown up in near poverty, missing out on a university education and the career path she deserved because, dead or alive, neither of her parents had sought a better life for their daughter. When Derek came along, she hadn't fallen for him as much as his lifestyle, but she had been a good wife and hostess. She had tried to be a good stepmother too, but it had all been for nothing. Derek hadn't appreciated a wife who had a will of her own, and when his interest had waned, he found fresh amusement by humiliating her. The first time her husband had pressed the sharp edge of a knife to her neck, Faith refused to be scared off. What followed was a race to secure a future at the other's expense.

It had been a close call as to who would cross the finishing line first. Faith had hoped to resolve the matter before Derek had completely stripped his company's assets, but she had to be careful. She had considered a confrontation and a scenario much like the one she had created with Nick. She had researched the most efficient wound to make with a knife, but had decided her best defence was to use a weapon that would leave no fingerprints. She had been at her creative best engineering an intermittent fault on the car that had been Derek's pride and joy. To cover herself, she had booked a hotel break hundreds of miles away from the scene of the crime before tampering with the brakes one last time. Suing the dealership for negligence afterwards had been a stroke of genius, and donating Derek's organs to save far more deserving lives had gone some way to assuage her conscience.

Faith had to give her father some credit for the efficient dispatch of an unwanted husband. He had taught her well during her unhappy childhood, although arguably the most important lesson had come from Faith's first failure. After watching her mother throw away her best years to a man who refused to drink himself to death, fifteen-year-old Faith had decided to expedite matters. An opportunity arrived unexpectedly one day when she saw her father working beneath a car, probably too drunk to stand. Sadly, he survived the crush because the jack she had loosened hadn't given way completely. The back injuries he sustained exacerbated his dependence on alcohol, and their lives had become more miserable as a result. Preparation was key; that was what Faith had learnt from her father, and it had almost been her undoing with Nick.

She accepted that she had acted impulsively that day, but it wasn't as if she had been motivated by any monetary reward. She had thought she was doing it for the greater good. She had believed the gossip April passed on to be fact, and had reacted instinctively. Or had she overreacted? Had Nick been nothing more than a selfish chancer with a dubious under-standing of love? As unthinkable as it was, had she made a mistake?

This conundrum gave Faith pause for thought as she mopped up the bright red jam with the last of her croissant. The pastry wasn't as buttery as Tara's, but Faith had no appetite for returning to Hale Village or seeing her so-called friends. Their loyalty had been tested and April and Tara were both found wanting.

Ella too had let her down. She had changed her phone number and would only speak to Faith via a solicitor. Faith suspected it was married life that had changed her. It was a shame because they had had such a close relationship, but if ties had to be cut, it would be on Faith's terms. Thanks to the generosity of the public, she had made an offer to buy Ella's share of the property, based on a reduced valuation, naturally. She awaited her response with anticipation.

Standing up to stretch her spine, Faith put the past behind her and gazed out of the window. The sun had broken free of the line of conifers that weren't as tall as they had been the week before. Mr Newton had sent his gardener over to trim them free of charge. He was a lovely man and had supported Faith at a time when others had waited expectantly for her to fall. She hadn't realised how lonely he had been since his wife died. Whatever else lay ahead for Faith, she would repay his kindness.

Acknowledgements

I should probably start with an apology to Hale Village for allowing my fictional characters to invade your community and take over your village hall: I hope my scene setting has done some justice to this little haven tucked in between the suburbs of Halton and Merseyside. I live only a short drive away from Hale and made many visits during the writing of this book, and I'd like to say a big thank you to the ladies I met at the village hall for allowing me to disturb their coffee morning. You were all so welcoming and friendly, and it was obvious that you love your village very much.

Thank you to my old workmates who I meet regularly at The Railway in Liverpool – to Julie Parry, Dave Holden, Ian Rogers, and Mike Thorpe – particularly Ian, who lives in Hale and gave me the idea for basing my latest novel there, and to Mike, who insisted Eastham got a mention. On the subject of Eastham, I would also like to thank my lovely friend Karen Sutton and her granddaughter, Jasmine, for giving me a personal tour of Eastham Country Park.

I am forever grateful to my sister Lynn Jones, her husband Mick and their group of friends, most especially Julie Lynn, for taking me under their wing one New Year's Eve during a short break to Wales only weeks after my son, Nathan, had died. 'I Predict A Riot,' was the song you chose to mark the end of what had been a tough year for me and my daughter, and I hope you don't mind me stealing what has become your anthem for this book.

A special thank you to my aunt and uncle, Chad and Evie Chadwick. As a writer, I've had some very strange conversations in the name of research and none more so than the one I had with Chad, which helped enormously with the planning of this novel. Your expertise was invaluable and any technical liberties I've taken are my own.

All my love and gratitude goes to the rest of my family and particularly to my mum, Mary Hayes who, at the time of writing, is celebrating her eightieth year and is one of the most incorrigible widows I know. Much love also to the friends who make me drink way too much and laugh far too hard for a menopausal woman.

I say it every time, but my life wouldn't be the same without the people who have helped me develop my craft and turn my love of writing into the career of my dreams. Thank you to my agent, Luigi Bonomi, my publisher, Kim Young, and my editor, Martha Ashby. You are unfailingly supportive, incredibly talented and generous dream-makers for the lucky authors you take under your wings, and I'm blessed to be amongst them. A huge thank you also to the rest of the team at HarperCollins who do an extraordinary job of bringing my words to life and releasing them into the world.

My biggest thank you goes to my daughter, Jess. You have been my source of joy and inspiration, and I'm not sure if I can take any credit for the beautiful and caring young woman you've become. Wherever the next chapter of your life takes you, I know you've got this. You make me so proud.

And a final note to my readers. Writing can be a lonely business, especially when I'm lost in the world I'm busily constructing (or dismantling, depending on the stage of writing and editing), so when someone leaves a review or contacts me on social media to let me know they've enjoyed one of my books, it's such an amazing feeling. You keep me going, and I couldn't do what I do without you. Thank you!

A good mother doesn't forget things.

A good mother isn't a danger to herself.

A good mother isn't a danger to her baby.

You want to be the good mother
you dreamed you could be.

But you're not. You're the bad mother
you were destined to become.

At least, that's what he wants you to believe...

OUT NOW